Poison City

Paul Crilley is a Scotsman living in South Africa. He also writes for television, comics, and computer games. His previous books have mainly been for children, among them The Invisible Order series about a hidden war being fought on the streets of Victorian London between mankind and the fae.

Poison City is his first novel written solely for adults.

PAUL CRILLEY

Poison City

HODDER &
STOUGHTON

First published in Great Britain in 2016 by
Hodder & Stoughton
An Hachette UK company

A CIP catalogue record for this title is available from the British Library

Hardback ISBN 978 1 473 63158 8
Trade Paperback ISBN 978 1 473 63159 5
Ebook ISBN 978 1 473 631618

Printed and bound by Clays Ltd, St Ives plc

Hodder & Stoughton policy is to use papers that are natural, renewable
and recyclable products and made from wood grown in sustainable forests.
The logging and manufacturing processes are expected to conform
to the environmental regulations of the country of origin.

Hodder & Stoughton Ltd
Carmelite House
50 Victoria Embankment
London EC4Y 0DZ

www.hodder.co.uk

For Caroline, Bella, and Caeleb

I

The first thing the dog does when I walk through the door is sniff the air and say, 'You forgot the sherry, dipshit.'

He stares at me, the colour of his eyes shifting between jaundiced yellow and soul-of-a-serial-killer black. He knows I hate that. It's his lazy-ass way of saying, 'You open that mouth it better be to say: *Sorry, dog. I'll get right on it, dog.*'

That's how he insists on being referred to, by the way. Just 'dog' or 'the dog'. I've tried giving him a name, but he's not having it.

I drop the rucksack filled with bullets on the kitchen floor. 'I'll get it later,' I say. 'Got stuff to do first.'

He growls, then whines and tilts his head to the side, trying to cover all possible responses to my failure to act as an enabler to his alcoholism.

I give him the middle finger.

'You know what?' he says. 'I *hate* you. With every fibre of my being.'

'Love you too, man.'

'Come *on*, London. You know I need my afternoon sherry. What's so important you couldn't stop at the liquor store and buy me a bottle? You got a date? Joined a cult? Is the circus in town? Tell me so I can laugh derisively in your face.'

I sigh. You know all those cute dogs in the movies you saw as a kid? Jock? Benji? Lassie? Well, the dog is nothing like that. He's the complete *opposite* of that. He's the dog equivalent of a pervert in a dirty raincoat, sucking methylated spirits through a loaf of bread while watching porn and cackling to himself. He looks a bit like a border terrier, but don't let that fool you. Cute and friendly he is *not*.

But you know what? He's OK.

Actually, no, I'm lying. He's not OK. Not by a long shot. He's like that one friend you've known since high school. The one who drinks too much and tells sexist and racist jokes. The one you wouldn't admit to knowing if you bumped into him with actual people from the real world.

But we're used to each other by now. And as long as I keep him stocked up on *OBs*, (Old Brown sherry – the cheapest, nastiest stuff on the market), he's golden.

I pull out a stool, park myself at the kitchen counter. 'We think we've found out who's taking the kids.'

That shuts him up.

Someone has been stealing kids from the townships. Kids who haven't gone through their naming ceremonies yet. Eleven in the past three months. The families went to ORCU – that's the Occult Related Crimes Unit of the South African Police Force – and they in turn passed it on to Delphic Division. Because let's face it, ORCU is a waste of space and the closest they've ever gotten to the supernatural is daring each other to say Candyman three times in front of the mirror.

ORCU is the public face of the country's supernatural police. Delphic Division is where the actual work gets done.

The families of the missing kids thought it was a tokoloshe, but I thought differently. That's why I requested the case. The ages of the missing kids, the way they just vanished into thin air . . .

It was *them*. It had to be.

After three years, they were getting back in the game. They thought it had all blown over, that they were forgotten.

They're very much mistaken.

'Come on,' snaps the dog. 'You know my bladder can't take

this kind of suspense. Who's the naughty thief stealing little kiddy-winks?'

'Babalu-Aye.'

The dog stares at me then erupts into wheezy laughter. Which in turn descends into a horrific coughing fit, making him sounding like an asthmatic coal miner with lung cancer.

'Seriously?' he says, when he finally gets himself under control.

'Seriously.'

'Would never have pinned that on him. Didn't think he had the imagination.'

Babalu-Aye is the orisha of disease and illness. (An orisha is what we call a Tier-One supernatural. The word orisha is supposed to refer to the Yoruba gods, but over the years it's become the catch-all term for anything . . . *other*: gods, demons, nature elementals, whatever. There are other tiers below the orisha, but they're the biggest pains in the arse.)

Everyone thinks of Babalu-Aye as this mild-mannered old god called upon by the sick to make them feel better. Only thing is, that's not the whole story, because Babalu-Aye likes to cause disease as well. Which he does quite often, apparently.

'You know where he is?' asks the dog.

I nod.

'And . . . what? You're going to just walk in and take him on?'

'No choice. Another kid went missing yesterday. Might still be time to save him.'

'Doubt it,' says the dog cheerfully. 'Come on. Forget it. Let's go out drinking instead. Drinking is *good*. Hunting gods is *bad*.'

'You know I can't. The gods are bad enough as it is. I'm not going to let him think he can just snatch kids whenever he feels like it. Let one get away with it, they all start getting ideas.'

'And tell me. Is this little escapade on the books or off?'

I hesitate. Delphic Division's budget is being squeezed by pencil-pushers in Parliament, and my boss, Armitage, is under pressure to only take on 'high-return' cases. Whatever the hell *that* means.

But that doesn't stop Armitage. Oh, no. She just surreptitiously passes me the case file, taps her nose, and tells me, 'Take care of it, there's a good lad.'

Plausible deniability is just one of the super-fun phrases I've learned while working at Delphic Division.

But I don't mind. Not this time. I've been waiting for this chance for three years now. It's the only reason I stayed on at the Division, when it would have been a hell've a lot easier to just sink into the drink and let oblivion take me.

The dog plods forward and sniffs the rucksack at my feet. 'What's that smell?'

'Pixie dust.'

'Yeah? Well, Tinkerbell's got cancer or something, because that stinks like a match factory and a methane farm fucked each other and had ugly babies.'

I ignore him, reaching into the cupboard by my knees and pulling out my antique double-barrel sawn-off. It's a thing of absolute beauty, filigreed and silver-plated. I won it in a game of poker with Mathew Hopkins, an utter psycho who started hunting witches in the 17th century. Last I heard he was still alive and doing his thing over in Russia.

I take a box of shotgun shells from the rucksack, crack open the gun, and slot two into place. I put the remaining six in my pockets.

The lead shot inside the shells has been removed and replaced with petrified dung balls, courtesy of Aka Manah, a Zoroastrian demon who's currently tenth in line for the throne of Hell. It's Aka Manah's job to take care of naughty demons down below. He's Judge Dredd to their Mega-City One citizens, and *every part* of him can kill an orisha.

Even his shit.

I really wish I had more shells, but at two thousand rand a pop, these have already destroyed my operational budget.

I shove the shooter inside the rucksack. There's another box inside, this one filled with thrice-hexed 9mm silver-plated rounds. I slot them into the magazine of my Glock 17, shove the pistol into the back of my trousers and toss the leftover ammo back into the bag. There are a few other little surprises in there as well, but I'm hoping I won't have to use them. They're not exactly . . . low-key.

I turn my attention to the dog. 'You coming?'

'What about the Covenant?' he says, giving it one last try. 'You can't just go around killing gods. Armitage should know fucking better than to even ask.'

He actually has a point there. The Covenant is the agreement made centuries ago between mankind and the gods/monsters/supers/orishas/whatever-the-hell you want to call them. It runs along the same lines as Mutually Assured Destruction, where both sides know that if one faction kicks off the whole world will burn. There's a book the size of a telephone directory filled with supernatural laws we're all supposed to stick to.

The operative word here being *supposed*. If everyone obeyed the law I'd be out of a job.

'Just have to make sure I don't get caught,' I say. 'You coming or what?'

The dog sighs. 'Got no choice, do I? If you die, who's going to buy me my sherry?'

'That's what I love about you, man. You're all heart.'

Durban, wedged up against the east coast of South Africa, is the dirtiest, strangest, most violent place I've ever lived. It's the soul of South Africa. A sweaty one-night stand of a city where anything goes and the warm Indian Ocean washes all your sins out to sea the next morning.

Durban is a schizophrenic mix of colours and impressions. A serial killer wearing a fake identity, struggling to present a facade of normality to the world. Grey 1970s concrete buildings, painted with dull greens and reds in an attempt to liven up the drabness. Dusty skylines, shading up from sepia to blue. Street signs advertising craft markets and muti doctors. (Mutidoctors – what us ignorant foreigners would call witchdoctors.) Litter everywhere, newspapers, pamphlets, fruit peel, broken glass, everything stepped on and pummelled into mulch, a carpet of dirty memories and forgotten troubles.

Then on top of this is the brightness. The yellow ANC signs, the red EFF billboards. The vibrant, clashing colours of the thousands of street traders who come here from all over the continent, about half of them smuggled aboard the ships that draw into the busiest port in Africa: Swahili, Tanzanian, Malawian, Indian, Zimbabwean (and, increasingly, Russian).

Walking through the streets is an attack on the senses. The bright clothes, the stabbing sunlight, the conflicting smells of fruit and spices, curry powder and cinnamon, marijuana and sweat.

That's the city itself. But then, right at the edge of all that you have a tiny oasis called the Golden Mile. A bubble of rich obliviousness, the expensive cream floating on top of the scum, uncaring of what goes on beneath.

The Golden Mile looks like it has been transported here from Venice Beach. Four miles of prime beachfront real estate stretching from the Blue Lagoon to the Durban Harbor. A wide, brick-paved promenade fronted by hotels and apartment blocks, populated by tourists and surfers, joggers and cyclists, dog walkers and hipsters.

This is where I live, right on the outer edge of the Obliviousness Bubble. A tiny apartment in Windemere Road. Not because I'm rich, you understand. But because I bought the place when the beachfront still belonged to the drug dealers and pimps. It kind of still belongs to them, but they've gone a bit more upmarket now. All that foreign money.

I step out of the cool lobby of the apartment building into a furnace oven. I squint. The sidewalk is steaming, the moisture from the recent storm hanging in the air, a wet heat that clings to me like damp clothing.

Summer in Durban. Nothing like it for humidity, hot weather, and bad tempers.

I unlock the door of my faded green Land Rover and climb in. She's an ancient thing that devours diesel at a rate I didn't think possible and breaks down about seventy per cent of the time she's on the road. But I'll never get rid of her. We've been through a lot together.

I flick a hidden switch beneath the dash. My own personal security device that cuts off the flow of diesel to the engine when I'm not using her. I'm not saying Durban beachfront is particularly crime-ridden – it's the same as anywhere in South Africa – but over the past year thieves have tried to steal my car thirteen times. That I know of.

The dog jumps into the passenger seat and checks himself out in the wing mirror while I peel out into traffic, do an illegal U-turn, and head along the Golden Mile. North Beach passes to our left in flashes of sun and shade as I head around the traffic circles and deeper into town. Our destination isn't too far away. About five kilometres as the bird flies.

'Hey, London,' says the dog after a while. 'Got a question for you.'

London. Or 'London Town'. My unasked-for nickname. My *real* name is Gideon Tau, but I got saddled with London because that's where I'm from. I worked in the Met for fifteen years before moving over here under something of a cloud. Oh, and 'London Town' because it sounds sort-of-but-not-really like 'London Tau'. All the wags at the Division think it's hilarious.

'As long as it's not like your last question. I told you that's what Google is for. Just make sure safe-search is switched off.'

'No, no. Nothing like that. You know that movie?'

'Which one?'

'The one about the incest. With the nazis. And the terrorists trying to take down the government.'

I do a quick mental search of all the movies we've watched recently. None of them match up.

'Not ringing any bells. Give me specifics.'

'Come on, man. You know the one. The space nazis and the brother and sister? And the dad cuts off the kid's hand and he's all like, "*N-o-o!*". '

I frown. 'Are you talking about *The Empire Strikes Back*?'

'That's the one!'

Space nazis and incest. I suppose that's one way to describe it. 'What about it?'

'Well . . . were you guys really stupid back then?'

'Huh?'

''Cause the guy's name is Darth Vader, right? And it's supposed to be a big surprise that he's the kid's dad, yeah?'

'It *was* a big surprise. This was before the internet. People went into a movie without knowing the whole plot beforehand.'

'Yeah but . . . the guy's name. Darth Vader. Vader is Dutch for father. Darth means dark. His name *literally* means Dark Father.'

I flick the visor down to block out the afternoon sun. Left my shades back in the flat again. 'Well . . .' I say defensively. 'So what? We didn't go into it expecting him to be someone's father. You're only acting the smartarse with hindsight.'

'Bull*shit*. I would have called that right there in the theatre.'

'Yeah, I don't think so,' I say, stopping behind a long line of cars. I lean out the window and see that a minibus taxi has stopped dead in the middle of the street to pick up passengers.

'I would have, man. We're not even talking spoilers here. Just common sense.'

I ignore him and drum my fingers on the wheel. My gaze drifts to the right. I can just see the metal fountain outside the entrance to uShaka Marine World. Families are filing inside to spend an enormous amount of money pretending they're in an upside-down shipwreck while they watch sharks swimming around behind safety glass.

Insider's secret: the water holds more than sharks. A Jengu water spirit calls the place her home and she steals a tiny piece of every visitor's soul to feed on. Not a lot, you understand. Just enough to keep going. The equivalent of a couple of cents out of every Rand spent. We do monthly checks on her to make sure she's not overstepping the mark.

The taxi driver eventually decides he's crammed enough bodies into his minibus and pulls off with a spurt of oily smoke, allowing us to get moving again. I take the next right onto Prince Street and find an empty spot to park.

'This it?' asks the dog.

I nod across the street at a dirty white wall covered with peeling paint. The peaks of a cluster of buildings jut up above the wall, stark against the blue sky.

'Addingtons,' I say. 'Used to be a kid's hospital. Been closed for thirty years.'

'Why the hell is Babalu-Aye hiding out here?'

'Word is, it's his den. Where he holds court. Not a bad choice, really. Central location. Easy access to the shops, the beach. It's prime real estate.'

I climb out of the Land Rover and spot a thin guy down the street wearing a lumo yellow safety vest. He jogs over, a huge smile on his face.

'Good day to you. I am Moses. I will watch your car, yes? Take care of it.' He looks me up and down. 'You are going to a wedding today?'

I frown. 'No. Why?'

'Oh. You are a very smartly dressed man, then.'

'Thanks,' I mutter, ignoring a sound from the dog that sounded suspiciously like a snort of laughter. I take a fifty rand note from my wallet and hand it over. Ten times what people usually pay car guards. 'You been on this patch long?'

He makes the money disappear. 'Two years.'

I nod at Addingtons. 'Anything strange going on over there?'

His smile vanishes. He shrugs, uneasy.

'Tell me,' I say.

'Lots of talk,' he says reluctantly. 'No one sleeps there. Not anymore. They say it's haunted. That's all I know. I don't ask about that place.'

I nod and grab my satchel.

'You're going in there?' asks Moses, surprised.

'Have to.'

'Oh.' He squints at me. 'If you don't come back, can I have your car?'

'Sure,' I say. 'If you come in and get my keys.'

The dog and I cross the street and do a full circuit around the property. It's pretty big, at least three acres. The gates are padlocked but someone has used a crowbar to bend the bars apart.

We slip inside, me being careful not to get rust and dirt on my shirt. The dog sees this.

'Why *are* you dressed like you're auditioning for a role in *Inception*?'

I look down at my clothes. A Gucci three piece, sans the jacket. White shirt, sleeves rolled up. It cost me an absolute fortune, but buying nice clothes is my one vice.

'It's how I always dress.'

'Yeah, but . . . you don't think this kind of thing is better suited to jeans and T-shirt? That shit is going to get ruined. I've told you this before.'

'Yeah, but you know I don't listen to a word you say.'

He's probably right. But I'm not going to let him know that.

I check out our surroundings. We're standing on the ruined driveway leading up to the hospital. Uneven grass spurts up in tufts and clumps. Weeds push through cracked asphalt.

We approach the building. Empty windows gaze down at us, like the vacant eyes of a retail worker at Christmas. The main door is wooden, recessed beneath a portico and balcony. Just below the balcony is a frieze of what looks like Jesus standing with some children. They're holding fruit, the only splash of colour on the dirty beige paint.

There's a silence here, a stifling emptiness that hangs over everything.

I take a deep breath, let it out slowly. 'You ready?'

'Ready,' says the dog.

'Hit me.'

A surge of . . . energy . . . *power* . . . rushes through my body, tingling through my veins, sparking into every corner of my being. I feel a wave of euphoria, a sense of well-being I haven't felt in three years. A golden warmth that slides through my soul like a liquid orgasm.

Little known fact, and not one they tell you before you join up. Wielding magic (or Shining, as I call it) is like using drugs. From the way it makes you feel, to the effects of the magic itself. It changes you inside. Your body comes to crave it, and every time you use shinecraft (again, one of mine), it picks a little bit of your DNA apart, unravelling you in ways you can never predict.

Keep using it and one day you're going to go for an X-ray on a routine medical and find an extra brain growing in your lungs. Or you'll wake up one day and find your chest has become transparent, a window looking out into another world. (This happened to a guy who used to work at Delphic Division. Near as we can figure it from checking the configuration of the stars in the sky through his chest, the world was a couple thousand light years away. The guy eventually got pulled through the hole in his chest, literally sucked inside out. I was there. It wasn't pleasant.)

So yeah, magic is a drug. Don't do it, kids.

I shudder in delight and try to pull the fragments of my mind back from wherever they're tripping out to. 'Jesus, that feels good,' I say.

'Shut up,' mutters the dog. 'You're making me feel dirty.'

I blink. My vision swims back into focus. I'm warded now. Protected by an invisible body shield constructed from shine-craft. Kind of like the Holtzman generator shields in *Dune*. It won't stop a bullet, but it *will* absorb most other kinds of attack. A fist, a hammer, a knife, that kind of thing. Up to a point, of course. No need to get cocky about it.

I'm filled with nervous energy. It feels like my skin is thrumming gently, ultra-sensitive. All my senses strain outward, trying to escape the confines of my body.

I push the door open. No creak. Odd. Beyond is an open-roofed atrium. Cracked terracotta tiles covered in loose earth and dried mud. No footprints.

'No one's been here for a while,' says the dog.

'Thanks, Sherlock.' I pull the shotgun out of my satchel, then slide the bag around so it's resting against my kidneys. Easier to reach. 'Smell anything?'

The dog pads softly ahead of me and sniffs around. 'There's something . . . I can't identify what it is. Nothing close, though.'

I walk through the atrium, past pillars covered with tags and stencilled graffiti. There's an alcove in the wall up ahead, a statue of a child with its arms broken off kneeling on green marble.

Through more doors into what must have once been the reception area. Paintings on the wall, faded and chipped: Li'l Devil, a cartoon character I remember from when I was a kid.

A ghost wearing a top hat. A badly drawn Daffy Duck knock-off.

A corridor beyond. The afternoon sun smearing through dirty windows, like walking through a hazy dream. The roof panels are mostly gone, gaping holes showing second-storey rooms. The paint is peeling from the walls like sunburned skin, sloughing off in ugly damp patches.

My heart beats erratically in my chest. I don't know if it's the after-effects of the shinecraft, fear, or anticipation. My shirt sticks to my back. Sweat dripping into my eyes. There's no sound except my breathing and my boots crunching across the detritus of the past.

We follow the corridor deeper into the ruined building. We turn left and it's as if the light has been turned off. No windows here. I pause as my eyes adjust. Wooden floors. Badly painted pictures on the yellow walls: a rasta girl with 'HAIR' painted beneath her. A little girl in a purple dress and high heels that are too big for her. Strip lights hanging from a high ceiling.

-*Where to?*- says the dog.

It takes a moment for me to notice he's talking mind to mind. He only does that when he's worried. When there's danger around.

I shrug. I have no idea. I peer into each room we pass: old, cast-iron cots, a wall chart of a skeleton that someone has drawn a moustache onto, broken sinks, a room filled with patient records in creased brown folders, rotting in the damp.

We find the stairs and climb to the next floor. The first room is huge, easily double the size of my flat. Somebody has ripped a load of doors from their hinges and piled them up on the floor. There are no paintings in here. Just two words written high up on the wall.

I thirst.

-*Could do with a drink myself,*- says the dog.

I don't answer. We move through the room to another corridor. This one is pitch black, all the doors closed. Something feels . . . funky here. Just . . . not right. Hard to explain. It's something you get taught in Delphic Division, how to pick up on the presence of an orisha, or even just magic in general. It feels like bugs are crawling under your skin, sliding along your nerves trying to get out.

A moment later the dog drops to the floor, his gums pulled back in a snarl. His ears flatten against his head and he squirms on the ground.

-*Jesus fucking Christ!*- he moans. -*How are you standing there? Can't you* hear *that?*-

I move my head around. I think I might be able to hear something . . . high-pitched, just on the edge of my hearing. But I'm not sure.

'What is it?' I clutch the sawn-off nervously, looking over my shoulder.

The dog doesn't answer. I stand protectively over him as he writhes, waiting for an attack I'm sure is going to come.

He finally pushes himself back to his feet, panting heavily. 'Fuck, man. That was *not* pleasant.' He squints up at me. 'You seriously didn't hear that?'

I shake my head.

'Lucky bastard. It was like every ultrasonic whistle ever made was being blown at the same time. Except it wasn't a whistle. It was screaming.'

'Screaming?'

'Yeah, man. Screaming.'

I peer into the darkness. 'What did it sound like?'

'The fuck you mean, what did it sound like? I just *told* you. Screaming.'

'I mean did it sound animal? Human?'

'London, it doesn't matter what it sounded like. If whatever made that noise is in here, we should be out there. End of.'

'We can't just leave.'

'We can. It's what our legs are for. And our brains.'

'You go. Wait in the car or something. I'll be out soon.'

The dog shakes himself in irritation. 'Yeah. Right. If I leave you, ain't no way you're coming out again.'

'Then shut up your whining and let's get this finished,' I snap.

The dog stares at me for a long moment before turning and walking into the corridor. I'm sure I hear him mutter 'cock weasel' beneath his breath. His favourite insult for me when I really annoy him.

The corridor branches into a second passage that has been ravaged by fire. The ceiling and floor are soot-black. The paint on the walls has bubbled and peeled. The little flakes of paint look like leaves, white on one side, black on the other. They're moving silently, shivering slowly back and forth as if someone was breathing gently on them.

There's an open door at the far end of the corridor. I approach it slowly. That's where Babalu-Aye is. I can feel it.

I pat my pockets. Shells close at hand. Two in the gun. Glock in the back of my pants. Tattoos ready and waiting. Shit. I'm not prepared for this. The dog was right. I shouldn't be doing this. At least, not alone. If this was officially sanctioned I'd have two teams of five backing me up.

I curl my hands around the grip of the sawn-off. I take a deep breath, then swing around the door, gun levelled, watching for the slightest movement.

Images and impressions flash through my mind. Large room, the largest so far. Green paint. Wall paintings faded by time. A swept concrete floor. Windows painted black. The smell of piss and vinegar.

Movement from the shadows to my left. I swing the gun. Something heaves through the darkness. Way too big to be the missing kid. The shape makes a growling sound and I pull the trigger. An explosion of noise. A flash of white that burns my retinas. Something drops heavily to the floor.

I squint, trying to readjust to the darkness. I move forward. The shape on the ground isn't moving. It's big. The size of a lion. A hairless, pink-grey face, all muzzle and yellow teeth.

'That was my dog, you piece of shit,' says a voice, and something slams into my back and sends me flying twenty feet through the air to smash up against the wall with enough force to actually break the concrete.

Thank fuck I'm Warded, that's all I can say.

2

I land on shattered stone and grunt in pain. If it wasn't for the wards I'd have more than a few broken bones right about now.

I'm yanked off the ground. I feel fingers tighten on my arms and legs, then a rush of air. A moment of lightness, then another sickening collision and I bounce off the wall again and hit the floor. My gun skitters away into the darkness.

I groan and try to push myself up. *Stay down!* shouts a voice in my head. *Pretend you're dead.*

But here's the thing. I was never very good at listening to advice. Even from myself.

'Why have you not burst?' says the voice, and I hear a sliver of interest in the tone.

I shake my head, trying to chase away the blackness. Once again I'm lifted up, weightless. But I don't feel fingers this time. I force my eyes open.

I'm hanging in the air in the centre of the room. An old man walks towards me. He has a wrinkled face, a neatly trimmed white beard. He's wearing . . .

I frown. For a moment I wonder if I'm hallucinating. He's wearing one of those pastel blue suits that Don Johnson used to wear in *Miami Vice*. Beneath that a pink T-shirt with ocean waves printed on it.

And cheap plastic sunglasses, the kind you get for five rand at the stalls along the beachfront.

'Hey,' I murmur. 'The 1980s called. They want their clothes back.'

He doesn't smile. I don't blame him. That joke was already *old* in the 80s.

'You are one of them, I think. Yes?' Babalu-Aye pushes the plastic glasses up so they're perched on his head. He leans forward and sniffs me. 'Yes. I can smell the first breath of the world on you. The power. Like a baby trying to perform heart surgery. That is what you all are.'

Babalu-Aye sucks air through his teeth and stares at me thoughtfully. I don't like that look.

'You know what I have not done in such a long time?' he asks.

'Felt the loving touch of a woman?' I say, as I glance around the room searching for the dog. I can't see him anywhere. 'No – dance naked in the rain. That's it, isn't it?'

'Eat a softskin,' he says.

Nope. Really didn't need to know that.

'I used to do it quite often. This was . . . oh – seventeenth century? Eighteenth? Time starts to lose meaning after a while. But it was one of my favourite treats. Children were the best. Such soft flesh. Succulent. Moist.'

He shivers with delight. His words bring the world sharply back into focus, bring the memories rushing back. Why I'm here. What I'm seeking.

'Is that what you did?' I whisper, fearing the answer. It would explain everything. The lack of bodies. All the blood. 'With the kids you took?'

Babalu-Aye frowns. He reaches up and slaps me hard. 'Do you not listen? I just said I have not eaten a child in a long time.'

I struggle in vain, trying to get out of his invisible grip. 'Three years ago,' I snarl. 'A house in the mountains. That was your doing, wasn't it? You told those guys to snatch the kids. Just like now.'

Babalu-Aye frowns, thinking back. He finally shakes his head. 'Not me.'

'Don't lie!' I shout. 'Five kids. All under eight. There were three men there. Two got away. They know where the bodies are!'

Babalu-Aye floats up so that he is hovering in front of me, face to face. 'You are not listening, human. I have no idea what you're talking about.'

'You're lying! It was you! It had to be.'

'Listen to me, my child. I was part of the creation of this land. I *am* this land. A hundred thousand years ago, your ancestors prayed to me when they barely understood the concept. Forty thousand years ago, they drew paintings of me in caves. I do not lie. What need have I for untruths?'

I shake my head in despair. I'd thought this would be it. That I was finally going to get the truth.

'Then why?' I whisper, my voice broken. Hoarse. 'Why are you taking those kids now? Why are you here?'

'Why am I here?' He spreads his arms out and smiles. 'This hospital feeds me – can you not feel the essence? How many diseased children died here? How many prayers were sent to me from this place?' He lowers his arms and smiles. 'But do not waste your thoughts on these children you seek. They are already dead.'

I stare at him blankly as his words sink into my soul, cutting fresh wounds across old scars. I want to reach out and rip his smug face to shreds. To gouge his eyes from his head and burst them in my hands.

'The boy? The one you took yesterday?'

'You did not see him while you were searching for me? No, of course not. You're still alive, how could you?'

'Show me. Take me to him.'

'No,' says Babalu-Aye. 'I am bored now.'

He twists his hands in the air. I feel my head being pushed to the side, my neck pulled in the opposite direction. I scream as bright, flashing agony surges through my body. No matter how strong my wards they're not going to prevent this orisha from eventually breaking my neck.

I feel vertebrae starting to pop. I'm looking sideways now, staring into rheumy yellow eyes, white teeth parted in a grin.

Fuck. No choice. Time to call in the big guns.

I close my eyes and repeat the words of awakening.

I feel them instantly on my skin as they stir to life. It tickles and repulses at the same time, a spider-walk sensation that crawls up my spine.

Light explodes in the room as my tattoos come alive. Twin dragons, green and red, bursting out through the gap at my collar to coil up in the air over my shoulders.

Babalu-Aye's eyes widen in surprise. The glowing dragons – still attached to my spine – lunge over my shoulders and wrap around him. They lift him off his feet and flick him away. He spins through the air, hits the wall and falls to the rubble.

I hit the ground too, landing on my knees.

The dragons are hissing and spitting, dragging me forwards along the dirt. I grit my teeth and bring them to heel, forcing them back behind me with sheer force of will. I can feel their hatred, their desire to devour me, to devour everything.

Goddammit but I regret getting them. They were the first piece of magic I ever picked up. *Sak yat*, a Chinese tattoo magic that's over two thousand years old.

Buddhist monks originally engraved the tattoos into warriors for strength and protection before they went into battle. I thought that sounded pretty cool. So I travelled to the Wat Bang Phra Temple in Thailand and asked them to ink me up. I had to do a few favours for the monks before they finally agreed. After that they took me below ground and left me to fast for two weeks. Then, when I was delirious and raving like a madman, they inked me the old-fashioned way, using a piece of bamboo tapped repeatedly against the skin.

And the ink isn't any run-of-the-mill ink. It's a special supply made from dried dragon blood, passed down through the centuries.

Only problem is, the tattoos – they're kind of alive. The dragon blood craves sacrifice, and every time I summon them I find them harder to control. They hate me. Hate being trapped. They'd give anything to break free.

Plus, every second they're awake they drain my life source, literally devouring parts of my soul. The dog helps me a bit, throwing in some of his own power so the tattoos don't suck me dry. But even so, I'm terrified of calling them up. I never know if they're sucking weeks off my life. Months. *Years*, even.

Still, if the alternative is actually being ripped apart by some old bastard of a god, I suppose you can't complain.

I move forward until the dragons are within reach of Babalu-Aye. They wrap around him, yank him to his feet, pull him towards me.

His eyes widen suddenly in surprise. His lips pull back from the teeth in a shout of pain.

I wonder what's going on. Are the dragons killing him? Draining him dry?

Then I see it. The dog has clamped his teeth on Babalu-Aye's balls. Yeah, gods have genitalia when they're corporeal. How else are they going to indulge in their favourite pastime – fornicating with mortals?

I focus my attention on the dragons and mutter the words of sleep. The dragons shudder, fighting me all the way. I push my focus into the words, repeat them over and over, and they finally release Babalu-Aye with a hiss of displeasure and snake back over my head, coiling back around my arms and down my back. As always, I feel like they're somehow trying to take me with them. Like they're trying to pull me into Nightside with them, where, I have no doubt, they'd have a lot of fun ripping me to pieces.

I stagger, a wave of nausea washing over me.

-London? Don't flake out on me, man. Got my mouth full here.-

I straighten up, take a few steadying breaths. I spot my shotgun a few feet away and scramble over to grab it. Babalu-Aye has pulled a knife from somewhere and is about to plunge it into the dog's ribs.

I place the sawed-off against the back of the old bastard's neck. He freezes.

'Dog,' I said calmly. 'Drop.'

The dog releases his grip. I take a shaky breath, relief flooding through my system. I break into a grin and glance down at the dog.

'Who's a good boy, then?' I say. 'Huh? You are. Yes you are!'

'Bite me, London,' mutters the dog.

I make sure the gun doesn't lose contact with Babalu-Aye's neck and use it to shove him ahead of me through the dirty corridors.

'You know you cannot harm me,' he says mildly. 'The Covenant applies to your kind as well.'

'You picked a good time to start worrying about the Covenant, old man.'

'I am not a man. I am a God. Capital G. And if you think you are going to walk away from this, you truly are a most stupid skinbag.'

I prod him roughly with the barrel, hoping he can't pick up on my nervousness. Hoping the dog, trotting along a few feet behind, can't either. He's right, of course. No matter what happens this afternoon I'm making enemies. That's what happens when you don't think things through.

Funny. That's what Armitage always says about me. I'm too impulsive. If I survive this I'll have to tell her she's right. She'll like that.

Babalu-Aye eventually leads me to the far end of the building. Into a long room with high windows to either side.

Dust motes flash and wink in the lowering sun. Glass partitions run the length of the room, painted with images that are supposed to be calming to children: a scene from 'The Cow Jumped over the Moon', with a cat that looks like it's high on cocaine playing a fiddle while the moon leers down at it, grinning like a serial killer. Badly copied versions of Bugs Bunny and Porky Pig, chipped and faded. And creepiest of all, paintings of kids on their knees. Praying. But all of them with their backs to the viewer.

'Where's the kid?'

Babalu-Aye points to a door at the far end of the room. 'Through there.'

We reach the door. It's thick, with a round window at the top. But I can't see through. There's a piece of warped cardboard stamped with the word 'sunlight soap' stuck to the other side.

'Open it.'

'That is a very bad idea.'

'Open it!'

The orisha sighs. 'Fine. But don't say I didn't warn you.'

Babalu-Aye pushes the door. I shove him hard, sending him stumbling into the room. I follow after.

Images flash before me, like photographs whipped past my eyes.

A huge room. White tiles, cracked, dripping with black fluid. An old metal bunk bed, six feet high, all the springs pulled out. A boy of about twelve tied spread-eagled between the frame of the top bunk, facing down to the floor. A fine sand-like substance siphoning from his nose and mouth, making little piles on the ground.

And on the floor some kind of black leathery cocoon. About ten feet long. There's movement in the cocoon, a rippling beneath the surface.

'What . . . ?'

Babalu-Aye looks at it in disgust. 'They can never control themselves,' he says. 'They are like teenagers tasting their first beer. All they want is more and more.'

'More?' I don't know what I'm looking at.

'More souls,' says Babalu-Aye. 'Unbaptized. Unnamed. Before they reach adulthood.'

I look around in dawning realization. The scene in front of me changes in my perception, like one of those pictures that can be either a young woman or an old crone.

The powder – manifested soul, stolen from the child.

The cocoon . . . not a cocoon at all.

As if hearing our voices for the first time, the mass on the floor undulates backwards and rises up. Black leathery wings unfold. Six sets. Two at the feet. Two on the back. Two on the neck.

They open up to reveal . . .

I stumble backwards. The creature in front of me has four faces. Not four heads, but four faces, north, south, east and west. Each of them has black eyes and a mouth wide open in a silent scream. The noses are coated with the sand. It's smeared across the cheeks.

I can't believe what I'm looking at. I wonder if I'm the first human to see such a thing.

An angel. But in its true form.

I've seen one or two angels in my work at Delphic Division. Not many. They tend to stick to Europe for some reason. But those I *have* seen were always projecting an image, something that wouldn't freak us poor mortals out. Marble statue features. Feathery wings, etc.

This ten-foot monstrosity is what they really look like.

It stares at me, but I see no awareness behind its eyes. I've seen the same look on crack-heads down at the beachfront.

This angel is getting high on the souls of children.

'He's becoming quite the addict,' says Babalu-Aye conversationally. 'I think I will have to move him to another city now. I can only acquire so many children before softskins start to complain.'

His words penetrate my shock.

I blink.

Then I shoot Babalu-Aye in the face.

His head bursts in a fine red mist. The explosion thunders through the room. Brain and blood spatter the dirty tiles. The orisha drops to his knees then falls forward to the floor.

I crack open the sawn-off, eject the empty shells, load two more. The dog is shouting at me, but I can't hear him. My ears are ringing. I'm not sure if it's from the gunshot or just shock. I jerk the gun, flicking it closed again. Pull back the two hammers.

Unload both rounds into the angel's face.

It shrieks, black blood spewing from its mouths. It flies back against the bed, knocking it over onto its side so the kid is now suspended sideways in the air. I hurry forward, try to untie him. I can't see any awareness in his eyes. I don't know if I'm too late. Can't get the rope undone.

The angel is thrashing around on the tiles, kicking and squealing. It's like Satan's own fingernails screeching across the blackboard of my soul.

I stop trying to untie the rope and jerk the shells out of the gun, load two more. Point the gun with my right hand and fish around at my belt for my knife – a present from Becca before she left me.

I find it. Cut the ropes of the kid's feet. He swings down into a standing position.

'Kid!' I slap his face. 'Kid. You hear me?'

The sand is still leaking from his nose and mouth, but the stream seems to have slowed. He blinks as I cut his hands free. The angel has stopped thrashing, is staring dully at me now, trying to speak around a ruined mouth. I'm sure I can see its flesh knitting together again, healing. I step forward and put the gun right against its head. It tries to bat it away but I pull the trigger. Brains or whatever the hell angels have spatter out the other side and it flops down again.

The dog's voice gradually filters back into my awareness.

'You are *so* fucked, London! What the hell are you playing at? You won't get away with this. Every orisha and super is going to be after your blood! This is what happens when you don't listen to me you stupid c—'

I turn and look at him. Something in my face stops his stream of abuse. He backs away. I turn back to the kid. He's looking around now, his awareness returning. I try to block his view of the angel behind me.

'Can you walk? Kid, can you walk?'

He blinks at me and moves his mouth. He spits. Sand drops to the floor. I wince, resisting the urge to tell him not to lose any more.

'Get out of here. Go downstairs. Out the front doors. You hear me?'

He nods, then stumbles out the room. I wait till I see him start to run past the glass-walled partitions before turning back to the angel, wondering how to finish it off.

It's standing right behind me.

The angel backhands me. I fly through the air and smash into the tiles, collapse to the floor. I lose my gun again. Need to glue that damn thing to my hand. It skids about ten feet away, out of reach.

The angel's face is reforming before my eyes, white-grey flesh knitting together. Its wings – the largest pair on its back – flare out, stiffening, smashing into the ceiling, punching holes in the tiles. The wings flex and move with each heavy breath the angel takes, pulling tiles from the walls.

There is a moment of emptiness. The breath of creation

waiting to see what happens next. Ceramic fragments fall to the floor with tiny *plink plink* sounds.

Then the angel smiles around its ruined mouths.

It uses its wings as leverage, stiffening them and launching itself straight at me.

I don't have time to think. I shove off with my feet, sliding through Babalu-Aye's blood. I make it out of reach just as the angel lands where my head was, crushing the floor tiles with its weight.

It gets stuck in the hole for a second, long enough for me to scramble for my gun. I unload the last barrel into its face, aiming for the eyes this time. It screams in pain and I turn and run. The dog is already ahead of me, halfway towards the door at the far end of the glass-partitioned room.

So much for my backup.

I pop the shells and load my last two. Not good. The shells aren't really having an effect on the angel. This is going to require something more radical.

I look over my shoulder just as the wall of the room explodes outwards, the angel simply shoving through the bricks. Dust billows towards me, followed by one extremely pissed off and extremely high angel.

I reach around and grab my satchel, pull it open and stash my gun. It's not going to help me.

Running. Holding my bag in one hand. Through the glass-partitioned room, along the corridor beyond. Down the stairs, slipping onto my back, pushing myself up as I hear the footsteps pounding behind me. Down to the first floor. The yellow corridor. Close now. Have to get out. The angel won't come out into the light. No matter how high the stupid thing is, an angel revealing itself to the public is a huge no-no. I hope. I don't know. But it's my only chance.

The corridor is long. I sprint as fast as I can, but even before I reach the end I know I'm not going to make it. The footsteps are closer. I can hear them, feel the vibrations in the wooden floorboards.

I glance over my shoulder just in time to see the angel launch itself at me, reaching out with huge hands. I spin around, bring my knife up. It pierces the angel's hand as it crashes into me. We fly back into the wall. Rotten plaster caves in, showers us in white dust. I can feel the dog's wards straining at the impact.

We're embedded in the wall. I hear the snapping of teeth. The fucker is trying to bite me. I yank my knife out its hand and stab it in the neck. Black blood gouts over my hand, steaming hot. I snatch my hand back but the angel doesn't seem to have noticed the wound. I push back on the angel's chin, forcing its neck taut. I bring the knife up to cut its throat but the angel jerks back, pulling us both out the wall.

I punch the knife repeatedly into its stomach. Over and over until it lets me go. I drop to the floor, scrabble between its legs, stand up, and do the only other thing I think might hurt it.

I use the knife to slice one of its wings off.

The angel shrieks in pain and fury, whirling around. One of the remaining wings hits me and sends me tumbling to the floor. I push myself to my feet and run. I run like I've never run before, fishing around in my satchel as I do so.

My hand closes around what I'm looking for. An insurance policy. Something I 'forgot' to hand in to the evidence locker after one of my cases.

I pull it out. It's a hand grenade, but I don't know what's inside it. Holy light, demon fire, swarms of flesh-eating locusts. Could be anything. Only thing is, if I use it, it's going to bring me to the attention of the Accountants, people I *really* don't want noticing me.

Hell, what does it matter? I've already broken the Covenant. The Accountants are going to be after my blood anyway. Might as well drag my life out as long as possible.

I keep running, heading for the front door. I can hear the angel following after me, but I've managed to pull ahead. I yank the safety pin on the grenade, holding the striker lever down. I wait till I'm only a couple of rooms from the front entrance then I drop the grenade behind me and keep on moving.

I make it through the reception area.

I'm in the open air atrium, passing the graffiti-covered columns, when the grenade explodes.

The detonation hits me in the back, throws me off my feet. I skid along the tiles, then scramble up and lurch through the wooden door, out onto the grass as the structure starts to collapse behind me. I run until I'm almost at the main gate, ducking and darting to avoid falling masonry.

I finally stop and turn around.

Stone and bricks are still pattering down around me. Black smoke billows up from a hole in the roof. As I watch, the outside walls buckle, those that weren't blown outwards now collapsing in on themselves.

I frown. So . . . the grenade was just an *actual* grenade? That's a bit anticlimactic. But at least it will have taken care of the angel. For a while. Long enough for me to get away.

Speaking of which, I should get out of here. I blink and look around. The dog is waiting by the gate. I trot over to join him.

'You happy now?' he asks.

'Where's the kid?'

'Long gone. I wouldn't worry. He seemed to know where he was going.'

I can hear sirens in the distance.

'You want to hang around, get arrested for terrorism, or you reckon we make ourselves scarce?' the dog asks.

I start walking. I feel as if my whole world has crumbled around me again. I got my hopes up. I knew I shouldn't have.

Never expect anything. That way you can never be disappointed.

We cross the street, heading back to the Land Rover. Moses is standing there, staring at the black smoke billowing into the sky. I fish around in my wallet and take out a two hundred rand note. All I have on me. I pass it to Moses.

'I wasn't here.'

Moses tears his gaze away from the smoke.

'What happened?'

'Gas leak,' I say. 'Moses, I wasn't here, OK?'

He looks at the money. Once again, he makes it disappear. 'You weren't here.'

'Thanks.'

The dog hops into the passenger seat. I start the engine and pull out into the street, moving slowly around the cars that are stopping to rubberneck. Hopefully none of them saw us leave the grounds.

'You should be happy. At least you saved the kid.'

I don't answer. What's to be happy about? If it wasn't Babalu-Aye then I'm no closer to finding out what happened three years ago.

I sometimes think I'm dead and stuck in limbo, doomed to repeat the same cycle of hope and defeat over and over again until the end of time.

It would be no more than I deserve.

3

Here's the thing. Shinecraft is everywhere. Always has been. Always will be. And there are a thousand different ways to use it. To name a few: binding. Demon summoning. Cursing. Golemancy. Necromancy. Magical sigils. Warding. Divination. Tasseography. Oneiromancy. Scrying. Illusion. Vivimancy. Runes. Heka. Mind reading. Alchemy.

And there are more. All different ways of channelling a power that has always been there. Tools to achieve a specific goal, tools that change over time as tradition, folklore, history, and religion all leak into the collective unconsciousness and influence the ways in which shining is invoked.

I mean, in Africa alone the different methods of shining number in the triple figures. The methods change all the time, shifting between tribal families, between ethnicity, even between age groups. A fifty-year-old user might do what he calls 'laying down tricks', forming patterns and sigils in the dirt then spitting into them to activate the spell. When the target walks over the lines, he or she is cursed.

But a teenager who's in the know might do the same thing with spray paint and graffiti, hiding the tricks in a piece. When his target walks past or looks at the art, the curse will activate.

It all comes down to what works for you. Shinecraft is like language, constantly evolving, never static, changing with the times.

In Delphic Division, we're given a basic education that covers as much as possible. But the sheer amount of information amassed over the centuries means there's no way we can learn it all.

Instead, we're told to find what works for us, to specialize. The Division wants its agents to be masters of one, instead of dabblers in everything, and you're encouraged to choose something that no other agent has picked. That way they have a wide spread of skills available to call on.

That was always my problem. My mind is too fickle. I'd pick something that looked like it had potential, something that suited me. But after a while I'd just lose interest. Either it didn't work the way I wanted to, or I decided it wasn't suitable to use in the field.

Take, for instance, calling on the ancestors.

I spent months training for that. Studying trance states, learning how to call up your bloodline, then bargaining with the ancestors, doing deals that would allow me to contact them in my hour of need, all that kind of stuff. But I eventually gave up because it just didn't work the way I wanted it to.

Which is a polite way of saying it was hell. Calling the ancestors is like having disapproving parents standing behind you twenty-four seven, judging every single thing you do.

Don't believe me? Here's how it worked. We have two worlds. We call them Nightside and Dayside. We're Dayside, obviously, and the other world is Night. So I'd put myself into a trance and call on the ancestors. The two worlds connect. (We can see this. You can't.) Everything becomes misty, insubstantial. The two worlds overlay each other. Everything is a bit . . . off. Like reality is off-kilter. The buildings are all there, same as in the real world, just . . . different. The windows are skewed, the buildings themselves are too tall, too thin, or lean to the side. The sky changes between storm black to apocalyptic orange. It's like you're in a Tim Burton movie.

Oh, yeah, and there are all sorts of creatures wandering around. Nightside is their home. Where all the orisha and supers come from. So you can have ten-feet-long hyenas wandering the streets, or packs of roaming ghosts, or even a city full of biblical demons.

It's always changing, so you never really know what to expect. There's a rumour going around that someone has a map of Nightside, but I'm not sure I buy it. We've been looking, investigating the possibility, but haven't turned up anything yet. We live in hope, though.

So . . . back to the ancestors. Say I'm in trouble. I need to use my shinecraft. It's not like in the movies, where I just hold my hands up and spit electricity at my enemy.

So I ask for help. The worlds connect, and suddenly I'm surrounded by my ancestors, going all the way back a few thousand years, the older ones receding into the hazy distance. I ask them to give me a hand. Politely. (Have to be polite. They take offence really easily.)

And you know what they do next? They stand there and *argue* amongst themselves about whether they should even bother. Then, when they decide that yeah, OK, maybe they will help me out, it's another discussion about exactly how much power I need. And all the while they're criticizing my life choices, fashion sense, taste in books, and anything else that comes to mind.

Which, if you're in an emergency situation, is not the best method of Shining.

So I gave that one up as a bad bet and haven't decided on a new method yet. Not sure I ever will. I might just skim the top of all available methods, dip in to something that catches my eye then move on to the next. I mean, calling on the ancestors was a bust. And my tattoos . . . less said about those bastards the better. Christ knows what I might might saddle myself with next.

But what that means is I'm stuck with the bone wand (stop sniggering) that every member of Delphic Division is given when they join up. The wands are supposedly made from the bones of famous magicians. Armitage says mine is from the shin of John Dee.

It was Armitage who presented it to me in the first place. I remember the day well. I think she was drunk. She took it from a velvet case and gravely handed it over, then looked at me and said, 'You're a wizard, Harry,' before doubling over with laughter.

Only thing is, we're supposed to outgrow the wands after the first year, when we specialize. I still have mine after four. Which explains my reliance on the dog to help me out with Shining and protective wards.

See, as well as the wand, every magician at Division is assigned a spirit guide, something to help him navigate those first confusing months and years.

It's kind of an initiation thing. You head down to the litter-strewn basement where an ancient stone circle has been relocated, cemented into the floor and sharing space with empty beer bottles and mouldering porn magazines.

You stand in the middle of the circle and the other conjurers at Delphic Division help open the gate to Nightside, and then in a ceremony not very magical at all, you're assigned your guide.

When the gate opened for me I saw some tall, horned, glow-ing creature walking confidently towards me. This being was . . . filled with wisdom. I could *feel* it shining through the gate, touching me with these mystical tendrils of knowledge. I had no idea what it was. Demon. Babylonian god, trickster spirit. I didn't care. Because I knew this thing was going to teach me everything.

Score, I thought. *I'm gonna bag me one of the Big Boys.*

Then what happens? The figure stumbles and falls to its knees, and I see the dog rip out its achilles tendon, cock his leg, piss in my spirit guide's face, and limp though the gate into the basement.

'All right, dipshit?' he says, sitting down at my feet.

And that was that. Rules are, you get the first guide that comes to you, no returns.

So I was stuck with him.

I didn't sleep well last night. The after-effects of using the tattoos left me feverish and ill, vomiting into a bucket until dawn eventually clambered into my room and told me to give up even trying to close my eyes.

Now, stuck in morning traffic as I make my way to work, I feel like I've got a bad case of the flu. Or the worst hangover ever. Queasy stomach. Throbbing head. Shaky limbs.

Whoever thought humans dabbling in magic was a good idea was a fucking moron. Our bodies are just not designed for it.

The Delphic Division headquarters are located in an abandoned cement factory bordering the N4 as you head out towards the old airport. It always reminds me of that place the bad guys hide out in at the end of the original Robocop. Grey concrete, huge chimneys, rusted metal lying everywhere, chain-link fences, and broken-down walls. A lovely place to work.

Of course, that's all a carefully maintained facade, bolstered with glamour shinecraft powered by aether generators stacked up in the basement.

I peel out of the Monday morning traffic onto a seemingly incomplete off-ramp, descending into a tunnel that loops beneath the freeway and out onto a newly tarred road leading to reinforced metal gates. (Anyone glancing over from the freeway will see rusted gates hanging from their hinges.)

My car has an RFID chip hidden inside and the gates swing wide and allow me to enter without me even having to slow down.

Anyone trying to get in without authorization will hit the wards Eshu has built up around the premises. I'm told it's like a million volts of electricity surging through your body while you're being read bad poetry by love-sick teenagers. Not sure about that last bit, but I don't really want to test it out.

I steer around the rear of the old factory, then down the ramp to the underground parking garage. I pull into my bay and switch the ignition off. I grip the steering wheel and stare at the yellow bollard in front of me.

Sitting here is a morning routine. Waiting while I try to slip into character. While I remember what it's like to be me.

Sometimes it takes me five minutes, sometimes twenty.

Everyone wears a mask. To fit in. To hide the real person inside. Because, let's face it. If we *didn't* have masks, if we all saw who we *really* were beneath the facade, beneath society's norms, and lies we tell ourselves, the human race would be extinct. We'd be too scared to leave the house.

I wear a mask because I sometimes forget what it feels like to be human. The mask is the me that existed before everything happened. It's a construct built up from memories and remembered responses.

I take a few deep breaths, trying to remember what I used to be like, dredging up the memories. The cockiness. The bad jokes. The sarcastic comments. Not exactly the best traits to aspire to, but they're the ones everyone expects.

It feels . . . nice, like welcoming an old friend.

I uncurl my aching fingers from around the wheel and climb out the car, jogging up the stairs to ground level. I could have just taken the elevator into the main building, but I'm hoping to talk to Armitage before I see anyone else to tell her what happened yesterday.

I emerge into daylight and skirt around the closest building, a towering, brutal grey silo with a radius of about two hundred feet. That's the Division's main building, where we have our offices.

I approach the first of six smaller silos that surround it, stopping before a smooth section of concrete.

I knock. A section of the wall fades to darkness and I step through, the concrete reforming behind me. Just before it does, the dusty sunlight illuminates a set of stairs leading down. Way, way down.

Energy-saving globes flicker to weak life as I descend, their anaemic glow lighting the way forward. I head down and find Eshu waiting for me at the bottom of the stairs.

Eshu is one of the Division's convict gods. He's a trickster deity, the Orisha of advice and communications. Which is why he's been put in charge of our comms and internet servers and . . . well, pretty much everything electronic really.

He looks like a seventeen-year-old street kid. Faded Levis. Converse high-tops and a George Romero T-shirt.

'Hey, London,' he says in greeting. 'Why do you never use the front door?'

'Uh . . . Don't know. Guess I'm just a backdoor kinda guy.' I wince as I re-run the sentence through my mind, but Eshu says nothing, just turns and walks away. No sense of humor, these gods.

'Armitage around?' I ask, following Eshu into his base of operations. (And his prison cell.)

The place never fails to impress me. It's as if a set designer from *Blade Runner* and *The Matrix* got together and created the ultimate SF computer room. There are monitors everywhere, drilled into the walls, bolted to the end of extendable swing arms, even piled one atop each other to form huge, multi-part screens.

Some are showing live CCTV feeds from all over the world. Others are playing movies, TV shows, music videos. Still others have 24-hour news channels on an endless loop while others are showing porn and cartoons. Thick black cables loop through the air and sprawl across the floor like burned snakes. There's a cot bed in the corner and boxes of instant noodles, the only thing Eshu eats.

I never actually found out what Eshu did to warrant his prison time here. It must have been pretty bad, though. I hear his sentence is a cool two centuries.

'She came in an hour ago,' he says. 'Said to tell you that if you came crawling in the back way like the yellow-bellied coward she knows you really are, you're to sit tight and wait on her call. She's dealing with Ranson.'

Ranson. Christ, I hate that guy. A politician. An officious pencil-pusher. He's our Divisional Commissioner and reports directly to the National Intelligence Co-ordinating Committee. And yes, he's as annoying as all those titles sound. Petty in the extreme. I could go my whole life without laying eyes on him again.

Only problem is, he's in charge of Delphic Division and seems to be doing his best to get us shut down. Or at least crippling our funding. He won't even acknowledge that shinecraft is real, for Christ's sake. How messed up is that?

I cross the room and duck through a heavy-duty blast door, emerging into a dimly lit tunnel. I duck through an identical door at the far end of the passage and I'm standing in the Hub, a round room with tunnels radiating off to the other sections of the Division, like spokes in a wheel.

There's a round metal plate beneath my feet. An LED light embedded in the plate flashes blue. Apparently this is where they keep our namesake, the Delphic Oracle, locked away and kept out of sight. I say apparently, because none of us really know if she's down there. We've never seen her.

I follow a tunnel into the heart of Delphic Division, the massive silo that I passed on my way to Eshu's door.

The inside of the silo is open all the way to the top. A massive post-modern office structure that wouldn't look out of place in London's financial district. The silo has been sectioned off into twenty floors, all holding offices, conference rooms, prisons, kitchens, sleeping quarters etc. A balcony circles each floor, a set of stairs leading between levels.

The entire bottom floor is taken up by our open-plan office, desks and partitions and white boards, the stuff you'd see in any police station. Except our white boards are covered with pictures ripped from fantasy books, D&D paintings of orisha, photographs of supernaturals, anything that helps us visualize work on our open cases.

The place is already bustling with activity. There are about thirty operatives in Delphic Division, and we all have a little space to call our own. I weave through the narrow lanes between the desks, nodding at people who insist on greeting me even though it's first thing on a Monday morning and that kind of thing should be forbidden. No talking till ten would by my rule if I was in charge.

I flop down into my ancient chair. It creaks and sinks down a few inches, the pneumatic gas long since dissipated. I pump the lever and it rises reluctantly upward.

A pile of coloured files has been placed neatly in the exact centre of my desk. My case load for the week. I stare at it resentfully, then prod it with a pencil. I grab a bottle of aspirin from my desk drawer and swallow a few dry. I can feel it already. It's going to be a long day.

Parker is sitting at her desk opposite mine, glowering at nothing in particular.

'Morning, sunshine.'

She grunts noncommittally.

Parker is our resident resurrectionist. Anything to do with dead bodies, zombies, death magic, hoodoo, voodoo, astral planes, whatever, she's your woman. We were recruited at the same time, so we learned about the hidden history of the world alongside each other. She's five-six and has a thin, muscular frame. Dark hair, dark eyes. Tattoos all across her arms and back. She may be small, but I pity anyone who mistakes that thin frame for weakness. She's got a punch that can fell an African Rhino and has a pair of knuckle dusters hidden away that spring to hand at a moment's notice.

She also has the most extensive T-shirt collection known to mankind. I've known her four years and I'm sure she hasn't worn the same T-shirt more than once. Today, she's wearing a faded Nick Cave and the Bad Seeds tour shirt.

She doesn't seem to be in a talkative mood. She's like that until she gets a few cups of coffee in her system. She lives on the stuff. I don't think I've ever seen her without a cup of thick tar close at hand.

I leave her to carry on with her system reboot and open up the first file on my desk.

It's a complaint from someone in the SAPS, a request to investigate the National Police Commissioner's in-house sangoma. The complaint alleges that the sangoma is actually a charlatan, and is using fear of the occult to influence the commissioner. Boring. Should never have come to us. That kind of thing is usually dealt with by ORCU.

The next file is a case being built around a bishop who mutilated children on the advice of a traditional healer. Apparently, the healer told him that mixing herbs and human tissue would boost his dwindling church numbers.

I toss it back to the desk. I hate these cases. No *real* connection to Night and Day. Just desperation and ignorance.

The next file is more interesting. An investigation into why more and more fairy circles are appearing in Namibia. Armitage's notes say she thinks it might be due to the migration of our own abatwa faeries. But that doesn't explain why they would be leaving their homes here in Natal. Faeries the world over are notoriously territorial, tied to the land itself. For them to leave meant something had to be driving them. We'd have to look into that.

The next folder is a series of suggestions to add secret amendments to the Human Tissues Act. These amendments are to give Delphic Division more power to carry out sentences against the country's vampires. Armitage wants me to read over her suggestions and add notes.

I groan. I hate that kind of stuff. Parker is much better at it than me. Maybe I can trade one of her cases for it.

I tuck the file to the bottom and move on to the next.

A report about Swaziland's ban on witches flying their broomsticks below 150 metres. I chuckle. That's not real. Witches didn't really fly broomsticks. Boil down the fat of children and coat themselves in it to fly, sure. But broomsticks? Nah.

Beneath the report is Armitage's untidy scrawl. *'How the hell are the poor buggers going to play Quidditch now?'*

Armitage is the one who recruited me into Delphic in the first place. I suppose I'm DS to her DCI, although we don't really have those ranks out here.

She came over from London on a case for the Ministry, the UK's version of Delphic Division. But she decided she liked the weather here better, so just sort of stuck around.

I asked her once if she didn't miss England and she squinted at me through wreathes of cigarette smoke, sipped her whisky and said, 'I won't lie to you, pet, I do, I do. And you know how I get over it? I get in the shower and stand under the cold water for ten minutes straight to remind me *exactly* what I'm missing. After that, I'm golden.'

She can be a miserable old sod, but we have a laugh together. The stories of some of our cases . . .

'Course that was before Ranson was appointed Divisional Commissioner, sent here from his last job as the Minister for Arts and Culture. (Yeah, South Africa, where skills mean nothing in government and it's who you know that counts. Or rather, who you knew during the struggle days.) Sure, it's probably the same all over the world, but at least in other countries the ministers seem to have some basic idea of what their job entails. Here, people just get passed around departments every year or so, make a lot of noise to look like they're actually doing something, inevitably running the department into the ground in the process, and then are moved to a new post leaving us to pick up the pieces.

And Ranson is the worst of the worst. Apparently, his remit is to slash our budgets by fifty per cent. No idea why. It's not as if we're not needed. Get rid of us, and the whole country would be swallowed up by supernatural crime in a month. The talk around the water cooler is that whoever he's reporting to in the National Intelligence Co-ordinating Committee is skimming whatever percentage Ranson manages to cut for him or herself, splitting the money with Ranson.

It's the only explanation that makes any sense. The Supernatural Divisions around the world are allocated budgets according to an international treaty agreed upon at a tip-top secret meeting that takes place in a different country every year. So it's not as if the government can just decide to cut us off.

I asked Armitage about it when Ranson started firing 'non-essential' personnel, and she said she was already looking into it. Haven't heard anything since, though.

I pull my thoughts away from politics before I get really worked up and focus on the folders on my desk. It's always the last file in my weekly workload that I look forward to the most. A list of odd happenings in the supernatural world. Bits and pieces that don't make up full cases, but give a general spread of events and happenings.

The first item relates to the fact that a lot of supernaturals from overseas were making their way to our lovely shores. Faeries from Ireland, djinn from North Africa, banshees from Scotland, goblins from Germany. Loogaroo from Haiti. Even the Fir Bolg were venturing beyond the shores of Ireland. And they *never* leave. Weird. Was it holiday season in Nightside? We'd have to keep an eye on that.

Next up is a note that Anansi is courting Mother Durban in the hopes of entering into some sort of marriage. I wince. That's bad news. Anansi is the infamous spider god. A trickster. He's one of the most powerful orisha in the country, and he's used that power to create a criminal syndicate that spans the length and breadth of the country. He's a gangster, a crook and a murderer, the Godfather of the supernaturals.

And the fact he's courting Mother Durban can only mean he's trying to extend his power.

See, every city has a soul. The memories, the histories, the lives of the inhabitants, they all seep into the background aether, creating an orisha that is the personification of the city itself, an extremely powerful goddess that we know next to nothing about.

What I *do* know is that if Anansi is after her, then we need to look into it.

I put the report aside for later. Next up is a mention that there is a truce in place between the Seelie and the Unseelie Courts in London.

I have to re-read the sentence twice. A truce? How did *that* happen? The Seelie and the Unseelie have been at war for *centuries*, using London as their battleground. There seemed to be no rhyme or reason to it. They just fight because that's what they've always done. Gods alone know how they managed to broker a truce.

I flip the page. The last entry reports that Adlivun – Inuit underworld spirits – are rising up above ground and stealing innocents, dragging them back to their underground cities. Apparently, this is the first time it's happened in a hundred years. I don't envy whoever it is in the Alaskan Bureau who has to venture beneath the ice to get their citizens back.

'Hey – you see this notice about the Courts in London?'

Parker finishes off her coffee and nods. 'Armitage says we might have to go for a visit. That our local faerie courts have been pestering her about it.'

I check the file again, but there's no mention about the locals getting pissy. 'Why?'

'The London courts seem to think they're in charge of *all* the fey. The locals don't like the fact that they're banding together. They think they're leading up to some sort of challenge to the fey leadership. They want—'

'All right,' says a loud voice, ever so slightly tinged with the accent of the north of England. 'Listen up, kiddies.'

I look up and see Armitage leaning on the second-floor balcony, staring down at us from what she calls her Pulpit. (A plastic milk crate.) She scowls at us with harsh grey eyes, waiting for the troops to settle down.

Armitage looks a bit like someone's scary mother. (Take that as you will.) And she wears an old macintosh no matter the weather. Her eyes can twinkle with humour one second and turn to flint the next. And you really don't want her shouting at you.

Not at all the type of person you imagine leading the country's supernatural police force. But there you go. Appearances can be deceiving.

She finally waves a piece of paper in the air.

'New memo from on high,' she says. 'Name change time.'

Everyone in the room gives a cheer and Russells, a plump guy who is the official liaison between us and ORCU, a good guy doing a job no one wants or likes, gets up and flips a white board around, revealing a list of names with betting odds scrawled next to them.

Here's the thing. Delphic Division, and even ORCU to a certain extent, are an embarrassment to the government. They seem to take it as a personal affront that the supernatural actually exists, so take great pleasure in making life as difficult as possible for us. (The only reason nobody's blabbed about us to the press is because Armitage casts binding spells on the entire parliament. She catches them every year at the Christmas party to renew the charm, the *one* time of the year they all actually attend parliament so as to get their share of the free food and drink.)

One of the petty ways parliament makes life difficult for us is that when we fill out requisition forms and expense reports for the guys who pay the wages and approve budgets, we're not allowed to mention magic, wizardry, magicians, sorcerers or anything like that.

Only problem is, they don't know *what* official language they want us to use. It changes every couple of weeks.

The first time we got a memo, they said we had to use the word hex instead of magic.

Which meant we were all . . . Hexers? Hex-people? None of us knew, so we sent a memo back to ask.

Silence. Then a week later another memo saying that we were now known as Augurs, and the term for what did was Augury.

Someone even higher up didn't like that. A week later we got a new memo and were told to use Theosophist, and to call magic Theosophy.

Russells loved that. Said it made him feel official. I hated it. Sounded like a subject you'd study in college.

So Armitage, Parker and I sat down to come up with our own possibilities. I came up with Dwemer and Dwemercraft. (It's Old English.) Parker hated it. She suggested mage, magus, or magi. I laughed in her face. No way was I going around calling myself a magus. I'd have to start wearing robes if I did.

Armitage wanted enchanter, but the head honchos responded with a resounding no, saying we weren't in a Disney movie.

I gave up and left them to it, deciding to just call the power shinecraft. It fitted for me. Sort of suggestive but not up its own arse. And I just refer to all of us as conjurers.

But here we are in a new week with a new memo, which means a new official name. Armitage theatrically clears her throat.

'The powers that be would like us all to know we are henceforth and forthwith to be referred to as . . .'

She draws it out. Too much reality television for her.

'. . . As *mages!*'

Groans roll around the room, loudest from Parker. The only one who doesn't groan is Simmons, a skinny guy who looks like he can hide behind a street light. He cheers loudly, which means he wins this month's pool. Lucky bastard. I could have done with that money. 'Course, there wasn't much chance my entry would have been picked. 'Pretentious arse-baskets' isn't really a term I see the president of the country using. At least, not officially.

'All right, all right. Settle down,' says Armitage. 'Start of a new week and all that. You've all got your case loads. Get to work. London?' She looks in my direction. 'My office.'

I heave myself up from my chair, ignoring the knowing looks from everyone who thinks I'm in trouble again. I throw a pencil at Simmons' head as I pass. He ducks and gives me the finger.

I wish I could say all this was atypical of life at Delphic Division, but it isn't. We once spent a whole week arguing about the colour of the paint for the fifteenth floor bathrooms. We split into two warring parties and eventually decided the winner with a day-long game of office Olympics.

I push the elevator button. A brass pointer ticks slowly down to the ground floor and the doors slide open. The elevator is one of those old-fashioned types and I yank the cage open and step inside, hitting the button for the top floor.

The elevator rises slowly, a muzak version of 'I should be so lucky' playing over tinny speakers. Armitage picks the music for the elevator, changing it every week. Before Kylie we had muzak versions of Rick Astley, Bananarama, and Led Zeppelin. She thinks it's the funniest thing ever but nobody really knows why. We just go along with it.

The elevator bumps gently to a halt and I walk around the curve of the silo until I get to Armitage's office. Two potted ferns flank a mahogany door bearing a brass plate with the words 'Boss Lady' etched into it.

I knock.

'Come in, then!' she snaps impatiently from inside. 'What are you waiting for?'

Entering Armitage's office is like stepping back in time. Everything is dark wood and leather, like a Victorian parlour. Bookshelves lined with ancient hardcovers (and one shelf of Mills & Boon). A massive leather-topped desk with a green-shaded lamp. Two high-backed reading chairs.

The place is a tip, though. Every available surface is covered with clutter: old reports, photographs, empty cigarette packets, fast food wrappers. The air is scented with cherry cigars and nectarines, her favourite fruit.

She's busy peeling one now, plopping the skin into an overflowing ashtray.

'I tried to call you last night. Your mailbox is so full I couldn't leave a message.' She frowns at me. 'You know how annoying that is? All this bloody technology and I can't get hold of you?'

'Sorry.' I was going to ask her why she didn't just text me, but then I remember how hopeless she is at using her phone.

'Well. You're still alive, so I'm assuming it went well?'

I flopped down in one of the chairs. 'I think "well" is a relative term. I survived.'

'And Babalu-Aye?'

'Gone. For now. I'm not going to be popular when he comes back, though.'

'We'll deal with that when the time comes. The bastard deserves everything he got. How did you do it?'

'Shotgun in the face.'

'Nice. And the kids?'

I shake my head. I hesitate, leaning forward in the chair. 'He was selling their souls to an angel, Armitage. I saw it. The thing was . . . *snorting* their souls. Like it was blow.'

Armitage blinks. The skin around her eyes tightens. 'Those bloody angels. I *told* you, remember? Watch out for the ones who say they're fighting for good. They're the ones that'll destroy a continent in the name of their god. Remember?'

I shrug. Armitage says a lot of stuff like that. She really hates the orisha. 'I saved the last victim, though. And I blew up the angel.'

She blinks at me, her plump face wrinkling in thought. 'You blew it up?'

'Hand grenade.'

'Hah! Serves the bugger right. Any idea which angel it was?'

I shake my head. 'No glamour. The thing was as its god intended.'

'Ooh, look at you! I'm slightly impressed, lad. Not many can face down an angel and survive.'

'A *psychotic,* high as a *kite* angel.'

'As you say. Well done. And . . . I hate to ask, but . . . ?' She raises her eyebrows at me.

'No official presence. But . . . like I said, I used a grenade. So I *did* blow up the hospital a bit. But the papers said something about a gas leak, so I think we're in the clear.'

Armitage smiles with relief. 'Good lad. Don't want to give that arse Ranson any more ammo, eh? Best to keep these ones quiet.'

Keep these ones quiet. In other words, the ones we don't really have enough evidence to convict. The ones we send me in to deal with. The heavy gun. The good boy who does what he's told.

If I wasn't using Armitage the same way she's using me, I'd be a bit offended about these dark ops. But doing stuff off the books is the only way I can follow up my own investigations without the Division getting suspicious.

Armitage's cell phone rings. She asked me to set the ring-tone for her so I set it to Queen's 'It's a Kind of Magic'. She hates Queen, though. Every time she hears the phone it makes her face crease with annoyance.

'Yes?' she barks. 'No. Yes. Where?' Armitage makes urgent hand gestures at me, miming writing with a pen. I get up and find one on her desk. She scribbles something down on her hand then hangs up.

'Come on, then, pet. The game's afoot.'

'Is it?' I ask. 'And what terrifying case awaits Mystery Inc. today?'

'Murder,' she says cheerily. 'Murder most foul.' She rubs her hands together. 'But first, a bacon sarni.'

4

Armitage drives her old Porsche along a dirt road while I try to log into GHOST – the Global and Home-based Occult and Supernatural Treasury – on my phone.

Our victim is a man called Jengo Dhlamini. Apparently, he's been the local *ramanga* to a tribal chief out in the midlands for the past two years, and Armitage said the word like I should know what it means.

Which I don't, but I'm not telling her that.

I stare out the window while I wait for a cell signal. Sugarcane rises to either side of us, green stalks vibrant against the blue sky. We leave a cloud of dust behind us as Armitage navigates the road, swearing furiously as she swerves from side to side in a futile attempt to avoid the massive potholes and tractor ruts in the hard-packed earth.

My phone whistles, informing me it's managed to log into the database. I wipe the sweat from my brow – no air conditioner in this car – try to ignore my worsening headache, and type in the word RAMANGA.

An image appears. A pathetic-looking man, skinny, haunted. Something of the animal about him. I scroll down and browse through the entry.

Turns out a ramanga is a sort of low-key vampire. They're known the world over, but here in Africa they generally work for the royal families out in the kraals. If the tribal leader gets cut, it's the Ramanga's job to lap up the blood so it doesn't go to waste. If the Chief cut his hair, the Ramanga has to eat it. Toenail clippings? Down the hatch. A severed finger? Yum-yum.

They started out as ceremonial vampires. Just servants who used to make sure the royal offcuts didn't fall into the wrong hands for use in black magic. But over the years, the ramanga tribe of vampires took over the position.

The local Chiefs seem to think having your own personal ramanga is a status symbol, but back in the city where the various tribes of vampires live, ramanga are considered the lowest of the low. Scavengers, really.

'Who reported the murder?' I ask.

'Anonymous tip-off. Went to ORCU first. They want it themselves, but some lazy bugger in their outfit passed us the wink.'

'Are ORCU there now?'

'Probably. Pissing their scent all over the crime scene.'

Wonderful. There's a seriously competitive vibe going on between ORCU and Delphic Division. Basically, what it boils down to is the fact that we're cool, and they're not. They hate us, but every single one of them is desperate to be called up to the Division.

I suppose they've got a right to be pissed off. We get all the real supernatural stuff while they're stuck with muti murders and the like. They're always trying to crack a real case before we do.

'You know a ramanga is a vampire?' I ask.

''Course I do. That reminds me. Better get on the horn to your boyfriend when we finish up at the scene.'

'He's not my boyfriend.'

Armitage grins wickedly. 'Well . . . BFFs is what I heard.'

She's talking about Kincaid, King of the East Coast vampires. I helped him out a couple of years ago when an orisha from North Africa was trying to muscle in on his territory. Since then we've had an understanding. He doesn't

break the law in any overt manner, he feeds me any information he thinks I might find useful, and I let him know if any of
our work turns vampire-related.

'London and Kincaid, sitting in a tree,' sings Armitage.
'K-i-s-s-i-n-g.'

'Oh my *God*. You are *such* a wrinkled little child.'

We carry on driving for another twenty minutes, going
deeper and deeper into the sugarcane fields. My window is
down and I can hear the dry stalks rustling in the warm
breeze every time Armitage slows down to avoid another
pothole. I close my eyes, feel the wind against my face. It's
peaceful.

I know it won't last.

There's a certain quaint image associated with the word *kraal*.
It conjures up pictures of wattle and daub huts topped with
thatched roofs. Of men dressed in animal skins, women grind-
ing down mielie-meal. Kids running around with stray dogs.
Dust and heat and sun.

The reality – at least here – is very different.

This kraal is more of a compound, completely surrounded
by a ten-foot-high electric fence. We have to sign in, and the
guard manning the boom takes note of Armitage's licence
plate as we drive past his little shed.

So those wattle and daub houses? Change them to white-
painted houses with brick-walled gardens. Fine, the roofs are
still thatch, but you'll see thatched roofs no matter where you
go in this country. Suburbs and villages alike.

There are about thirty houses in the compound. Most of
them pretty small. But one dominates the rest. A double-
storey structure with a landscaped garden and a sparkling
blue swimming pool. That would be the Chief's house.

Armitage ignores it completely and drives up the slope of a
small hill that overlooks the little village. Police vans and

unmarked cars are parked at the top of the hill, clustered around a tiny house like vultures around a body.

We park around the side of the house, far away from the other vehicles (Armitage is paranoid about getting her car scratched), and head towards the house. We're not greeted by the Crime Scene Manager, something that immediately puts Armitage in a foul mood. She's always quick to anger, but nothing gets her goat more than careless or stupid police.

There's a box of blue paper suits on the doorstep. We put them on, then pull the paper slippers over our shoes.

Armitage pushes the door open with her arm, careful not to touch it with her fingers. I'm following right behind her as she strides into the house and surveys the open-plan lounge with rage.

'And just what the actual *fuck* is going on here?' she shouts.

Everyone in the lounge jumps. And there are a lot of them, (the reason for her rage).

'This is a crime scene, not a bloody social club. Did none of you pass training? Or are you just so bloody stupid you don't know how to act during a murder investigation? If you're not out of here in three seconds I'm bringing you up on report. Actually – bugger it! I'm putting you all up on report anyway. Out!'

Armitage has a point. There are four uniformed officers, plus three plain-clothes, all of them standing around the lounge, staring down at the body of the ramanga. And not one of them is wearing protective clothing. Which means they're dropping DNA all over the place. Hair, threads, footprints, you name it.

This crime scene is well and truly contaminated.

The uniformed officers scamper quickly out of the house, doing their best to avoid eye contact. But the ORCU guys just glance at their boss, Mark Anders, a prick of the highest order. He waits a while, then casually tilts his head, indicating they can leave. Only then do they make a move.

Anders stops before Armitage. Armitage isn't tall. Plus, she's
pretty old, but she radiates . . . *something* that makes people not
want to mess with her. Anders tries to stare her down.

Tries.

Anders looks away first, frowning and glancing around the
room as if he has a choice in the matter. I grin at him. He says
nothing, walks straight towards me as if expecting me to move.
I don't.

He tries to shove me out of his way with his shoulder. I'm a
pretty big guy and I just shove back. He stumbles, hits the
wall. Straightens and takes a threatening step towards me, his
face flushed red.

I smile at him. 'Come on then, prick. Have a go.'

He hesitates, then storms out, slamming the door behind
him.

'What an absolute cock,' says Armitage. She pulls two pairs
of gloves out of her pocket, passes one pair to me, then moves
deeper into the house.

Probably pointless now, but I blow into the gloves to loosen
them and put them on. Only then do I follow Armitage.

I look around. A small sitting area. A tatty lounge suite,
holes covered over with grey duct tape. A breakfast bar to the
right, three cupboards on the wall and a two-plate grill covered
in grease and old food next to the sink. One door, leading into
the bedroom.

And one very dead Jengo Dhlamini.

He's lying on the floor next to the coffee table. Both his
hands are resting in his chest. Literally *in* his chest, where a
huge hole has been gouged out of him. There's blood and
meat on the couch. I glance over at the wall behind the couch.
Pieces of flesh, major blood spatter. I follow the trickle of
blood down and, sure enough, sitting on the floor, the actual
heart. Whoever did this ripped out Jengo's heart and flung it
against the wall.

His head has also been removed. It's sitting a few inches away, perched upright on its stump. The head is facing the body, the features stretched into a look of horror and pain.

Armitage leans down to study the corpse. I stay back, feeling my stomach lurching. Never really liked this part of the job. Plus I've got to contend with the magical hangover I'm currently experiencing.

'Weapon?' I ask.

'Come and look.'

'No thanks.'

She looks at me with amusement in her eyes. 'Come on, you big jessie.'

'I'm good.'

'Well, to answer your question, it looks like whoever did this used their hands.'

'Those are pretty strong hands.'

'Agreed.'

'And chance of fingerprints?'

Armitage straightens up and grins at me. 'That'd be a first, eh? Fingerprints *in* the actual death wound. I doubt it, though.' She takes her cigarettes out and is about to light one before she remembers she's standing in a crime scene. She reluctantly puts them away again. 'Doesn't look like the place was turned over,' she says, glancing around. 'Check the bedroom.'

I open the only other door in the house. A small room. Curtains are drawn, casting everything in shadow. I pull them open, letting sunlight reluctantly pick out the old faded bedsheets, the painting above the bed, the stained yellow carpet.

I frown at the painting. It's one of those kitsch ones from the seventies, a boy and a girl holding hands and walking away from the camera through a corridor of autumn trees.

This is something I come across again and again with vampires. They all have absolutely terrible taste. In decor, in clothes, in *everything*. It's like they're aliens who decide to fit in by watching television shows from the previous five decades and adopting bits and pieces at random.

I check the bedside table. Antacid tablets (Huh? He's a vampire. What the hell does he need those for?), a pen, a pad of post-it notes, and a diary. I flip through the diary but there's nothing of interest. I even run the pencil lightly over the pad to see if there are any impressions. Nothing.

I check under the bed. Dust. I lift the mattress up. Nothing. Not even any porn.

The cupboards: old clothes, nothing interesting at all.

I head back out to the lounge. 'Anything?'

Armitage shakes her head and sighs. 'Time to ask around the village.'

I groan. Door-to-door inquiries are the absolute worst. 'Can't we get the uniforms to do it?'

'No. They'll just balls it up.'

I sigh, open the front door—

—and find myself staring into the glaring yellow eyes of two seven feet tall . . . *creatures*. Man shaped. Lithe, ropey muscles, heads of dark skin with muzzles that are forced outward, skin pulled back in a snarl to reveal sharp canines.

It takes me a moment to figure out what they are. *Bultungin* – were-hyenas from East Africa.

I tell you, therianthropy gives me the creeps. Always has. Never mind your boring run-of-the mill werewolves. That's the cliché now. Nowadays they *all* come out to play. Were-hyenas, were-cats, were-panthers, you name it.

The two standing before me don't make any threatening moves, which is reassuring. I wonder if they're humans changed to hyenas, or hyenas changed to humans. (Works both ways for Bultungin.)

In the background I see a fat man in bright bermuda shorts and a string vest sauntering up the path towards us. He's talking on his cell phone, acting cool, like he's too busy to even notice us. I know immediately he's the Chief. Everyone who thinks they've got a lick of power has that same attitude. *I'm more important than you.*

He stops before us, but carries on chatting. 'Uh-huh. Yes. No. Of course not, baby. Not to you.' He listens a bit then breaks into a wheezy laugh. 'Tonight, then. Looking forward to it.'

He hangs up and finally turns his attention to us. His eyes are bloodshot *and* jaundiced. An impressive feat. His stomach is so large it distorts the string around his belly. This is not a healthy man.

'You are trespassing,' he says.

Armitage holds out her identification. 'Police. Major Armitage and Lieutenant Tau.'

I wave my warrant card, but the Chief barely glances at it.

'You have no power here.'

I snort. 'Don't be stupid. What – you think this is a foreign embassy or something?'

The bultungin growl. I jerk my thumb at them. 'And tell Thing 1 and Thing 2 to simmer down or I'll have to neuter them. What are you doing with Bultungin anyway?

'They are good bodyguards.'

'Bullshit. They're terrible bodyguards. They barely have two brain cells to bang together. Admit it. You think it gives you status, that's why you have them.'

'I do not *think* they give me status,' says the Chief. 'They *do* give me status.'

Annoying thing is, he's probably right. People like him *would* be impressed by orisha acting as personal slaves.

I glance at Armitage. 'Isn't it against the Covenant or something?'

She shakes her head. 'Not if they're acting of their own free will.'

'Whatever.' I wave it away. 'We want to know about Jengo Dhlamini.'

'He is dead.'

'Yeah, we got that, Sherlock. We want to know *why*.'

The Chief shrugs. 'He was not a well-liked man. They never are, ramangas. People think of them as . . . unclean.'

'So he had enemies?' asks Armitage.

'Many.'

'Anyone specific?' I ask. 'Anyone threaten him recently?'

'No. Not enemies like that. He stayed out of the way, and people stayed out of *his* way. I've no idea why he was killed. It is quite a pain, because now I have to apply to the vampires for a new ramanga, and it is quite a laborious process, let me tell you. So many forms to fill in. They do not like it when their ramanga are lost.'

I start to get even more annoyed. The Chief is trying to impress, letting it drop that he knows about Night and Day, about vampires and the like. I admit I'm curious. It's not often civilians know about the behind-the-scenes stuff. But not curious enough to give him the satisfaction. He wants me to ask how he knows. Screw him.

'He wasn't lost,' I say. 'His chest was gouged out and his head ripped from his body.'

The Chief shrugs. 'Same thing.'

I'm always suspicious when people don't have a healthy fear of authority. You approach a normal member of the public, flash your badge, and they immediately think they're guilty of something. Most of them trip over themselves to help.

Then you get those who actively antagonize you. The people trying to prove something. Either to their mates or themselves. Who try to act like they don't give a crap who you are. They *do*, though. And all it takes is five minutes in handcuffs for them to start blubbing for their mummy.

But the absolute worst are the self-entitled. The rich. The powerful. Those with 'friends'. Those who *honestly* couldn't give a shit who you are. Who know they're untouchable. People like the Chief here.

'Just for the record,' I ask. 'Where were you last night?'

'Me?' he says with relish. 'I was with my mistress. This is quite exciting. Am I a suspect? Are you going to take me "downtown"? What an interesting story for me to tell at my next dinner party.' He holds out his hands, clasped together, waiting for the cuffs.

Armitage has watched this exchange while cleaning her nails with a small pocket knife. She finally straightens up and glances past the Chief. I follow her gaze and see a white van stopping at the bottom of the hill.

'That will be Maddoc and Jaeger,' she says.

Maddoc and Jaeger, Delphic Division's very own orisha forensic pathologists. They're sisters, and they . . . well no one really knows what they are. Not human, that's for sure. Supernatural creatures that take an almost obscene delight in rummaging around inside corpses.

'I'd advise you to clear the area, sir,' Armitage says to the Chief. 'It's still an official crime scene, and if it's tampered with I really will have to arrest you. You might think it's all fun and games, but a night in the cells will soon change your mind.'

The Chief reluctantly stands aside. Armitage smiles brightly at him and heads down the path to have a few words with Maddoc and Jaeger. I stay by the door, arms folded, as they climb out the van. Maddoc is already wearing a pale blue paper suit and has her photographer's bag slung over her shoulder. Her skin is as white as the first sheet of photocopy paper from a new ream. Same with her hair. Her eyes, however, are lemon yellow.

She climbs the path towards me, followed by Jaeger and Armitage. Jaeger is the complete opposite of Maddoc. Her skin is pitch black. Like new oil. And it has a sheen about it, making it look almost viscous. Her eyes are the same yellow as

Maddoc's. I don't know what Armitage is saying to her, but she bares her teeth and looks in the direction of the Chief. I'm not sure if it's a smile or a snarl.

The Chief notices this as well and steps into the shadow of his bodyguards. I don't blame him. Jaeger is pretty terrifying.

Maddoc draws level with me and I nod respectfully. 'Maddoc.'

'London.'

She enters the house and puts her bag down carefully in the hall, squatting down to assemble her lenses and equipment. Then she takes some paper overshoes from her bag and slips them on, finally pulling a mask over her mouth to complete the incredibly fetching ensemble of crime scene respondents everywhere.

Jaeger draws level and grins at me. 'Hey, lover boy,' she says.

I flush with embarrassment. I don't know why, but Jaeger always makes me feel like a teenager. She and Maddoc have never told us what they are, but I suspect they're some form of succubus.

She cackles, showing her white, serrated teeth, and lunges past me, forcing the Chief and his were-hyenas to stumble back a step.

'You three, fuck off,' she says. 'I don't want dog hair on my crime scene.'

I grin as the Chief hastily makes his way back down the path, his bodyguards following behind.

'What are you laughing at? I meant you as well. Who was the FOA?'

FOA – First Officer Attending. I shrug. 'Not sure. But you're going to have a long afternoon of it. ORCU *and* uniform were traipsing around the scene without any protective gear.'

She swears loudly. I pull my notebook out and jot down the names of the officers that I recognized. I tear the page out and hand it over.

'There are a couple of names I'm not sure of. And I've no idea what time they got here.'

She takes the paper and pins it to the clipboard where she keeps her crime scene log. She'll fill in the details later and most likely contact all the cops to get DNA samples from them.

If this all sounds surprisingly boring and mundane for a supernatural police force, it is. But that's just the first phase of crime scene processing in the Division. Once Maddoc and Jaeger have gone through the physical evidence, they'll sweep the area for shinecraft and aether disturbances. By end of the day tomorrow we should have a pretty good idea of exactly what went down here.

In the meantime, it's left to me and Armitage to do the legwork.

You'd be surprised how many cases are solved just by talking to neighbours, writing everything down, and joining the dots. Making connections between seemingly disparate bits of information.

Oh, Jimmy Connors always walked the same way home? Everyone knew that? Thank you ma'am. Oh, Mr Smith left the pub early that night? And he never does that? What time? 11:30 on the dot? How do you know that sir? Because Jimmy Connors leaves the same time every night and he'd just stepped out the door. Thank you very much, sir.

It's all disappointingly . . . *normal.* But it's how most crimes are solved. Because here's the thing. Most criminals are pretty fucking stupid. They're not Professor Moriarty or Hannibal Lector. They make stupid, pathetic mistakes that get them caught, mistakes that could easily have been avoided if they'd only stopped to think. Some bury the body in their back garden. Others are witnessed buying twenty kilograms of lime at the local hardware store. Others kill after having a huge argument with someone. An argument twenty people witnessed.

Call it what you want. Heat of the moment. Momentary madness. I call it the human condition – stupid to the last man. Or woman.

In this case, though, nobody has any information for us. We spend the next two hours doing door-to-door, questioning anyone who will talk to us. But nobody saw anything. Nobody heard anything.

And nobody is sorry the poor bastard is dead. He wasn't well-liked, our victim.

Which makes our job a whole helluva a lot harder.

Sometime after two in the afternoon, Armitage calls it a day. We leave Jaeger and Maddoc to do their thing and head back to home base, but not before I buzz the Chief's intercom system.

'Yes?' It's the Chief. He sounds drunk.

'Detective Tau here. I notice you have CCTV cameras mounted above your gates.'

'Yes.'

'I'd like a copy of the feed. The past forty-eight hours should do. Take it up to the ramanga's house and hand it over to one of our pathologists, OK?'

A pause.

'OK? Otherwise, they'll have to come knocking on your door.'

'Fine.'

The sky is the colour of faded nicotine.

The clouds have turned purple and grey, week-old bruises that stain and bleed into the jaundiced sky. It's like I'm looking at everything through tinted glasses, the world around me leeched of its normal vibrancy and tinged the colour of old bone.

I stare absently at the clouds, wondering if we're going to get stuck on the freeway when the storm hits. I hope not. At this time of the afternoon, the traffic will be bumper to bumper.

Plus, the first hint of rain and South African drivers become possessed by stupid.

I'm still staring at the sky when I notice a vague shape taking form. It takes a while for it to register because it's so far away, nothing more than a tiny dot against the sallow sky. But it gets bigger. Closer.

I frown. Some sort of bird? I definitely see wings flapping. But it's huge. It *can't* be a bird.

It's—

'Pull over,' I say urgently.

Armitage doesn't ask questions. She steers the car to the side of the road and switches the engine off. Her hand moves to her hip, touches the butt of her police-issue berretta.

'What is it?'

'Trouble.'

I push the door open. Climb out the car. The afternoon heat crawls across my skin, stifling, oppressive. The threat of rain is heavy in the air. I wince and squint up into the sky. The figure is much closer now, soaring towards us much like Superman does in the movies.

That is, if Superman happened to be seven feet tall with wings.

The angel plummets straight towards the ground. At the last moment it flares its wings wide and stops abruptly, pulling sharply up and bobbing in the air.

The figure blocks out the sun, a silhouette of holy fury. It hangs there for a moment, watching us, then descends to the ground, slow-flapping wings raising a cloud of dust.

I wait, my heart hammering. What to do? I'm not going to attack another angel. Two in as many days is a bit much, even for me. My fingers are clasping and unclasping. I'm itching to grab my wand, but I don't. I'm not very good with it and I barely survived a fight against a demented angel that was spaced out and high. I wouldn't stand a chance here.

Unlike yesterday, this angel looks exactly how you imagine an angel to look. A face like a cold statue, hard lines and smooth skin. Curly hair that falls to his shoulders (it looks like a he, but it's hard to tell with angels). As he walks towards us his wings fold down around him, draping over his shoulders and changing, forming into a dark brown trench coat.

Neat trick.

I resist the urge to take a step back, something I'm pretty fucking proud of. An angel is a pretty scary figure.

I raise my hands in the air. 'In the immortal words of one of our forgotten, modern-day poets – "It wasn't me".'

The angel stops walking and folds his arms. 'What wasn't you?'

'Uh . . . whatever. Anything. Nothing. What is this anyway?'

Yeah. Cocky denial may not be the best route. Babbling confusion might be better.

I hear a match scraping to life, turn to see Armitage lighting a cigarette as she squints up at the angel. She's not looking very impressed.

'Do you know who I am?' says the angel.

'The Easter bunny?' I say.

'I am Michael, Lord of the Archangels. Prince of the Heavenly Hosts. I am the Angel of Deliverance. My name is a battle cry. My wrath is the wrath of God. I am the Archistrategos. I am the defeater of the Dragon.' He sighs and looks around, frowning at the sky. 'And I fucking *hate* it here.' He turns back at us. 'It's the heat, you know? Reminds me of you-know-where.'

'Texas?' I say. 'Australia?' Michael stares at me. 'Sorry. I get snarky when I'm nervous. Not that I'm nervous. Why would I be?'

'Yeah, why would you be?' asks Armitage, amused.

'Shut up, Armitage. So, why are you here? If you hate it so much, I mean?'

I tense, waiting for him to bring up the angel at Addingtons. Not that he has any moral high ground to stand on. One of his own was buying kids and snorting their souls. But still, you have to be careful how you handle these guys.

Michael sighs. 'You must stop pursuing this inquiry.'

I pause, the words of denial and righteous indignation dying on my lips.

'What inquiry?' asks Armitage.

'This death. The ramanga. I will find the perpetrator. I will punish him. This is not for you to deal with. If you continue on this course, you might be in danger.'

Armitage blows a cloud of smoke into the air. 'Sorry, pet, was that a threat?'

A pained look flashes across Michael's face. 'Don't be ridiculous. Believe me, you would know if I was threatening you. But there are . . . things going on here—'

'What things?'

'*Delicate* things. Things you are in danger of getting caught up in.'

'We're already caught up in it,' I say.

'Then extricate yourself. I do not want to have to come back here again. If I do I might have to peel your skin from your body and dip you in vinegar.'

I blink.

'*That* was a threat,' says Michael kindly. 'In case you didn't catch it.'

'No, no. I caught it all right.'

'Good. I do not wish to see either of you again. Good day.'

The trench coat unfurls over his shoulders, spreading out to either side to form Michael's wings. He flaps them a few times, rising up into the sky. He stares at us the whole time he does this. Then, when he is about thirty feet up, he turns and puts on a burst of speed, disappearing into the liver-bruised clouds.

There is a deafening crack of thunder and the storm hits.

Armitage tuts and shakes her head. 'Bloody angels.'

It's already four in the afternoon by the time we get back to the Division, so I spend the last hour starting my report into the ramanga's death and typing up the first few statements from those we interviewed. (If you don't like paperwork, don't become a cop. We spend about seventy per cent of our time filling out expense reports, balancing personnel budgets, filing crime reports, and typing out interviews that we *already* have on tape and video.)

I stop as soon as the clock strikes five. We've been told that there's no overtime any more, so it's pointless carrying on. I shut down my computer and lean back in my chair, stretching.

I glance across at Parker. 'What are you doing tonight?'

'Nothing much. Dinner and some TV. You?'

'I need a drink. A few drinks.'

Parker makes a face. 'The Cellar?'

I nod. 'I don't know what you've got against that place.'

'It's so . . .'

'Down to earth?'

'. . . *Disgusting*. The place is a dive.'

I shrug. She's right, but I know the owner and he lets me run a tab till payday, which is a huge plus in my books. He also makes the best club sandwich in town. Sweet chilli sauce, chicken, bacon . . . my mouth's watering just thinking about it.

I get to my feet grab my keys. 'See you tomorrow then. Same time, same place—'

'Same shit.'

'You got it.'

Back at the flat and I can feel the stiffness creeping up on me. My joints ache, and my muscles are seizing up. The magical hangover has been with me all day, but this is my body reacting to the battering it took yesterday. Walking around at the kraal staved off the pain, but it's coming on hard now, armed with heavy bats and crowbars. The wards the dog applied saved my bones from breaking and my insides from spilling inconveniently out my mouth, but the beating still had an effect.

'Honey, I'm home,' I call out as I enter the flat.

'Did you get my sherry?'

I hold up the brown bottle. 'Is that all you can say? We don't talk any more. I feel like you don't even care about me.'

'Pour the booze and I'll listen to you whine about your day all you like.'

'God, it's like I'm a kid again. You even sound like my ma. Same throaty growl.'

I pour the entire bottle of sherry into the dog's huge bowl.

'So how was *your* day?' I ask.

'Epic. I watched movies and licked my balls. You?'

'A ramanga was murdered out in the boondocks. Been out there all day cooking in the heat.'

'Lovely. Now we're all caught up, let's have some silence. I need to drink.'

I leave him to his afternoon tipple, grab a beer from the fridge, and head into the bathroom to run a bath. Steaming hot and filled with all that relaxation shit Becca used to buy. I have no idea if it will help, but it can't hurt.

I wince as I strip off my clothes and slowly lower myself into the scalding water, sinking down until only my head is exposed.

I close my eyes and drift as the steam and heat attempt to relax my muscles. My thoughts float to Becca, drawn towards her by the scents floating around me.

Maybe I should call her.

Then again, why bother? She's made it clear on numerous occasions she wants nothing to do with me. I can't blame her, either.

So, no. No phone calls. The past is in the past. Leave it there. At least until I have something concrete to tell her. Something to put her mind at rest. One way or another.

The best thing for me to do is to give the dog my mobile phone, head down to the Cellar, get drunk, talk crap with anyone who will listen, come home, try (and fail) to get my phone back to drunk text Becca, then fall into bed and wake up tomorrow with a *natural* hangover so bad it will make demons weep.

I soak for another half hour and finish my beer, then heave myself out of the tub. I choose a Dolce & Gabbana suit, leaving the jacket in the closet. (Too hot.) I pick a white Veneta shirt with pink pinstripes, a grey waistcoat and a dark grey tie. I slip my phone into a zip-lock bag and toss it onto the dog's chair.

'Going out. Getting drunk.'

He opens one eye. 'Don't ask for it back.'

'That's the whole point.'

'What if it rings?'

'Take a message.'

'I'm not your secretary.'

'Ignore it, then.'

I grab my wallet, my keys, and I head out into the summer evening to get spectacularly wasted.

5

The dream always starts with the rain.

It pours from the night sky. A torrent. A flood. Sheets of solid water cascading across the pine trees, over the mountains, turning the road into a river of mud. The noise – a thundering roar, a constant, heavy assault on the ears.

His car breaks down a kilometre from the lodge. He can see it, nestled against the craggy backdrop. The windows are just visible, yellow light struggling to lift the darkness.

He gets out the car and is instantly soaked. Like he's jumped in a pool. He slithers around to the trunk, yanking it open for his torch. He sees his gun case, pulls it towards him and flips the catch to reveal his shotgun. He loads the shells, slips extras into his jacket pocket, then starts to run.

The man with the gun falls over, pushes himself up and keeps moving. The rain is blinding, pushing against him, the wind trying to force him back. He fights against it, struggles on.

The lodge is so far away. He doesn't seem to be getting any closer. The panic sets in. He thinks he's stuck in a nightmare. The one where he's trying to escape something but can't get anywhere.

The mud flows past his legs. His feet are numb, freezing cold. His bobbing flashlight picks out brief snapshots of his surroundings – leaves, the bark of a tree, the sharp rocks, the flowing mud. His breath sounds harsh in his ears. His chest is on fire, getting worse with every step.

The panic is driving him on. Pushing his feet one in front of the other. He didn't think he could get any more scared, but he was wrong. The fear keeps rising. A sickening, heart-wrenching darkness that is cresting higher and higher, driving his sanity away.

He realizes he's uttering words as he forces one leg in front of the other, wading through the mud.

'Cally.'

Step.

'Cally.'

Step.

'I'm coming, honey.'

Step.

'Hold on.'

Step.

When he finally gets to the lodge, all his training deserts him. He doesn't do a perimeter search. He doesn't assess. He doesn't make a judgement based on observation.

He kicks in the door, the shotgun levelled before him.

Into the lounge. Looks around.

And sees the blood.

So much blood.

It covers the wooden floorboards. A massive puddle. A lake of crimson.

Three figures. First threat, the big one. Hulking, massive. Easily six feet six. Shaved head, with a bushy black beard. He's standing with his hands resting on the head of a second man. The second man is facing away from the blood, kneeling in a doorway, his eyes closed, head bowed.

He looks like he's praying.

The third figure is seated in the centre of the pool of blood. Smiling. Running his hands over the blood in wide circles.

He lifts the shotgun. The big man spots him, lunges through the door, trying to escape, shoving the kneeling man ahead of him. The shotgun goes off, tearing a huge hole in the doorframe.

He runs forward, but the corridor beyond is empty. He hears a door slamming on the other side of the house. He hesitates, glances over his shoulder.

The man sitting in the blood is getting to his feet, blinking and looking around in confusion. The man with the shotgun turns back to him, knowing his priority is to find the kids, find his daughter. The sitting man has . . . he has blood around his mouth, caked beneath his nails.

He lunges forward and hits the figure with the butt of the shotgun.

'Where is she?' he screams. 'Where's my daughter?'

The man slips, falls back into the blood. 'Wh-who?' he says. 'I don't . . .' He shakes his head, looks around in confusion.

'Where is she?' the man screams.

'*Who?*'

He needs to search the house. She could be dying. Locked away somewhere. But he has to make sure this man doesn't get away. Not till he's told him everything he knows. He pulls the man's leg out, angles the foot to the side, and then hits his ankle as hard as he can with the gun.

The crack of snapping bone. The man starts to scream.

He leaves, frantically searches every room in the house. But there are no kids. No Cally.

He comes back to the lounge. The man is still lying on the floor, his face clenched with pain. The man with the gun doesn't care about that. All he cares about is finding his daughter.

'Where is she?'

The man blinks at him. 'I . . . I don't know. I don't know why I'm here. I don't . . . don't remember—'

'*Liar!*' He hits the man in the face with the gun. 'Where is my daughter?' he screams. His daughter is supposed to be here. All five kids are supposed to be here. This is where the informant said the kidnappers took them.

'I have no idea!' the man wails. 'I don't even know where I am!'

The man with the gun doesn't understand. It's as if he really doesn't know. The look on his face is too genuine to be faked.

He looks around at the blood, despair washing over him.

He's too late. He knows it. The blood is hers. And those other kids. And later DNA tests will prove him correct.

An inhuman howl erupts from him, a scream of loss and pain. A primitive shout of emptiness and loss. He turns and unloads the last barrel into the man on the floor.

The dream might start with the rain.

But it always ends in blood.

6

Your mind breaks when you lose a child. You have to go a bit insane, because there's no actual logical way for the human mind to deal with something like that.

It's like your limbs have been torn off, like some demon has injected an empty void into every waking moment of your life and you know you'll never be able to fill it again. Memories are torture. Reminders of your failure. A lead ball forms in your stomach and weighs down every single moment of your life. Guilt is no longer a simple emotion, something you feel then eventually get over. It becomes the dominant presence in your life. A new companion to everything you do. A treacherous whisper in your ear. *Why are you smiling? Why have you woken up without tears? Why aren't you thinking about Cally? Who are you to think about the future? How dare you contemplate a life that might some day involve happiness.*

Anything that gives pleasure becomes a catalyst for the guilt, until your whole life, every waking moment, revolves around the pain and loss.

And then you give in to the guilt. You have to. There's no other way. Like an abused spouse you realise it's right, even as it's hurting you. You let it destroy your life, your marriage. You let the pain win. Because the pain is right.

And then three years have passed and you realise you're still no closer to finding the people responsible.

*   *   *

It's always worse in the mornings. When I wake up covered in sweat, the facade built up the day before hanging in bloody tatters, my soul exposed to the harsh reality of life without the daily filters in place.

On bad days, like today, when the nightmares last all night, I just want to make the world burn. For *everyone* to suffer, for everyone to feel exactly what I'm feeling. I'm utterly . . . *enraged* that other people have normal lives. How dare they? Who the fuck do they think they are? Nothing is normal anymore. Everyone should know that. The whole world should know that.

Other times, when I'm not so angry, when the dreams fade into dull grey images that hover just out of reach, I want to warn everyone that the world is bad. That the world is a horrible place and they need to take their kids and hug them and never let them go. To play with them. Read to them. To take those moments and hold them tight. To remember them now, because the bad days are coming, and these little moments will be all you have left. You have to stack them up inside your soul. They're what keep you alive when nothing else seems worth it.

And you have to fight for them. Because your mind will forget, it will just let them drift away like ash from a fire.

And other times, when I wake up remembering Cally from before that night in the mountains, when the memories aren't of blood and horror, but of us playing with her Star Wars toys, or us goofing around in the pool, I want to protect everyone. I want to go out and catch every bad guy alive, round them up and drop them into the ocean. I want to show the world that there's still someone out there who wants to help. That no matter how it looks, not everyone is corrupt.

Those days are few and far between.

I crawl out of bed and into a scalding shower, trying to burn away the dreams. I only partially succeed. I blink, realising the water has turned freezing cold while the images from the nightmares play over and over in my head.

I get dressed and retrieve my mobile phone from beneath a snoring and snorting dog. I take it out the zip lock bag and check it. There are five missed calls from Armitage, all from last night. No text messages or voicemail, though.

I'm about to call her back when there's a knock at the door.

I open it to find Anders from OCRU and a young woman waiting for me.

The woman is wearing the pale blue shirt/dark blue pants of the police. Anders is in a neat suit, cheap, looks like he bought it from Woolworths.

'Yeah?'

The guy actually holds up his I.D. 'Sergeant Anders, SAPS. This is Constable Ndlovu.'

'Yeah, I know who you are, Anders.'

'We'd like you to come with us, Mr Tau. We have a few questions we'd like to ask.'

I sigh. Was this about yesterday? Giving him attitude back at the kraal? I have a sudden thought. Maybe it's about the kids' hospital? Had Moses the car guard sold me out?

'Does it have to be now? We've got a murder to deal with, Anders. You know that.'

'It has to be now, yes.'

Might as well just get this over with. If it is about the hospital I'll just deny everything. I should be back at work for a bollocking from Armitage by noon.

I glance over my shoulder to see the dog watching all this. 'See you later, dog.'

'You want to phone someone to come take care of . . .' Anders looks at the dog and his face furrows with distaste, '. . . *it?*'

I frown. 'Why? Am I going to be gone long?'

'That all depends on you.'

That sounds ominous. 'He'll be fine,' I say.

Anders leads the way down the stairs while the constable walks behind me. There's a white and blue police van waiting for me outside, another worrying sign. I'm one of them. I should be transported in an unmarked car, not a meat truck like every other perp they pick up.

I'm bundled into the back and the door slams shut behind me. I sit on the bench behind the metal grill as Anders and Ndlovu climb in to the front, Ndlovu driving. The back of the van smells of vomit, sharp and vinegary. There are stains on the wooden bench opposite me, very clearly old blood.

The police radio is crackling and beeping. Anders turns it down as we pull into the traffic, heading west through the streets of Durban and finally out onto the M3 freeway. I frown. Why are we heading out of Durban? There are plenty of police stations inside the city limits.

'Where are we going?' I ask.

Anders glances over his shoulder. 'Hillcrest Station.'

Hillcrest? Why the hell are we going there?

Hillcrest used to be one of those sleepy villages, a one-road town all the way up to the early 2000s, when the rich people from Johannesburg suddenly realized it was there and started buying the land up cheap and building their huge houses. Now it's a bustling town with shopping malls, housing developments, and a way-too-high cost of living, and it *still* only has one main road, although they *had* widened it to two lanes each way.

Oh yeah – and they'd put traffic lights up every thirty feet or so, just to make your blood pressure rise every time you needed to get anywhere.

It takes us about fifteen minutes to get into Hillcrest from Durban, a thirty-kilometre trip, and then another ten minutes to travel the two kilometres along the main street to the police station.

We turn left at the traffic lights, then left again into the *Mr Price Home* parking lot. (Mr Price is a huge furniture shop with a massive parking lot, while the actual police station across the street is tiny, and hasn't been upgraded since the 1980s. Priorities. Gotta love them.)

Anders opens the back door of the van and I climb out. The three of us cross the road and enter the brick building. A tiny reception area no bigger than my kitchen lies beyond. It's packed with people waiting to fill out reports on stolen cars or housebreakings. Anders takes me around the back of the faux-marble worktop and into a dingy corridor, walls painted nicotine yellow, then into a room with a steel foldout table and three plastic lawn chairs.

'Wait there,' he says.

I sit down. Anders comes back a moment later with some paperwork, a couple of thick files, and an ink pad. He puts everything on the table and gestures for me to stand up.

'Hand,' he says.

'Am I under arrest?'

'Just give me your hand.'

'You've got my prints. They're on file.'

'*Hand.*'

'Do I need a lawyer?'

Anders finally looks at me. 'Yeah, reckon you will.'

I'm starting to get a bit worried. I thought this was just a basic questioning. I don't think there's any real evidence to tie me to the destruction of Addingtons, except for Moses' say so. But this looks more serious. They had something on me. Had Moses taken pictures on his cell phone? Was there CCTV footage?

I put my hand out and Anders takes my fingerprints, smearing them across the little boxes on the arrest report. He gestures to the corner of the room. There's a tiny cracked sink there with a hard, ink-smeared block of soap. I do my best to get the stains off my fingers, then tear some paper towel from an industrial-sized roll sitting beneath the sink.

Anders leads me deeper into the station, into another room.

A scratched wooden table and two chairs, foam padding poking out through slits and holes in the material.

We sit down and I wait to see how Anders is going to handle this. If there's no evidence it means they need me to confess. The fact I haven't been put in cuffs means they're not a hundred per cent sure what I've done, or if I've done anything. I don't know whether to be hopeful or not.

Anders opens one of the files and starts copying information from it onto the arrest report. I peer across the table and see it's my SAPS personnel file.

'The fuck is going on, Anders?'

He smirks at me. The prick is loving this.

I lean back in my chair, give him the dead-eye stare. (I learned that from Armitage. She has a look on her that could melt iron into a puddle of molten metal.) 'What are you? Twenty-seven?'

'Twenty-nine,' said Anders.

'Whatever. I'm not going to sit here and have some snot-nosed fast-track gym-bunny judge me because he's got an inferiority complex and a power buzz. Tell me what's going on. Now.'

He smirks at me. Again. I'm pretty proud of the fact that I don't lean over the table and punch him. I *really* want to.

'Where were you last night between nine and three?'

I blink. Wasn't expecting that.

'Last night?'

'That's correct. Can you account for your whereabouts?'

Why the hell does he want to know that? All that stuff at the hospital happened two days ago.

I straighten up in my chair. 'What's this about?' I ask. 'Why am I here?'

'Do you know Major Olivia Armitage?'

'Don't be stupid. You *know* I do. Christ, what's she done? Is she here? Have you locked her up for something? I *told* her to stay away from Point Road.'

'She's not locked up, no.'

I lean forward, feeling a small tug of satisfaction when Anders leans quickly back. I'm not a small guy. Six-two without my shoes. I can be scary if I want to.

'Then what's this about? Why are you asking me about Armitage?'

'Because she's dead,' says Anders, biting off each word and watching me carefully for my reaction.

I don't say anything. I hear his words, but I don't believe him. It's that cliché, isn't it? When you're involved in some tragedy or another it doesn't feel real. It's like you're watching it in a movie.

'No, she's not,' I say stupidly. 'She can't be. I just spoke to her yesterday.'

'Nevertheless, she's dead. Murdered.'

I blink. I shake my head slightly. My thoughts are racing, my heart hammering as if to keep up. I feel sick. It can't be true. It's a joke. Has to be. This whole thing. This can't happen again. I can't go through all this a second time.

'You're taking the piss. Where is she?'

Anders pulls some glossy photographs out of one of his files and lays them out on the table. I glance at them, then look away, feeling the bile rise in my throat. My insides are churning. My heart sinks into my stomach.

I don't want Armitage to be dead. I always thought she'd outlive me. I could easily see her giving the finger to Death when the skeletal bastard came for her.

I force myself to look at the first photograph.

Armitage lying on tiles. I recognize them as being from her lounge. Suddenly it makes sense why I'd been hauled all the way to Hillcrest Station. She lives here. The death happened on their patch.

Armitage's chest has been ripped out. Exactly like the ramanga. A huge gouge scooped away revealing her spine.

She's baring her teeth in a snarl. I can almost hear her thoughts, the anger at going out this way. Her fury at being killed.

Another photo shows her heart sitting on the couch, a little numbered marker pinpointing it as evidence.

Armitage's hand is reaching out to the side, her fingers covered in blood. There are smears beneath her fingers . . .

Anders slides another photograph on top of the previous. Not smears. Writing. Armitage had dabbed her fingers in her own blood and written on the tiles. How that was even possible is beyond me, but she always was a stubborn old cow.

But it's what she's written that makes everything clear. I suddenly understand why I'm sitting in this interview room.

Written on white tiles in her own blood is what looks like the word:

Tau.

'Got anything to say for yourself, *Tau*?' asks Anders.

'Come on!' I snap. 'You think I did this? Because she wrote my name? We were working on the same case. Chasing down whoever did this . . . !' I stab the pictures with my finger.

'I'll ask again. Do you have anything to say in your defence?'

I lean back in my chair. 'Yeah. I want my fucking phone call.'

I call Parker and tell her to get over here and get me the hell out of jail. While I'm waiting I get to enjoy the comforts of our wonderful state hospitality. A Spartan cell with a plastic-covered mattress and a toilet that doesn't work.

I pace. I keep thinking of Armitage. It was obviously the same killer that had murdered the ramanga. Which meant someone didn't want us investigating the case. *Really* didn't want us investigating.

The angel. Michael. He'd told us to back off. Warned us away. Could he have done this? Surely not. Even sanctimonious angels would stop at cold-blooded murder.

Wouldn't they?

I remember all the missed calls on my phone. She'd tried to call me. Probably even tried to leave messages, but I still hadn't cleared out my voice mailbox. Shit. And while she was being murdered, I was out getting rat-arsed drunk.

I shout in frustration and punch the wall. Which does absolutely nothing except make my hand really hurt. I sink down onto the thin mattress and put my head in my hands. Stare down at the pitted concrete floor.

This was my fault. If I'd had my phone. If I'd answered the call, gone to her . . .

Then you might both be dead, says a voice in my head.

I can't believe she's gone. My mind won't accept it. Doesn't *want* to accept it. I think back to the cases we worked on, the nights we spent drinking together. We even drank here in Hillcrest. A place called The Station Masters Arms, a pub built in an old train station building, the outside tables butting right up against the unused tracks.

I shouldn't be feeling like this. After everything with Cally, I thought I was immune to feeling *anything* for anyone else.

In this job, you're supposed to develop an acceptance for the end of life, and you deal with it in one of two ways. You either become a pragmatist – you live, you die. It's all random, and there's nothing after you croak.

Or you become spiritual. You decide there's more out there, that maybe death isn't all that bad because you move on to another plane, or you come back, or you go to heaven, hell, whatever. The point is there's something *more* than you. Something more than the job.

I still remember the day I chose my own path. This was before Delphic Division. Before Becca, before Cally. Back when I was a normal cop. I was called to a crime scene in the suburbs. High walls. Electric wires running along the top. Burglar bars on all the windows. Two cars. Swimming pool. Pretty standard stuff.

The husband had lost his job, racked up gambling debts. Wanted to commit suicide. But could he do the decent thing and just take himself out? Hell no. He killed his family first. Two daughters, one son, and his wife.

Then he chickened out. Couldn't do it to himself. He eventually got off. No jail time. Mentally unfit to stand trial.

Where's the justice there?

I worked that crime scene all morning, trying not to look at those three kids lying on the kitchen floor. I can still see that image in my mind, fresh as if it was yesterday.

I left work that day and drank myself into a stupor, and when I woke up I just felt . . . hopeless. Like I was a tiny sandbag against a metaphorical flood. That nothing I did mattered.

I took a week's leave and I thought about where I was, what I believed, what the job was *making* me believe. I just kept thinking, if this is all there is to life, I might as well shoot myself in the head right there and then. I even considered it. I really did. Why not? Nothing I did was going to make a difference anyway.

But over the course of that week I came to realise, to wish, and eventually to believe, that there *had* to be something more out there. Had to be more to life than simply – you're born, you live, you die. I couldn't accept that this was the sum total of human existence.

I wasn't talking about God, though. Fuck no. Any God who puts up with the shit that I've seen can fuck right off. I just felt there was something . . . else. And I didn't know what.

A few months after that I met Becca. Then we had Cally and my world changed. *She* gave my life meaning. *There* was hope. And I realized that *this* was part of the reason we kept going. Our kids. We lived to protect them from the world.

Something I failed to do.

Christ, I would give anything to have Cally back. Switch places with her in a micro-second. Die every day for eternity if it only brought her back to us.

But failing that I decided I could only do what I believed was right in the face of evil. Because, yeah, that's one thing I *did* come to believe in this job. Evil is real. I've seen it. I saw it that night in the cabin up in the mountains. I've seen it hundreds of times since.

The Devil is not some hideous monster ruling over the many courts of Hell.

He walks among us.

And I will not stand by and let him win.

So what do I believe now that I failed my daughter?

One thing.

I believe in justice.

Not the law. That's a different thing. The law is man made. Justice comes from the soul.

An hour later Anders arrives at the cell with his keys. He unlocks the door and holds out a form on a scratched Perspex clipboard. 'Sign.'

'What is it? Admission of guilt?'

'You're being released.'

'About time.'

I thrust the clipboard back at him, sending him stumbling back a few steps. I head down the hallway to the front desk and find Parker waiting for me. Her eyes are red. She doesn't say anything, just folds her arms around me. I freeze. Physical contact has never been my thing.

But then I just let it happen, meld my arms around hers. It feels good. The human contact.

She breaks first, leaning back and looking at me. I look away, worried I'd see accusations there. *Why weren't you with her, London? You should have been with her.*

The desk officer tosses a brown A4 envelope onto the worktop. I take out my watch and my wallet. I check inside. Cards, driver's licence, but no cash.

'There was five hundred bucks in here,' I say.

The desk sergeant looks down at his form. 'Not according to this.'

He hands it over. Sure enough. An itemized list of the cards inside but next to the column for Cash was a big fat zero.

'It was here.'

'That your signature?' The sergeant taps the bottom of the form.

It is. I hadn't even bothered to read it. Had other things on my mind. I toss the clipboard back at his face. He flinches and catches it, half-rising from his chair. I stare at him, waiting, hoping he'll do something. I want to lash out. To hurt, to cause pain. I don't care who to.

'Get out,' he says.

I don't answer, just head through the door and across the street into the parking lot. I wait for Parker to catch up.

She leads the way to her old silver BMW. I open the passenger door. The seat is covered in junk. Old CDs, newspapers, fast food wrappers. I sweep them to the floor and climb in, glumly staring out the window.

Parker climbs in the driver's side and starts the car.

'What happened?' I ask.

'No one knows. She didn't log her actions. She was on her own time.'

'It's the same killer. The ramanga we saw yesterday.'

'Yeah. Jaeger said.'

'Where's her body?'

'In the Division mortuary. You want to see her?'

'Not yet. Let's check out the crime scene first.'

Parker drives deeper into Hillcrest, turning off the main road and heading into the suburbs. We drive past the library then a primary school. Parents arriving in their cars at the end of the school day. Kids screaming and laughing, running around. Enjoying their lives.

I look away as Parker slows to let them cross the street.

'I'm ... sorry,' she says. 'I know you and Armitage were close.'

'She was a pain in the arse,' I say softly.

Silence. Parker starts moving forward again. 'Ranson's already talking about her replacement.'

'She's only been dead a couple of hours! Who is it?'

Parker scowls as she slows down for some speed bumps. 'Don't know. Some guy from Cape Town.'

'Christ.'

I hate Cape Town. Everyone raves about it, saying it's the jewel of South Africa. The ultimate tourist destination, yadda-yadda-yadda.

It's not. It's where all the pretentious wankers move to when they get money. Where all the rich people live. Give me Durban any day. Durban is the soul of South Africa. Johannesburg's the heart. Cape Town is the rectum, shitting out refuse and pretension in a never-ending stream of hipsters and writers and filmmakers.

Parker turns into a cul-de-sac. Armitage's house is easy to spot. It's the one with all the police vans parked outside. We park behind them and climb out. A crowd has gathered outside the perimeter of blue and white tape. They have their cameras out, taking pictures and recording everything that's going on. Scum. Vultures hoping to profit on pain by selling their images to the papers. I'd arrest them all if I could.

'Get this lot out of here,' I snarl at a uniformed officer.

He looks at me fearfully, the fear of a rookie given instructions he has no idea how to carry out.

'Tell them it's a gas leak. Health and safety.'

I grab a paper suit from the back of Parker's car, duck under the tape, and trudge up the path. Neatly trimmed hedges flank me on both sides, flowerbeds carefully tended. I remember how surprised I was the first time I came to Armitage's house. Gardening was the last thing I thought she'd be interested in.

I pull on the suit and overshoes, Parker doing the same. I take a deep breath. Then we enter the house.

The sharp, tinny smell of blood hits me. I don't stop walking, even though I want to. Too many people around. Can't look weak. Along the hall, past Armitage's stainless steel kitchen, into her minimalist lounge.

It used to be white and grey.

It's red now.

I blink, look away. But no matter where I turn I see it. Dark blood, frozen rivulets, dark spatters. Across the LCD television. Across the white tiles. Even up across the ceiling.

'Evidence?'

'Nothing yet,' says Parker.

'Was it quick?'

'No . . . She put up a fight. It starts in the bedroom, ends up here.'

I sigh, look around the room. 'Did Jaeger say when she can tell us anything?'

'She's already done the post-mortem on the ramanga.' Parker checks her watch. 'She started on Armitage a couple of hours ago.'

I nod.

'Uh, one thing before we go.'

Parker leads me to Armitage's bedroom. I enter the room and look around. More blood.

Lots of it.

And also medical equipment.

Lots of it.

An EEG monitor. A dialysis machine. Monitors, tubes, drips, and various other medical paraphernalia.

'Was Armitage sick?'

'That's what I was going to ask you,' says Parker.

'Not that I knew of.' I check the readouts on some of the machines, but it's pointless. I have no idea what I'm looking at.

'No charts?' I ask hopefully. 'Files?'

Parker shakes her head.

'And then . . . there's that.' She points behind me.

I turn around. The entire back wall of the room is covered in crucifixes. There had to be over a thousand.

I look at Parker. She just shrugs. 'No idea. Didn't even know she was religious.'

'She's not,' I say.

We both stare at the wall.

'Maybe we can access her work records,' I say. 'If she was sick the Division might have been paying for it.'

'Maybe.'

There's nothing more to be done here. I had to come. I knew there'd be nothing left for me to do, but I had to take a look for myself. I owed it to Armitage.

We leave the house and head back to Delphic Division. We use the front entrance, entering a huge, echoing foyer that looks like something from a seventies science fiction movie. All grey stone and high ceilings.

Through a second set of doors and into the corridor that leads to the central hub, then into our offices.

A heavy silence drapes across the room. There's an emptiness that seeps into every corner, an Armitage-shaped hole that will never be filled. Everyone turns to look at us. No one says a thing. For all intents and purposes, Armitage *was* Delphic Division. She helped build it up. She recruited every officer in the room. There wasn't a single person here who didn't feel her loss as if it was a family member who had gone.

I glance up at the pulpit, half expecting to see her standing there waving her cigarette around while she debriefs everyone, ash raining down onto the desks below like snow.

I flop into my chair and stare at my monitor. Why the hell hadn't I just answered the phone? Why hadn't I stayed in?

Why, why, why? The questions everyone asks when something terrible happens. Why didn't I leave the house when I meant to? Why did I go back for my sunglasses? Why did it have to rain? Why did God decide to take a dump on me? I played this game when Cally disappeared. It doesn't end well.

My phone rings and I reluctantly pick it up. 'Tau.'

'London,' says Jaeger. 'I'm finished.'

Delphic Division has its own mortuary. It has to. The kind of bodies the unit deals with can't exactly be taken to the morgue at the local hospital.

It's nothing at all like the mortuaries you see in cop shows, though. You know the ones, with the mid-century cracked tiles, the exposed pipes, the old, porcelain tubs, all the moody lighting.

Our mortuary is state of the art. Brushed aluminium sinks and tables. Bright strip lights, plus a movable spot directly above the autopsy table that can be pulled down to inspect wounds more closely. One wall is floor-to-ceiling morgue drawers. The walls and floors are tiled. But the tiles are huge and spotlessly clean. Not a crack to be seen.

Jaeger is waiting for us. Her usual grin is absent. She just looks angry. Maddoc is standing in the corner holding a clipboard. She's staring at the floor, not moving a muscle.

An involuntary shiver runs through me. I don't like it when orisha act oddly. Most of them have adopted our mannerisms and behaviours so they can fit in. But when they get upset, all that falls away and I have no idea how to read them.

Two autopsy tables have been wheeled into place above drains in the floor. The ramanga – Jengo – and Armitage. Both bodies are covered.

I hover in the doorway, unwilling to enter. Parker keeps

walking, then pauses and glances back at me. She reaches out
her hand. I hesitate, then take it. Her fingers squeeze mine.

Goose pimples rise on my skin from the cold air. I shiver,
wait for Jaeger to take the lead. I feel lost. Don't know what to
do. My eyes keep skittering away from Armitage. I find myself
approaching Jengo instead.

'You want to do this one first?' asks Jaeger.

I nod, not trusting myself to talk.

'Fine. Both injuries are identical anyway. Definitely the
same attacker.'

Jaeger pulls back the pale green sheet and folds it over the
ramanga's stomach. Jengo's head is absent. I look around and
see it sitting on a table on the other side of the room. I feel like
it's watching us.

The hole in Jengo's chest looks worse in the harsh fluorescent lights. Purple and deep red. Like meat at a butcher's
shop. The same smell as well.

'OK, we're talking major sharp force trauma to the chest. In
both victims the chest plate has been ripped away. Crushed
first. Then pulled out at the same time the attacker scoops out
the heart. One movement. Not easy.'

Jaeger points into the hole with a ballpoint pen, although
I'm not exactly sure what I'm meant to be looking at.

'Carotid and subclavian arteries are torn. Happened at the
same time as the heart was taken.'

'What was the murder weapon?' asks Parker.

'Well, we have a combination of sharp and blunt force
trauma. It's more of a chop wound—'

'So an axe?'

'Let me finish.'

'Sorry.'

'The pattern of the wound is similar to those seen in animal
attacks. But the margins of the wound indicate someone used
their hand to do this.'

Parker frowns. 'A hand?'

'Yes. Look inside. See those furrows at the top of the lungs? Nail markings.'

'Are we talking claws?' I ask.

Jaeger taps the pen against her teeth. 'I wouldn't think so. The furrows are too wide. But whatever caused this injury is phenomenally strong. There are no probing wounds. This was one confident strike, scoop out what you want, and bye bye vic.'

I nod, take a deep breath, then turn to face Armitage.

Jaeger starts to pull the sheet down, but I stop her when it gets to her neck. I don't need to see the wound. Don't need to see her unclothed. Let her have some dignity.

I stare down into the pale face of a person who used to be my friend.

Blood spray covers her neck and chin. At least her head is still attached. The killer didn't feel the need to decapitate her. Probably because she wasn't a vampire.

'What were you doing, you stupid cow?' I whisper.

'She seemed . . . agitated. Excited,' says Jaeger.

'What?' I look up, confused. 'When?'

'Last night. She wanted me to get started on the ramanga's post-mortem straight away. She stayed to watch.'

'She was here? After hours?'

Jaeger nods.

'When did she get excited?' asks Parker.

'When we emptied the contents of the victim's stomach.'

'What was in it?'

'Goat. Salad leaves. Beer. And a coin.'

'A coin?'

Jaeger nods. 'An old-fashioned one. She took it with her when she left. This was about nine o' clock.'

Right when Armitage first tried to call me.

'Where are her possessions?'

Jaeger nods at a stainless steel table behind me. A clear plastic evidence bag sits in a tray. I open it up and tip the contents out. A box of cherry cigars. Her old pocket watch. (Really, who uses a pocket watch? What a poser.) Her purse. I open it up and look inside. Some money, business cards, a shopping list (Washing powder. Cake. Socks. Condoms – multi-pack. Massage oil.) I grin and shake my head, imagining her walking up to the checkout with those items in her basket.

I turn to Jaeger. 'Where's the coin?'

Jaeger points to a second metal tray on her desk.

I pick it up and examine it. It's not really a coin. It looks more like a token of some sort. Like the sort you used to get at games arcades. But Jaeger's right. It's old.

'Why is it in the tray?' asks Parker, peering over my shoulder. 'Why not with her possessions?'

'Because it was in her stomach,' says Jaeger.

I look at her. 'In *her* stomach?'

Jaeger nods.

'So . . . the killer made Armitage and Jengo swallow it before killing them?' says Parker.

'No. That's a different coin.'

I frown, confused. 'So . . . you find a coin in Jengo's stomach. Armitage takes it, disappears somewhere, then she turns up dead with the same type of coin in *her* stomach?'

Jaeger nods.

'And you're sure they're different?' asks Parker.

Jaeger goes to her desk and picks up a photograph. She shows it to me. It's similar, but the two are clearly different. The patina and colouring are distinct.

'So the killer forces them into the victims' mouths?'

'Or Jengo and Armitage both swallowed them voluntarily,' says Parker.

'Why would they do that?'

She thinks about it. 'To hide them from their killer?'

I study the coin again, but it still doesn't reveal any secrets. 'Can I take it?'

Jaeger point to an itemized list on her desk. 'Sign it out first.'

I check the list and sign my name against 'Stomach contents: coin – unmarked'.

'What do we do with the body?' asks Jaeger.

'Keep it here. I don't think she has any next of kin, but I'll look into it.'

Jaeger nods. 'Have you had a chance to look at the footage yet?'

'What footage?'

'From the kraal. We think the Chief's CCTV picked up the perp.'

I stare at her, eyes wide with shock. 'You're kidding me. We have footage of the killer?'

'Possibly. Not sure if it's him or not. I uploaded it to the server couple of hours ago.'

I hurry back to my desk and log in to the Division intranet. I find Jaeger's file and open it. Parker peers over my shoulder.

Four different images flicker to life. Different angles from the Chief's cameras. Jaeger has trimmed them down to the exact point where the suspect comes into view.

My breath catches in my throat. My skin goes cold, prickling. Hair standing on end. Like seeing a ghost in an empty window smiling at you.

I stare at the image before me, my mind catching up with what I'm seeing. It . . . it can't be. Can it?

I rewind the footage and freeze it. My heart is hammering erratically. I feel dizzy as I stare at the screen.

At the face of Armitage's murderer.

At the face of the big man from the mountains. The guy with the shaved head and beard who ran out the back way with the other perp.

It's him.

One of the people responsible for Cally's death.

7

Seven-thirty that night and I'm walking along the esplanade.

The cicadas are out, hiding in the trees along the sidewalk, their shrill shrieks a summer chorus as the sun drops behind the tankers and container ships queuing up on the horizon.

I pass a guy pushing a mobile ice cream fridge along the street. He nods at me, eyebrows raised. I usually buy a Cornetto from him but tonight I shake my head. I need something stronger. I need to sit down. Stop moving so my brain can catch up with everything that's happened.

My heart is still hammering. I'm excited. Nervous. Terrified. This is the first real lead I've ever had. The first clue that the man actually exists. That he wasn't a figment of my own imagination. (Because believe me, it's something I've considered every day since that night in the mountains.)

I've already printed a copy of the perp's face and circulated it to all the law enforcement agencies throughout the country, marking it as highest priority.

Never mind wondering how he connects with the ramanga, what his motive is for killing him. I'll figure that out later. (I know why he killed Armitage. She got too close.) Right now I just have to focus on catching him. Making him talk.

Making him tell me where Cally's body is buried.

After that I can get him for Armitage. For the ramanga. But Cally comes first.

The Cellar is a pub that was built below street level. Hence the incredibly original name. I hurry down the stairs and shove the reinforced door open. My feet immediately stick to the linoleum, and that's about as classy as you're going to get in the Cellar.

A pool table takes up the space to my left. An old jukebox straight ahead, one that still plays records. Booths around the walls to give the drinkers their privacy. Old movie posters hang on the walls. *Plan 9 from Outer Space. The Maltese Falcon. Metropolis.* That kind of thing.

Charlie is leaning against the bar that runs along the wall to my right. Charlie is a retired cop. Bald, with a trimmed grey beard. His face is weathered, lined and creased by the wind. He goes surfing every morning. Apparently he's out in the water from sunup to midday. Crazy bastard.

He's chatting to Mick, the old guy with one leg who I suspect actually lives here. He has a little dog that never leaves his side. Some kind of Jack Russell hybrid. It sits on the stool next to him, looking between Mick and Charlie like he's following the conversation.

The rest of the pub is empty.

'London Town,' says Charlie. 'Back again?'

'Charlie.' I nod at Mick, and, before I can stop myself, at the dog. 'Glenmorangie. Double.'

Charlie pours the drink and slides it to me. No ice. No water. Just as God intended. Down in one go.

He raises his eyebrows. 'Rough day?'

I gesture for a refill, which he does without any more questions. That's why I like it here. It's never full, and no one talks to you when you don't want to talk.

I take my drink to a booth with a torn *Blade Runner* poster hanging above it. I slide in and stare at the TV mounted above the bar. The sound is down and some soccer game is playing. I sip my drink this time, letting my brain do its own thing. Not trying to pin anything down. Not yet. I don't have nearly enough information to make any deductions. I know from past experience that it's best just to stay out of my brain's way for a few hours.

After the third double whisky I'm feeling maudlin. Armitage was such a huge part of my life over the past five years I'm finding it hard to accept I can't just pick up the phone and call her.

I stare at my phone, sitting in a little puddle of sticky . . . *something* on the counter.

It's the suddenness that always gets me. That instantaneous severing of life. And everyone is supposed to just . . . adapt. Immediately. It makes you think in clichés. Life is short. You never know what's around the corner, live each day like it's your last, yadda-yadda-yadda.

But I'm feeling even worse because my grief is mixed with hope. A combination that feels . . . wrong. Hope is something I haven't experienced in a long time. But I felt it flicker to reluctant life when I stared at that bearded face on my computer monitor.

Could this be it? Am I finally going to find him?

I pick up the phone and scroll to Becca's number. I haven't called her in . . . what? A year? Not my choice. She doesn't want to have anything to do with me. Wants to move on with her life. To not live in the past. But . . . this is big. This is something, isn't it?

My finger hovers over the call button. I stare at her name on the screen, take another sip of my Glenmorangie. I let the peaty taste swirl around my tongue, and a moment later the phone is dialling and I'm not sure if I hit the button accidentally or not.

She picks up after three rings. 'Hello?'

She sounds the same, which is a weird thought to have. Why wouldn't she sound the same?

I hesitate.

'Hello?'

Why isn't she saying my name? She should have my name programmed into her phone, right?

Unless she's deleted me from her address book.

I lick my lips. 'Becca?'

A pause. 'Gideon?'

'Yeah. . . .'

Silence. I swallow nervously. 'How are you?' I ask.

'How am . . . ?' I can almost see the incredulity on her face. That look of amazed wonder at the stupidity of some people. 'What do you want — has something happened?'

Yeah, you could say that. I open my mouth to tell her. But then I freeze. What am I going to say? That I saw a grainy image of one of the men involved in the murder of our daughter? Then what?

'No – yeah . . . It's not . . .' I sigh. 'I . . . just wanted to hear your voice.'

'Goodbye, Gideon.'

'Becca—'

She hangs up.

I stare at my phone. And *that* is why I'm supposed to leave it with the dog. No good comes from having access to comms when you're feeling the way I do.

It's about ten o' clock now. The bar has filled up a bit. Charlie's wife, Sandra, has come down to help out from their flat above the pub. I say help out, but Sandra is sitting on this side of the bar with a glass in her hand as she chats to Charlie. They burst out laughing at something and I feel a twinge of jealousy. I want that. I want the easy understanding that comes from knowing someone completely. That feeling of companionship. Did I ever have it with Becca? I can't remember. We had good times, sure. We loved each other. But there were problems there as well. Problems that were starting to outweigh the positives even before . . . before Cally went missing.

I sigh. No point in hanging around here anymore. Any more drinks and I'll be on the other side of the buzz line.

Maybe the best thing would be bed. Look at all the evidence tomorrow with the team. Write everything up on the board and start searching for connections, points of convergence, that kind of thing. I don't feel like it's a real case until we start sticking photographs on the board, drawing in links and theories with our markers.

I step out into the humid night air. I can hear the waves from here, a whispered susurration, a gentle reminder of the tide of life.

Christ, the tide of life? Maybe I'm already on the other side of the buzz line.

I climb the steps to street level and start walking the half kay back to my flat.

I'm still a couple hundred metres from home when I realise I'm being followed.

The street is alive with traffic. Young kids heading to the clubs and pubs along the beachfront, an older couple heading home after supper, the beggars and the homeless who call the sidewalks their home. Cars drive past, honking at the girls. Taxis too, always the taxis, kwaito music blaring from the huge speakers in the backs, the bass actually vibrating windows in the flats as they drive past.

All perfectly normal.

But then, as these people, chatting, laughing, shouting, get to around twenty metres behind me, they go quiet. A lull in life as Armitage used to call it.

I know what that is. It's the uneasy silence that generates around Joe Public when they experience something . . . *other*. Like – to take an example entirely at random – when an orisha is following me.

The normals don't see whatever it is, but they can feel it. Hence the uneasy silence that opens up, then drops away again as they pass by.

I slow my pace. Maybe not the brightest move, but I'm trying to think what to do. I don't want to lead whatever it is back to my flat. It's the only place I've got, and if it gets trashed then I'll be out on the street.

I've got my wand with me. *Never leave home without it, Harry Potter*, was Armitage's command. And later, when I still hadn't found a replacement focus, *Seriously. I know it's hideously embarrassing for you, but don't leave home without it. You'll thank me one day.*

I did indeed thank her as I pulled it out of my pocket and reversed it, laying it up along my forearm.

I draw level with the Southern Sun hotel. Faux marble steps leading up to glass doors. I look around, getting desperate. Too many people for a confrontation here. Need to take this off-grid.

I cross the street, giving the finger to a taxi driver who decides to pull out right in front of me. I dodge around his bumper, taking the opportunity to glance over my shoulder as I do so.

Something there. A patch of movement in the shadows. An indistinct figure. Big. At least seven feet tall. Pedestrians flow around it like a stream around a rock.

On the other side of the street is the main thoroughfare of the Golden Mile, a twenty-feet-wide esplanade where people stroll and rollerblade and walk their dogs. I jog across the sand-dusted concrete then hop over the low wall onto the beach itself. My feet sink into the sand. There's an old pier about a hundred metres to my right. The pilings are cloaked in darkness. No pubs or restaurants facing it. That will have to do.

I'm not sure whether to run or just stroll casually. Strolling implies I haven't spotted my tail, so hopefully whatever it is will give me time enough to get to cover. The flip side of that is that they might be sprinting directly for me at that very moment.

My neck prickles at the thought. My ears are straining, hyper alert, listening for the slightest sounds of footprints in the sand. The water is a constant woosh and sigh to my left. The moon is full, the tips of the waves glowing white. I can see ships far out in the ocean, lights twinkling, waiting for their turn to be pulled into the harbour.

I wipe my sweaty hands on my jeans, then grip the wand again. I don't want to draw any attention, so I'm thinking anti-light, kind of like a reverse fire. It burns cold but doesn't let off any visible fireworks.

I call up the sequence of conjuration in my mind, feeling the shinecraft building up in my chest. It feels like you're on speed, a tightness, a rapidity, an . . . awareness of everything. My scalp tingles, the sensation flowing down my body like a shower of electrified sand. At the same time I can feel my surroundings being leached of power as I suck in energy from the world around me.

The pilings are about twenty feet away now and I see they're not the traditional kind that I can hide behind or use for cover. These pilings are concrete and are actually joined together without any gaps between them. I'm actually leading myself into a trap.

Shit.

I can't help it. I glance over my shoulder.

The huge shadow is loping towards me, bent over on all fours. Others come behind it, creatures I can't quite make out that are moving with an odd jerky gait.

I fling my hand out and unleash some of the power. Dark tendrils of black lightning burst out of the wand. The air freezes as the tendrils shoot towards the creatures, mist exploding into being, then dissipating in the humid air.

I make it to the pilings and whirl around, the wand held ready before me.

Only then do I falter.

When I see what's coming for me.

It's a Matchstick Man. That's what we call them. Real name *Mpakafo* – or heart stealer. Another tribe of vampire.

Over seven feet tall, limbs thin and abnormally long. The creature's skin is pallid white and blotchy, like dirty marble. The colour of its eyes are reversed. White pupils in black.

The Mpakafo is wearing an old-fashioned velvet suit – dark purple or black, hard to tell in the light. But the suit is too small for it, the sleeves pulled up past the forearms.

And behind it, the creatures with the odd gait, are Smilers – *Aigamucha*. Again, vampires. They have no eyes in their heads. Their mouths are massive, ugly slits. Wounds that almost slice their heads in two.

I say no eyes in their heads, and that's true. But they have eyes in the soles of their feet. That's why their gait is so odd. They're walking on their hands, their feet raised up before them so the eyes can see where they're going.

One by one they put their feet down into the sand, rising up to their full height. I can hear snuffling sounds coming from the black holes in their faces where their noses should be. They've caught my scent. They don't need their eyes any more.

Christ. I should have kept the tattoos for today. Looks like I might need them more than I did at the hospital. That's the problem with calling the dragons. They weaken my will, my life force. If I summon them again so soon after the last time, they'll defeat me. I won't have the power to send them back.

Of course, there's always the off chance that this is some kind of social call, that the creepy snuffling vampires might need Delphic Division's help with something.

'Anything I can do for you?' I ask.

The Matchstick Man edges forward in a jerky motion. 'Where is it, Mr Tau?' it says.

'Can you be a bit more specific?'

The Smilers have spread out in a line so that I can't get past them. I'm trapped. Five Smilers and a Matchstick man. These are odds I'm not going to walk away from. Even if the dog was here, we'd still get our arses handed to us on a plate. It's just a simple matter of numbers. I have a horrible, terrifying feeling I'm about to join Armitage.

'Specific. Yes. We would very much like to have the soul, if you please.'

I blink. 'Soul?'

'The soul, that is correct, yes please.'

I have to admit, I'm stumped. I have absolutely no idea what it's talking about.

'Do you want my soul?' I ventured. 'Because I'm pretty attached to it.'

'No please. The soul you very much know we would like yes.'

I wait, still none the wiser.

'The ramanga's soul, yes please. That is the one we seek, yes.'

The Smilers shift slightly at the mention of the ramanga.

'Listen, mate. I have no idea what you're talking about.'

'This is . . . displeasing to us,' says the Mpakafo.

And then, with a suddenness that I'm totally unprepared for, it lunges forward, crossing the fifteen feet between us before I can even raise the wand above my waist.

A blow to my chest. Air sucked out of my lungs. Flying through the air, then I smack into the concrete pilings. Light explodes behind my eyes. I hear a crack. Not sure if it's my back or a rib. Blood trickles down my neck where my head hit.

I fall into the water. Slump forward. Try to steady myself.

The water comes halfway up my forearm. Cold wet sand beneath my fingers.

Still, I manage to hold onto the wand. That's something.

I shake my head. Little flashes of white erupt before my eyes. Hands on my shirt, yanking me out of the water.

'Where is the soul?' asks the Mpakafo.

Before I even get a chance to respond, it flings me back towards the beach, sending me straight into the pack of Smilers.

I hit the sand and roll a few times. Look up. See the moon, suddenly eclipsed by the faces of the Smilers as they come for me. I bring the wand up, release the anti-light. It writhes out of the wand like diseased lightning, wrapping itself around the closest Smiler.

It stumbles back with the black tendrils locking around its face like a scene from *Alien*. I release more bolts, sending them randomly around me as I struggle to my feet.

A flashing, cutting pain in my back. An explosion of red hot agony. I cry out, stumble around and see a Smiler holding a long strip of skin with a layer of fat still attached. I stare incredulously as it eats it, black tongue darting out to fork my skin into its mouth.

'That's my fucking skin!' I scream.

I pump bolts into the creature. It wails and falls back onto the sand, its whole body shuddering and twitching as the anti-light leeches life (or un-life) from its body.

Something grabs my left arm, yanking it back. I hear the bone break, cry out in agony. I'm whirled around by my broken arm. I scream. It's like nothing I've ever felt. I'm convinced my arm is about to come away from my shoulder and fall to the sand. I'm shoved back and forth a few times then released to stumble back into the water, arm hanging uselessly at my side.

I stare dumbly as the Smilers and the Matchstick Man walk slowly towards me. I fire more anti-light, but it's weaker. No power left. (Magic is directly proportional to the strength of the user.) The Matchstick Man bats the writhing blackness away. It hits the sand and fuses a patch to black glass.

I know I'm done. I can't win this fight. This isn't an underdog movie where the hero finds an inner strength he didn't know he had. This is real life, and I'm outnumbered, fucked over, and about to die, and there's not a thing I can do about it.

Knowing this brings a certain curious calm. Was this how Armitage felt? I always thought there would be panic, a maelstrom of regrets and fears. But all I have is . . .

. . . wait.

Ah. Not calm. That's going away now, replaced by . . .

Anger.

Fury.

'Fuck you, you toothy bastard,' I mutter. 'I will not die today.'

I charge the Matchstick Man. I summon the last of the power and the black lightning surges into the Matchstick Man's chest. It sinks into his skin, disappearing.

The Matchstick Man stops walking. It makes a curious sound, like a child's whimper.

'This is . . . not pleasing,' it whispers.

The Smilers stop moving, turning to face their leader, their body language radiating fear, uncertainty.

I almost feel a tiny sliver of hope. Maybe this *is* like every underdog movie from the eighties. Maybe I'll defeat the bad guys and Becca will come back to me and we'll live happily ever after. Maybe I'll get out of this after all.

Then the Matchstick Man opens its mouth and the black lightning crawls out and flops to the sand like a dead spider. As one, the Smilers turn in my direction, smiling hideous, bloody smiles.

Then again. Maybe not.

The Smilers snarl and leap at me. All I see is wide open mouths and serrated teeth. Then I'm pushed to the ground. Water pouring over my face, up my nose. I choke, try to fight. The Smilers snap at me like dogs. Worrying at my flesh, pulling small chunks loose, getting the blood flowing. I've still got my wand. I lash out with shinecraft, feel weak lighting trying to push the Smilers away.

A barked command from the Matchstick Man. The Smilers jerk away, hurry to stand behind their leader, crouching down and fawning, reaching up to hesitantly touch its velvet suit.

I turn in the shallows, try to crawl away. I'm too weak. I'm losing blood. My arm is broken.

And I'm a bit impressed to realize I'm still trying to come up with a plan. Looking for a way out. That's me. Good old London Town. Always looking for the angle.

I realise I'm pulling myself deeper into the sea. The water flows over my head. I rise up. Choking. Spitting. Then a wave hits me in the face and I'm back under. Struggling. Fighting the current.

Why do you fight me, child?

The darkness folds over me and I'm suddenly hanging in eternal nothingness. Pitch dark water, deep and ancient. It's all around me. I'm swallowed up by it.

A lithe, dark-skinned woman floats before me. She's naked, her dark hair floating around her full face.

I wonder if I'm dead. If this is the final vision of a brain starved of oxygen.

Who are you? I don't speak, but somehow she hears my words.

I am Yemanja, says the woman. *You are in my home.*

Yemanja? I mentally flick through my internal catalogue of gods. Yemanja is an orisha of water and rivers.

Bit far from your patch, aren't you?

All rivers flow to the sea.

Fair enough.

Can you help me?

That depends. How would you have me help you?

I rack my mind for any information regarding vampires. I didn't have to think long.

Bless the water for me.

She smiles. *I think not.*

Why?

I only perform blessings for my people.

Oh. How do I become one of your people?

The smile widens. *Why, you must give yourself to me. A sacrifice.*

Isn't all the blood I'm leaking enough?

No. I require . . . a fuller commitment. Do that and you attach yourself to me for the rest of your life, Gideon Tau. You will be mine, and I yours.

A fuller commitment.

I have a horrible feeling I know what that is.

Yemanja floats towards me and strokes my face gently. Her fingers are like little pleasurable electric shocks. I stare into her eyes, eyes as dark as the deepest ocean trench. Filled with the primeval darkness we all crawled from.

Well? What will it be?

Let's be realistic here. It's not as if I have much of a choice. It's either give in and let them kill me, or I take matter into my own hands. There are no other options. I'm outmatched. Whoever is behind this wanted to get information and then kill me, so they sent a team big enough to do that. No messing about.

Yemanja floats backwards, receding into the darkness. I reach out for her, but something's wrong. My throat is on fire. My chest feels tight. My entire body is in hideous, agonizing pain.

I open my eyes, feel the salt water stinging them. Water laps up my nose.

Then I'm dragged back out of the shallows. Flipped over and lifted up. Staring into the face of the Matchstick Man. It tilts its head to the side.

I sigh. Might as well get it over with.

'Come on then, you wannabe blood licker. *Nosferatu* was a shit movie. Christopher Lee can't act. You're all pathetic. Scared of garlic? Do me a fucking favour.'

Then, just to get my message across, I lift my hand and stick my thumb in its eye, gouging as deep as I can.

The Matchstick Man snarls in pain and fury and drops me to the sand. I manage to keep my feet beneath me. 'Do your worst, laughing boy.'

The Matchstick Man lashes out. A lunging pain in my neck. A sudden wind on my throat. Cool air caressing muscles that are not meant to be exposed.

Blood bubbles out of my shredded throat, pouring down my chest.

I smile.

And collapse back into the ocean.

The waves pull me out. I'm turned over by the current, staring into the dark nothing of the sea. I taste metal in the water. My blood. It's cold. Freezing. I can't see anything. Darkness closes in on my mind. I feel a sudden panic. This is it. I'm dead. But I don't want to die. I'm pissed off it happened this way. A stupid ambush after a night out drinking. Pissed off I wasn't prepared. Pissed off at everything, basically.

Your life doesn't flash before you when you die. You just realize what a complete prick you've been. How small a difference you've actually made in the world.

Then Yemanja is floating before me. She touches me and the pain winks out. Vanishes. She comes closer, her hands caressing my face. I'm drawn into her eyes. Can't look away as she leans in and her lips brush mine.

A burst of freezing heat. My body jolts. My skin tingles. Every nerve end on fire. Her tongue darts softly into my mouth, touches mine.

I try to pull closer but then the touch is gone and she's floating backwards again.

You are mine now, Gideon Tau. And my blessing is yours.

My wand is in my hand. The blackness recedes and once again I'm floating face down in the sea. But I feel refreshed. Like I've slept for twenty hours straight. I hesitantly reach up with my free hand and touch my throat. The wound is gone. My arm is healed.

Yemanja has claimed me. She is my goddess now.

I smile and push myself to my feet. I've floated far enough out that the ocean comes up to my hips. I start wading back to shore. The Matchstick Man and his Smilers are walking away.

'Hey!' I shout. 'I haven't finished with you yet!'

They turn. I hear their hisses of fury and the Smilers come for me, loping on all fours.

I raise the wand like a conductor and the seawater obeys my summons. It rises in a wave behind me, a wall of dark, ancient water.

Blessed water.

Holy water.

I flick my wrist and the water surges past me, parting around my body and engulfing the Smilers in a mini tsunami. Their shrieks of pain and terror echo across the beach as the water coats their skin, gets in their mouths, down their throats.

The Smilers fall to the sand, rolling, howling. Their skin is sloughing off their bodies, dropping away in huge, peeling chunks. Their fluids pool around them, leaking and soaking into the sand.

Their cries grow weaker, turn into mewling whines. Foul smelling smoke wafts into the air.

I peer through it and see the Matchstick Man making a break for it.

I start running, sprinting across the beach. I flick my hand and the water comes with me, a surging wave that keeps pace to either side.

The Matchstick Man glances over its shoulder, sees me coming. It trips, falls to its knees.

I stop and let the water carry on. It smashes into the creature, sending it tumbling across the sand. It pushes itself to its knees and just stares at me as its skin slides off its face. All of it just ... melting away like it was burning beneath a blowtorch.

'I will see you soon,' it says, its voice a wet gurgle. 'The war ... the war is coming, Mr Tau.'

A final puff of cloying smoke, and the Matchstick Man's head falls from its neck, hitting the sand and collapsing to sludge.

8

New discovery: being stalked and then murdered by a pack of psycho, slit-faced vampires makes a person a bit twitchy and paranoid.

Who'd have figured?

Physically, I feel fine. Great even. But psychologically? Not so good. I can feel those claws ripping skin off my back, gouging out my throat. I keep reliving the utter, body-freezing pain of it.

I died. I felt my presence slip away into the water, the blackness coming to claim me. Not many people come back from that. Which is something, I suppose. A topic for the next dinner party.

I crouch in the shadows of a palm tree, checking both ways to make sure there are no more surprises waiting in store. I keep expecting another attack. I'm checking faces, eyes, worried that the late-night revellers are just waiting for me to step out of cover.

I can't stay here all night, though. I force myself to move, jogging across the esplanade and onto the sidewalk bordering the hotels and flats. People swerve to avoid me, staring at me with wide eyes.

I glance down.

Then stumble to a stop.

'God-fucking-*dammit!*'

A woman squeals in fear and scurries away from the crazy man standing in the street swearing. Screw her. That's another suit ruined. Ripped to shreds and covered in blood and vampire death-jizz. I need to take out some insurance or something, because this is just getting ridiculous.

I straighten up and force myself to calm down. I need to get home. Need to reassess and decide on my next move. Whatever it is, it's going to have consequences. Big ones. Kincaid is – *was* – a friend of the Division. The vampires have long been supporters of the Covenant, and for his subjects to so easily break it and attack a member of Delphic Division is pure insanity. They're calling down the wrath of the entire SA supernatural police force onto their heads.

I mean, there's a chance he didn't know about what went down. But if so, that raises a whole shitload of questions about him not controlling his subjects. But if he *did* know about it, it means he's involved in Armitage's death.

I really hope he's not. I actually looked on him as a bit of a friend.

But . . . another thing to think about. The killer. The big guy from the mountains. If Kincaid *is* involved, does that mean he knows who the man is? Can Kincaid give me a location? The name of the man who killed Cally?

I make it back to the Windemere building without collapsing, vomiting, or killing anyone in a fit of paranoia, stagger through the glass doors and up to my flat. I stumble inside and slam the door, locking everything. Grab a bottle of Glenmorangie from the top of the fridge and gulp some down.

I wince as it hits my stomach, lean on the counter, breathing heavily.

The dog looks up from his chair. 'Good night?'

'No.'

'Christ, you're not still moping about Armitage, are you? You have to move on. The past is in the past.'

'It only happened twelve hours ago!'

'Oh.' Pause. 'It feels longer. So what's bugging you?

'I was just attacked by a pack of Smilers and a Matchstick Man.'

The dog tilts his head to the side, puzzled. 'But ... the Covenant ...'

'Yeah. I know. Seems a lot of orisha don't really hold with the Covenant anymore.'

'How did you get away from—?'

'I didn't.' Swallow. Wince. 'It ripped my throat out. I died.'

'Oh. You look pretty healthy—'

'Yemanja brought me back. But only after I sacrificed myself to her.'

'And she killed them?'

'No. She blessed the ocean water and I used it to destroy them.'

The dog turns back to the TV. 'There you go then. All's well that ends well.'

I just stare at him, unsure if he's being genuine or trying to wind me up.

'You're supposed to be my guide,' I say, deciding to just move on. 'Have you heard anything about the Covenant no longer holding?'

'Nope. Not a thing.' He doesn't look away from his movie, but half-glances my way when I don't reply. 'It's worrying,' he adds.

'Gee, you think?' It's a waste of time. Sarcasm is lost on the dog. Or he simply ignores it. Not sure which.

My phone is ruined from the seawater. I head into my room and dig out one of my older models (I'm a serial upgrader). I take the sim card out of the ruined phone and wipe it down, making sure there's no salt left anywhere. Then I insert it into the older phone, hook it up to my laptop, and restore all my contacts from the backup.

I grab my iPad while it's doing its thing, log into GHOST, and scroll through the entries for Kincaid's number. All orisha who have contact with the Division have their details listed. It's a voluntary thing, so those that give us their numbers are generally friendly. Or at least neutral.

I find his number and dial it on the landline. The phone rings for a long time before it's finally answered.

'Talk,' says a voice.

'Kincaid,' I say. 'Long time no speak. It's Gideon Tau.'

Silence.

'Kincaid?'

'Yeah, sorry. What can I do for you, my man?'

'I need to see you.'

'Might not be a good idea.'

Is it my imagination, or is he sounding nervous? Not sure, really. I've never talked to a nervous vampire before. He doesn't sound right, though. I'll say that.

'Unavoidable,' I say. 'Things have been going down the past couple of days that have got Division worried. Remember our deal?'

As well as helping Kincaid out with that attempted coup, he's also friendly to us because he's on probation. He's allowed freedom as long as he doesn't try to enslave the government of the country. Again.

'Yeah, I remember.'

'Good. We need to meet.'

'Fine.'

'You still at that old warehouse in the city?'

'No. I mean, yeah, but I can't meet you there. Look, can't we do this over the phone?'

'Sorry. This is face to face only. Some of your subjects have been a bit naughty.'

'Christ, fine. Look, you know the BAT centre?'

I shudder. A cafe/cocktail bar for hipsters and folk music. 'I know *of* it.'

'A boat will be waiting for you there.'

'A boat? I don't like the ocean, Kincaid.' I look around guiltily as I say this, hoping Yemanja isn't somehow able to hear me.

'That's the deal, London. I'm taking a risk meeting you. This has to be done on the down-low.'

I chew on my lip for a moment. That doesn't sound good. 'Fine. But I need a guarantee of safe passage.'

Silence on the line.

'Kincaid?'

'Yeah.' Another pause. 'Fine. You have safe passage. But only you. No one else from Division.'

'Guaranteed? In the name of Ekimmu?' Ekimmu was a Sumerian vampire, the first of their kind. It's sort of like swearing on the bible. But a lot more serious.

'Guaranteed. On the name of Ekimmu.'

'See you soon.'

I hang up. The dog is watching me with that look on his face.

'You . . . ah . . . heard all that?'

'I *heard* it. I don't *believe* it.'

'What?' I say defensively.

'Are you *really* going to a meeting, alone, with a vampire, at night, out in the middle of the ocean, when a vampire pack just tried to *kill* you?'

'Well, when you put it like *that* . . . '

'Don't be a smartarse.'

'Sorry. But yeah, I am.'

'Then enlighten me. You have Division backup hiding somewhere?'

'Nope. But you're coming with me, so it will be fine. Actually, you're not leaving my side till this is over, OK?'

'Lucky me.'

'Speaking of which, where *were* you tonight? Couldn't you . . . I don't know . . . sense a disturbance in the Force or something when those vampires came after me?'

'Doesn't work that way. Besides I was watching my soaps. You know I don't notice anything when I'm watching my soaps.'

'It's really great you have your priorities in order, dog. Come on. We're going for a boat ride. And I really hope you get seasick.'

The BAT centre is only a couple of kays away along the beachfront so I grab my semi-charged phone and walk, hoping the exercise will clear my head. When we arrive we wait around the side of the building, standing next to an old graffiti piece spelling out the initials of the centre by someone called *Lyken*.

I got the dog to cast the protective ward on me before we left the house. I feel hyped up, filled with energy. Buzzing.

'Keep still,' mutters the dog. 'You're making me nervous.'

I ignore him, bouncing on the soles of my feet, listening to someone attempting to play Cat Stevens up in the cafe. I still can't figure out what's going on here. I'm supposed to be a detective, but don't let that fool you. It's nothing like it is on TV. No grand leaps of logic or anything like that. It usually comes down to joining the dots, following one aspect of the case to its eventual dead end, then following another, and another, until one of them connects to something interesting. Wash. Rinse. Repeat. But right now all I have is a dead ramanga, a dead friend, the fact that the murderer was involved in my daughter's death, and that it looks like the vampires are somehow involved.

But then . . . Jengo was a ramanga. A vampire. Why would they kill one of their own?

'Hey,' says the dog. 'Time to get into character.'

He's staring out into the ocean. I follow his gaze and see a small speed boat bouncing over the waves towards us. It doesn't have any lights on, but whoever's driving seems to be handling it just fine. Not that it can be that difficult. Point it in the direction of the shitty music and put foot down.

The engine cuts out about twenty feet out and the boat coasts the rest of the way and slides part way onto the sand. There are two figures inside. I hop over the low wall onto the beach and approach them. They're both vampires – male and female, but I can't tell what caste.

'You London?' the girl asks.

'Yeah. Kincaid told you I had guaranteed safe passage, right?'

'You think we're going to eat you? Don't flatter yourself. You're not my type.'

'What's your type?'

'O negative.'

'Har-de-fucking-har,' I say. Just what I need. A vampire who thinks she's a standup comedian.

I climb in the boat. The dude looks at the dog doubtfully. 'Kincaid said only you.'

'Come on, man. He's my dog. He goes everywhere with me. He gets upset if I leave him in the flat. Don't you, boy?'

-I'm going to piss in your bed- says the dog in my mind.

'Let's just go,' says the chick. She leans against the front of the boat (what is that? The prow? I've never been big on nautical terms), and effortlessly shoves the boat back along the sand until it's bobbing in the water. She pushes it around so it's pointing back out to sea and hops in to start the engine.

A couple of seconds later we're heading out into the open waters, the cold sea spray soaking my face and doubts collecting in my mind.

After about twenty minutes, the boat shifts direction slightly and I realize we're heading towards a cargo freighter, one of those flat container ships that carries goods in truck-sized metal boxes.

The freighter is huge, easily 150 metres long. Arc lights surrounded by haloes of mist light the deck, illuminating the red, yellow, and green containers, hundreds of them stacked one atop the other like massive Lego blocks.

'Who owns that? Kincaid?' I ask.

'Kincaid has many business interests,' says the girl. 'What – you think we're just bloodthirsty animals who wander round the streets looking for our next meal? This is the twenty-first century, man. We have corporations, business deals. You name it, we've got our finger in it.'

'Shut the fuck up, Huntley,' says the dude.

'Christ, Jarvis. I'm just saying. The prick thinks we're simple.'

'Insecure much?' I ask.

Huntley whirls around and bares her teeth at me. The moon glints rather dramatically on her fangs.

'Diplomatic immunity,' I say. 'I don't think Kincaid is going to be happy if you disobey his orders.'

'Kincaid can suck my—'

'Huntley!' barks the other vampire. 'Enough.'

She glares at him, but turns back to focus on the steering.

The sheer scale of the container ship becomes apparent as we draw closer. It dominates the ocean, rising high above us, a giant metal monstrosity. Huntley guides the tiny speedboat around to the rear, jouncing and skimming over the crosscurrents thrown up by the huge hull.

There's a massive open space at the back, a black mouth that looks like it's spitting out seawater as the container ship moves slowly forward. Huntley takes us inside, the light of the moon winking off as if a switch has been thrown. Orange lights bolted into the metal hull illuminate the interior. The speed boat slows, the engine dropping to a throaty growl as it bumps up against the side of the ship.

Huntley and Jarvis hop out onto a narrow deck. I start to pull myself up after them, am yanked the rest of the way by the inhuman strength of Huntley. She tosses me to the side and I stumble against the hull. Jarvis opens a rusted metal door. White light spills out, revealing a narrow corridor beyond.

'Move,' says Huntley.

'Where to?'

Huntley growls and shoves me aside, taking the lead. The dog and I go next and Jarvis takes the rear. Bulbs bolted behind thick safety glass illuminate the way. The metal grating in the floor rings with our footsteps.

After a few turns we arrive in a wider corridor. A set of stairs leads up to what I assume is the bridge. Huntley ignores it, heads through another door into a brightly lit hold.

Our footsteps echo as we step inside. The hold is easily the size of a school gymnasium, the curved metal walls painted white. There are more metal containers in here, towering high above us to either side.

Thirty metres in and we arrive at a separator wall. We duck through the door into a second, identical hold.

'What's in the containers?' I ask.

'Clothes. Food,' says Jarvis promptly. 'Shipping them to Cape Town.'

'What, for charity?'

'Don't be stupid. Kincaid is a wholesaler. He supplies the big chain stores.'

I burst out laughing. 'The King of the East Coast vampires is a clothing supplier? Are you shitting me?'

'*Manufacturer*, actually. He has textile companies in Nigeria. He's a millionaire.'

'Good for him. You think he'll lend me any money?'

'Doubt it,' says Huntley. 'He doesn't invest in lost causes.'

We enter a third hold, and this one is different. There are still metal containers piled up around the hull, but the room is carpeted. Immaculate Persian rugs, hundreds of them, laid one atop the other.

Sound is muffled as we walk across the hold. Against the far wall is a small round table. One of those nasty things from the seventies. Hollow aluminium and red Formica, peeling and pitted with cigarette burns.

Kincaid is waiting. A metal bar has been wedged between the two sides of the hull, and he's hanging from it by two curved iron hooks that sprout from his knees.

Kincaid is an *Asanbosam*. A huge vampire that basically looks like an extra from *The Lord of the Rings* orc army, except his teeth and claws are made from iron. His kind usually spend their time hanging from tree branches, waiting for their prey to walk past below. Kincaid decided that wasn't his thing and trekked here from North Africa in the fifties. He's been building his empire and consolidating his power ever since.

Huntley shoves me and I stagger forward, catch myself before tripping. The dog trots forward to keep pace with me. He's looking around us with interest, sniffing the air.

-*Anything?*-

-*Something odd. Not sure what.*-

-*Jesus, what good are you?*-

'Come forward, my friend,' says Kincaid.

I walk across the soft carpets. Kincaid drops from the bar and summersaults, landing elegantly on his feet. He pulls out a chair and sits down, folding his hands on the Formica. He looks ridiculous. A giant sitting at a doll's table.

I pull out the chair opposite and sit down, playing it cool, ignoring the presence of Huntley and Jarvis hovering behind me.

'You can go,' says Kincaid, glancing over my shoulder.

I get the feeling there's some kind of protest going on behind me so I turn quickly in my chair. Huntley quickly brings her hands down from whatever gestures she was making.

'Yeah, you can go,' I say. 'I'll call you when I need a ride back.'

I turn around again and make myself comfortable. I wait till

I hear the metal door slam shut in the hold before I finally relax, though.

Kincaid wags a massive finger at me. 'You are a very naughty man,' he says. 'My people do not like you.'

'I'm not really crushing on them myself.'

-And they stink,- mutters the dog. *-Like week-old carrion.-*

I didn't notice that myself, but I'll take his word for it.

'Now, my friend, what did you want to speak to me about?'

Call me suspicious, but when people call me 'my friend' twice in the space of thirty seconds, I get a bit uneasy.

'Here's the thing,' I say. 'Yesterday, one of yours was murdered. A ramanga.'

Kincaid makes a sour face. 'I do not like ramanga.'

'OK. But they're still classed as vampires, right?'

'I suppose. For official purposes only, though.'

'Right. Then my boss, a member of Delphic Division, was also murdered. In the same way as the ramanga.'

'What way is this?'

'Their hearts were gouged out, and in the case of the ramanga, his head was ripped off.'

'I see. Carry on.'

I stare at him for a moment. 'Do you know anything about these deaths, Kincaid?'

He looks surprised. 'Me? Why would you think I would know anything?'

'Because not two hours ago I was attacked by a Matchstick Man and five *Aigamucha*.'

Kincaid's eyes widen. He leans forward. 'That cannot be. The Covenant forbids any attacks on a peacekeeper.'

'Yeah, I was pretty surprised myself.'

'But you survived! You are strong, yes?' He frowns. '*How* did you survive? One against six – these odds are not good.'

I shrug. 'You don't fuck with Delphic Division, Kincaid.

That's what we always tell you guys. What I want to know is, why was I attacked?'

'You are asking me?'

'You see anyone else in here?'

'How should I know?'

'Come on, Kincaid. You're the King of the East Coast. If you don't know then you're losing your grip on your people. Either way, you're in trouble here.'

'Me?'

'Yes, you. If you can't control your subjects, we'll have to find someone who can.'

Too much? Kincaid's eyes flash angrily. He struggles to keep himself under control.

'You think . . .' he clears his throat, '. . . you think you have the authority to depose me?'

'Maybe not depose. But if you went missing, someone would have to take your place.'

'My friend,' Kincaid says softly, regretfully. 'Are you threatening me? In my own territory?'

I clench my fists. 'You want to talk about territory?' I shout. 'Armitage was killed in her *home*. I was killed – *attacked* – half a kay from my flat. Cut the self-righteous bullshit, Kincaid. I'm not in the mood for it.' I force myself to calm down. 'We had a deal. I'm not even talking you and the Division. I'm talking you and me. I thought we were mates.'

'We were.'

I freeze. '*Were?*'

Kincaid sighs heavily. He bares his teeth in a grimace. The light glints on the iron inside his mouth. He rubs his face in a gesture that is almost weary. He straightens up and looks me in the eye.

'Where is the soul, London?'

I slump back in my chair, staring at him in disappointment. Had I known? Deep down inside? The attacks couldn't really have happened without Kincaid's authority, could they?

'What the hell, Kincaid?' Softly. Regretfully. I really thought Kincaid was a friend. We'd spent many nights chatting about his old life. I'd stuck up for him at the Division. I *vouched* for him.

'I am sorry, London. This is not my fault. None of this is.'

'Then whose fault it is? The buck is supposed to stop with you.'

'Not anymore.'

-I don't like this,- says the dog.

-Me neither.-

'Who do you answer to?' I ask.

'I can't say.'

'Kincaid. You *have* to tell me. If something's going down in vamp society, the Division needs to know.'

Kincaid laughs bitterly. 'In vampire society? My friend, you are thinking too small. What is happening now involves the entire world.'

I pause. 'What?'

'The ramanga's death wasn't even the first move. He is just another link in the chain.'

'What chain? What did he do?'

'It is not what he did. It is what he knew.'

'But . . . what's all this about his soul? The guy's dead.'

'Do not act as if you do not know. He . . . what is the term? He backed it up before he was killed. No, that is not right. He put his soul into safekeeping. His body was on autopilot when he died. He must have known he was being hunted.'

I stare at him. 'You're saying the ramanga's soul is hidden away somewhere? That it's in – what? A safe-deposit box or something?'

Kincaid nods.

'And you think I know where it is? You thought *Armitage* knew? *That's* why she was killed?'

Kincaid says nothing. I lean back in the chair. What a waste. Armitage dead for something she didn't even know.

'Fuck, Kincaid. We knew nothing about that. This is the first I've heard of any of this.'

-Is that even possible?- I ask the dog. *-Hiding a soul like that?-*

-Yeah. It is. Pretty common, actually.-

Kincaid frowns. 'I do not like being lied to, London.'

'Join the club. Does safe passage mean nothing to you guys anymore?'

'You have not been hurt.'

'Yet.'

'Just give us the soul, then you are free to go on your way.'

'Kincaid, I *told* you. I have no idea where it is.'

'Armitage must have told you. There were calls to your cell phone—'

'I didn't answer! I was out drinking! Why are you so convinced she even knew?'

'Because,' says a woman's voice from somewhere above us, 'she did the same thing with her *own* soul.'

I see Kincaid's face twist with fear. That, more than anything else, makes me realise I'm in serious trouble here. Again. Twice in one night might be a record even for me.

I look up into the shadows of the hold. A balcony circles the top section. A shadowy figure stands there, hands spread across the railing, watching us.

Then the words actually hit home. I stand up.

'Wait – you're saying Armitage put her soul somewhere? For safety? That it wasn't in her body when she died?'

'Correct. She suspected she was in danger. She is a clever woman.'

The shadowy figure moves, heading towards the stairs that lead down into the hold.

-Any idea what's going on?-

-None. But I'd like to take this opportunity to mention that I was against this from the start.-

The figure descends, reaches the floor. Kincaid glances

over his shoulder, gets up and carefully holds the chair back.

'You do not rise when in the company of your betters?' says the voice.

I say nothing, just wait as she approaches the light. She's about six feet tall, wearing a black vest and black trousers. Her arms are bare, toned with muscle. She has long dark hair that's parted in the middle, falling to either side of an angular face. Faint lines in the skin. Not wrinkles, but the hint of what is to come in the years ahead. Dark brown eyes, expressive. Showing amusement and slight annoyance.

She's . . . well, she's majestic. Beautiful. She radiates intelligence. Awareness. Power.

She sits down and smiles slightly, a slight crease to the side of her mouth. She breathes in deeply.

'Busy night?' she asks.

'You could say that.'

'We have not been properly introduced.'

'No.'

The woman looks to Kincaid.

'Uh . . . Gideon Tau,' says Kincaid quickly. 'This is Lilith. The First. Mother of the Illium. Mother of the Watchers. The First Ruler of Eden.'

-Oh, fuck,- says the dog. *-London, you need to get out of here. Now.-*

-Why? She's not . . . She's not the *Lilith is she?-*

-Adam's first wife? The one who told God to go fuck himself when he expected her to bow down to Adam? Yeah, she is.-

I blink in surprise. I had no idea that was a real story. It's kinda hard to tell, you know? Some myths are real. Some aren't. The Division is still finding this stuff out as we go along.

'So you're the one responsible for my friend's death?'

'She is not dead. Her soul lives on.'

'Fat lot of good that does her if she's the only one who knows where it is.'

She leans forward on the table, stretching her arms out slowly across the Formica, almost as if she was enjoying the feel against her skin.

'Do you enjoy your life?' she asks.

'Um . . . sure. Ups and downs. Swings and roundabouts, you know?'

'It never seems that way. Your kind, you are like privileged rich children. Handed everything you could possibly want, yet you do nothing with it. Always bored. Always searching for excitement. Never happy with what you have.'

'O-k-a-y. You heading towards a point here?'

'Just that I am going to make your lives exciting again. Interesting.'

'And how are you going to do that?'

'What is it your kind call our two worlds? Night and Day?'

I say nothing.

'You are the Day. Sunshine. Life. Laughter. We are the Night. Death. Darkness. Fear. Correct?'

I shrug.

'Who decided this?'

'Who decided what?'

'That our kind were to be relegated to the shadows.'

'You're asking me? Shit, lady. I have no idea. It's just the way it's always been. To be honest, I thought you guys *preferred* lurking around in the dark. Some of you . . . you're not exactly fit for the catwalk, you know?'

Too much. I see her eyes darken. The skin tighten around her eyes. I raise my hands.

'Apologies. That was out of order. I have no idea who decided. It's just always been that way.'

'Not always. Three hundred thousand years ago my kind – the orisha – were the dominant species. Then your kind turned up.

Threw all sorts of problems into the mix. You breed like rabbits, you see. We couldn't keep up. You overwhelmed the world. A plague. Pushed us aside. Kicked us out of our own home.'

'I think that's called survival of the fittest.'

Lilith smiles. 'I'm so glad you agree.'

I hesitate. 'Sorry?'

'Survival of the fittest. You are correct. And now it is time for us to retake the world. I've been waiting a very long time for this.'

'Have you?'

'And all we need from you is the location of the ramanga's soul.'

'OK, even if I *did* know, which I *don't*, what makes you think I'd be crazy enough to tell you now? After what you just said?'

'Because you know I'm right.'

I blink. 'I do?'

'Yes. Your kind – you have made a mess of everything. Corruption is endemic. Poverty is increasing. Overpopulation threatens to destroy the world. Diseases are left unchecked because pharmaceutical companies make more from treatment instead of cures. I mean, give it a hundred years and you will probably be on the way out anyway.'

'So why not wait?'

'Because you seem intent on a scorched earth policy, destroying the world before you go. We do not want to inherit a desert.'

'Well . . .' I say uncertainly, uncomfortable with the fact that I sort of agree with everything she just said.

Lilith leans forward. 'Also, if you do not tell me where the soul is we will kill everyone you know. Starting with your ex-wife, Becca.'

I don't say anything. The fear, the familiar pain and terror of someone close to me dying because of something I've done, rises up and utterly engulfs me.

'You surprise me,' says Lilith, one perfect eyebrow raised in amusement. 'No, "If you touch her I'll kill you"? No, "If you lay one finger on her I won't rest until you are destroyed"? I'm disappointed.' She pauses, cocks her head to the side, thinking. 'Or am I impressed? No pointless threats. No blustering. It's quite refreshing, actually. You should have heard your boss. Such language. I was afraid my poor delicate ears were going to fall off.'

I clench my jaw a few times. Things are moving too fast here. I'm messing this up. Keep it cool, London. You're here for information. You're here for Cally.

'The man. The big guy who did the killing for you. Where is he?'

'Resting. Far away.'

'What's his name?'

'Why would I tell you that?'

She stands up and walks slowly around the table, moving out of sight behind me. I feel her breath on my ear. A tingle courses through my body. She smells of jasmine and summer afternoons, a heady mixture of heat and pleasure. Aren't there legends about Lilith being a succubus as well?

'We are taking back the world, Gideon Tau. A war is coming, and those we let live won't recognize what is left behind. You would be advised to pick your side wisely.'

She moves around the table and sits down again.

'I'll ask one more time, and if you don't tell me I'll assume you are of no use to us. Where is the soul?'

In answer, I reach beneath my shirt and yank two water pistols from inside my pant line. One pistol is dayglo orange. The other dayglo pink. I rest my elbows on the table and point them at Kincaid and Lilith.

-Dude,- says the dog. *-If you'd told me you had a death wish I could have ripped your throat out for you. I wouldn't even have had to leave the house.-*

'And what are you going to do with those?' asks Lilith, amused.

'Here's the thing. First, you're going to tell me where the killer is. Then I'm going to walk out of here. I'm going to take your boat and head back to the beach, where I'll leave it for you to pick up. You will not bother me again.'

'London—' begins Kincaid, but Lilith holds a hand up and he instantly stops talking.

'I'm curious as to your thought processes here,' says Lilith.

-Yeah, me too.-

'Usually I can predict what the food will do. But you . . . not so much.'

'Ninety per cent of the time *I* don't even know what I'm going to do,' I say. 'It makes life more . . . interesting.'

Lilith nods solemnly and places her hands together, resting them against her mouth while she studies me. 'Then proceed.'

I pull the trigger on the water pistol.

A stream of water squirts out and hits Lilith in the face.

An embarrassed silence follows.

-Dude,- says the dog in awe. *-I don't even know what you're doing right now. This is* amazing.-

I frown at my water pistol. Give it a shake. Then fire again. Still nothing.

'Are you done?'

I shift my aim and pull the trigger. The water shoots out and hits Kincaid's hand. He leaps to his feet with a cry of surprise and pain. Greasy smoke writhes up from his blistering skin.

'Tau! What the fuck, man!'

I gesture at Kincaid with my water pistol. 'See, that's the effect I was going for.' I scratch my forehead with the barrel. 'Guess holy water doesn't work on you, huh?'

'Some call me a vampire, but I was created by God. What do you think?'

I nod. 'Noted.'

Kincaid is cradling his hand in his arm, looking at me with wounded eyes.

'Oh, don't look at me like that, you two-faced prick. You set me up. I wouldn't even be in this situation if you'd kept your word.'

'I wonder what you will do now,' says Lilith.

In answer, I leap to my feet and place one water pistol against Kincaid's head, standing behind him to keep out of sight. The guy is huge. I have to stand on tiptoe just to get my arm around his neck.

'London, this is stupid,' he says. 'Be nice to her. She'll give you a place in the new world.'

'As what?'

'We will still need peacekeepers,' says Lilith. 'All supernatural creatures are not of one mind. Many will break the law. Many will need to be punished.'

'Yeah, somehow I don't think that will end well for me.'

'So you plan on just walking out of here?' asks Lilith.

'Sure. If you value our old pal here.'

'Be my guest.'

I wait for the punchline but it doesn't come. Lilith stays sitting at the table. Watching.

I turn Kincaid around and we start walking back through the hold.

We make it to the middle of the room before a loud screeching sound echoes around us. I freeze, looking wildly around.

The doors to all the metal containers are swinging open.

To reveal hundreds of vampires.

Nosferatu, hipsters, goths, bikers, homeless, children. A cross-section of society, the only difference being these guys are all pale as maggot flesh, have black eyes, and massive fangs.

Oh, and they all want to eat me.

Some of them lean casually against the container doors, watching. Others drop down into the hold. They move slowly forward and more and more join them.

I look to the hold door, wondering if I can make a break for it. Before I can make up my mind, it swings open and more vampires stream through. Those containers I saw as I moved through the ship. It looks like they all contained vampires.

-Now might be a good time to call up your tattoos,- suggests the dog.

-Too soon. They'll kill me if I do.-

I back up, but there's nowhere to go. Kincaid gently lifts my arm from around his neck and steps away.

'Coffins are so passé,' says Lilith as the crowd of hissing and spitting vamps opens up to let her through. 'Now, you've had your fun. I admit to being slightly amused. But what do you think your next move is going to be?'

'A deal,' I say quickly. 'You tell me who the guy is that killed Armitage and Jengo, I give you his soul.'

'That was never an option, I'm afraid. I need our large friend. He is important to me.'

She holds out her hand. I reluctantly hand over the water pistols.

'Now,' she says. 'I ask again. What do you think your next move is going to be?'

'I'm going to take you to the ramanga's soul,' I say heavily.

'Good boy,' says Lilith.

-You don't know where the ramanga's soul is,- mutters the dog.

-Yeah, but they don't know that.-

-You are such an idiot.-

9

It's been said before (by Armitage) that I'm some kind of stupid mix of naivety and cynicism. It's a pity she's not here to see this, because it pretty much proves her point and she'd be laughing her arse off.

It's an hour after midnight and we're driving along the deserted freeway. I'm squashed between Kincaid on my left and a twitching Nosferatu on my right. The Noss are old school. It's actually pretty rare to see one hanging around Africa. They tend to stick to their European hunting grounds, shunning modern society as much as they can. They're the Amish of the vampire community.

Lilith is sitting in the passenger seat and a young vampire with slicked back hair and sunglasses is driving.

I watch him for a while. He's aware of it, his jaw clenching and unclenching in what he probably thinks is an intimidating manner but really just looks like he's taken too many E's.

'So, are they remaking *The Lost Boys?*' I ask him.

Kincaid elbows me in the ribs.

'Shut up, man. You're going to get yourself killed.'

-*What* is *your plan?*- asks the dog. -*And I ask merely out of curiosity. You know, so I can let people know exactly how you died.*-

I had to argue with them to let me bring the dog in the car. It's an Audi A5 and the driver wasn't too keen on having the mutt sitting on his spotless seats. A compromise was reached and he's now squatting on the floor by my feet.

-*Can't tell you. It's a surprise.*-

-You don't have one, do you?-

-I do! I'm just not a hundred per cent sure if it's going to work.-

'Neo,' I say, 'take the next off-ramp.'

-Tau, what are you doing? You're not seriously *taking them to the Division, are you?-*

-What choice do I have? Don't worry. I've got it figured out.-

-London, you haven't even figured out how much milk to put in your cereal yet. Consider me worried.-

'Turn right at the dirt track,' I say, leaning forward and pointing to the unlit road. 'Just follow it into the tunnel.'

Lilith glances at me over her shoulder as we exit the tunnel on the either side of the freeway. 'I hope you're not going to do something stupid, human. I am not the kind of person you want as an enemy–'

Her face twists. A flash of pain overshadowed by fury. She opens her mouth in a scream of anger at the exact same moment the driver jerks and spasms, smashing his head into the side window and shattering the glass. The Noss bucks next to me, hissing in pain. Kincaid roars with agony.

All this time Lilith does not take her eyes off mine. She reaches for me. The car veers to the left, skidding off the dirt road. It bounces, hitting deep ruts at sixty kays an hour. It ramps up and slams back into the ground. Hard. The driver's foot is jammed down on the gas. The car picks up speed.

Just as Lilith's fingers find my arm the car slams into the brick wall of an old outhouse. Lilith and the driver jerk forward. I'm watching in slow motion as she hits the windscreen head first. The glass shatters into a thousand tiny pieces. She and the driver fly through and hit the wall with wet, meaty thuds.

Always wear your seat belts, kids.

The Noss's face is covered in blood. It's making a childlike keening sound. I ignore it, push the side door open and scramble over its wiry frame.

Something grabs my leg before I make it. I turn. Kincaid. His fangs are on full display. He's struggling with his safety belt. (Not as stupid as he looks.) His grip is tight. I kick out but I can't break his hold. He starts to pull me back into the car.

My fingers scramble in the dirt, trying to find a handhold. But there's nothing to grip. I flip around, half on my back, and kick him in the face with my free foot. Once. Twice. Nothing. He doesn't even blink.

The dog appears behind him. His mouth is open, tongue hanging out as if he's panting. But I know better. That's him laughing.

'A little help here?'

'There is no help for you, my friend,' says Kincaid, thinking I'm talking to him. 'Not anymore.'

Then the dog rips out the side of his throat.

Kincaid lets go of my foot and grabs his neck. The dog hops delicately over his lap and onto my chest, over my face, then out of the car. I flip around and follow after. Push myself to my feet and sprint.

I only stop running when I know I'm way past the wards that protect the Division. Even then I don't stop for long. Just a quick look, and when I see Lilith getting to her feet at the front of the car, I dart behind an old rusted cement truck and use it for cover while I make for the nearest hidden entrance.

Along the corridors and into Eshu's lair. He's already watching the monitors, all of them showing a view of the dirt road leading into the compound.

'Have they gone?' I ask.

Eshu leans back in his chair and glances over his shoulder. 'They have now. The chick sent the Nosferatu against the wards a few time, but she gave up when he kept catching fire.'

'Thank Christ. I wasn't sure they'd hold.'

'Of course they'd hold. They're designed to withstand an attack of a thousand spiritual amps. *And* I've got backup aether batteries powered by the souls of the dead. I can plug those in if it looks like the wards are going to crack.'

'Which still doesn't say how you're going to sort this little mess out,' says the dog. 'This place is supposed to be hush-hush.'

'What choice did I have? I had to get rid of them. This was the only way.'

'I told you going into this it was a trap.'

'Yeah, thanks. Shut up now.'

'Don't take it out on me. You're the one who's going to have to explain to Ranson why the high-security tip-top super-secret headquarters of the supernatural police force is now known to Lilith, she-bitch of the orisha.'

'That was *Lilith*?' says Eshu in a small voice.

'Yup,' says the dog happily.

'London, what did you *do*?' Eshu's voice is filled with awe. Or wonder. Or amazement at my stupidity. Not sure which.

I head to the door. 'Call me if they come back.'

'Yeah, sure.'

Jaeger is sitting in her office spooning congealed yellow gunk into her mouth. I wonder what it is. Pureed flesh? Manifested mana?

I hesitate in the doorway, unsure whether to go in or not.

'What are you waiting for?' she says without looking up. 'An invitation?'

'Uh . . . yeah, actually.'

'Come in.'

I enter and sit down on the other side of her desk.

'What's that?' I ask, not really sure I want to know the answer.

She looks down at the cup, then at me. 'It's custard,' she says.

I blink. 'Oh. OK.'

'Never got the hang of making it. It always comes out lumpy.'

'You have to keep stirring,' I say. 'If you leave it, that's when it all goes to shit. Wait, are we talking about the powdered stuff? Because I have no idea how to make it from scratch.'

'Is that why you're here? To discuss custard-making techniques?'

I flush. 'No. Sorry. It's about Armitage. When you saw her last – at the Ramanga's post-mortem – did she discuss anything about . . . backing up her soul? Putting it somewhere for safekeeping?'

Jaeger just stares at me for a moment. 'You know, I'm pretty sure she didn't? That kind of thing would stick in the mind, make me think it might be relevant.'

I note the sarcasm. Couldn't help *but*. It drips from her words like . . . well, like congealed custard.

'Sorry. OK, different question. If someone *had* . . . removed their soul from their bodies. Would you notice? I mean, while doing the post-mortem?'

'No,' says Jaeger. 'The reason being I only do autopsies on dead people. And dead people aren't known for having souls.'

I sigh and rub my face. 'Look, I've been told that both the ramanga and Armitage had stored their souls somewhere for safekeeping before they were killed. That they knew they were in danger and took steps. I'm wondering if it has something to do with those coins. Did Armitage give *any* indication why she was excited by it? Anything to explain a connection?'

Jaeger thinks about it, then shakes her head. 'No. She ducked out of here pretty quick after that.'

I sigh in frustration. 'Thanks.'

I leave the office, fishing around in my pocket for the old coin as I go.

The Division is empty at this time of night. The glow of screen savers flicker and flash, illuminating the dimness. Pictures of someone's kids. Someone else's fantasy art slideshow – dragons, *Lord of the Rings*, that kind of thing.

Me? I still use the moving pipes that came with Windows 95, the operating system we still use, shored up with Delphic Division proprietary patches and software installed over the top, all of it stored behind firewalls guarded by the ghosts of dead software programmers.

I sink into my chair and flick the desk lamp on. I check my watch. One forty a.m. I don't want to leave yet, just in case Lilith and Kincaid are lurking around outside. I'll take the alternate route out anyway. Better safe than sorry.

First things first. I pick up the phone and call Becca.

The phone rings for a long time before finally being picked up.

'Hello?' A man's voice. Annoyed.

I swallow. 'Uh . . . yeah, I need to speak to Becca.'

'What the fuck time is it?'

I resist the urge to ask who the hell it is I'm speaking to. 'Late. It's an emergency.'

'Who is this?'

'Gideon. Gideon Tau.'

A pause. Then the phone line goes dead.

'Son of a whore!'

I dial again. It rings and rings, until finally Becca answers.

'What?'

'Becca. Listen, you have to get out of the house.'

'What are you talking about?'

'You're in danger. Some people know your connection to me. They . . . they want to use you to make me do something.'

'Tau, I can't deal with this now. Tomorrow—'

'No! Not tomorrow. I've pissed them off and they know about you. Do you understand? If you stay there you will die.

I'm not kidding. You and your boyfriend. Get the fuck out of there. Go to a hotel or something.'

A pause. 'You haven't changed, have you? Still the reason people get hurt.'

'Yeah, really not the fucking time for this, Becca. Just promise me you'll go.'

She sighs. 'Fine.'

The phone goes dead. I tap it against my chin and stare up at the ceiling.

'You're a lucky bastard, you know that?' says the dog.

I look down. He's sitting in his bed beneath my desk. 'I don't feel lucky.'

'Then you're an idiot as well. You just walked into a vampire nesting ship, shot Lilith with a water pistol filled with holy water, and you got away to talk about it. So yeah, I'd say you're a pretty lucky guy.'

I thought about this. I can't help a little weary grin. 'Yeah. It *will* look good in my memoirs, won't it?'

I examine Armitage's token beneath the desk lamp. What did she find so interesting about it? There are no identifying marks, nothing that says what it is. It's so old it's been worn smooth of any writing.

I frown, holding it close to the light, tilting it this way and that. Is that a line? Barely visible? I'm not sure. I nudge the dog with my foot and hold the coin out.

'Sniff this.'

The dog obliges, then puts his head down and closes his eyes.

I nudge him again.

'Do that one more time and you lose your toes.'

I snatch my foot back. 'Sorry. But did you smell anything on the coin?'

'Desperation. Sadness. Fear. And that's just from it sitting in your pocket.'

'Yeah, laugh it up, fuzzball. Anything else?'

The dog sighs. 'Hope. Relief. But those two are buried under the desperation. And I don't mean yours.'

I stare at the coin, rubbing my thumb over it. I can feel slight indentations. I have a thought, and head over to the office scanner. I put the coin onto the scanning bed and scan both sides into the PC at 300 dpi, then I open up the image in Photoshop.

I push the contrast way up, then fiddle with the brightness and saturation levels.

I sit back and stare at the monitor.

A picture has been revealed, outlined in harsh black and white lines.

It's a symbol. A tree.

I run it through GHOST's image search and it brings up a hit.

I read the entry with growing excitement. The tree is the symbol of *Tiurakh*, the orisha of treasure and hoarding. Wealth and success. His place of worship is at the foot of a tall tree.

I follow the hyperlinks embedded in his name and find out he runs a bit of a pawn shop empire crossed with a safety deposit business. He looks after people's property in return for a hefty fee. The tokens from Jengo and Armitage are chits used to reclaim the items left with him.

I do a bit more reading and discover that Tiurakh operates out of a tower block in Pinetown, about twenty kays from our current location.

Is that what happened? Did Jengo store his soul with Tiurakh?

More to the point. Did *Armitage?*

Something occurs to me and I pull up the crime scene photographs from Armitage's house. I scroll through them until I get to the one where she wrote *Tau* in her blood.

Except, now I'm looking at it, I can see it doesn't say Tau. It's *Tiu*. She was writing Tiurakh in an untidy scrawl, but died after the first three letters. Anders saw Tau because that's what he wanted to see.

I frown. Even if they did store their souls with Tiurakh how does that help? Can we talk to the souls? Communicate with them? Lilith must think so. Why else would she want to know where the ramanga's soul is?

I clear the search bar in GHOST and look up the entries on souls, removal of, communicating with, survival of. Anything that will help with figuring all this out.

There are multiple entries on communicating with ethereal entities and souls. I brew myself some coffee and start to click through them. First up is your basic astral projection. Going into a trance state and leaving your body behind while your consciousness floats around the astral plain. I don't fancy that. I can't even still my mind long enough to meditate. Plus, it doesn't say *how* you communicate with a soul once you've managed to project.

Next option is drugs. Peyote cacti, mushrooms, acid, that kind of thing. Again, not my thing. I was the guy who was never allowed drugs back in college. My friends said I was too tightly wound. They were worried what would happen if my inhibitions suddenly vanished. They were probably right.

The next entries are about experiments going on with brainwave stimulation using audio waves, pushing the brain into trance states. The page links to articles on EEG, brainwaves, neural oscillators, wave spikes, that kind of thing. Too much info. Next page.

Ah. The good old-fashioned Ouija board.

To be honest that appeals to me the most. The UK version of the Division – the Ministry – grew out of some secret society called the Invisible Order back in Victorian times. They have whole rooms devoted to Ouija boards. The Victorians knew their stuff when it came to ghosts and the spirit world. Maybe I can get in touch with them to see if they could help out.

But then I click on something that makes me straighten up and concentrate.

Creating a revenant. Or bringing someone back from the dead.

A revenant isn't like a zombie. It's someone who comes back to life, but who still has their consciousness and soul intact and doesn't have that pesky craving for human flesh.

I lean back and stare at the ceiling. Can I do that to Armitage? Bring her back? She won't like it. Hell, who would? But she's the only link I have with Cally's killer.

Sorry, Armitage. I need you back here.

I scan the article, then put in a call to Parker. It rings for a long time before she picks up.

'London? What the fuck? What time is it?'

'Time for action!'

'What?'

'Sorry. Always wanted to say that. I need you back at Division.'

'Can't it wait till tomorrow?'

'No. I know who's behind the killings.'

'Who?' Her voice sounds more alert now.

'Lilith. You know, from the bible? Well, not the actual bible. The Apocrypha.'

'I know who Lilith is. You sure?'

'Pretty sure. I was attacked by vampires tonight, ended up in a boat out in the middle of the ocean where I met her. It's . . . complicated. Can you get over here?'

'Why?'

'Um . . . I want to resurrect Armitage as a revenant.'

'Oh.' A pause. 'You got permission from Ranson?'

'Of course! Wouldn't be calling you otherwise.'

'You know we need her soul, right?'

'On my way to get it right this minute. Should be back in an hour.'

'Seriously?'

'Yup.'

She sighs. 'Fine. But don't complain if I'm grumpy tomorrow, OK?'

'Parker, you're always grumpy. How am I supposed to tell the difference?'

She hangs up on me. I smile, grab the keys for one of the company cars, and head out to find Armitage's soul. I nudge the dog gently and quickly pull my foot back. He opens one eye and glares at me.

'The game's afoot.'

The building that Tiurakh operates from is called The Towers, a twenty-three floor apartment building shaped like a three-pointed star. It's been there for decades, dominating the Pinetown skyline, the only tower block in the entire city and impossible to miss. I've noted it every time I drive along the freeway, but I didn't know Tiurakh used it as a warehouse.

I take the off-ramp and turn right, heading across the bridge. I follow the road around the Knowles shopping centre and onto a slip road that curves towards the residents' parking lot. The boom is down and I don't have a card, so I reverse and park by the side of the road.

The dog and I approach the glass door leading into the building. There's a security guard sitting behind a little metal desk. I wonder how I'm going to get past him. I could try the Jedi mind trick I've been practising. It's basically using your own strength of will and mild shinecraft to overpower the will of another. I'm not very good at it, though. My whole being reacts badly to that kind of violation. I think it hampers the effects if your heart's not in it.

I knock on the door instead. The guard looks up and frowns. He makes shoo-ing motions and doesn't move. Cheeky bastard.

'Show him the chit,' says the dog.

Good idea. I take the little token out and press it against the glass, knocking on the door again. The guard sighs and puts down the book he's reading (*Fifty Shades of Grey*, I notice). He heaves himself out of his chair, acting as if I've just asked him to move a mountain for me.

He frowns at the token, then takes a keycard from his pocket and swipes it over the lock. The door opens but he doesn't step aside to let us in.

-*He's an orisha*,- says the dog in my mind. -*Low level. Nothing impressive.*-

Makes sense. If Tiurakh is operating from here he's going to want a supernatural guarding his business.

'Tiurakh in?' I say.

'You collecting?'

I hold the token up again. 'What do you think?'

He chews his lip and finally steps aside, indicating one of the elevators. 'Hold the token in front of the keypad.'

The elevator doors slide open as we approach. I wave the token around in the general area of the buttons. The doors slide closed and we start to rise.

Loud music bursts full blast from the speakers, making me leap about five feet into the air. 'Jesus Christ!'

'. . . *Don't fear the reaper* . . .'

'Nice song,' mutters the dog. 'Appropriate.'

'Yeah.' I straighten my clothes and watch the elevator numbers count upwards, all the way up to twenty-three, the top floor. Except it doesn't stop there. It carries on up another floor.

The doors open into a huge circular room with small windows running in a band all the way around, the glass shielded by angled concrete ribs on the outside of the building. I step out of the elevator and turn in a slow circle, impressed despite myself.

The room is how I imagine Aladdin's Cave must have looked. Gold and silver are strewn everywhere. Goblets, necklaces, trays, swords and shields with Celtic symbols engraved on them.

Huge cauldrons hold glittering emeralds and rubies. Persian rugs are tossed carelessly around. About a hundred tapestries hang on frames inside a wooden construction, each frame mounted on coasters that can be moved aside to view each one. Statues, some marble, some bronze, some, I think, gold, stand in random positions around the room, some of them clumped together so that it looks like I've just interrupted a party.

To my right are five full-length mirrors framed in antique wood.

There's a person standing in the mirrors, the same guy in all five. He nods at me and smiles.

'You Tiurakh?' I ask.

'I am the god of belongings, the orisha of objects, the valiant lord of–'.

'Save it for the tourists.'

Tiurakh frowns. 'Come on, man. I don't get to do my schtick anymore.'

'Not interested.' I hold up the token. 'Someone came in here yesterday, a deposit.'

'I can't give you whatever it is unless you are the depositee.'

'Don't talk crap. I've got the token.'

'You might have stolen it.'

'I didn't.'

'I don't know that.'

'But I do.'

'Yeah, but . . . you know. Why should I believe you? You could have killed the owner.'

'As it happens, she is dead. But I didn't do it.'

'You might have.'

'I *didn't*,' I say, feeling my temper start to rise.

'But you *might* have, is what I'm saying. Only the person who brought me the item can reclaim it. I have a reputation to uphold. I mean, look around. Some of this stuff has been with me for thousands of years.'

'Yeah, I noticed. You ever think whoever brought it all here might not be coming back?'

'That's not the point!'

I sigh and walk deeper into the room. I look around and realise I'm standing in the circular concrete crown on top of the Towers. I look out the window. It's a clear night. I can actually see the lights of ships out in the harbour from here.

The dog is sniffing the carpets.

'Don't,' I warn him.

'Don't what?' asks Tiurakh from the mirror. 'I can't see. What's your dog doing?'

'Where are you anyway?' I ask. 'Why aren't you here?'

'I'm in Jozi.'

'God, you call Johannesburg Jozi? Really? Doesn't everyone hate that?'

'Yeah, that's why I do it.'

'So . . . how does all this work?'

'I have mirrors all over the country. When I need to deal with a client, I can appear before them.'

He does a little twirl. The blackness around him snaps out of focus briefly, and I think I catch a glimpse of snapping teeth, rending jaws ripping flesh, blood pouring over bodies. I blink and it's gone. I'm not a hundred per cent sure it was even there. The briefest flash of something . . . *other*.

'To tell you the truth, I'm thinking of starting a franchise.'

'A franchise?'

'Sure. So I don't have to appear in person all the time. Except for my most important clients. Solomon. Judas. Those types.'

I have no idea if he's screwing with me. I hold up the chit. 'It's urgent.'

Tiurakh spreads his hands in the mirror. 'Sorry, man. I can't. Like I said, got my reputation to think of.'

I gave him a chance. Nobody can say I didn't. I pick up a heavy goblet and throw it at the closest mirror. The glass shatters, the noise obscenely loud in the room. I see flashes of broken bones and ripped skin in the falling fragments, a fire-lit sky and people screaming at the clouds. Christ, where the hell was that mirror from?

'What are you doing?' shrieks Tiurakh. His reflection is facing the empty frame. I note with interest that there is blood on his left arm, as if the falling glass wounded him. 'That . . . that was over two thousand years old!'

Huh. Didn't think they had mirrors that far back. I pick up another goblet and heft it in my hand. 'Your call. Where do you want to go from here?'

The orisha gives me a look of disgust and waves his hand. A glowing green line appears in the air, thin like a piece of string. One end is attached to the token in my hand and the other end disappears out the door.

'Follow the light,' says Tiurakh. 'And I won't forget this, human. You'll rue—'

'Yeah yeah. Rue the day. Yadda yadda yadda. Come on, dog.'

I head back into the elevator. The glowing string is touching the button for the fifteenth floor so I hit it and lean back against the mirror, tapping my foot.

'He was annoying,' says the dog. 'You should have broken all the mirrors.'

The elevator pings and the doors slide open onto a tiled corridor illuminated by harsh white strip lights. The green string disappears into a door a few feet away.

'What now?' asks the dog.

I shrug, then knock. The door opens to reveal an old man. He frowns, staring left then right, but not directly at me. I wave my hand in front of his face. He doesn't blink.

That makes it easier. He steps back and starts to close the door. I slip inside before he does so and follow the glowing string into the lounge. The TV is on, some programme with hot vampires and manly werwolves. The string vanishes into an ancient ashtray, one of those metal ones with the collapsing lid to keep the ash inside. I open it up and shake it. The ash parts to reveal what looks like a little black marble.

I pick it out. The green string comes with it, attached to the ball, but it fades away as I let the marble nestle in my palm.

'This is it?' I say to the dog. 'This is a human soul?'

No answer. I turn around and see him sitting on the couch next to the old man watching TV.

He glares at me. 'You see what you're doing? You're making me miss my shows.'

I sigh and hold the marble up to the light. I see a tiny flash of red, an even briefer flash of white, but the rest is complete blackness.

Pretty representative of Armitage, all things considered.

10

By the time the dog and I get back to the Division, Armitage's body has been laid out on the post-mortem table, dressed in her old mac and a spare set of clothes she kept in the accommodation block. Her face has been cleaned of blood.

Parker is waiting for me, sipping from a cup of steaming coffee while staring at Armitage's body. She rounds on me as I enter the room.

'You can't bring her back.'

'We can. I looked it up.'

'I don't mean that. I mean you *shouldn't*. She's dead. Leave her be.'

'She's not really dead, though. She backed up her soul because she was worried something like this might happen. That means she *wanted* to be brought back.'

At least, that's how I'm justifying it to myself. I quickly explain everything that's happened since I last saw Parker. She doesn't look impressed.

'I still don't like it. It's not natural.'

I laugh. I can't help it. 'Not natural? You're Delphic Division's resident resurrectionist. It's your specialty.'

She scowls. 'Point,' she says grudgingly.

'So, are you going to do it?'

She puts her coffee down and leaves the room, reappearing with a cardboard box filled with paraphernalia. She places it carefully on the desk and starts laying out her tools in neat rows.

'What do I do?' I ask.

'You stay out of the way.'

'I can do that.'

Parker takes a thick piece of chalk out the box and draws a closed double circle around Armitage. Next, she unstoppers a clay vial. An acrid smell fills the room. Vinegar, garlic and some kind of sharp spice. She taps the powder out between the lines of the circle.

'Did you bring her things?' she asks me.

I'd just come from Armitage's office. I hand over a shopping bag, and Parker takes out Armitage's cigarettes, her pocket watch, and her 'special' magazines. Parker glances at the cover. It shows two male models posing without shirts.

'Seriously?'

'You said to bring things that mean a lot to her. Those mean a lot to her.'

Parker places one of the magazines over Armitage's solar plexus. The cigarettes go onto her throat and her pocket watch over her heart.

'Her soul?'

I take out a yellow Lion matchbox and shake it. The soul rattles around inside.

'Yeah, if you *wouldn't* shake the immortal soul of our boss I'd very much appreciate it,' says Parker.

'Sorry.'

'Place it on her forehead.'

I step forward.

'Don't scuff the circle.'

I step carefully over the chalk and open up the matchbox. Armitage's soul gleams dully inside. I take it out, surprised again at how heavy it is. I place it over Armitage's forehead and move my hand away. The soul rolls off, smacking loudly against the metal table.

'Jesus,' snaps Parker. 'Be careful!'

'It's a ball! What do you expect me to do?'

'Just make it stay in one place.'

'Can I hold it there?'

'No, you can't hold it there. Not unless you want to end up like that dude from *The Fly.*'

I shudder. Me and Armitage fused into one body? While the sitcom possibilities are endless, it's not really something I'd be up for. I duck out the mortuary to the office, returning a minute later with a roll of duct tape.

Parker sees it and bursts out laughing. 'Are you serious?'

'What?'

'You're going to duct tape her soul to her head?'

'Why not? It's a remarkably adaptable product. I've used it to bind demons before. No good exorcist should leave home without it.'

'Fine. Just get on with it.'

Two minutes later we're standing on either side of the autopsy table, staring down at Armitage. Her face is pale. Composed in death. At rest.

With a great big strip of grey duct tape stuck to her forehead holding her soul against her skin.

'Well . . . it works,' says Parker doubtfully.

I step out of the circle and stand against the wall. Parker picks up an old jam jar filled with yellow gloopy stuff. She takes the lid off and spreads it onto Armitage's hands, feet and face.

'What's that?'

'Unguent. Made from griffin fat, the tears of possessed children, the tongue of a liar, and skin scrapings from an innocent man hanged for murder.'

'That's . . . disturbing.'

She puts the jar down and picks up a sheet of clear plastic. Actually, it's two pieces of Perspex with a page of old parchment wedged between them.

'And that?'

'This, my friend, is a talismanic scroll. It's what encourages her soul to re-enter her body.' Parker holds it up for me to inspect.

'Nice,' I say, because she clearly expects me to be impressed. 'Very . . . antiquey.'

'It was created by the Mad Emperor Fatim Caliphate in Egypt. He used to conjure demons to entertain at his parties. He was obsessed with them. Wanted to be one. It's written in Kufic text.'

I point to the top of the parchment. 'And the picture?'

Something in blue. It's so faded I can't see what it is. A pentagram, possibly?

'Solomon's Seal. It's said Emperor Fatim had Solomon's ring – that he used it to control the demons once he conjured them.'

'Solomon's Ring? Like, with the name of God written on it?'

'That's the thinking.'

'Where's the ring now?'

She gives me a look. 'Come on, London. If anyone had the ring, you think we'd even have a job? We'd just order the orisha to do what they were told and that would be it.'

'Fair enough.'

'Right. Be quiet now. I need to concentrate.'

'Don't you need to light candles or something? Incense?'

'Would it make you feel better?'

'Not really.'

'Then I'm good. Don't disturb me when I get started, yeah? That's very important. If you interrupt the invocation, anything can happen.'

'Anything, as in . . . ?'

'As in,' she says, deadpan, 'Armitage's body is about to become a beacon, a spotlight in the eternal darkness of Limbo, and the foulest creatures of hell and the nether planes are going to be swarming towards her, hoping to use her as a gate through to our world. If even one of them gets a foothold, they'll claw their way out her body, ripping it apart and opening up a permanent door that will condemn the world to hell on earth in a matter of days.'

'Ah. Then—'

Parker raises an eyebrow. I close my mouth, mime zipping it shut and throwing away the key.

Parker turns her back on me. She holds the parchment up, clears her throat, and starts speaking in a language I've never heard before.

I always thought this kind of thing was done in Latin, but this . . . this is . . . *alien*. One minute it sounds like Parker is gargling on glass, then it's like liquid hypnosis, her voice a warm, wet touch, a lover's embrace that slides into my being, fills my mind with entwined limbs and silky caresses. Only thing is, the entwined limbs and silky caresses are not human. They're shared between demons, all twisted limbs and scaled hides.

I can't escape the sound, the images. Her voice grows louder, throbbing in my ears, between my legs. This is ancient magic. Primeval spirits talking directly to the amygdala, bypassing society, modern man, communicating with the primitive caveman huddling in his cave, terrified of the storm outside. I can no more escape the feelings than I can chase away a lightning bolt.

Not that I want to escape. Parker's magic reverberates through my being. Her voice is everything. I know that if it stops my heart will stop as well. My brain will just switch off. I want it to go on forever. I want to wrap her words around me, let them seep into my skin.

My heart is beating rapidly. I groan, and I'm not sure if it's pleasure, or fear, or pain. Maybe all three. Her words grow louder. The heat in the room grows. I'm sweating now. I realise my eyes are closed. I force them open. The lights have dimmed. Black smoke whirls through the air, twining above

Armitage's body. The silhouette of Parker pulses. She is taller, more powerful, a towering mage astride ancient worlds.

Her voice rises, growing even louder. Shouting. Now it's like the very first wave crashing against the very first shoreline. Powerful, dominating, irresistible. I need to obey it, but I don't know what it wants me to do. Purple-white flashes of gristle and bone and horned gods bestriding ancient heaths.

The horned god comes for me, a powerful presence that smells of musk and sweat. It seems to know who I am. I feel a connection, that somehow I have met this being. Or am *going* to meet it. It points a clawed finger at me and smiles. And I'm suddenly hanging above London, watching the city crumble and fall, creatures rampaging through the streets, slaughtering any who get in their way.

Then it's not just London. The creatures of the past come back and move through England, then Scotland, ancient, primeval creatures from the dawn of consciousness re-emerging into the world.

I grimace, struggling to find myself, fighting to keep my mind from fragmenting into a million pieces.

Then Parker shouts a single word. Three times.

'Dolm-aata. Dolm-aata. Dolm-aata!'

The smoke rears back like a snake about to strike. It hovers, then rushes downward, disappearing into the little bump on Armitage's forehead.

An incredible implosion of air. My ears pop. I smell ozone, smoke. Blood and fear.

An invisible wind rushes in to fill the void of reality. It batters me to my knees, rushes through my ears, a roar of fury.

Then nothing.

I blink. Stare at the tiles, condensation droplets glinting in the light. My head pounds. My body feels like it's run the Comrades Marathon. Twice.

I haul myself heavily to my feet. Parker is leaning back

against the desk, watching me, breathing heavily, a triumphant gleam to her eyes, a wicked grin on her face.

'Was it good for you?' she asks.

'Fuck me, woman,' I say, steadying myself against the wall. 'You could have warned me.'

'You wanted to stay.'

'Yeah. I did that.'

A noise from the operating table brings us both around. Armitage is sitting up, pulling a cigarette from the creased box we left on her throat. She flicks it into her mouth and lights it. Inhales deeply.

Smoke trickles out from the between the stitches Jaeger made to the wound in her chest.

We all stare at this for a while. Then she looks slowly up. First at Parker. Then at me.

I'd like to say it was like the end of a Saturday morning cartoon. That we all burst out laughing and Armitage gives us a sly wink. 'You *guys*.'

I'd *like* to say that. But it would be a lie.

She goes bat shit insane.

Throwing the desk over, screaming in anger, bending the metal tables in half. (Seriously. Great strength upgrade, being a revenant.)

Parker and I flee outside and pull the door closed, listening to the destruction unfolding not five feet away.

'Jaeger is going to be *pissed*,' says Parker.

The dog wanders into the corridor. -*What's that noise?*- -*Armitage.*-

-*Oh.*- He turns and walks away again, utterly unconcerned.

The noise goes on for about five minutes before an uneasy silence falls.

Parker looks at me expectantly.

'I'll just check if the coast is clear, shall I?'

'Off you go then,' says Parker.

I cautiously open the door. A scene of chaos greets me. Nothing has survived unscathed. Jaeger's desk is in pieces. Tiles smashed. Shards littering the floor. Twisted metal surrounding Armitage, who's sitting amidst the wreckage, head bowed.

'Armitage?' Hesitant.

She looks at me with such anger and fury in her face that I take step back.

'You know what you are? An absolute cock-tonsil. A selfish, fucking jizzcock. That's what.'

Right. Well. I've been called worse for less.

An hour later and Parker, Armitage and I are standing awkwardly around in her office.

Armitage is slumped in her comfy chair, a lit cigarette dangling from her fingers. She doesn't look too bad for a member of the undead. Pale, sure. But that's what comes from having no blood circulating around your body. But it still looks like her. She even sounds the same. A bit raspy, but again, that's to be expected seeing as her vocal cords have been in deep freeze for the past day.

I look at Parker. She shrugs and makes shoo-ing gestures at me.

I clear my throat. 'Armitage?'

She stirs, looks at the cigarette, then turns her sad eyes onto Parker. 'How could you let them do this to me?'

Parker stiffens. 'Hey – I was against this. I told them not to do it.'

'So what am I? A zombie? Am I going to start craving human flesh?'

I give her a forced smile. 'Ah, no. Parker was very clear on this. You're a revenant. All the benefits of being a zombie without that desire to eat brains.'

She glares at me. I sigh. 'Look, I'm sorry, all right? If we had any other choice we would have taken it. But this case . . . it's serious, Armitage. Big.'

I tell Armitage about what's happened since her death. About Lilith's serious hard-on for the ramanga's soul, wanting to start some kind of war.

'Only problem is, I have no idea why she wants it. I was hoping we could . . . wake you up and you'd tell us where it is. I mean, I'm assuming you used the token? Picked it up from Tiurakh?'

Armitage nods. 'I picked it up all right. When I looked inside the box Jengo had left with Tiurakh I realized what he'd done. I thought it was a pretty bloody good idea too. You know why?'

'Why?'

'Because I was being followed. I'd lost them by that time, obviously. I wouldn't lead them to Tiurakh. But still, I was feeling a bit paranoid. So I did the same as Jengo. Called in a couple of favours from an old sangoma I know, extracted my soul, and left it with Tiurakh – after making sure my tail hadn't found me again.' She shudders. 'It's . . . not a great feeling, let me tell you. The emptiness . . . Like you're hollowed out. Utterly devoid of life, of *everything*. Kind of what I feel like now, actually.' She trails off, then shrugs. 'But still, I'm kind of glad I did it. When I got home I realised why they weren't following me anymore. They'd decided to just wait for me in my house.'

'So what did you do with Jengo's soul? Where is it now?'

'Now? It's in the evidence room.'

I look at her in surprise. 'Here?'

'Of course here. Where the hell else would it be safe?'

'So can we communicate with it?' I ask. 'Try find out what happened?'

'I have no idea,' says Armitage. 'I suppose we can ask Eshu. He's supposed to be the expert in this kind of thing.'

★   ★   ★

'This is bullshit,' says Parker.

We're sitting around a foldout table in Eshu's room. There's a Ouija board sitting on the table, and resting on the board is Jengo's soul. It's similar to Armitage's, although there is more red and purple in Jengo's.

Parker looks at Armitage, then me. 'We're really going to do this?'

'It will work,' says Eshu. 'Trust me.'

'What makes you so sure?' asks Armitage.

'Because I've used my aether generators to boost our psychic powers.' He flicks the light switch. The fluorescent strips wink out. Then he goes around the room, switching his monitors off one by one.

He leaves his LCD television on. It's showing the space battle at the end of *Return of the Jedi*, the dim room lit up by red and green laser blasts.

Eshu sits down next to me and holds his hand out. I stare at him.

'Come on. Link up.'

I sigh and take his hand. It's warm and dry. Parker is on my right and she grabs mine and grips it tight. She takes Armitage's on the other side and Armitage completes the circle with Eshu.

'So . . . what do we do?' I ask.

'Close your eyes,' says Eshu.

We do as we're told. I can still sense the TV, light flashing and strobing through my eyelids.

'Jengo Dhlamini. Are you there, Jengo?'

Silence.

'Jengo. Talk to us, Jengo.'

More silence. Then the temperature in the room drops by a few degrees. Parker squeezes my hand tighter.

'Who wakes me?'

My eyes snap open. There's a pale shape hovering before us. I recognize the features as Jengo's from the decapitated head.

Armitage looks at Eshu and he nods.

'Why were you killed, Jengo?' asks Armitage.

The ghost looks around. He seems lost.

'Jengo?'

Jengo turns slightly, focuses on Armitage.

'Why were you killed?' she repeats.

'Ul Khu tavu.' The voice is faint, like a whisper.

'Ul what?' Armitage looks at me. I shrug.

'Ul Khu tavu.'

'What does that mean, Jengo?'

Eshu pulls his hand away and gets up from the table. He disappears into the darkness and fiddles around with something at one of his computers. Jengo's ghost brightens suddenly. He blinks, focuses on us all sitting at the table. Eshu rejoins us.

'Better be quick. I've upped the amps but he'll burn out soon.'

'Where am I?' whispers Jengo.

'Dude,' says Eshu, 'you're dead.'

I punch Eshu in the shoulder. He winces. 'What? Best to be upfront with these ghosts. Get it out the way.'

'Dead?' says Jengo.

'That's right,' says Armitage. 'You were murdered. Your heart scooped out. And you were um . . . decapitated. Sorry.'

'Oh.' Jengo frowns suddenly. 'Yes. Yes, I remember. He was a big man.'

'What did he want?'

'He wanted my sins.'

I frown. 'Your sins? You got a lot of them?'

He frowns at me. 'You do not understand. They were not *my* sins.'

'You're right. I don't understand.'

'I took them from people. I helped them. I took them inside of me.' He holds his hands against his chest. 'I was their sin-eater.'

Armitage and I exchange looks. A sin-eater? What the hell?

I've never come across a sin-eater before. To be honest, I didn't even think they were real.

The stories I'd heard were mostly from England and Wales, and put them as these sad, lonely old men who went round to a house when someone had died and took on the sins of the deceased, absolving the soul of all wrong doing.

'Do you know who your murderer was?' asks Parker.

'I have never seen him before.' Jengo looks around, frowning. 'I do not like it here. It's cold.'

'Just a few more questions,' says Armitage.

'No. I am done now. I am tired.'

He starts to fade away.

'Wait,' says Armitage. 'We want to help you.'

He looks sadly at Armitage. 'I am beyond help.'

The ghost winks out of existence. Eshu gets up and flicks on the lights again.

'Can you bring him back?' asks Armitage.

'No. Not for a while. His soul is drained. It will take a while for him to recharge.'

'What good are your bloody generators then?' snaps Armitage.

'You think that was a normal séance? You think in Victorian times they had their ghosts actually turn up and chat to them like that? You should be thanking me. Now come on. Get out. I need to catch up on my feeds.'

We head back to her office. Sin-eaters? Is that why Lilith wanted the ramanga – no, the *sin-eater*? So he would take *her* sin? She didn't really seem like the repentant type, to be honest. Besides, Jengo's dead. He can't take any more sins.

So why did she need his soul?

Armitage sits on her desk. 'Do some research into these sin-eaters,' she says. 'See if we have a list of names or something. And look up those words. Ul Khu tavu? Try as many different spellings as you can.'

'What are you going to do?' I ask.

'I am going to sit in my dark office for a while. I need some alone time. To come to terms with my death and resurrection.'

Parker and I leave her office and head down to our desks. I yawn. It's after three now, and I've had what could only be termed as a busy day. I plan on putting my head down in the accommodation block, but I log in to GHOST and do a quick search on sin-eaters. Just to satisfy my curiosity.

Nothing.

And by that I mean all we have is a link to a Wikipedia article. I frown. That's not right. Every single orisha on the planet is supposed to be listed in the database. Why not sin-eaters?

In fact, there's more info on the public internet than we have in our own files. That's *really* not right.

I try to find a reference to Ul Khu tavu, but likewise come up with a blank. Parker has no luck either.

I stare at the monitor, but I can't think straight. My brain is too scrambled. I think I'll have to pay a visit to one of my contacts in the morning. A guy who goes by the name of Harold Grimes. If anyone knows anything about these sin-eaters it will be him.

I log out. Parker is already asleep, folded over her keyboard like a dropped marionette. I prod her but she just gives a little snort and carries on sleeping.

I take the elevator up to the accommodation block on the tenth floor and open the closest door. The room on the other side is like every generic hotel room you've ever stayed in. I half expect to find a Gideon bible in the drawer.

I open it to check. No bible. Just a business card for 'Sexy Solange, mistress of the night'.

I close the drawer with a tired grin. I wonder who used this room last? Bet it was Russells. Dirty bugger.

I fall onto the bed and am asleep within a minute.

II

I wake up to the sounds of shouting.

I stare at the ceiling, blinking, trying to make sense of the world.

Trying to shake off the dreams.

They weren't so bad last night. Still there, but I slept through. Didn't wake up every hour in a cold sweat.

The shouting is getting louder. I think I hear Armitage's voice.

Armitage.

Shit.

I scramble out of bed and pull on my shirt. Head through the door and lean over the balcony. It's Armitage and Ranson. Ranson is standing behind a desk in the office below, looking terrified and furious while Armitage tries her best to pummel him into submission with her rage. The rest of our co-workers are watching this with wide eyes. Most of them are staring at Armitage in wonder.

'Do I *look* dead to you?' she screams. 'Do I? Because I don't feel dead, you odious piece of shit.'

Anger transforms the fear in Ranson's face. 'You can't talk to me like that! I'll have you up on charges.'

I grab the elevator and ride it down to the bottom floor.

'What's going on?' I ask, hurrying to Armitage's side.

Armitage waves at Ranson in disgust. 'Mr Hopeless-Case here doesn't want to accept I'm alive.'

'Oh. Well . . . you're not. Not exactly.'

'No. But it doesn't interfere with my ability to run this unit.'

Ah. Now I understood. If Ranson couldn't even admit to magic being real, he's not going to be happy working with a revenant.

'It's a clear conflict of interest,' he says, appealing to me in an incredibly misguided belief that I was on his side.

'How so?'

'She's one of them now. An orisha.'

'I bloody well am not.'

'Actually, she's not.'

We turn around to find Parker approaching with a file stuffed full of printouts. She hands it to Ranson. 'All the details about the procedure I undertook, background details on revenants etc. She is *not* an orisha. If anything, you would call her physically challenged.'

'I am *not* physically challenged,' protests Armitage.

'Fine. Not *physically* challenged,' says Parker. 'Spiritually-challenged? Life-challenged?'

Ranson winces. Something-*challenged*. The word strikes fear into any office manager's heart. Especially if we're talking about discrimination.

'I don't know about challenged,' says Armitage. 'But if you try and fire me because I'm a revenant, I'm pretty sure that's racist, species-ist, dead-ist, and any other amount of -*ists* I can think of. I might need to have a word with the National Intelligence Co-ordination Committee.'

Ranson frowns. He pages through the file Parker gave him, then glares at Armitage. 'This isn't over,' he says, and stalks away to the elevator.

Armitage turns to face everyone else.

'Right,' she says. 'I'm sure you're all wondering what's going on. Let's just say that reports of my demise have been greatly exaggerated, and leave it at that. I'm still me and I'm still your boss.'

The crowd broke into a slightly self-conscious cheer. Armitage's eyes widen in surprise.

'What the bloody hell is that? Don't tell me you're *glad* I'm back. Right. First thing you all need to do is look up Stockholm Syndrome, then get back to work. Move!'

The crowd slowly disperses. Armitage watches them go, then turns her attention to me. 'Anything on the sin-eaters?' she asks.

'Nothing in GHOST. Not even a mention.'

Armitage frowns. 'That's odd.'

'That's what I thought. I've asked Eshu to track back through the database and see if there have been any changes or updates.'

'You think someone's deleted it?' She thinks about this, then shakes her head. 'No. The database is global. How would they get into it?'

'Hackers? It might be difficult, but it's certainly possible.'

'Fine,' says Armitage. 'Let me know if he finds anything. And that word? Any translation?'

'Nothing. I reckon we should pay a visit to Harry Grimes.'

Armitage's face twists in distaste. 'Grimes? Don't like that man. He's got too many friends. Never trust a person with a large group of friends.'

'Well . . . sure. But he also has the largest list of contacts in the country. If anyone knows something about sin-eaters, it'll be him. And if *not* him, he might know someone who does.'

Armitage chews her lip, then nods. 'Fine. We'll have a word with him. Meet me out front in twenty minutes.'

I head back to my desk. The dog is still sleeping. I nudge him with my foot.

'Heading into Durban. You coming?'

'Is it hot out?'

I glance at the skylight high above. Blue sky. 'Looks like it.'

'Then no. I'm not coming.'

'Suit yourself,' I say, and take the elevator back to the accommodation block so I can shower and change.

Durban has many nicknames, but the one that springs to mind as Armitage and I make our way along Grey Street, cooking in the morning sun, is Poison City.

Users huddle in doorways, stand in alleys, swaying like pieces of cloth in a breeze. You know straight away they're high. There's an emptiness to their stare, a vacancy of spirit that makes them stand out. Like zombies in a crowd of the living.

The drug of choice used to be Tik, more commonly known as crystal meth, but now it's Whoonga, a lethal mix of brown heroin, rat poison, and detergents mixed with dagga and tobacco to stretch it out. Twenty bucks a hit, four hits a day, and your life withers away like a slug in a bath of salt.

It's only eleven in the morning but already the heat is like a physical presence, a weight that rests across my shoulders and back, prickling sweat from every pore despite trying to keep to the shade.

'How does it . . . you know?'

'Feel?'

I nod.

'Like I'm watching myself on a movie screen.'

I frown, not getting it.

'All my emotions are still here. But it's like I'm watching them being felt by someone else. Like I'm on the outside look-ing in. I spoke to Parker and she says that might pass. That revenants are actually the closest you can get to being human without actually, you know, being human.'

'I *am* sorry,' I say softly. I glance at her sidelong.

'For what?'

'For doing this . . . without permission.' I hesitate. 'But I'm not sorry you're back.'

She grins at me, the old twinkle in her eye. 'Not getting sappy on me, are you, London?'

I don't reply. We pass stalls selling Indian spices. I smell cinnamon, curry, and paprika. Heat waves rise off another stall, the sizzle of cooking samoosa growing louder as we approach. My stomach rumbles, but there's no way I'm buying anything from one of these stalls. I did it once and ended up flat on my back with food poisoning for three days.

'Besides,' she casually says, 'it's probably for the best.'

'How so?'

'At least now my insides won't spontaneously shift backwards and forwards in time. Seeing as they're dead.'

It takes me a moment to hear what she just said. I stop walking. She carries on ahead, hands stuffed in her long coat.

'What?'

She stops and turns. Nods cheerfully. 'You know how it is. A lifetime of using shinecraft. Comes to us all in the end.'

I remember all the medical equipment in her room. 'What was wrong with you?'

'My internal organs. They were . . . taking holidays along my timeline.'

I think about this, then shake my head. 'I don't get it.'

'At night. I'd wake up feeling like I was having a heart attack. Or my joints would seize up and I couldn't move. Turns out my organs were swapping places with their . . . other selves. I'd get an eighty-year-old heart in my chest, or my kidney suddenly regressed to a five year old's. Had a lot of health issues when I was a bairn. Doctors never could figure it out. Now I know.'

'How long had this being going on?

'About six months. But it didn't happen every night, like.'

'How long . . . You know . . . Until . . . ?' I trail off.

'How long did I have left?'

I nod.

'It was getting worse. Lasting longer. My brain took a trip last time. Had Alzheimer's for a night. Went wandering around in the garden in my nightie. Then there were the demons. But that was a separate thing.'

'The . . . ?'

'Demons. They tried to possess me. Like in *The Exorcist?* Apparently the build-up of shinecraft in my body over the years attracted them.'

I just stare at her.

'I had to get a priest in. Looked nothing like Max Von Sydow, though. Was a bit disappointed in that.'

'Did he succeed?'

'No. Got torn apart. Wasn't strong enough. There were bits of him everywhere. After that, I just tried to handle it on my own.'

'Why didn't you say?'

'What for? It comes to us all in the end. Nothing you could have done.'

She starts walking again.

'And . . . now?'

'Seems to be all gone. Demons and time-hopping body organs.'

'So . . . I actually saved your life?'

She gives me one of her looks. 'Don't push it, lad.'

'Sorry.'

We pass a second-hand shop with a rack of clothes displayed on the sidewalk. A shop assistant sits in a white plastic chair, one hand gripping the rack in case someone decides to make off with it.

'That's what this job does to you,' say Armitage.

I glance at her questioningly.

'It was brought on by . . . you know. What we do. Magic.'

'You're sure?'

She nods. 'Jaeger said so.'

I mentioned before that using shinecraft is not conducive to a long life? That's the kind of thing we've all got to look forward to.

About twenty feet farther on we turn into a narrow alley between a barber shop selling pay-as-you-go phones and a boarded-up pawn shop.

We stop walking.

There's a large van parked next to a garage door up ahead. The van is rocking violently, bouncing back and forth as if the Hulk and She Hulk are having some private happy time.

The van doors slam open. Something huge grabs the sides of the vehicle and pulls itself out, crushing the metal beneath its hands. The creature straightens up and stretches as two armed figures appear out of the building to the left.

The huge creature casually backhands them, sending them sailing over the van to slap painfully onto the pitted asphalt beyond.

'Hey,' I say. 'That's Buno.'

Buno is a *Bungisngis* – a type of cyclops from the East Indies. This particular cyclops is a repeat offender, in and out of our Division multiple times over the years.

The massive creature blinks its bloodshot eye and focuses on us.

'Hey there, Buno,' I say. 'You were supposed to be in court last week. What happened?'

Buno starts to giggle, high-pitched and unpleasant, then lumbers towards us. His huge mouth is filled with serrated shark teeth and he has two lethal tusks to either side of his upper lip.

Shit. I fumble for my wand. Armitage steps to the side, watching Buno approach with interest.

'Hurry up, Potter,' says Armitage encouragingly.

I frown, then clear my mind and summon up the wind. There's not much around, though. No moisture in the air at all. So I end up sucking the surrounding air in and using it as a battering ram, throwing it into Buno. The force lifts him off his feet and slams him against the alley wall, holding him there.

He doesn't stop giggling once.

The door at the end of the alley slams open and Harry Grimes runs out with a long pole clutched in his hands. There's a metal collar on the end of the pole. Grimes pushes it towards Buno and it snaps around his neck. The cyclops immediately stops giggling, hanging slack against the wall.

'He controlled?' I ask.

'Yeah.'

I nod and step away, flicking the wand to cancel the summoning. Grimes uses the pole to drag Buno along the alley. We follow after as he guides the cyclops towards the garage.

Harry Grimes. Bail-bondsman to the orisha. He's a bit of a double-edged sword, is our Harry. See, not all orisha are gods and angels. Most of them are just Tier 1s and 2s. Regular supernaturals, the equivalent of petty criminals, pimps and users stealing for their next fix. And someone has to put up the money to cover their bail (or the orisha equivalent of money. Sometimes gold, sometimes souls, sometimes favours. It can be anything, depending on the judge).

Grimes is the person who puts up the bond, for a hefty fee, of course. In the process he's earned a reputation as being a tough son of a bitch with knowledge of and contacts within the orisha world that are second to none.

The garage door slides up with a metallic rattle and he pulls Buno inside. We follow him into a large empty room then into a short hallway. There's an old rusted bicycle with no wheels sitting on the floor. A sun-bleached photograph of a family on holiday hangs on the wall.

We enter his reception area. It's so generic as to be almost invisible. Ancient aluminium chairs, a table with ten-year old magazines, and a wilted fern. His receptionist, Lydia, sits behind a desk covered with bulging folders. She's holding a phone in the crook of her neck while she types on one of those old clickety-clackety keyboards. Her monitor is CRT, no fancy LCD screens for Harry Grimes. He's a known cheapskate.

Grimes pushes Buno into one of the chairs. The metal legs creak then give with a groan, depositing Buno butt-first onto the floor.

'Oh, for fuck— you know what? Stay there. OK?'

'OK,' says Buno.

The fact that Buno is being so obedient might impress Joe Average, but the truth is we gave Grimes the method for manufacturing these collars. He has a freelance conjurer on his payroll, and when he has to put up the bond for an orisha, the conjurer draws out some of the client's spirit and attaches it to the collar. The client also has to enter into a binding magical spell that acts as a contract, giving command of themselves over to Grimes when the collar is in place.

'Course, none of them think he'll get a chance to use it on them. Those that run off before their court dates think they'll get the hell out of Dodge before Grimes even knows they're gone. But he hasn't lost a single orisha yet. Those that run are always caught, usually by freelance bounty hunters. I've taken on a few jobs myself when money was tight.

'Yeah, I'm not sure about that, honey,' says Lydia into the phone. 'You say your bail has been set as "the dreams of the Djinn Al'aka as he sits trapped for a millennium in his bottle"? What's that? *Two* millennia? Let me guess. The judge was that Victorian ghost? Mr Ravenhill? Yeah, thought so. Look, I'll talk to Harry, see what he says, OK?'

She hangs up and looks at Harry. He shrugs. 'Give me a few hours to call around.' He glances at us. 'You want tea? Coffee?'

I shake my head. Armitage does likewise and we follow him through a door behind Lydia's desk.

The three of us can barely fit into the room. It's more like a walk-in closet than an office. There are no windows, so the heat is stifling. Two desk fans placed in opposite corners of the room battle to push the turgid air around.

I look around for a place to sit. No chance. Filing cabinets are lined up around the walls and an old chipboard desk takes up the rest of the space. There are files everywhere: piled up to either side of his chair, on his desk, on top of the cabinets.

'Christ, how can you work in here?'

Grimes looks around as if seeing his surroundings for the first time. He shrugs and sits down, reaching under his desk for a bottle of water. He gulps some of it down.

'So,' he says after he's drained half the bottle. 'Hot enough for you?'

Armitage smiles sweetly at him. 'You know, I actually arrested someone who asked me that once.'

'Did you now? And I take it you're Armitage? His long-suffering boss?'

'That's right.'

'Great. Now we all know each other. What can I do for you? You looking for more work?'

'Uh . . . no.' I throw a sideways glance at Armitage. The Division has a bit of a strict policy on moonlighting. 'We were hoping you could tell us a bit about a class of orisha.'

'Sin-eaters,' says Armitage.

'Sin-eaters?'

'Yeah. You know the stories. They go to the house of the deceased—'

'I know the stories,' he says. 'But that's all they are.'

'You mean you've never dealt with one?'

'Never.'

'But . . . somebody has to know *something*,' says Armitage.

'Well, sure. *Somebody* might. But not me.'

Shit. Another dead end.

'Actually . . .' says Grimes.

'What?'

'How do you feel about the fae?'

'I find them very annoying, smug, and obtuse. Why?'

'Because there's one – a lore-collector. It's a holy position among the fae. Her official title is the Lord High Lore-Keeper and Guardian of the Ancient Rites and Hidden Histories of Mankind.'

Armitage snorts. 'Jumped up and full of themselves, the lot of them. What does everyone else call her?'

'Gran.'

'Seriously?'

'Seriously.'

'Where is she?' I ask.

'The Sleeping Market.'

'That's started up again?' I say in surprise. 'Where?'

'Warwick Junction. She's there every night on Muti Bridge. Least, until they move on. But I reckon that will only be in the autumn. They like the sun too much.'

'Thanks.'

'No problem. You'll have to get there before the normal markets close for the day, though. No way in once the gates are locked down.'

We leave Grimes' offices and head back along Grey Street. I skirt around a shop owner pushing plastic crates of bread into his store, shaking my head at a dude trying to sell me an old Japanese knock-off cell phone.

My phone rings. Parker.

'What's up?'

'There's been another murder.'

I stop walking. 'A sin-eater?'

'Could be. Same MO.'

'Where is it?'

'The Oyster Box hotel. Out in Umhlanga. Victim's name is Caitlyn Long.'

'Isn't the Oyster Box that five star place? Where all the Hollywood big shots stay when they come here?'

'The very same. As you can imagine, they're very keen to keep this as quiet as possible.'

I tell Armitage and we climb into her car.

'Oyster Box, eh?' she says, glancing over her shoulder, then pulling out into traffic. 'I think this is going to be a long investigation. They might have to put us up for the night.'

'Yeah,' I say. 'Good luck with that. I'm not a hundred per cent confident they'll even let us in the front door.'

Immaculately scrubbed cobbles lead to an open air foyer outside the hotel. Huge ferns planted in intricately painted pots line the walls. Palm trees flank the building, flags on the roof fluttering in the warm breeze.

The glass doors are watched over by a tall black man wearing a glaringly white colonial uniform. He looks nervous, ill at ease.

He glances at Armitage in her old coat and scuffed shoes and steps forward to block our way. We show him our IDs before he gets a chance to ask us to leave.

'Where's the manager?' Armitage asks.

He doesn't get a chance to respond. A short guy in a charcoal suit walk-runs towards Armitage and me. He peers around me, checking the parking lot. I follow his gaze.

'Don't worry,' says Armitage. 'No big nasty police cars to scare the rich guests.'

He bows slightly, managing to combine the bow with a cringe. 'Ha-hah. Yes. No. Of course. No offence. Sorry.' He straightens up and tries to smooth his suit. 'Bit of a rough morning, as I'm sure you can imagine. Um . . . the name's Mason.'

I nod. 'Where's the body?'

He winces at the word. 'If you'll just follow me. I'll ah . . . take you to the unfortunate . . . guest. She's in the presidential suite.'

He stands aside and gestures for us to enter. We walk through the doors, onto brown tiles. Cool air wafts over us, but from hidden air-conditioning vents, not the slowly circling ceiling fans. Ferns and greenery lurk in alcoves, concealed lighting illuminates oil paintings.

Mason takes us past the reception area, heading straight for an elevator. Two uniformed SAPS officers are standing discreetly in the shadows, almost swallowed up by the foliage of the pot plants. Armitage and I flash our IDs at them and the manager swipes a card over a sensor. The elevator doors open immediately and we step inside. The doors close and I feel a lurch as we get moving. I check out the wall. No buttons.

'How does it know what floor to go to?'

'This is a private elevator. For the Presidential Suite.'

Armitage whistles. 'Not bad. How much would a night there set me back?'

'Ah . . . the cost of a night's stay is fifty thousand rand, madam.'

'Shut the bloody hell up,' says Armitage immediately.

'Uh . . .'

'What my esteemed colleague is trying to say is, that's not cheap.'

'Ah. I see. But that cost does cover many benefits. Access to our gym, our spa—'

'For fifty kay a night, I hope it includes a half-naked male masseuse permanently on call. Because that's the only thing that would justify that kind of money. So? Does it?'

She stares at the manager. I'm feeling kind sorry for the guy.

'Does it what?'

'Include a male masseuse.'

'No.'

'Bloody rip-off.'

The elevator *bings* softly and the doors slide open onto an opulent lounge. Mason is about to step out but I put a hand out to stop him. Armitage is already taking out the paper overshoes she grabbed from her car.

'We'll take it from here,' I say. 'How many people have been into the room?'

'Well, the butler obviously. He's *incredibly* traumatized. He's going to need psychiatric leave. I don't know where I'm going to find a replacement. Um . . . then me, of course. And the police, but there were only three of them.'

'I'll need the keycard.'

He hands it to me and I pull on my overshoes. Armitage is already standing in the lounge, staring around with an unimpressed look on her face. I follow after and swipe the card over the sensor so the doors slide shut in the manager's face.

I take a deep breath and check out the surroundings.

'It's very . . . white,' I say.

Everything looks like it's just been freshly painted. White lounge suite, white wing-back chairs, gold-rimmed mirrors. Huge white pillars and a long white dining table – *two* dining tables.

'Why do they need two dining rooms?' asks Armitage.

'No idea. I don't even have one.'

'Well, no, but you're a savage, aren't you?'

'Thanks,' I say absently. I walk across the diamond-shaped tiles and take the stairs to the upper level. It's the bedroom with an adjoining sitting room. Two bathrooms – his and hers, I suppose. I enter the closest. A massive bath dominates the room, positioned in front of a huge bay window looking out over the ocean. I sniff the soaps. Wrinkle my nose at the pungent odour.

'Out here,' calls Armitage from the bedroom.

I retrace my steps. I see Armitage through the windows, out on the balcony. I step through the doors. The sea breeze hits me, fresh, warm, the smell of salt and seaweed. I take a deep breath and gaze out over the ocean. The red and white light-house that's become a bit of a landmark around here stands proud against the sky.

Nice view.

'If you've quite finished sightseeing?'

I reluctantly turn away. My eyes drop down to the body.

It's a woman. She's lying on the balcony in a pool of congealed blood. Her chest has been ripped out. But this time there's something different. An odd, yellowish powder that coats the body.

I squat down and gently touch it. Fine. Like ash. I bring it up to my nose to take a sniff.

And end up hanging over the balcony puking my guts out into the bushes below the terrace. The powder smells like week-old corpses left out in the summer sun.

'Come on, now, London,' says Armitage disapprovingly. 'You're letting the side down.'

I wipe my mouth and turn back, leaning weakly on the balcony. I take a cautious sniff of the air. Nothing. But something that strong, it should stink out the whole place, shouldn't it?

'Bag some of that powder.'

'Ooh, giving orders now are we?'

'Please?'

Armitage salutes. 'Yes sir.'

I take a deep breath, trying to clear my lungs of that stink. I nod at the body. 'You think she's a sin-eater too?'

'If she is, she did a lot better at it than the first victim. To make this kind of money.'

I nod. Of course, she might not be a sin-eater at all. It could just be coincidence. Or maybe Lilith wanted her dead for some other reason.

'Find her appointment book,' says Armitage. 'Her laptop. Whatever. Let's see if we can find out why she was in town.'

My phone rings. It's Jaeger. Her and Maddoc have arrived at the hotel. Armitage and I search around till we find the victim's phone and laptop, then we head back down to the ground floor and hand the keycard over to the orisha.

'When are you going to take me to a place like this?' asks Jaeger.

'Sorry. Way out of my price range.'

We head outside. It's about three in the afternoon. Grimes said we should be inside the market before it closes for the day, which happens at five. Just time to grab a quick bite to eat before we try to track down this lore-keeper.

I'm really not looking forward to it.

12

The Warwick Junction market is a little piece of chaos nestled in the heart of the city. A taste of the entire African continent squashed into a cramped, claustrophobic location in the centre of the city's main transport hub.

The market is made up of about eight thousand traders separated into nine distinct markets, all of this squeezed up against two major freeways, a railway station, five bus terminals, and nineteen taxi ranks. Half a million commuters use the roads, walkways, and pedestrian bridges that crisscross the area every day.

The market itself is a hundred years old, started when Indian merchants set up camp here after their time as indentured labourers was up.

Then apartheid reared its ugly head in the forties, and the area became the hub for the African workers heading into the city. Street traders were prohibited anywhere near the city centre, but trade persisted despite the harassment of the blackjacks – the apartheid police. The place just couldn't be shut down. It had a life of its own. No matter how many times the blackjacks tried to clear the stallholders out, they were back a few days later. It was a losing battle and they eventually just gave up.

When the apartheid policies began to loosen in the eighties, the trade at Warwick Junction exploded, but the infrastructure was laughable for the amount of people it catered to, and from the nineties onward, the area was earmarked for expansion and upgrade.

The fact that this hasn't been completed yet is all thanks to a government initiative called the Urban Renewal Scheme, a little scam that is used to line the pockets of cronies by way of corrupt tenders and major kickbacks.

Armitage and I stroll through the taxi ranks on the periphery of the market, jostling with workers fighting for space in the hundreds of white minibus taxis covered with advertisements for soap powders and cell-phone operators.

We're flowing against the tide, heading for the stairs to the pedestrian bridge that crosses the freeway. The hubbub and shouting of commuters assaults my ears as we hurry up the steps, trying to get inside the market before the gates close.

Before the 2010 World Cup came along there used to be one fatal accident here every week. But when the government realized this didn't look very good to visiting tourists, they built a viaduct and pedestrian bridges across the freeways, meaning people didn't have to play chicken with 120 km an hour traffic anymore.

We hurry over the bridge and down the wide steps into the market proper. My senses are going into overload. The bright colours of the stalls, the smell of meat grilling over stolen metal supermarket carts, the thumping bass of a hundred different sound systems, the stench of sweat.

We head through the Bead Market, rainbows made up of little plastic balls strung up on twine, bracelets and necklaces laid out on display for all to see. Bright clothing hangs on racks, the last shoppers of the day browsing for bargains.

We cut through a stall into the Impepho and Lime Market, trestle tables displaying balls of red and white lime the size of my head. The area is filled with sweet and savoury smoke battling each other for dominance. Incense used to communicate with ancestral spirits.

Next, we pass into the Bovine Head Market. A huge area

covered with a gently curved corrugated roof: frozen cow heads rest on the tables outside the shelter, defrosting in the still-sweltering sun. Aisles of wooden benches are covered with mielies, sweet potatoes, and onions. The heavy *thunk* of cleavers chopping through meat into wood.

Steam clouds the air. The smell of meat, raw and cooked, clings to the back of the throat. Plastic trays holding neatly sliced lamb and beef, salt, pepper and tabasco sauce laid out for those wanting a snack before heading home.

Outside the Bovine Head Market are stalls of fresh produce covered with beach umbrellas. Potatoes, onions, mushrooms, herbs.

We head through the narrow aisle and take the stairs up to the Music Bridge – a wide pedestrian flyover lined with stalls selling CDs and cassettes, mp3 players, rasta hats, and counterfeit designer caps. There's no point even trying to talk here. Each stall blasts out a different type of music: gospel, pop, kwaito, maskanda.

We take yet another bridge to finally arrive at our destination, our senses battered and bruised.

The Muti Market sprawls across an incomplete motorway overpass, the construction abandoned due to some idiot making mistakes in the planning. When the builders realized their error they just upped and left, leaving behind a concrete cliff that literally drops away onto the road below.

It didn't take long for the traders to move in. Houses and shops sprouted up overnight. It was prime real estate. Easy access to the market and taxi ranks, but high off the ground so there was no danger of flooding in spring.

I stop walking and look around, just ... enjoying the quietness.

The difference is intense. The echo of silence rings in my ears. From the blaring music to this sudden quiet calmness, where the Izintanga – the healers – brew up their medicines in small covered kiosks, where shoppers browse for traditional medicines – herbs, tree barks, roots and spices.

All we have to do now is wait. I lean on the railing, staring at the market down below while Armitage wanders off to browse the stalls. There's a barber booth right below me, a huge poster showing cartoons of the available hairstyles, most of which look like they're from the seventies and eighties.

Armitage re-joins me some time later, handing me a can of orange Fanta and leaning over the railing at my side. She squints at me, the afternoon sun hitting her square in the face.

'So,' she says. 'You want to tell me what's going on?'

I look at her in surprise. 'What? Nothing – why?'

'Come on, love. I've known you for years now. You're acting . . . off. Like before. You know. All that with your daughter.' She stops talking, frowns and looks away. 'There's something in your eyes,' she finally says. 'Something different.'

'You're imagining it.'

'Am I?' She stares at me, and when I don't answer, I see a brief flash of hurt. She shrugs and looks away. 'Suit yourself. Never let it be said I pry into another's business.'

I hesitate. Then sigh. 'The guy we're looking for. The one who killed the sin-eaters. He . . . He was there. That night. In the mountains. He's involved.'

She knows instantly what I'm talking about. 'That night' has defined every waking moment of my life since it happened. 'So . . . are you saying this case is connected to the murdered kids?'

I wince at her words, turn away to look over the market. 'I don't know. I don't think so. Except for the fact that the same guy is involved.'

I take a deep breath, tighten my grip on the railing till my knuckles go white. 'I want him, Armitage. I want him for what he did.'

'You don't need to tell me that,' she said softly. 'I'll do everything I can to help.'

She holds a fist out to me. I stare at it in confusion, then realise she's waiting for me to fist bump. I can't help it. I burst out laughing.

'What, are we in high school?'

She smiles, the sun reflecting in her eyes. 'Don't leave me hanging, London. I taught you better than that.'

I shake my head but hold out my fist. She bumps hers against mine.

'In it till the end, pet,' she says, which I can't help feeling might be an unfortunate turn of phrase.

The healers have started to pack away their wares, storing them inside their kiosks and locking down the shutters. The setting sun is level with the bridge opposite us, limning the concrete in bright orange light, shadows stretching out towards us across the half-completed flyover.

A guy in a green shirt approaches us. He's one of the Urban Management Zone security guards who watch over the market at night.

'Hi, guys,' he says. 'You'll have to leave now. We're closing up.'

Armitage flashes her ID. 'We'll come find you when we need to get out. Official business.'

He nods and turns away, chatting to one of the healers as they head towards the stairs. I finish my drink as the market slowly empties of life. The sun sets and huge spotlights burst to life around the perimeter of the ten-feet-high fence, creating sharp contrasts of white light and midnight shadows.

'How long do you reckon we'll have to wait?' asks Armitage.

I shrug. Who knows with the fae. Nobody can predict anything about the capricious bastards.

We could be in for a long night.

When the fae do finally arrive, it happens almost without

me noticing it. A silence has fallen over the market, a quiet peacefulness that floats through the warm evening air. A light breeze carries the remnants of cooking food. A dog barks in the distance.

The lights dim slightly, as if a cloud has passed in front of the moon. And then the fae are slipping from shadows and from behind stalls and kiosks, stepping into the summer night as if they were always there.

Now, get all those Hollywood ideas of the fae out of your mind. They're not like that. No bright colours or glittering wings. No pixie dust and pan flutes. The fae are a race of being as dissimilar to each other as we are.

I see ten-feet-tall giants with huge bellies and dirty over-alls, like they've just finished a day's work down a mine. I see knee-high gnomes with bark-coloured skin and black eyes, their heavily lined faces breaking into laughter and chatter as they spot friends. I see dryads, their skin a muted olive colour, lithe, tall. Their faces are alien, eyes too wide apart, mouths too thin. They move around the stalls in a slow and steady manner, their steps so light it's like they're floating in the air.

All the fae wear earth-toned clothing and it's lived in. Worn out. Creased and dirty. The fae are a living race and they work every day just like we do. Don't ask me doing what. That's something the Division has wanted to know for years now.

The air is filled with the sounds of different languages. The sibilant hiss of visiting selkies, their bodies wet, their teeth sharp and black. The guttural growl of dwarves, who sound like they're angry every time they speak. The high-pitched clicking of an insect-man, huge compound eyes inscrutable, black tongue darting out to taste the air.

As always, I'm immediately uncomfortable in their presence, a general uneasiness that a seemingly harmless word or gesture could get me locked away in a faerie mound for the next hundred years. They're so fickle, you never know what might upset them.

Some of the fae take up positions next to the kiosks, opening up their own shops for business. But their wares are different to what had been on sale earlier in the day. I glance at a table covered in jars. Handwritten labels hang from little pieces of twine: *The Tears of an Abandoned Wyvern. The last breath of murdered playwrights (18th cent.) The despair of a lost battle. The soul of a betrayed lover (Suicide.)*

Another table holds all kinds of dead mythological (at least to us) animals, such as basilisk feet, for a particular soup the fae enjoy. (The feet are added to bark taken from the World Tree that grows deep beneath London's streets.)

One shelf holds only unicorn horns, their pearlescent sheen dulled in death. The fae grind down the horns and use them as a particularly virulent poison. As far as I know, trading in unicorn horns is highly illegal seeing as the species is on the endangered list. We can't do anything about it now, though. If we cause a scene we're likely to get thrown out, at best, or more likely attacked. I make a mental note to send someone down here tomorrow night. Just to check if the horns are real or fake.

We ask around and eventually find our way to a kiosk right at the edge of the overpass, where the concrete drop-off is linked to the newer pedestrian bridge.

Two imposing fae block our way. They're tall, thin, their skin rough and cracked like bark. They look like trees given human shape.

'Uh . . . hi. We're looking for . . . uh . . . Gran?' I feel stupid saying it but I can't for the life of me remember her full name and title.

'Who would ask?' says the treeman on the left, his voice deep and booming, like an English actor overacting in a Shakespeare play.

'Delphic Division. We just want to ask her a few questions.'

'Many would ask. Few are satisfied with the lore-keeper's answers,' says the treeman on the right.

'Maybe so,' says Armitage. 'But we need to have a word.'

'Then you must answer five riddles,' says the first treeman. 'Three are false, two are true, but of the five only one will speak to the heart, and that is the one you must answer.'

I blink. Do I have a piece of paper handy? Somewhere I can write the riddle down so I can try and figure it out? I turn to Armitage to ask if she has anything, see the slight smile tugging at her lip, the amused glint in her eye.

I frown, turn back, and the treemen suddenly break into laughter.

'Sorry, man,' says the one on the right. 'We're just fucking with you.'

'Right.'

The treeman on the left wipes his eyes. 'Ah . . . that's funny shit. I'll see if she's free.'

He turns and disappears behind a tatty white curtain.

The second treeman is still laughing at us. A ringing sound starts up behind him. He glances over his shoulder, grabs something from the table, then turns back with a cell phone pressed to his ear.

''Scuse me,' he says to us. 'Gotta take this.'

He walks away, talking into the phone. 'No, Randle. I said two thousand on the *dragon* winning. Why would I bet on the human . . . ?'

He walks out of earshot. I look at Armitage, but she just shrugs.

The first treeman reappears and gestures for us to enter. He stands aside and we duck through the net curtain. He doesn't follow. The kiosk is too cramped for us all to fit inside.

A lantern hangs on the wall, but the flame is turned down, casting a low, flickering light throughout the interior, picking out shadows rather than illuminating anything.

There's a click and the kiosk floods with electric light. I blink, squinting against the brightness. The kiosk looks remarkably less mysterious now. A messy room filled with junk and pot plants.

It turns out that Gran is the perfect name for the lore-keeper. Her face is chubby, her expression good-natured. Her black eyes are almost swallowed up by a mass of deep wrinkles, crevasses that map out the years in her skin.

She's sitting behind a fold-down table with an iPad leaning against a half-empty jar of coffee. I glance at the screen and see the paused image of what looks like an action movie. One of the Fast and the Furious films, if I'm not mistaken.

She's also wearing a knitted tea cosy on her head.

'So,' she says briskly. 'What can I do for you?'

'We're looking for information on sin-eaters,' says Armitage.

'We were told you might know about them,' I add.

'Who told you that?'

'Harry Grimes.'

Gran throws her hands up in the air in frustration. 'Urgh. You break *one* of your stupid laws and you owe that guy forever. He's a leech.'

'So? Can you help?'

'Doubt it. There's not much to know. They're very secretive.'

'Anything you can tell us would be great,' I say. 'We know the basics. That they turn up at a dead person's house and take on the dead person's sins, but that's it.'

'Ah. Now. Maybe I *can* help you. Because that's a very old-fashioned view of sin-eaters. It's like saying that all vampires live in castles in Transylvania. No, the sin-eaters have evolved way past that now.'

'How so?'

'They're organized. A group – no – a corporation. And they don't take on the sins of the dearly departed anymore. No money in it, y'see. They hire themselves out to take on the sins of the rich and connected. I heard rumours that their company is one of the top earners in Europe. People pay a lot for absolution.'

'What, you mean . . . like the Catholic Church?' I ask. 'Ten Hail Mary's and all is forgiven?'

'It's a bit more concrete than that, but yes, that's the general idea.'

'Do you know what this company is called? Who's in charge?'

The fae shakes her head. 'No. All I know is the gossip.'

'All very interesting,' says Armitage, 'but it doesn't get us any closer to our buggering killer, does it?'

'No.' I sigh. 'But at least we know why the last victim was so rich. This sin-eater company must pay their people well.'

'What about the ramanga? He was dirt poor.'

'Maybe he was a rookie? Bottom of the ladder?'

'What is this?' asks Gran.

I hesitate, then decide to tell her about the deaths. (Without mentioning Lilith. No need for her to know that.)

'So this killer is targeting sin-eaters?' she asks.

'If Caitlyn Long is one, then yeah. Two so far.'

'Tell me, was there any residue left at the scenes of these murders?'

Armitage and I exchange looks. She takes out the bag of yellow powder that she gathered from Long's body and hands it over. Gran opens it up and takes a big sniff. I step quickly back, but she doesn't throw up.

She returns the bag to Armitage. 'Your killer is another sin-eater,' she says matter-of-factly.

'What?' I step forward. 'How do you know that?'

She gestures at the bag. 'That residue. It is manifested sin. What is left over when sin is taken from a sin-eater.'

I frown. 'I don't understand. I thought sin-eaters took the sin from normal people. Not another sin-eater.'

'Yes. But sin-eaters . . . they're not immortal or anything. Understand? When they die they must pass on the sins they have collected to the next in line, otherwise the sins return to those who first committed them. It's an apprentice-master thing. So a sin-eater nowadays can hold sins stretching back hundreds – thousands – of years, passed down to them from previous generations.'

'OK. What's that got to do with these deaths?'

'Because passing down the sins voluntarily is not the only way to do it. Another sin-eater can take sins forcefully, can draw them from a sin-eater's soul and absorb them as the victim dies.'

'Why would they do that?'

Gran shrugs. 'Information? Blackmail? Industrial espionage?' She leans forward. 'See, the sins are not just sins. They hold memories and feelings. Everything associated with where and when the sin took place. The sin-eater takes all that into his very soul when he takes on a sin.'

Is that why Lilith is so obsessed with the ramanga's soul? Because it holds the sins he's collected? But why does she want them? Is it about blackmail? Does she intend her pet sin-eater to absorb the sins Jengo held? To blackmail those who committed the sins in the first place?

That doesn't sound right.

'I don't suppose you happen to know what *Ul Khu tavu* means?' asks Armitage.

'*Ulkhuta-what?*'

'*Ul Khu tavu.* Three words.' Armitage glances at me. 'We think.'

'Where did you hear these words?'

'The first sin-eater that was killed. He kept saying them. Well, I say *he* said them. But it was more like his ghost. Long story.'

'It sounds like it could be one of the ancient tongues. Pre-Sumerian.'

'But do you know what it means?'

'No.'

Another dead end. But before I can start complaining to Armitage about how shitty our luck is, Gran picks up her iPad and starts swiping across the screen until she finds what she's looking for. She taps an icon, looks sharply at us, then tilts the iPad away so we can't see what she's doing.

'Not for human eyes,' she says.

My interest is piqued. 'What is it?'

'My reference books.'

'I thought you'd . . . I don't know, have a library somewhere.'

She gives me a look of scorn. 'Keep with the times, boy. Why should I keep a library when I've got one of these?' She brandishes the iPad. 'Everything I ever collected can be stored in here.'

'Kinda takes the magic away from it all.'

'Pah. Magic is overrated. And before you get any funny ideas about stealing this, it only works for me.'

'Hey, I'm one of the good guys,' I protest.

Which is true, but I *had* been thinking about ways to get my hands on it. That kind of reference library would be worth a lot back at the Division.

Gran starts typing on the screen. After a couple of minutes she leans back, looking worried.

'What's wrong?' asks Armitage.

'I was right. It is pre-Sumerian. *Ul* is easy. It means *the. Khu* is a bit trickier. It means . . . one, to be the best, or . . . to be first at something. And *tavu* means evil. No – not quite evil. But . . . *personal* evil. '

'Personal evil?' I say. 'That's sin, isn't it? Personal evil can be described as sin.'

Gran locks eyes with me. 'Yes. Yes it can.'

'So it means . . . what? One sin?' asks Armitage.

'No. In this context I would say it means *the first sin.*'

I frown. 'What the hell's the first sin?'

Armitage gives me a look. 'Well, seeing as we're dealing with sin-eaters and words in a pre-Sumerian dialect, I'd hazard a guess that it refers to the first sin that the first sin-eater took on. And that's what you-know-who is after.'

'Maybe . . .'

'Maybe nothing.'

'It could mean the *ramanga's* first sin. The first sin he absorbed when he became a sin-eater.'

'No,' says Gran. 'He would have said *my* first sin. Not *the* first sin.'

I chew my lip. 'Is that even possible?' I ask Gran. 'Can Jengo, the first victim, *have* this first sin?'

'I *suppose*. As I say, the sins *are* passed down each generation. So it's theoretically possible a sin-eater nowadays holds this first sin. Whatever that may be.'

'Something powerful enough to kill for,' says Armitage.

'Obviously.'

'Is that all you can tell us?' I ask.

'Is that all?' snaps the fae. 'Isn't that enough? And you tell Grimes that wipes my slate clean, understand?'

I nod, distracted. So our killer is a sin-eater? Where does that leave my investigation into Cally's death? If he's a sin-eater, what was he doing back at the lodge that night? I remember he had his hands on that one guy's head, the one who got away.

And what about the other one? The one who was left at the lodge. The one who acted like he had no idea what I was talking about.

What if he really *didn't* know?

What if the guy with the shaved head and the beard isn't the killer at all? What if he was just taking on the killers' sins?

'Do . . . do sin-eaters – when they take the sin, do they take the *memory* of the deed as well? Like, if I used a sin-eater, if he took my sin, would I remember that I'd done something?'

'No. Everything about the sin is taken away.'

My throat constricts. I swallow, feeling the rage building up inside. That meant the other guy got clean away. The man who helped murder five kids and hide their bodies, he's out there right now, walking around without any knowledge of what he's done.

Christ, what if he's done it again? What if he'd done it *before*? And every time he just paid a sin-eater to take away his crimes?

'Hey.' Armitage is frowning at me. 'You OK?'

I take a deep shuddering breath. 'I'm fine. Let's go.'

I duck back under the curtain and step outside. I hear Armitage thanking the lore-keeper before coming to join me.

'So what now?' I ask.

'Now we head back to the Division and focus on finding out who our sin-eater is. He's the key to all of this.'

Yeah. He is. And I'm going to catch the fucker.

We take the stairs down from the herb bridge and into the market proper, winding our way through the noisy, smelly crowds as we head back to the gate.

At the Congolese barber stand, a skinny creature about eight feet tall cuts the hair of a squat fae with hair that sprouts all over its body, keeping up a constant stream of chatter while he does so.

As we pass a circle of tables that have been pulled into a makeshift beer garden we're approached by one of the fae. The creature doesn't even come up to my knees but has a belly so large and distended it's supported on a tiny unicycle. If he didn't have the support I think he'd just fall onto his stomach and roll around like an upended turtle.

We stop and look down at him.

'Nomkhubulwane wants to talk to you,' he says to me.

Nomkhubulwane is the African goddess of rain and fertility. I suppose she's the African equivalent of Danu, the Celtic

Earth goddess. Her powers are at their height at this time of the year.

'What have you done now?' asks Armitage, glaring at me.

'God knows. And if he does, he's not telling.'

We follow the little fae and his squeaking belly-wheel back around the side of the unfinished overpass on which the Muti market was built. He pauses beneath the drop-off. There's a huge mural of Nomkhubulwane painted on the final concrete support. The mural shows her leaning forward, her hands outstretched as if reaching in for a hug.

I wait, but nothing happens. I'm about to ask the little guy what's up when he suddenly starts dancing.

Seriously. Rolling around in circles, his hands up in the air, then down to his chest, his wheel giving him a squeaky accompaniment. He sketches a wide circle, grinning at us as he wheels past.

'The time is on us when all of us are timed.'

I look at Armitage. She shakes her head and shrugs.

A movement ahead of me catches my attention. The mural of Nomkhubulwane is moving. She's leaning out of the painting, the top of half of her body becoming three dimensional. I step back. Armitage stays where she is. The little dude squeaks past us again.

'When all are timed, the race must end.'

What. The actual. Fuck?

But if all that isn't weird enough, Nomkhubulwane, now hovering above me like some massive hologram, smiles and says, 'I have a message from my sister, Yemanja. The message is as follows: When you see the five rand coin, pick it up.'

That's it. She fades back into the mural, becoming a painting once again.

Little dude squeaks past. 'Pick it up. Pick it up.'

I glare at him, then turn to Armitage. 'When the fuck did we start living in Twin Peaks?'

I turn away and start making my way back towards the gate. Armitage catches up and we walk across the purple bridge that arcs across Brook Street Market. It's the biggest market in Warwick, currently filled with fae doing their grocery shopping.

The glow of cell-phone screens can be seen all over the place. I wonder what types of apps the fae use? How to be really annoying and cryptic? How best to confuse humans?

Although, to be fair on them, Nomkhubulwane isn't actually fae. She's a goddess – Tier One. And she *was* just passing on a message. From my fairy godmother.

I snort and shake my head.

We're let out of the market by either an orc or an ogre. I'm not sure which. As soon as we step through the gates the hubbub behind us instantly stops, as if someone hit the mute button. I look back and see only empty stalls and deserted bridges.

'Well,' says Armitage, clapping her hands together. 'Today has been a long day filled with what-the-fuck and I-don't-know-what. I'm tired, I stink, and I'm going home to veg in front of the TV for the rest of the night. You? Wait – don't tell me.' Armitage puts a hand to her head as we cross the street, heading back to her car. 'I'm picking up an image. I see . . . something murky in your future. Something disgusting. An evil odour and taste. It's . . . it's whisky.'

'Har-de-har-har.'

We arrive back at the car. The street is deserted. No clubs or pubs down this end. Too far out. Light from shop windows spills out onto the sidewalk.

Something catches my eye. A glint of metal.

I look down and see a shiny coin next to my foot.

A five rand coin.

I frown at it.

'Hey . . .' I say. I hesitate, hearing the words in my head.

Pick it up. Pick it up.

I bend down.

And a spray of bullets shatters the window behind me, showering me with broken glass.

Automatic gunfire explodes around us. I dive behind the car. Armitage scrambles around from the driver's side to join me. She already has her gun in her hand. I pull out my Glock.

The gunfire carries on. The shop displays in front of us are being shredded, bullets ripping through the buildings. Bottles of whisky and beer exploding in the liquor store. Clothing and pillows bursting into floating feathers and shredded material. The heavy *thunk-thunk* of bullets hitting the car, metal vibrating beneath my back.

'You see anything?' I shout.

Armitage shakes her head. She crawls slowly forward so she can peer around the front of the car. I head to the back.

The gunfire stops. I slowly put my head around the bumper. Muzzle flash from a building across the street. Upper storey window. I jerk back. Bullets skit across the ground where my hand was, thump into the bumper.

I put my hand around the car and fire off five or six shots in the general direction of the muzzle flash. Armitage is doing the same.

'How many?' I shout.

'Multiple muzzle flashes. Five at least.'

Shit. We're pinned down.

Another burst of gunfire aiming for the front of the car. Armitage and I hunker down and I'm praying a bullet doesn't ricochet beneath and bounce into one of us.

'So who the bloody hell are they?' screams Armitage.

Who indeed? This didn't have the smell of magic about it.

'We can't stay here forever, Tau.'

No. We can't. I scan the street, then fire a couple of shots at a shop about ten doors down, shattering the glass in the door. Hopefully our friends across the road don't notice.

'Cover me,' I say.

Her eyes widen. 'What—'

But I'm already moving, running from cover. She swears and fires frantically over the hood of the car as I dive through the empty window of the liquor store we'd parked next to. I land in a lake of whisky and brandy, slide forward until I hit into a shelf, knocking the remaining bottles over.

I catch one. Glenfiddich. It'll do. I yank the cork out and take a mouthful.

Then I'm moving, heading towards the back of the shop. Past the till, into the office at the back. There's a locked door here. I kick it open and step into a dark alley. Crates of bottles waiting for recycling are piled against the wall. I peer around them, scanning the darkness.

Nothing.

I run to the right, counting ten shops before stopping before a metal door. This one has a huge padlock on it. I shoot it off, pull the door open. Step inside and make my way through a dingy office and into the shop.

Which just happens to be a sex shop. I head to the glass door I shot out, crouch down next to multi-coloured dildos and peer outside. Armitage is still firing off occasional volleys. I keep my eyes on the building across the street as she does so.

There are flashes from the second and third storey. Nothing from the first floor. I check the location of each attacker, then wait for a lull in the gunfire, assuming our attackers are using the time to reload.

I sprint across the street, expecting to feel bullets ripping me to shreds as I do so. I make it. Smack into the glass door of a second-hand furniture shop.

I slide along the wall until I'm standing beneath the windows that hide our attackers. I try the door. Unlocked. Push it open. Slowly. Waiting for gunfire.

Nothing. I duck my head around then jerk it back, just in case someone is waiting for me to appear. Again, nothing. An empty corridor, light from the street revealing graffiti-covered walls, stairs leading up, and an old bicycle leaning against the wall. The place looks like a disused apartment building.

I duck inside, gun swivelling, taking in all points of attack. I move to the stairs. They're concrete, no chance of creaking. I slide up the wall, gun pointed above me. I can hear more gunfire, Armitage with another distraction. Not sure how much ammo she has, though.

It's dark in here. No lights. I get to the second landing, peer into the corridor. Movement. I pull my head back as someone comes out of one of the rooms facing the street, heading in my direction.

I push my gun into my pants and pull out my knife. Wait for him to approach.

He turns into the stairs. I'm face to face with night vision goggles and a mouth stretched in an 'Oh!' of surprise. I jam the knife into his throat, silencing him before he can make a sound.

He drops. I catch him, ease him down, wait to see if anyone has been alerted.

Nothing. I pull his night-vision goggles off, strap them onto my own head. My vision turns green and black, my surroundings lighting up like a video game. I pull the dead perp down the stairs out of the way, then hurry back up to the corridor.

It's hard to tell which of the rooms hold the shooters. I peer into the closest. Empty. Four more rooms on this floor. I check the next. This one is occupied. Another figure in black tactical gear, standing to the side of the window as he shoots what looks like a SIG MPX semi-automatic rifle at Armitage. I'm jealous. Not the shooting at Armitage part. I mean about the gun.

I want to take him down quietly too, but as I step into the deserted room he spins around and places his back against the wall as a few of Armitage's bullets punch holes in the ceiling.

He stares at me in surprise and I yank out my Glock and shoot him in the chest. Bullet-proof vest. Fuck. I raise the gun and shoot out the night-vision goggles. His head jerks back and he slumps against the wall, drops into a sitting position.

Shit. I wonder if his mates heard? Realised it was a different type of gunfire.

I get my answer a second later when the wall to my right starts exploding, bullet holes ripping through the plaster at ankle height.

Clever bastard. Thinks I'll drop to the floor to avoid the gunfire. The line of bullets cuts towards me and I make a leap for the window, landing on the dead perp and hopping onto the windowsill just as the bullets reach me. The dead guy jerks and rocks as the bullets thud into him. He slides over onto his face.

I reach down and grab the guy's SIG, brace myself against the window frame, and return fire, swinging the rifle around in random patterns until I hear someone cry out.

I hop back onto the floor. Three down. How many more to go? Two? But they were one floor up, I think.

I grab the dead guy's spare magazines from his combat vest, eject the clip in the SIG and ram the full one home. I check the landing outside. No one waiting for me. Out and heading towards the stairs.

I put my foot on the first step and someone comes hurrying down towards me. He doesn't shoot, so he must reckon I'm one of them. I'm hoping he'll try to pass me so I can grab him, but he realises the truth a couple of feet away and launches himself straight at me.

We sail back off the stairs and I land on my back. He scrabbles for my face, attempting to yank the goggles away. I try to hit him, but he's kneeling on my right arm. The gun is in my left hand but it's too long for me to get it pointed at him. I drop it, punch the guy in the head. Once. Twice. His teeth are bared in fury as he finally gets my goggles off and goes for my eyes.

His thumbs press in. I scream in pain, try to push him back. But he's too big. Too heavy.

I can't get to my knife or my wand either. I don't have any other weapons so I straighten my hand and ram it as hard as I can into his throat.

He rolls off me, clutching at his throat. Gasping for air. I scramble to my feet, pick up the SIG, point it at him. No need. His face is turning blue. I can see a depression in his throat where I hit him. Must have collapsed his larynx. His eyes are wide and bulging. The sounds he's making are terrible, pained heaving gasps that gradually trail off to nothing.

Running footsteps above me. Fuck. Nowhere to go but down.

I put my foot on the first step then realise someone's coming up from the bottom floor. Where the fuck had he been hiding? I fire off a burst, then head back to the room where I killed the second guy. Bullets punch into the doorframe, showering me with splinters. I dive through the door, skid across the boards, then scramble up and bolt for the window.

I fire behind me, keeping them out the room. Lean over the ledge. Second floor. Fifteen-foot drop onto the roof of a car.

More gunfire behind me, cutting straight through the wall to either side of the doorway. I hunker down, return fire, spraying bullets across the room.

Nothing else for it.

I climb onto the ledge, hesitate, and glance over my shoulder. The two remaining attackers choose that moment to enter the room, guns firing.

I jump. Hit the car roof with a jolt that sends my knees hard into my chest. Tuck and roll off the car and onto the ground just as bullets pepper the vehicle. Armitage spots me and fires towards the window. The attackers jerk back, disappear from view. I give them a couple of seconds, then sprint to the car.

Armitage is pulling herself into the driver's side. I yank the back door open and throw myself in as she fumbles with the keys.

I poke my head up to look through the rear window. The two attackers run out of the building, straight into the street. They raise their rifles.

I grab my wand. Take a deep breath and focus, drawing in the power around me, pulling in the electricity from the shops and street lights. The wand vibrates, thrumming with energy. Little arcs of electricity crawl across my hand.

I wait till all the lights around us wink out, plunging the street into darkness. Then I hold the wand up and, resisting the urge to shout out 'Lumos', I release the power.

Intense white light bursts into life, like a hundred flares exploding at once. Harsh, monochrome shadows slam into the street. I wince against the glare, grinning as the two remaining attackers scream in pain, their night-vision goggles multiplying the light and hopefully burning out their retinas.

They struggle to pull the goggles off. I try to see their faces as they do so, but only catch a brief glimpse of one of them as they dive behind cars. He's in his late forties. Thin. A heavily lined face.

Armitage finally gets the car started. She pulls off, tyres screeching on the asphalt, and speeds off down the street. There's steam billowing out from under the hood. The car isn't going to last much longer, but as long as it gets us away from here I don't much care.

I look out the back window. One of the attackers is back in the street, his rifle aimed at us. I fire a couple more shots at him and he dives to the side.

I flop down in the seat, my heart hammering brutally in my chest.

So who the hell were they? Who the hell have we pissed off now?

When we get back to Division I phone a contact in the Albert Park police station. I tell him Armitage and I were attacked while pursuing inquiries and that if they hadn't already, they should head out to clear the body and debris.

He tells me they'd already had a call out for gunfire. Major damage to shops and cars, but no bodies.

Armitage and I decide to sleep at the Division. There's no telling how much our attackers know about us so we can't risk going home.

I wonder briefly if our attackers tonight are linked to Lilith, but I dismiss the thought. It didn't seem like Kincaid's style. He would have just sent another pack of biters after me.

No, this was someone else who wants us dead.

13

At nine o' clock the next morning I take my coffee and stumble into our operations room on the eighth floor. The whiteboard wall is filling up with photographs. The ramanga, the kraal where he was killed, Armitage's body, her lounge, the killer's face.

Down one side of the board are notes written in Parker's neat handwriting. Red lines drawn between the photographs detail definite connections, while blue lines denote possible connections we haven't managed to confirm yet.

Parker is already here, adding the photographs of the second sin-eater from the Oyster Box Hotel. I sit down and yawn as Armitage strolls in and glances at the board.

'Bloody hell, people. A little empathy wouldn't go amiss. Do I have to be on the board?'

'You're part of the case,' Parker points out.

'Well . . . cover my face or something, will you? I don't want to stare into my own dead eyes first thing in the morning.'

'I suppose you got enough of that looking in the mirror when you were alive,' I say.

Armitage throws a whiteboard marker at me. I dodge but I'm not quick enough. It hits me in the ear.

She's not upset, though. Armitage is old school. Laughter is the best medicine. Stiff upper lip. Grimace painfully and carry on, that kind of thing. I'm just doing my bit to stop her dwelling on everything. It's a public service, really.

She approaches the board, scans it quickly, then turns to me. 'Our attackers last night. Human?'

I nod. 'There's blood at the scene. Definitely human.'

Parker frowns. 'What attack is this?'

I quickly tell her everything that happened yesterday, ending with our night-time ambush.

'They sound like pros,' she says.

'They were. It was a hit squad.'

'We don't know that,' snaps Armitage.

'Of course it was. How else do you explain it? Mistaken identity?'

Armitage sighs, a habit more than anything else. It's not as if she needs air. She waves at the board.

'OK, fine. But let's put a pin in the mysterious assassins for now. Let's go back to the beginning. Start with the ramanga. Our dead sin-eater. Talk to me as if I don't have a clue what's going on.' She points at me without even looking. 'And no smart arse comments.'

'We think he was new,' I say. 'Going on what the fae told us, he must have recently followed on from his own teacher. Master. Whatever they call it. Else he wouldn't still be a local ramanga. He'd be living it up somewhere else.'

'They don't inherit anything from their master? Belongings?' asks Parker.

'No. I reckon this . . . corporation or whatever it is takes everything. The sin-eaters get to enjoy the money while they're alive, but after that it's sucked into the company coffers.'

Armitage nods thoughtfully. 'Follow that up with the second victim's records. Check her will, her bank statements that kind of thing. Where's her laptop?'

Parker nods at the table up against the wall. A new MacBook Air and a cell phone sit there.

'Good. What else do we know about her?'

'Nothing,' I say. 'That's on the agenda for this morning.'

'Get on it. Search for any links between her and the ramanga. Maybe we can use them to trace more of these sin-eaters. If there *are* more, they're in danger from Lilith and her attack dog.' She's silent for a while, then makes a tutting sound. 'All this stuff about the first sin – I don't like it. It stinks of religion.'

'Which one?'

'Lucifer. God. All that stuff. Wasn't Lucifer the first being to sin? Pride, wasn't it? That's what's supposed to have kicked the whole thing off.'

'What – you think that's what Lilith is after?'

'You tell me.'

'That doesn't make any sense,' I say. 'Even if the sin-eaters *have* been around for that long – and we have no way of verifying that – what could they do with Lucifer's pride? And it's not as if a sin-eater took his sins from him anyway. He's still reigning down below, isn't he?'

Armitage shrugs. 'No idea. That's Level ultra-alpha-tip-top-super-duper-secret security clearance. They don't let the likes of me into those files.'

'Don't forget that archangel you both saw,' says Parker. 'He's involved somehow. That kind of implies it's a Christian thing.'

'Or Jewish,' said Armitage. 'They have angels too. So does Buddhism, Islam, and Hinduism.'

'Yeah, but he said he was Michael, remember?' I say.

'Good point,' says Armitage. She claps her hands together. 'Righto. I see we've got a busy day ahead of us. I'm going to have a chat with Jaeger to see if she can do something about this hole in my chest. Her stitching's come loose.'

Armitage pulls her shirt open to reveal the wound. Parker and I both cry out in protest and turn our heads away.

'Oh, that's very nice, that is,' says Armitage. 'And just how do you think that makes me feel, eh? Just be thankful Parker's spell stops me decaying. Then you'd all be in the shit.'

She storms off in a huff, buttoning up her shirt as she goes.

I sigh and grab Long's laptop while Parker focuses on the cell phone, plugging it into her own PC so she can clone the entire system before fiddling around with it.

I boot up the computer. No password. Very careless. There's a photograph as a desktop wallpaper. The victim and two kids. I swing the laptop around to show Parker.

'Has anyone notified next of kin?'

'Don't think so.'

I swivel the computer back. I'm not doing it. I hate breaking that kind of news to anyone. It brings everything back. Becca's face when I told her about Cally. The way her features just seemed to . . . collapse with grief. I tried to hold her, but she wouldn't let me. I could see it in her face. The blame. *Why couldn't you save her? Your own daughter. What good are you to anyone if you can't even protect your family?*

I frown and shake my head, loading up the computer's calendar. Lots and lots of bookings. She was a busy girl, our Caitlyn Long. Only problem is, all the appointments are marked with just the initials.

I check yesterday's date, when she arrived in Durban. Nothing there. But there *is* an entry for tonight at eight o'clock, Marked with the initials, MD.

I check through her emails, but there's nothing of interest. Certainly nothing from someone with the initials MD. Family stuff. Friends getting in touch, that kind of thing. Her internet history is just as boring. Hollywood gossip sites, Facebook (logged out, can't access it), local news sites.

No smoking gun. No emails from the head of this mysterious corporation detailing who they are and where they're based. Typical.

'Here's something,' says Parker.

I look up.

'SMS messages,' says Parker. 'The first came through Wednesday night. "Can you come to me Friday?" Her response, "Why? Will see you Sat." Next SMS, "Need you sooner. Have a feeling I might be a naughty boy." Her response. "Double the last price." Then he texts back, "Not a problem. See you Friday night." '

'No name?'

'Just a number.'

'You think whoever this person is wanted her services as a sin-eater?' I ask.

'Either that or she's a hooker on the side.'

—Hey, London.—

I look around but can't see the dog anywhere.

—What's up?—

—You've got some problems down here, man. Serious ones.—

—What problems?—

—I think you're about to get arrested for murder.—

I blink. That wasn't something I expected to hear.

—Where are you?—

—Under your desk. I wouldn't come down here, though. Not unless you want to get taken in by the SSA.—

SSA? The State Security Agency? Those guys are our answer to the CIA and MI6. What the hell are they doing here?

I hurry to the door and open it a crack. Look both ways. Nothing. I can hear shouting from the main office on the ground floor. I move forward and peer over the balcony.

I see them straight away. Men in suits. Five of them. And one, the leader, arguing with Armitage. He looks familiar. Cold face. Lined. Experienced.

Their voices rise up towards me from where I'm watching a few floors above.

'You and Tau will just have to go quietly,' snaps Ranson. He's standing next to the lead spook and looking like he's enjoying every minute of this.

'We have to do no such thing,' snaps Armitage. 'We're both employees of the Crime Intelligence Division. Any problems you have need to be taken up with the Divisional Commissioner—'

'–And a warrant issued in your names,' finishes the SSA guy. 'We know that.' He hands over a folded piece of paper. Armitage snatches it from him and scans it, then looks at him in amazement.

'Murder of State Security Agency personnel? What the hell are you talking about?'

And then I realize where I've seen the man before. Last night. The guys shooting at us. He was the one whose face I saw when he ripped off his night-vision goggles in the street. Shit. They were SSA?

'Last night, you and your officer Gideon Tau interfered in an operation being conducted by the SSA. You both opened fire after I clearly identified myself, killing four of my men. I'm sure the ballistics retrieved from the scene will match one of your sidearms.'

'Clearly identified yourself?' Armitage steps forward until she's right in his face. 'You and your lapdogs attacked *us*. Without any warning. In fact, I'll be laying charges against you!'

'You're more than welcome to do so. But in the meantime you and Tau need to come with us. Arrest her.'

One of his men steps forward and slaps a pair of cuffs on Armitage. While he's doing this she looks involuntarily up at our floor. The SSA guy follows her gaze.

We lock eyes.

Oh, shit.

'There!' shouts the spook, pointing up at me. 'Get him!'

I run back into the room. Parker sees my face.

'What's wrong?'

'Last night. I killed a few SSA agents. I'm wanted for murder.'

Parker doesn't ask questions. Just unplugs Caitlyn's phone and tosses it to me. I dart around my desk to the police computer I was working on. I quickly scroll to the SMS messages and log into the National Police Database, typing in the code for number retrievals.

It takes a while. Our computers are ancient. I think they still operate on some version of DOS software. Supposedly unhackable. Great for security, but really crap for me.

I glance at Parker while I'm waiting. 'Get out of here. Stay by the phone. If I get out of here I'll be in touch.'

She doesn't hesitate, but heads straight for the door.

'Not the elevator!' I call out.

'Got it!' Her voice trails back into the room as she sprints off around the curve of the wall in the opposite direction, heading for the stairs on the far side of the silo.

I chew my lip while I wait for the computer to do its thing. The passing of RICA – the Regulation of Interception of Communications and Provision of Communication-Related Information Act – made our jobs a whole hell of a lot easier. Everyone who buys a cell phone nowadays has to register the number against their personal ID number. Sure, it's easy enough to fake it – false documents, fake ID books, that kind of thing – but I'm hoping our mark didn't feel the need to do any of that.

Jesus. This is taking too long. I dart out the room, lean out over the balcony. The elevator is only two floors down. I can see SSA guy staring up at me through the glass.

I run back into the room.

The information is waiting for me.

The guy who sent the SMS messages is Menzi Dumelo.

M.D. The initials from Caitlyn Long's calendar.

'Got you.'

I memorize his address and sprint from the room. I run in the opposite direction from Parker, not wanting to draw them after her. This takes me right past the elevator. I hear it *bing* as I sprint past. The doors start to open and I duck inside the closest room, watching through a crack in the door as the SSA spooks burst out of the lift and run towards the operations room, weapons drawn.

I wait for them to line up against the wall outside the office, then slip out and carry on running. I arrive at the stairwell at the exact moment they realise I'm not in the room.

'*There!*'

I don't wait to see if they're pointing at me, but take the stairs three at a time, yanking myself around the corners of the stairwell.

–*Dog? Get to the Land Rover.*–

–*Yeah, 'cause I can't think for myself and have absolutely no survival instinct. I'm already here. Hurry up.*–

I hear the door slam open above me. Gunfire erupts in the stairwell, echoing back and forth. A bullet ricochets against the handrail. I snatch my hand away and glance up. The SSA dude is peering down at me. I jerk back as he fires again. Sparks burst from the metal.

Down the last few floors and into the parking garage. I pull the fire axe from its mount and jam it between the door and the wall.

I sprint for my parking bay, stumble to a surprised halt when I see Armitage waiting for me.

'How the hell did you get away?' I ask, fumbling for my keys.

She holds up her wrists. The cuffs are still there, but the chain between them is broken. 'Being a revenant gives me a bit of a strength upgrade, remember?'

'Lucky you.'

I pull open the door and unlock the passenger side just as the spooks burst out of a second stairwell. I ram my foot down on the gas and the Land Rover lurches forward. Bullets slam into the door. One flies right past my stomach and hits the dashboard.

Armitage leans over and grabs the steering wheel, giving it a violent yank so the Rover veers straight towards the agents.

They dive out of the way and she screams out the window, 'Bastards!' before we hit the ramp with a burst of sparks and then emerge into daylight.

An hour or so later, Armitage stares out the window into the traffic. 'So? What now, bright spark?'

I didn't like her tone. 'This isn't my fault.'

'Well, *I* certainly didn't shoot the SSA agents, did I?'

I frown, open my mouth to argue. She sees this and smiles slightly. 'Relax, pet. I'm not blaming you.'

We pause at a red light. 'The question remains, though. We don't have access to any of our normal resources. Plus, we're wanted criminals now. Going to be hard to get any solid police work done.'

She's right. This case has gotten messy – *messier*, I should say. The SSA are bad news. Sure, the CIA have a bad rep, but in this country it's worse. There's no public accountability here. The SSA is as corrupt as they come, a self-serving agency more concerned with enriching themselves and doing the bidding of powerful politicians than actually protecting the country.

Which leads to the question – why are they after us?

Armitage turns to look at me. 'Do you think the SSA know about the sin-eaters? Are *they* investigating them? Are we stepping on their toes?'

I shake my head. I highly doubt that's the reason. Even if they were investigating sin-eaters, that wouldn't justify trying to kill us.

I have a sick feeling in my stomach, because the only reason I *can* come up with for the SSA wanting to take us out is that someone very high up doesn't want us investigating this case.

Who, though?

★   ★   ★

It's late afternoon and we decide to hole up in a Wimpy at a truck stop on the N2. We still have a few hours to kill before the sin-eater was supposed to be at Menzi Dumelo's house and we don't want to turn up early.

The dog is still out in the car, much to his annoyance. No animals allowed. I order a cheeseburger and coffee. Armitage doesn't order anything.

'On account of me not getting a chance to talk to Jaeger about fixing this bloody hole in my chest. Don't think the kiddies will enjoy their food if they see chewed up french fries slipping out of my wound.'

I grimace.

'I seem to recall,' says a voice from the booth behind us, 'asking you – very politely I might add – to stay away from all this.'

I peer over the divider and find the archangel Michael sitting on the red vinyl bench, a half-finished Bar One milk-shake in front of him.

'Who's that?' asks Armitage, who's too short to see over the divider.

'Michael,' I say.

'Michael who?'

'You remember? The angel? Tried to put the frighteners on us.'

Michael's perfect eyebrows rise up. 'You mean I did not succeed in making my wishes clear?'

'You did,' I say. 'But there's not much we can do about it when people are dropping dead around us. It's our job to investigate.'

Michael rises to his feet. Armitage nods a greeting at him.

'All right there? I meant to ask you the other day – did it hurt?'

Michael looks momentarily confused. 'Did what hurt?'

'When you fell from Heaven?'

'I did not *fall* from Heaven. That would make me one of Lucifer's demons. I do not understand what you're saying.'

'Aye, I can see that. Lighten up, Golden Boy. You'll live longer.'

I stifle a grin. Probably not the best move to laugh at God's chief enforcer and muscle man. He might get weird about it.

'Hey,' I say. 'Seeing as you're here, why don't you tell us what you know about all this.'

'Why would I do that? I am here to warn you away from it.'

'Not really working though, is it? Just tell us – why are you so interested in sin-eater deaths?'

Michael doesn't answer straight away. His face is expressionless, but I get the impression he's trying to stop himself from smiting us where we sit.

'Who said anything about sin-eaters?' he finally asks.

'Come on, fancy man,' says Armitage. 'Give us some credit. We're investigators. It's our job to find this stuff out.'

'I do not know anything about sin-eaters.'

'Then why are you warning us off? Is it because of Lilith?'

Another silence.

I laugh. 'You didn't know Lilith was responsible for this, did you? She's one of your lot, isn't she?'

'She is not "one of our lot". She was expelled from the grace of God's presence a long time ago.'

I sip my coffee. I'm enjoying this. 'Yeah, she's not really happy with that. Has a few choice words to say about you and your god.'

'Your god, too.'

'Not mine, mate,' I say coldly. 'Never was.'

'He created you. Created this world.'

'So you say. I know a few orisha who'd argue with you, though. Reckon some of them have been around longer than the big man.'

'You will go to hell for speaking this way, Gideon Tau.'

'If breaking your list of ten commandments is all it takes, I was all set for hell when I shoplifted a Kit-Kat when I was eight. Now, you going to help us with this case? It's probably in your best interests.'

'There is nothing I can tell you that will help.'

'No? What about the first sin? Can you tell us anything about that?'

Michael surges forward. He grabs me, lifts me from the table. I slap at his hands, but his grip is like stone.

'Where did you hear those words?' he says softly.

'The ramanga. The one who got killed. Why? What does it mean?'

Michael leans close to me. I'm looking directly into his eyes. I thought they were black but I can see stars in there, the unimaginable gulf of galaxies. 'This is your last warning, human. Step away or die.'

Somehow Armitage manages to slide between us. 'Hey, come on now. You're frightening the bairns.'

Michael bares his teeth and drops me. He backs up a step, looks around. The other patrons stare at us in shock.

'Heed my words. I do not want to see either of you again.'

He whirls around, his trench coat flaring out, and strides out of the Wimpy, slamming the glass doors behind him. Armitage looks around, then flashes her ID.

'It's all right. We're police.'

I'm not sure that reassures them.

I call the waitress over and gesture at my food. 'Can I get this to go?'

14

Menzi Dumelo's house is in the upmarket Durban suburb known as Morningside. The houses on the street all have multi-acre, well-manicured gardens, their six-feet high walls stamped with the logos of private security companies.

One house had even put a picture frame around the security company sign. Not sure if the person living there really liked their security or if it was just an aesthetic thing, though. Watch, everybody will be doing it soon.

We park across the street and watch the house. It's seven o'clock, an hour before Caitlyn Long was supposed to turn up.

We wait for half an hour, but nothing interesting happens. There are lights on in the ground-floor windows, but we haven't seen anyone moving around inside.

I screw the suppressor onto the barrel of my Glock and glance at Armitage. 'You ready?'

''Course I am.'

'Can I come?' asks the dog.

'As long as you promise to be good.'

'Mmm . . . no,' says the dog. 'Can't do that.'

I sigh. 'Fine. Just don't piss on anything.'

'Can't promise that either.'

'Jesus,' I snap, pushing the door open. 'Do what you want then!'

We climb out the car. The sun has set by this time, dusk creeping in towards night. We cross the empty street and I throw the dog blanket from the car over the metal spikes on the wall.

Armitage goes first. I help her over, pushing her up from the bottom in a manner that is not very dignified. She's not the most . . . athletic of shapes, and while turning into a revenant might have given her super strength, it didn't do much for her agility.

I pass the dog up to her and she unceremoniously drops him over the other side. I hear his muffled complaining and follow after.

The garden is immaculate, flower beds weeded and discreetly lit with hidden lights. Crickets chirrup in the bushes. A bullfrog croaks from somewhere on the other side of the house.

'Should we knock?' asks Armitage as we approach the front door.

I shake my head. 'Whoever this guy is I want to catch him *in flagrante delicto.*'

I try the door and am a bit shocked to find it unlocked. This is South Africa. *Nobody* leaves their doors unlocked.

I push it gently open, revealing a warmly lit entrance hall. Tasteful paintings line the walls, expensive throw rugs cover the Italian tiles. We step inside. A set of stairs leads up to the second floor and a wide arch to our left opens into the sitting room.

We go left. Deserted. A white leather lounge suite, a wooden coffee table. Massive LCD television mounted on the wall.

There's a drinks table beneath the window. I pull the curtains closed and pour myself a whisky. I hold up the bottle to Armitage but she shakes her head. She's frowning, looking around uneasily.

The dog trots in from the entrance hall. 'Nobody upstairs.'

We check the kitchen. Nothing. Just a half-empty bottle of Johnnie Walker Blue sitting on the worktop. No dishes in the sink. No coffee-stained mugs lying around.

'I don't get it,' says Armitage. 'Why set up a meeting with Long if he's not here?'

'Maybe Lilith came for Dumelo as well?'

'Why? He's not a sin-eater. And where's the body? Lilith and her crew have never bothered with cleaning up before.'

I look around in frustration. I need this guy to be here. He's my only lead on the sin-eaters and their possible link with Cally's death. I track back over the evidence in my mind, looking for something we've missed. Another route to take. But there's nothing. We hadn't managed to trace Long's bank account details before the SSA came calling.

Maybe we could call Parker, get her to check up on it. There might be something there we can use . . .

A clunking sound comes from a door to our right.

We turn just as the door opens and a man enters the kitchen, covered head to toe in blood. He stops abruptly when he sees us.

'You're not her. Where is my sin-eater?' He giggles. 'I have a feast for her. So many sins.' His eyes take on a haunted look. He glances nervously over his shoulder, where I can see a set of concrete stairs leading downward. 'I think I'd really like to see my sin-eater now,' he says, in much the same tone of voice as one would say, 'I'd really like to see my lawyer now.'

I grab him and shove him through to the lounge while Armitage draws her weapon and heads slowly down the stairs. I push Dumelo roughly into a chair.

He stares into space, twitching slightly. 'I'd like to see Miss Long now,' he whispers. He nods vigorously. 'Yes, I really think that's the best thing right now. For everyone concerned.'

He tries to get up but I hold him down. He frowns, blinks, and finally focuses on me. 'Who are you?'

I hear a noise behind me and turn to see Armitage rushing towards us, her gun aimed directly at Dumelo. I grab her arm and shove it to the side. The silenced gun goes off with a muted, airy *thud* and hits the wall. Armitage fights me, trying to force it back towards Dumelo.

'Bastard!' she shouts. 'You sick bastard!'

Dumelo curls his feet up beneath him on the couch, shaking his head. 'No, no. Not me. Miss Long says I'm not sick. It's perfectly normal behaviour, she says. Always fine.'

'Armitage! Hey – boss! Look at me!'

Armitage tears her gaze away from Dumelo. I've never seen her this angry before.

'What is it? Talk to me.'

'Go look for yourself.'

I hesitate. 'I think it's better if we all go.' I don't trust her not to put a bullet in Dumelo as soon as I turn my back.

Her jaw tightens. She grabs Dumelo by the back of the neck and yanks him from the couch. 'Move.'

She shoves him into the kitchen. As soon as he sees the door, he skids to a stop.

'No, no. I can't go in there. Miss Long will sort it out. She always does. She's a magician, you see. She makes everything go away.'

Armitage pushes him and he stumbles through the door. He slips on the blood and tumbles down the steps with a cry of pain.

I put my hand on Armitage's arm. 'Easy!'

She shakes me off. 'Don't tell me to go easy. Go look. Go look for yourself.'

Our stares lock for a second. I don't want to look. Whatever it is I'm going to find I don't want to see it.

I tear my gaze away, look to the concrete steps. Bloody footprints stain the concrete, new and old. So many that the steps are almost black.

I head down into a cellar, trying futilely to avoid stepping in the blood. No point. Impossible. I note the walls first, padded. Soundproofed. There is music playing. Softly. A Disney song, I think. That famous one from the movie about the ice princess. The words accompany me as I descend past the level of the ground floor, the basement slowly coming into view.

Overhead strip lights illuminate everything in a harsh, surgical glare. Metal benches, tables, all spattered with pooled blood. The smell of iron and tin. Sweat and fear. Faeces and urine.

On the floor, the remains of what I think are two people. Cut into pieces. Body parts posed and swapped over like a jigsaw. The skin covered in cuts and burns. White glimpses of bone, a pile of purple and grey organs sitting in a bowl in the centre of the room.

'They wouldn't stop screaming,' explains Dumelo from where he's lying at the bottom of the stairs. 'You understand, don't you? I had to stop them screaming.'

I drag him up the stairs again. I snatch the bottle of whisky and shove him into the lounge. I push him into the couch and force his mouth open, pouring the whisky down his throat, hoping it will snap him out of whatever insane little safe place he's drifted into. He coughs and splutters, tries to push me away.

I slap his face, twice. Hard.

I'm not sure if it's that or the whisky, but he finally blinks and shakes his head, the confusion drifting away from his eyes. He looks at me. At Armitage.

'Who are you?' He wipes his face, sees the blood, tries to wipe it on his drenched shirt. He tries to get up but I force him down again.

'The fuck you think you're doing?' he demands. 'Do you have any idea who I am?'

I look at Armitage. She shrugs.

'I am member of your government. I'm a close personal friend of the President.'

'Yeah. And I'm Harry Potter. I've even got a wand.'

'You dare to joke with me? I'll have you arrested. I can make you disappear.'

'You recognise him?' I ask Armitage.

She shakes her head. 'Can't be anyone important.'

'How dare you! Where is Miss Long? What have you done with her?'

'Miss Long ain't coming,' I say. 'She's a bit dead right now.'

Dumelo's eyes widen. Not sure if it's panic or surprise. 'You . . . you have no idea how much trouble you're in,' he says.

'Whatever. We didn't kill her. Look, you need to understand something here. We're cops. OK? Long—'

Dumelo laughs. 'You are police? Then you are very stupid police. I am protected.'

'Who protects you?'

'Everyone.' He shakes his head and laughs again. 'You have no idea how much trouble you are in.'

'Us?' says Armitage. 'You're the one with an abattoir in your basement, you sick bugger!'

'I am allowed to do that.'

'Who says?'

He shrugs. 'I am done talking to you now. I think you should call one of your superiors. I will speak to him.'

'You're done when we say you're done,' says Armitage.

'No. I am done now.' Dumelo looks at us, his gaze filled with the arrogance you see in politicians everywhere. That look of entitlement, of superiority. 'You are nothing. Understand? A speck underfoot. I am a member of parliament. My friends are some of the most powerful people in this country. You think you can just barge into my house and start ordering me around?' He chuckles and picks a bit of skin from beneath his fingernail. 'You know nothing.'

He takes the bottle from me and downs another gulp, watching us beneath hooded lids. I want to punch him. A member of parliament? Our government is so bloated I bet he's never even set foot in the Parliament buildings. I want to shoot him in the knees. I want to cut his fingers off and stuff them down his throat.

Instead, I take a deep, steadying breath.

'What's happening tomorrow night?'

'I've no idea what you're talking about.'

'When you texted Long. She asked why you couldn't wait till tomorrow. What's happening tomorrow?'

'I've already told you. I will not talk to you. Summon your superiors.' Dumelo smiles and leans back. 'Perhaps I should do it? Where is my phone? I'll call them.'

'Bugger this.'

Armitage leans past me. I see the flash of a blade, but before I can do anything she slices it along Dumelo's inner thigh. He screams and throws himself back into the couch as blood gushes from the wound.

'That there is the femoral artery,' says Armitage. 'If you leave the wound untreated you're going to bleed out in about two to three minutes.'

Dumelo tries to get up, but she hits him in the face with her gun. He looks at her in utter amazement. As if he can't fathom anyone raising a hand to him.

'Talk,' she says.

'Call a doctor!' screams Dumelo.

I swallow nervously, watching the blood pour out of Dumelo's leg. Armitage has killed him. The cut was deep enough to completely sever the artery. There's no way he can get help in time.

'Tick-tock,' says Armitage.

'You fucking bitch! You whore! I'll kill you. I'll cut you into pieces and piss on your body.'

Armitage yawns and looks at her watch.

'I'd really start talking,' I say.

'What? What do you want to know?'

'Everything. Who's involved in this sin-eater thing?'

'Everyone who has any real power is involved, you idiot!'

'The government?'

'Yes, the fucking government. *Every* government. The

church. The World Bank. The IMF, everything. This isn't some local operation. The sin-eaters – they're worldwide. A secret society. Like the Templars or . . . or the Illuminati. They hire themselves out to take on the sins of the rich!'

Dumelo tries to hold the cut on his leg closed.

'We'd have heard about them if that was true,' I say.

'Not if they didn't want you to.' I notice that he's shivering now, the blood flowing freely between his fingers. 'You . . . don't get it, do you? They're rich. Bilderberg rich. You think getting a clean slate comes cheap? All those war criminals, corrupt ministers, spies, you name it. They want to live without sin. They'll pay anything that's asked of them. The sin-eaters are the most powerful group in the world. They control govern-ments, organized crime, everything.'

He looks down at his once-white couch and moans. 'That's too much blood. It shouldn't be outside.'

'So what's happening tomorrow night?'

'A . . . a gathering. A party. They . . . the corporation – the sin-eaters – do it once a year. Throw a party for their impor-tant clients. Their . . . leader. Or whatever he is . . . the senior sin-eater, attends. It's the most important event in the social calendar. It's where . . . where policies get discussed. Where businesses decide on . . . on prices for the year ahead. Where foreign policies are agreed upon.'

I knew it. I fucking knew it. Everyone thinks I'm a cynical bastard for hating politicians. Now look. Everything I say is true. We're talking secret meetings, handshake deals, billion-rand tenders handed out with a wink and a nod. Exactly how everyone used to think the Freemasons operated.

And we can expose the lot of them.

I pause at the thought. Could we do that? Get evidence? Record them, perhaps? Leak it to the media? Christ, it would be huge. The whole government would implode.

Then I think of something. 'You say all the powerful people

are involved in this. Do you mean law enforcement? Like the State Security Agency?'

Dumelo laughs weakly. 'Of course.'

Armitage looks at me. There we go. That explains why the SSA spooks are after us. Either they, or their bosses, found out we were investigating sin-eaters. And obviously, the powers-that-be don't want that.

But how did they know?

Then I realize. GHOST.

Only someone really high up could have hacked into GHOST and wiped out the entries on sin-eaters. That's why there was no information. And I bet there was some sort of call-back embedded in the code. So that whenever anyone calls up the sin-eater entry, it triggers an alarm that tells them who's looking. We all have to sign into GHOST using our personal IDs.

I shake my head, almost impressed. This is big. *Huge.*

Does Lilith know about it? Is she going to expose it to the world? Is that how she was going to 'shake everything up' as she put it?

'How do you get into the party?'

'An . . . invitation.'

Dumelo's face is grey. His breathing is slow and laboured. He doesn't have much longer.

'Where is it?' asks Armitage. He doesn't respond, so she slaps him until his eyes flutter open. 'Where is it? The invitation.'

'In . . . my suitcase. By . . . by the stairs.'

I find the suitcase and bring it into the lounge. I unzip it. Smart clothes, toiletries. An A4 envelope made of thick, gilded paper. I turn it over. No marks. No address.

I open it up. There's something big inside. Some kind of . . . mask? I shake it out. A wolf mask. But just the top half. So it would cover the eyes and nose but leave the mouth free. There's something else inside the envelope. A card.

It's the invitation. Has to be. A time and a date in a simple, stylish font. Beneath that an address up in Johannesburg.

Dumelo sees what I'm holding. 'Nuh . . . no. That is . . . mine.'

He tries to get up, slips in his own blood. His face cracks hard against the tiles. He moves weakly, wallowing on the floor like a beached whale for a few seconds before finally sliding to a stop.

I hear his last breath slide softly from his body.

'And good riddance,' snaps Armitage.

'Can we go now?' says the dog, who has been watching from the doorway, not wanting to get his paws bloody.

'In a minute.'

I study Dumelo's body. He looks to be about the same size as me. I toss the mask and invitation back into the suitcase and zip it shut. Then I track down his car keys.

'What are you doing?' asks Armitage.

'I can't very well turn up at an exclusive party in my old Land Rover, can I?'

'So that's the plan? You're going to pretend to be one of them?'

'Why not?'

'Because,' says the dog, 'ten minutes with that lot and you're going to go loco.'

'We don't have much choice, do we? Unless you've got a better idea?'

Nobody does, so we slip out the house and head round to the garage. Dumelo's car is a BMW X6, the newest on the market. Courtesy of the taxpayer. So really, it's not actually stealing, is it? My taxes paid for this car.

Armitage drives behind me in the BMW till I find a shopping mall where I can leave the Land Rover for a couple of days. Then I climb into the BMW and we head west towards Johannesburg.

'Road trip!' says the dog from the back seat.

Then, a few seconds later, 'Are we there yet?'

15

Five o'clock the next day and we're driving along the winding back roads about forty-five minutes west of Johannesburg, heading towards the address on the invitation.

None of us are talking to each other. It's been that kind of day.

It's only a five-hour drive to get to Gauteng. Dragging it out as much as we could, stopping at every service stop along the way for coffee and energy drinks, meant we still managed to arrive at a rundown bed and breakfast on the outskirts of Johannesburg by four-thirty this morning.

Which was still too early. The place wasn't even open yet.

We spent the next hour and a half playing I-spy with the dog. Armitage and I wanted to get some sleep, but every time we tried to quit the game he threatened to stink out the car.

And that was the best part of the day, to be honest. The next ten hours were spent cooped up in a tiny bedroom with the dog and Armitage, each of us wondering who would snap first.

It was Armitage.

The dog was watching some old movie on the TV where women were running around screaming, calling for the big manly men to save them.

The dog grinned at me. 'Ah, the good old days.'

Armitage whirled around and smacked him on the nose.

The dog couldn't believe it. He looked at me beseechingly. I shrugged and took a sip of my beer. The dog looked back to Armitage.

'You . . . you *hit* me!' he said accusingly. He actually sounded hurt. Not physically, but emotionally.

Armitage said nothing. Just grabbed her mac and left the room.

The dog turned to me. 'Reckon I'll stick to being a voice in your head from now on.'

'Probably better that way, anyway. What if a member of the public hears you?'

'Fuck 'em. They'll just think they've gone mad.'

'Either that or they'll steal you and sell you to the circus.'

So now we're out in the middle of nowhere, the flat, green landscape stretching away to either side of the endless road. Blue-grey clouds are building up on the horizon, piling up higher and higher into the hazy summer sky. Too far away for us, but someone's about to get a hell of a storm.

The aircon is on full blast but we have the back windows all the way down. Yeah, so sue me. Global warming is one thing, but travelling anywhere with the dog in an enclosed space is another thing entirely. I think his smell is actually sticking to my penguin suit.

'So what's the plan, exactly?' asks the dog.

'The plan is I use the invitation to get in, scout around while the bigwigs do their back room deals, and keep an eye open for the head sin-eater. Then I politely ask him what this first sin is, why Lilith is after it, and what it can do.'

And then once that's done I make the fucker tell me who Cally's killer is. Because he has to know. If he's in charge of all the sin-eaters he has to have a list of some kind. A database.

I feel a rush of fear and nervousness at the thought. This is the closest I've ever gotten to finding out what really happened that night. Three years of disappointment. Three years of pointless searches and false leads. Thousands of hours of viewed CCTV footage, tens of thousands of rands paid to informers – all for nothing. Nobody knew who had taken the kids. Nobody knew the men at the house. Nobody knew anything.

This time tomorrow, will all that have changed? Will I know the names of the people who killed Cally?

We drive though a tiny village about twenty kilometres from the address. The main attraction here seems to be a rundown liquor store where the locals hang around drinking quart bottles of Black Label and Castle Milk Stout. I could do with a drink myself, but I'm not going in there dressed like this.

We pass through the village, keep going for another ten kays or so. When I'm sure we're out of sight of any witnesses, I pull over. I pop the trunk and we climb out and head round to the back of the car.

Armitage and I stare into the cramped space.

'It won't be for long,' I point out.

'You realise I blame you for this,' she says. 'All of it.'

'What the hell did I do? I didn't take the ramanga case. You did.'

She waves her hand in irritation. 'You're my subordinate. It's always your fault.'

The dog leaps into the boot and sits there, giving us a bright-eyed-bushy-tailed look, tongue hanging out the side of his mouth.

'If you even *dare* – and I cannot stress this enough – *even dare*, to generate *any* kind of smell, I will shoot you in the head,' Armitage says.

The dog stops panting. Closes his mouth and looks at me.

-She serious?-

-Want to risk it?-

Armitage scowls at her surroundings then holds a hand out for me to help her climb in. She lies down, pushing herself as far to one side as she can go.

'You stay down there,' she snaps, pointing at the dog.

I close the trunk. Not all the way. Armitage holds it with her hand so she can get out later. I climb back into the front and put on my mask, checking my reflection in the rear-view mirror. It's good. No one can see who I am. Just another anonymous corrupt minister. One of thousands.

I drive for another few kays, then turn off the main road into a long tree-lined driveway. There's a warm wind picking up. The sun flashes and darts through the swaying branches, blinding me with late afternoon light. I take a deep, steadying breath. Have to stay calm. Keep in character.

The road leads to a set of huge double gates, ornately carved with tree motifs. Two armed guards stand on the other side, R5 rifles held in the resting position, fingers resting along the trigger guard.

A third guard comes out of the gate house to the right. The gates open and he approaches the car. I don't say anything to him, just stare straight ahead. (I'm in character here. A South African politician does not deign to acknowledge those lesser than him or herself.) I crack the window just enough to flick the invitation through the gap. The guard checks it, then waves at the armed guards.

They step aside and I drive past, watching the gates close in the rear-view mirror. I'm inside. For better or worse.

I turn my attention to the winding cobbled road unravelling ahead of me. It's about a kilometre long, flanked by more massive, stately trees.

The driveway eventually loops around a huge, swimming-pool size fountain outside the house. I stop the car, peering up through the windshield and mentally correct myself. That's not a house. That's a mansion.

No, it's an *estate*. It's five floors high, and it stretches away to either side, square, neat windows frowning down at me as if daring me to step inside.

There are a couple of cars here already, masked figures

climbing out to hand over their keys to smartly dressed valets. I squint, but don't recognize any faces. But I suppose that's the whole point.

There's a knock at my window. I start, then see a young dude in a bow tie and white shirt waiting for me. I get out the car and he hands me a valet chit.

'Thanks.'

He doesn't answer. His eyes look kind of vacant, as if he's been watching reality TV for hours on end.

'Busy night ahead, huh?'

Again, no answer. He climbs into the car and drives off around the rear of the house, leaving me standing next to the fountain all by my lonesome. I walk over to check it out, just to look busy in case anyone's watching. There's a statue of the Greek goddess Hebe, bearing her traditional cup for the gods. Water spews out of the cup. I lean over and see the other Greek gods have been inlaid in a mosaic at the bottom of the fountain.

There are more cars coming along the drive. I take a deep breath and turn towards the house, climb the stone stairs to the entrance. The huge door is standing open, a young girl waiting with a tray of champagne. She has the same vacant stare as the valet.

I take a glass, trying to catch her eye, but her gaze slides away like ice over stone. I send out a few subtle strands of shinecraft, immediately picking up on the tendrils that hang over her. She's been glamoured, her mind locked away for the night. She won't remember a thing come tomorrow.

I look around, casually sipping my drink. The entrance hall is *huge*, with full-on English-haunted-mansion in decoration choices. Polished wooden floor, oil paintings of knights and oddly dressed men, two staircases that wind up either side of the wall to meet on the second-floor landing, and dark mahogany wall panelling. It feels like I've stepped back into Victorian times.

A few guests are milling around chatting. I quickly duck through one of the doors that open off from the foyer in case any of them decides to draw me into conversation.

The door leads into a huge library. Despite the summer heat a fire is roaring in the hearth. There are more guests in here, standing around in small groups exchanging low conversation. They look at me suspiciously as I enter, drawing closer together. I ignore them, pretend to glance at the books on the shelves, then head through a second door on the far side of the room.

I wander through the house for the next hour. Never pausing for too long, constantly moving as the rest of the guests turn up and the house gradually fills with expensive cologne, superiority complexes, and hundreds of different masks: faeries, wolves, dogs, butterflies, snakes, crocodiles. All of them expensively made, and, if I'm not mistaken, covered with real jewels. Diamonds, sapphires, and rubies.

I don't think Dumelo's mask has anything of that kind of value, though. Maybe he was entry level. Not as important as he obviously thought he was.

I try to fit in, but it's hard for me not to run screaming from the house as I hear these people mumbling about their problems.

'. . . *Oh, and they were all out of Beluga Caviar, darling. I couldn't believe it.*'

'. . . *I said to him, I want the A6 tomorrow, delivered to my house with a silver bow on it, or I'll get Audi to pull your dealership licence.*'

'. . . *My boy is very sensitive. I mean, obviously it was the other boy's fault little Donny threw him out that window. Hmm? No, the school made it all go away. It's what we pay for.*'

'. . . *I said to him, yeah, it's eight thousand jobs gone, but really, it's nothing personal. You have to separate the sense of self from business dealings. Hmm? What did he do? He killed himself. Nose dive from the overpass.*'

I grit my teeth and drink my champagne.

-Dog? How's it going?-

-Wonderful. Your boss found me some booze in the kitchens and tossed it out the window. She's very considerate.- There's a pause as the dog thinks about this. *-Actually, now I think about it, I had to dodge pretty quick to avoid the bottle.-*

-Where is she now?-

-No idea. She just told me to sit on my arse and drink my booze.-

It's about eight o clock now, and most of the guests are loudly drunk, trying to outdo each other in their poor-rich-me stories. I've been watching these people closely. Obviously some of them know each other, or how else would their big deals get done? In fact, I've seen small groups heading into the various rooms, closing the doors behind them while they have their private pow-wows.

But the others . . . those who are *not* supposed to know each other? They *really* seem to *want* to be known. Proclaiming loudly for all to hear what they did last week in their job. Dropping hints about this or that government policy, about who they know, about who was at dinner with them last week. It's like they all want to rip off their masks and scream out, *Look at me! I'm important!*

I'm doing my second circuit of the house when I sense a ripple of movement running through the guests. They whisper to each other excitedly, leaving the rooms and heading towards the front of the house. There's excitement in the air. A tension that is slowly rising.

I flow with the crowd as it spills into the entrance hall. I'm at the rear of the crowd, a hundred or so guests standing in front of me. I make a half-hearted attempt to get closer to the front, but all that earns me are dirty looks and elbows in the ribs.

'Can I have your attention, please.'

We look up. Conversation falls away to excited mutterings and hopeful sighs. A tall man wearing a charcoal grey suit is standing on the second-floor balcony directly above the foyer. His face is deeply creased, with eyes so startlingly grey they're almost white.

'Good evening to you all. I just want to take this opportunity to welcome you to our little soirée.'

He speaks with what sounds like a Scandinavian accent. He scans the masked faces staring rapturously up at him. 'Now, I know you've all had a very stressful couple of months, if the many emails and letters I've received are anything to go by. This is understandable. You are hard workers. The best in your fields. You make the world go round, yes? This is very stressful, I think.'

He leans slightly over the balcony, staring down at us all. 'That is why I am here. I am your psychiatrist. I am your priest. I am a-hah-hah, Dr Feelgood, yes? You have problems, you come to me. I make them go away. Forever. I take them from you.' He holds his hands to his chest. 'I lessen the burden of life. That is my job.'

He smiles. He's pretty good, I have to admit. I almost believe he cares about us. About me.

'My friends, tonight is your night, yes? Your night to enjoy yourself. To let loose. To relieve the pent-up frustrations of the past months. To purge your systems and do what comes naturally to us all. Because, let us face it, yes? Society and its laws are not for us. A veneer of lies to help the sheep sleep better at night. You are the one per cent, the ones who know what it means to be human. You are the ones who embrace all sides of your nature. You do not deny who you are. Why should you? Let your true nature rise up, my friends. Enjoy who you are. Embrace the lust.' He smiles at us all and presses his hands together, almost in prayer. 'And now? Go to it. *Tak.* Thank you.'

The crowd bursts into cheers. Frenzied, animalistic howls and ululations. I raise my glass and voice like the rest of them, trying to hide my unease. There's danger here. The danger of a mob let loose to do as they will. I've seen it often enough in my work. The mob becomes a single organism, feeding itself on the emotions the more powerful members generate. I can feel it here, as the self-styled Dr Feelgood looks down on us with a smile of ownership, like a master looking on his dog.

Then all the doors that were locked during my exploration of the house open up and long lines of naked men and women walk out to join the party. I watch them file past, moving into alcoves and along passageways, some of them heading deeper into the house. They have that same vacant look as the valet and the girl at the door. Glamoured. Or drugged.

A sense of anticipation hangs in the air. A feeling of urgency. The guests stop talking. They eye the naked people hungrily, licking their lips.

One of the new arrivals – a young man, beautiful and flaw-less – climbs the stairs and comes to stand next to Dr Feelgood.

'And now,' says Feelgood, 'to start the night off in the proper manner, we will indulge in one of our . . . special traditions. Who will open the bidding?'

The guests shout and raise their hands. I look around in confusion. What are they bidding for? A sex slave?

'What was that?' says Feelgood, leaning forward. 'Did I hear one million? Come now, my friends. That is loose change to you all.'

'Ten million!' shouts a voice.

Feelgood smiles. 'That is more like it. We have ten million. Do we have fifteen?'

'Fifteen!'

'Twenty!'

Twenty million? What the hell? What are they paying for?

Feelgood smiles down upon the masses and takes out a gold knife. He holds it up.

'The winning bid will also receive this exclusive knife. It is a one of a kind piece from my own private collection.'

'Twenty-five million!' shouts a woman's voice.

'We have twenty-five. Twenty-five million for the honor of first blood. Do I hear thirty?'

Feelgood scans the crowd.

First blood?

'No rise on twenty-five million? No? Then sold to the lady with the vulture mask.'

A polite round of applause strikes up. The crowd parts to allow the winning bidder access to the stairs. She climbs to the landing and Feelgood hands over the knife.

'Do your worst, my dear, then come to me for absolution. I will be waiting for you.' He gestures to a room behind him, then lays a hand gently on her head 'For it is your right.'

'It is my right,' the woman murmurs back, as if responding to a benediction.

I look around in horror, realization of what is going on finally sinking in. I was expecting a drug-fuelled party. Maybe a bit of an orgy later when some of the guests got out of hand.

But this . . . this is a *sin* party. The rich and powerful getting to indulge in their sickest fetishes and still leaving free of sin. Free of guilt. Free of the memories of what they've done.

I swallow the bile in my throat, reach behind my back for the Glock shoved into my pants. I'm not going to just stand here and watch this.

That's when I smell cloves and jasmine, and a hand rests lightly on my arm.

'No, no, my friend,' says a deep voice. 'Let us keep the weapon hidden away. There's a good boy.'

I glance to my right. See a figure wearing the mask of a demon. Look to my left. Another figure. This one wearing a red devil mask.

But they're not wearing tuxedoes. They're wearing black trench coats.

Angels.

16

The angels pull me away from the foyer, moving deeper into the house. To be honest, I'm not sorry to be going. The other guests are starting to get into the swing of things. I hear shouts of joy, screams of agony. The cackle of giddy laughter as the veneer of society is stripped away and the animal inside let loose.

From the lower half of their faces I can see one of the angels looks old. Tanned skin, creased with wrinkles. The other looks younger, with that generic, cold-statue look I mentioned before.

I struggle against the older one's grip, but I can't budge. I might as well be trying to lift a ton of metal. Doesn't stop me trying, though.

'Such a strong will,' says the older angel. He leans close to me and inhales. Then he gently strokes my hair. I jerk away and he clicks his tongue in disappointment.

The younger angel leans close. 'Michael sends his regards,' he says.

I glare at him. 'Seriously? You just here from a Godfather retrospective?'

His mouth purses with annoyance. He turns to the older angel. 'Ramiel?'

The older angel – Ramiel – sighs. 'He means you are talking in clichés, Azazel.'

Ramiel and Azazel? I've heard those names before. And recently, too, when I was reading up on Lilith. The Book of

Enoch, I think. They're part of the Grigori, the fallen angels who came to earth to fuck their way through the human population. (And to teach us how to make weapons and shit. They're probably the kickstarters of civilisation.)

'Aren't you supposed to be chained in a hole in the desert or something?' I ask Azazel.

'No,' says Ramiel. He reaches behind me and gently strokes Azazel's cheek. He obviously likes physical contact, does old Ramiel. 'The "hole in the desert" – this was never true. But Michael *has* temporarily released us from prison to come and . . . take care of you. He does not wish your death to stain his soul.'

'You want to talk about staining your souls? Shouldn't you be doing something about all this shit going on here?'

Ramiel shrugs. 'It is in their nature. Would we stop a lion from hunting? A vulture from devouring a corpse? Of course not. Now come. Let us find a quiet room.'

Azazel pulls me and we move deeper into the house.

-Dog. Could do with a hand here.-

-Hah! Thanks, London. You won me my bet.-

-What bet?-

-How long it would take before you needed help. I said two hours.-

-What did Armitage say?-

-Twenty minutes.-

-Nice.-

-So what's the problem?-

-Two angel hitmen.-

-Huh. Michael must be going soft. He used to do that shit himself.-

-I need a distraction.-

-How big?-

-Big. I've eyeballed the head honcho here. Once I shake these two loose I'm going to have a word with him.-

-Right. Just to make sure. Are we talking like, BANG! big, or Big-badda-boom big?-

-Big-badda-boom, Leeloo. Definitely. And quick.-
-Leave it to me.-
By this time, the angels have me in a long, wood-panelled corridor. Ramiel picks a room at random and opens the door.
'Clear,' he says, peering inside.
-Rear of the house, dog. First floor. Middle of the building.-
-Got it. You're gonna like this, London. You know they've got their own gas pump here? How upmarket is that?-
I wince. The dog and fire never go well together.
-Just hurry up. Running out of time.-
Azazel shoves me in the back and I stumble into the room. It's a study. A huge desk facing the door, leather-bound books arranged by colour on the shelves behind it.
There's a large window straight ahead. I think I can see something flickering outside. Something orange. I position myself so that the two angels stand between me and the glass.
'I'm curious,' I say. 'How do you square this with the big man and his ten commandments? You know, "Thou shalt not kill"?'
Ramiel frowns at me. 'It is not for us to question the Will.'
'Ah. Got it. Just following orders, eh?'
Ramiel raises his arm and a sword appears in his hand. The blade bursts into flame, blue fire coursing along the blade. The light reflects against his face, illuminates the study.
I immediately want one. With every fibre of my being. Heavenly lightsabers. How goddamn fucking cool is that?
'Am I really such a big deal to you guys?'
'Not you. What you are doing.'
'Yeah. Sticking your nose into stuff that isn't your business,' says Azazel.
'Oh, come on.' I look appealingly to Ramiel. 'You can't kill me with him spouting this shit.'
'You are correct,' says Ramiel. 'Azazel. Shut the fuck up and cut his head off.'

Azazel grins. 'Sure. Afterwards, can we visit the city? Before we have to go back to heaven? I want some pizza.'

'We'll see.'

Curiosity gets the better of me. 'I thought you said you were in prison?'

'*I* am not in prison,' says Ramiel defensively. 'I am a guard.'

'But he just said heaven.'

'Not the *real* Heaven, cock-head,' sneers Azazel. 'That's what we call the prison. Where the Fallen are locked away—'

'Enough,' snaps Ramiel. He hands the sword to Azazel. 'End him.'

'With pleasure.' Azazel grins and steps forward.

The explosion, when it comes, is spectacular.

The windows explode inwards, shards of glass cutting into the backs of the angels, sending them staggering forward. A huge fireball soars up past the house.

The sword flies from Azazel's hand, hits the floor next to my feet. I grab the hilt, and almost drop it again when I feel the freezing cold burning my hand. Azazel straightens up and lurches for me. I grit my teeth and swing the sword. He lifts both arms to protect himself and the sword slices through them at the elbows. Like they weren't even there.

His arms hit the carpet, fingers clenching up like dying spiders.

Azazel stares at them in horror, then glares at me. 'Look what you did, man! How am I gonna eat pizza now?'

I swing the sword again. His head flies through the air and hits the bookcase. His body drops to its knees and then just sits there.

I advance on Ramiel.

'Don't be stupid, human. You kill me, you make a very powerful enemy.'

'More powerful than Michael? Because I think I'm already on his shitlist.'

He tries to smile. 'Fine, fine. What about . . . what about a gift? You want anything? Women? Money? No? Your tastes run different, yes? A child—'

I rush him.

He holds up his hand and a second sword appears, this one blazing with red fire. The swords connect.

Purple fire explodes in the room, magical lighting writhing around the blades, bathing our faces. I step back, swing for his head. He blocks it and kicks me in the stomach. I stagger back, arms cartwheeling, but still manage to hold onto the sword. I hit a bookcase and push myself upright just in time to meet Ramiel's counter-attack.

His blade almost hits my neck. I bring my own sword to stop it just in time. The purple light glints in his eyes. On his teeth.

'You have no idea how much trouble I'm in now,' he snarls. 'Azazel was my ward. I'm probably going to have to face a committee. You realise how boring committees are? Especially committees of angels?'

'My heart bleeds for you.'

I duck, and the force he was putting on his blade sends him staggering to the left. He swings his arm behind him, stopping my sword from cutting into the backs of his legs. He turns to face me, still holding the blade down, blocking my own.

'Paperwork. I'm going to have to fill in a missing prisoner file. In quadruplet.'

He pushes me back. I can't move my own blade. It's holding his down. If I move it, he'll use the momentum to cut me in half. I glance over my shoulder. A few steps from the wall. I'm going to be stuck in a corner. I won't be able to swing.

I briefly consider using the tattoos, but then remember it's only been a couple of days. The strength they'll have gained from me will still be coursing through them. It's too soon. What's the point of using them to combat one threat if they just turn around and devour me once they're finished?

Shit. Nothing else for it.

I let go of the sword, falling back against the wall. Ramiel staggers to the side as my resistance suddenly vanishes. I lean around him and grab his arm, yanking and twisting. I hear something break and his fingers spasm open.

I grab the hilt of his dropped sword before it hits the ground. This one is burning hot. I shove him back towards the window. His eyes are wide. Panicked.

'Wait. Wait . . . I can—'

I cut his head off before he can finish the sentence. As soon as I do, both swords wink out of existence. His head tumbles to the carpet but the body just stands there, framed against the fires outside. I kick him in the chest and he tumbles back-wards into thin air.

I look out the window. The cars belonging to the guests are parked in neat rows. But one of them has been driven into the gas pump, knocking it away from its base and catching fire. I'm assuming Armitage did that. Otherwise the dog has learned a few tricks I didn't know about.

I turn away, pull my gun out. Have to get to this Dr Feelgood before the fire spreads.

I open the door.

There's a man dragging one of the glamoured staff along the passage outside, pulling her by her legs. I hit him on the head with the Glock. He drops to the floor, howling in pain.

I stare at the person he was dragging. She's already dead. A huge wound opens up her abdomen from chest to stomach.

I drag my eyes away, feeling the bile rise in my throat. I stumble along the passage and into a large sitting room. I stagger, stop walking.

The first thing I notice are the white plastic sheets laid over the furniture.

The second thing is the blood. It's everywhere. Spattering the plastic, pooling in little hollows and trenches formed by creases in the material. Body parts litter the couches. Arms, legs. Two torsos sitting next to each other. No guests. The victims have just been left here, abandoned.

I move into the next room, trying to escape.

But there *is* no escape. No place to hide.

It's like I'm walking through a biblical apocalypse. I try to ignore it. *Keep walking,* I tell myself. *Think about the bigger picture.* Walking around the blood, the bodies. Feeling my humanity stripping away with every step, with every ignored cry of pain.

Just keep moving, I tell myself. Get to the head sin-eater. Find the man who killed Cally. That's all that matters. That's why you're here.

Then I hear a high-pitched scream.

I freeze, look around for the location. The scream comes again and I'm running, heading down another corridor, this one lit with red lights. I kick the door open. Three men turn to me, and I see . . .

I see a child, a girl no more than nine years old, struggling to get out of the grip of one of the men.

I scream, run forwards. I fire the gun, hit the closest in the head. He jerks back, falls over a chair. The one holding the girl releases her, tries to reach for something beneath his arm. I see a holster. I fire. He tries to dodge aside and my bullet wings him in the right arm. He drops behind the couch as the third one turns on me. I shoot him in the groin. He shrieks in pain, dropping to his knees. I turn to the other one but he's already gone, vanished through a second door.

The girl . . . she's gone too. Vanished. I look around frantically. Can't find her. Did the third guy take her?

I hear a noise. Kneel down to see her hiding beneath a table.

Her eyes are wild, terrified. But they don't focus on me, they stare at nothing. She still seems glamoured, but somehow the terror of her situation forced its way behind the spell.

I take my mask off, drop it to the floor.

'Hey,' I say softly. Her eyes drag around to look at me. I try to smile. 'Hey there. Come on. You want to go? You want out of here?' I gesture at her. 'Come on. I'll take care of you. I promise. I'll protect you.'

And suddenly it's as if I'm talking to Cally.

'Trust me. I won't let them hurt you. I promise you.'

She hesitates, then slowly crawls out towards me. I'm relieved to see she's still clothed. The fuckers hadn't had a chance to do whatever they were going to do. Her head jerks around, looking around the library, searching for danger.

I put my gun into my belt and hold my arms out and she runs into them, burrowing into my chest.

I straighten up, make meaningless sounds, trying to calm her down, to reassure her.

I turn and stare at the man I shot in the groin. He's lying on the ground now, bleeding out, whimpering in fear. I look at the other one, sprawled across the table.

I feel rage. A deep, soul-destroying rage.

This. This is what we are. This is what we do to each other. Forget the orisha. Forget the monsters under the bed. *We're* the fucking monsters under the bed. We're the ones who do this. *Mankind* is the bogeyman. The word humanity doesn't mean kindness, caring. If it represents us as a species then it means evil. Perversion.

When we prey on the innocent, when we can't protect our own children, that's it. Game over. We might as well all give up.

Lilith was right. We've fucked everything up.

I can feel the girl shivering against me. I stare at the man, watching him as his convulsions eventually slow, then stop. But I'm not really seeing him. I'm making comforting sounds to the girl, stroking her hair.

'It's OK,' I whisper. 'It's OK.'

But it's not.

I head over to the fire. I'm not thinking about it anymore. Just acting. Stopping this.

I take a piece of burning wood from the grate and touch it to the curtains. The material catches, the flames crawling rapidly up towards the ceiling. I stand still, watching the flames grow stronger, listening to the screams of pain from other parts of the house. Listening to the murder and insanity of these sick bastards.

The black smoke curls across the roof, staining the white paint. I watch. It's hypnotic. It draws me in. How easy would it be to just stop? To let the smoke take my breath. To go to sleep and let the darkness claim me?

How easy to end everything?

The girl coughs.

I blink, look around, realizing I've been standing there for nearly a minute now. The flames have spread to the wall, crawling down to the furniture. I can feel the heat from all sides. The smell of the flames and smoke crawls into my nostrils.

-Dog.-

-Yeah?-

-All those cars outside. Burn them.-

-Seriously?-

-Burn everything.-

I need to move. Not much time. I still need to get to the sin-eater.

I stride from the room, eyes straight ahead. Someone screams for help. I turn. A young man is reaching out to me. His eyes are aware, the glamour burned away by the pain. Some hugely fat woman is trying to pull him along the tiles to a back room. I shove her away. She falls against the wall, her eyes wide with fear.

'Get out,' I say to the young man. I don't recognize my

voice. It's cold, alien. A killer's voice. 'This whole place is going to burn.'

I take out my phone, call Armitage.

'Where are you?' I say.

'Outside the front door. The dog said—'

'Wait there.'

I make my way back to the entrance hall. There's an orgy going on in the foyer. I cover the girl's eyes as we pass and pull open the door. Armitage is waiting on the steps, nervously holding her gun. She looks briefly into my eyes, and obviously doesn't like what she sees there, because she immediately turns her attention to the girl.

'And who's this bonny girl?' she says in a tremulous voice and a failed attempt at a comforting smile.

I hand her over. 'Put her in our car. Then get back in here and start getting these glamoured kids out. Quick.'

She nods and takes the girl down the steps. I rush back inside, take the stairs three at a time. Try the door on the second-floor landing, the one which Feelgood said he'd be waiting behind. Locked. I step back and kick it. Once. Twice. The door flies open.

Feelgood turns to me in surprise. His hands are hovering over a guest's head. There's a sickly, yellow glow hovering around them.

I fire the gun at the wall. The guest squeals in fear, jerking away from Feelgood.

'Get out.'

'You can't,' says Feelgood. 'Interrupting the process at such a time—'

I fire my gun again. But this time I misjudge. The bullet ricochets from the metal bedpost and hits Feelgood in the hand.

He stares at it in amazement. Watching the blood flow freely from the wound. 'You . . . shot me.'

I turn my attention to the guest. 'Out. Now.'

He bolts from the room, leaving the two of us on our own.

'What's your name? Your real name?' I ask Feelgood.

'Stefan,' he says, flopping down to sit on the bed.

'Stefan, you're coming with me.'

'I . . . I assure you I am not.'

'Fine. You can stay. But you're going to talk to me now, Stefan. You're going to tell me the things I need to know so I can catch a killer. Do you understand? Just nod.'

He doesn't nod. He's just staring at his hand. Blood is pooling on the bed between his legs.

'This . . . really is quite astoundingly painful,' he says.

'Hey. Stefan. Focus. I know what you are. I know about the sin-eaters. I know how widespread you are—'

This finally makes him look up from his hand. 'Then . . . you know you will be made to pay for this. My colleagues will hunt you. My clients will put you in jail.'

'I don't care anymore, Stefan. I really don't. And if you interrupt me again I'll shoot you in the dick.'

-London? You there?-

-I'm busy, dog.-

-Sure, sure. But you know the house is on fire, right? The whole back section is burning.-

I tilt my head and listen. I can hear screams, different screams, louder. Not just the glamoured victims anymore. But the guests too.

-Is Armitage getting the the vics out?-

-Yeah.-

-Good. Wait in the car. We'll talk later.-

His presence leaves my mind. I turn my attention to Stefan. 'Tell me about the first sin.'

His eyes widen in shock. 'How do you know of this?'

'I just do. Explain to me exactly what it is.'

'I . . . I can't.' He winces and move his hand. As he does so blood actually shoots out of the wound. It's a spurter. Must have got a few blood vessels.

'I . . . need medical attention.'

'Later.'

'Now! I must stop this blood, you fool.'

I sigh. 'You have a first-aid kit in here?'

He eyes light up. 'Yes. There are drugs. Bandages. In the next room.' He nods at an interconnecting door.

I hurry across and open the door into a second, larger bedroom. I look around, see a first-aid box mounted on the wall. I yank it free and take it back to Stefan, dropping it on his lap. He scrambles around inside and grabs a thick bandage, wrapping it around his hand. Then he finds a bottle of clear liquid and a syringe. He sucks the liquid up and injects it into his arm.

The effects are immediate. He slumps back against the bed, his eyes fluttering closed. I kick him.

'Hey. Wake up.'

He looks at me and smiles dreamily. What the hell was in that bottle? Morphine?

'What . . . do you wish to talk about?'

'You know what. The first sin.'

'Ah yes. The . . . first sin. Of course.'

'So? What is it?'

'It is . . .' He smiles again. 'It is the sin of God.'

I blink. I open my mouth, then shut it again. Finally, I say, 'What?'

'The sin of God. That is what the first sin refers to.'

I shake my head in confusion. 'How? How can God sin? Explain.'

'To do that I must take you back. Back to a place and a time long, long ago.' He giggles. 'And a galaxy far, far away.'

I kick him again. His eyes snap open, focus on me.

'Concentrate, Stefan.'

'It . . . started before the great flood. Apparently God was making . . . questionable decisions. Sodom and Gomorrah. Gob. Abraham. All the old testament stuff. He . . . was like an abusive spouse. Wrathful. Envious. Prideful. Greedy. He wanted everything for himself.'

Wrath. Envy. Pride, Greed. 'Those are four of the seven sins.'

Stefan points at me and winks. 'Exactly. Spot on. Well done.' He giggles. 'The archangels were uneasy, but they didn't feel they could act against him. He was God, after all. But he . . . got worse. The sins, they . . . it was like they were . . . alive. They were eating him up inside, taking over. He was giving in to them. And then he . . . discovered something that pushed him over the edge. He released the great flood. That was when the angels realized if they didn't do something, God would destroy the world.'

'What did they do?'

'Michael and Gabriel came up with an idea. They created a being – something called the Sinwalker. Someone who could take the sins from God, take them inside of himself. This . . . Sinwalker was to hold them, experience them, so God didn't have to.'

'Did it work?'

'It . . . seems so. After they created the Sinwalker we get the New Testament. A wholly different God.'

'So this . . . this Sinwalker. What happened to him?'

'He went mad. Utterly insane. It was inevitable, really. If God couldn't handle the sins, how could anyone else? Michael and Gabriel had to come up with another . . . solution. They created a . . . a coterie. The sin-eaters. It was their task to . . . siphon off some of the sin from the Sinwalker. To lessen the burden. Forever after.'

'What do you mean forever after?'

'The Sinwalker is . . . still alive. Immortal. God's sin never lessens, you see. It does not dissipate with time. Quite the

opposite. It . . . builds. Grows stronger. Hence the continued
need for us. We . . . get surges. Of . . . of sin. Every now and
then the sins come to us from the Sinwalker. When it is . . . too
much for him to contain. But we . . . cannot hold it all. There
are too few of us now. And many are dying without passing on
their sin to the next in line.'

'What happens then? If you die without passing the sin on?'

'It . . . returns to where it came from. To the Sinwalker. Or
to all the people who paid us to take their . . . deeds. The sins
always have to be held. Someone must feel the guilt.'

I shake my head, trying to take this all in. 'So, what – you're
saying this Sinwalker is still pumping you guys full of God's
sins?'

'Yes. But . . . as I say, we cannot contain it all. It . . . spills
out into the world, corrupting people, destroying what it
touches.' He winces and tries to sit up straighter. 'The . . . ills
of mankind do not come from the fact that God gave us free
will. Or because we ate from the tree of knowledge. It is
because his sins are staining the world, corrupting the earth.
Still, to this very day.' Stefan grabs my arm. His fingers dig
painfully in. 'It is *God* that is the cause of all that is bad in
the world.'

I pry his fingers off. He slumps back against the pillows and
closes his eyes.

'Why, though?' I ask. 'What did he discover? What made
him create the flood?'

'I . . . I am finished with you now. I will say no more.'

I grit my teeth in frustration. I grab the morphine bottle
and load the syringe up with another dose. I jab it into his
arm.

Stefan's eyes flutter open. He stares at me. 'That . . . feels
nice.'

'I'm glad. Come on now, Stefan. You were telling me a story.'

'Was I?'

'About the Sinwalker? You were telling me what God discovered. Why he created the flood.'

'Was I? Are . . . you sure? That is top secret.' He lifts a finger to his lips and tries unsuccessfully to make a shushing sound.

'So?' I prod Stefan. 'What did God find out?'

Stefan looks at me, his eyes slits of glinting amusement. 'He . . . he found out he did not create man.'

I wait for the punchline, but it doesn't come. 'Say again?'

'He . . . found out that it was the other way around. That *man* created *him*. That he grew from the beliefs and dreams and superstitions of our primitive ancestors. The angels tried to keep this knowledge hidden from him but he found out.'

'How could he not know he didn't create man?'

'Even gods suffer from self-delusion. He . . . convinced himself he created the entire universe and everything in it. That man was his possession to do with as he wanted. When he found out otherwise, he brought on the flood in a fit of fury.'

Christ, so God is exactly the same as all the other orisha. Self-deluded. Power hungry. Selfish. And an A+ asshole.

My thoughts are running furiously through my head. I can smell the smoke. It's getting stronger. I need to hurry. 'Why would someone be seeking this first sin?'

'I . . . do not understand.'

'Someone is searching for it. For the first sin.'

'Then they are searching for the Sinwalker. If they find him, they will find it.'

'Why are they looking for it?'

'I . . . do not know.'

His eyes drift closed. I poke him in the hand with my gun and he snaps awake again with a cry of pain.

'Pay attention. The one who's looking for the Sinwalker – she has a sin-eater on her payroll. He's killing your kind and absorbing their sins. How does that help him get closer?'

'Ah . . . I see. Clever.'

'What is?'

'That is how he will find the location of the Sinwalker. He is searching back through the sins and memories of our predecessors. We . . . take on the memories and sins of our masters, just as they took on the memories and sins of *their* masters. So it goes, all the way back to the first sin-eaters. If he looks back far enough, he will reach the first memories. The first sin. Find the Sinwalker's location.'

'How many sin-eaters will he need to kill to do that?'

'I . . . I do not know.'

'If they find him, what happens?'

'It . . . depends what they want to do. He is asleep you see, the sins held in his dreams.'

'What if he wakes?'

Stefan shrugs. 'The sins might . . . leak out, infect his surroundings. Corrupt the world. He is utterly mad, you see. Only in his dreams can he control them. If he wakes . . . who knows what will happen.'

'And if he dies?'

'Then the sins return to God. I am . . . not sure how he will react to that. He does not remember these sins. He has no knowledge, no memory of the evil he did. The angels will have made sure of this. Can you imagine how he will react if those sins return to him? If he suddenly remembers what he has done. If he remembers *why* he did it? He will do what he failed to do last time. Destroy the world.'

Lilith's revenge. How Night becomes Day. She doesn't even have to do anything. Just kill the Sinwalker and God will do the rest. Wipe out most of humanity.

The smell of smoke is getting stronger. I turn to the door and see it curling underneath. Time's up.

'Is there anything else you can tell me?'

'No. That is all I know. Now please. Help me. Help me escape.'

'Help yourself.'

I hurry to the door, pull it open and jerk back as the heat slaps me in the face. Smoke and flames are crawling across the ceiling. The stairs leading down are a wall of fire. I can't see ten feet down the corridor. Shit. Have to go up.

I take the stairs to the top floor. The walls are starting to smoke up here. I can feel the heat through the soles of my shoes. I move fast, find what I'm looking for at the end of the corridor. A small door with cramped stairs leading up.

I take them two at a time and emerge onto the roof of the manor house. The sky is choked with orange-tinged smoke. I can hear screams and shouts from down below.

I cover my mouth with my sleeve, skirt around the perimeter of the roof in search of a ladder, some way of getting down. I make a complete circuit before realizing with a sinking heart that there isn't one.

I hurry back across the roof. I need to find another way down. I open the door and a surge of flames leaps out, enveloping me in a wall of heat.

I shove the door closed. Stagger away, squinting through the smoke. I look around desperately. There has to be another way.

Then I see something odd. One section of the smoke is moving oddly. I frown, moving towards the edge of the roof. The smoke is swirling in little vortexes, and as I draw closer I see why.

Michael.

He's hanging in the air about ten feet away from the house, wings flapping slowly as he watches the scene unfolding below him. I peer over the edge and can just make out the lines of cars on fire, the guests streaming from the burning house.

-*Dog? Where are you?*-

-*With Armitage. She just finished getting everyone out. Fuck, London, did you see—?*-

-Later. Tell Armitage to get the car round to the fountain. I'll be there in a minute.-

Michael hasn't noticed me yet. I stare at him, feeling the heat on my back, pulsing up from below. The arrogant bastard is just hanging in the air, watching the tragedy unfold beneath him. Doing absolutely nothing.

I ready my gun, climb up onto the lip of the roof. I teeter there, waving my arms for balance. Thank Christ the smoke obscures most of the ground. I'm really not good with heights.

I watch Michael, trying to judge the distance. It's going to be close. There's a good chance I won't make it.

And the thing is, I don't really care. I'm tired. Tired of us. Tired of them. Tired of the powerful taking advantage of the weak. I'm tired of the entire fucking human race. If I die now, so what? I'll join Cally, wherever she is. Or I won't. Either way, it won't make a lick of difference.

I crouch down, then throw myself forward. The smoke whips past my face. Michael senses something, starts to turn. I grab hold of his wing with my free hand. We lurch to the side, my weight throwing him off balance.

'What are you doing?' he shouts.

He rights himself and flaps his wings. They hit me in the face but I hold on tight. He's starting to rise. That's not what I want.

I shoot him in the face.

He screams. We drop, but his wings are still flapping. He's not dead. I didn't think he would be. But he's hurt. He tries to control the descent as much as he can but we hit the ground hard and I'm thrown aside. I roll, come to a stop. My breath has been knocked out of me. I lay on the grass, wheezing for air. Michael is off to my right, sobbing in horror.

'What ... have you done to my face?' His words are mumbled, broken, but I understand them well enough.

I wince, feeling for broken ribs. 'Better watch out for that vanity,' I croak.

I push myself to my knees, then to my feet. My side is throbbing, hot flashes of pain stabbing through me. I stagger off to find Armitage, leaving Michael on all fours behind me.

'Have you seen my teeth?' he says. 'I can't find my teeth.'

I search frantically for my gun. Find it in the grass a few feet away. Eject the clip. Load a new one, point it at Michael.

But he's not coming for me. He's limping in the opposite direction, heading for the trees. When he's halfway there his wings start flapping and he rises jerkily into the sky, looking like an old Harryhausen stop-motion monster.

I put my gun away. There will be a reckoning there, I'm sure. Add another name to the list of creatures who want to kill me.

I look around. I'm at the rear of the house. The cars are all ablaze. I can smell burning rubber and fuel. There are clumps of guests milling around, staring at the cars in horror, wondering how they're going to get home.

I take out my cell phone and dial 10111.

'Police, what's your emergency.'

'There's a huge fire out at . . .' What's the place called again? '. . . Ainsley Manor,' I say, remembering. 'Lots of people dead. You better send everyone you can. Fire. Police. Everyone.'

I hang up, take a picture of the burning house, then forward it to the press contacts I have in my address book. I give them the address and title the email, 'Sex party goes wrong'. That will get them here.

But even as I send the email I wonder if it will make any difference. The people at this party are the ones who *own* the papers. They'd never let this story go to press.

But I have to try.

I can feel the heat even from this distance. The flames have taken hold of everything now. Pouring up out the windows, crawling up the outside walls like they're alive. I squint and think I see movement in the flames. Fire demons called up by the pain and suffering that went on here.

The front of the house is a scene of utter chaos. The guests are running around like headless chickens, crying, sobbing. Pointing at the house in horror. Yeah, cry me a river, fuckers.

I see a flash of headlights beyond the fountain.

-Dog. That you in the car?-

-It's us.-

I jog towards them, climb into the passenger side. I check the back and see the little girl, mesmerized by the fire, watching the figures silhouetted against the bright flames. I follow her gaze. A portion of roof suddenly caves in, accompanied by a terrific crunching, splintering sound. The flames reach higher, climbing into the night.

'London?' Armitage, prompting.

I don't take my gaze from the flame. I'm transfixed, caught in the moment.

So she drives, and finds the nearest hospital. Armitage takes the girl inside, saying she found her wandering around on the street. Armitage lays a hand on the girl's head. I feel the shine-craft from the car as Armitage cancels the glamour and wipes out her memory too. No need for her to remember what went on tonight.

The girl immediately turns and looks at me. Armitage ducks back through the doors and into the car. She starts the engine.

The little girl lifts a hand slightly in goodbye.

I lift mine in response, then Armitage pulls back into the street.

'Where to?' she asks.

'Back to Durban.'

17

I don't talk during the trip back to Durban. I can't. All I'm seeing are images – flashes of what happened back at the house, things I hadn't even been aware of seeing at the time. Jagged bursts of red and white. Of blood and bone. Of hunger glinting behind masks, of the terrified screams of the dying, the triumphant, animalistic howls of the killers.

I'm struggling to come to terms with it. It was as if a hundred thousand years of progress was simply . . . stripped away in an instant. As if society was nothing more than a feeble veneer, a group lie that we all hide behind so we can think we're better than we are. More advanced.

But we're not advanced. Lurking inside every single one of us is the animal, all fangs and hunger, waiting to be let off its chains.

It's making me feel sick. More than anything because I recognize that animal in myself. Every time I think about Cally I hear the snarling, raging beast, locked away in its cage, howling to be let loose, a force for revenge that will destroy everything before it if I just gave in. If I just opened the door.

But I can't. Because I know that if I let it out, it would devour me whole. That I wouldn't be able to come back from it.

I shiver, watch the tail lights of the car ahead of us. They look like glowing red eyes, watching me.

Waiting.

★   ★   ★

Armitage drops me back at the shopping centre where I left my car. It's about four in the morning. I'm exhausted. I feel beaten down, defeated.

'You given any thought about what you want to do next?' Armitage asks as I open the back door for the dog.

'I've no idea.'

'Because those SSA fellas are still going to be after us.'

'I know.'

'So—'

'Christ, Armitage. I *don't. Know.* I told you what Stefan told me. You figure it out.'

She stares at me for a second. 'No need to be a dick about it,' she says, and pulls out of the parking bay. The back door slams shut with her momentum.

I sigh and unlock the Land Rover. The dog hops in.

'You OK?' he asks as I drive out of the parking lot.

'No.'

'You . . . I don't know . . . Wanna talk?'

'No.'

'Thank Christ for that,' says the dog, relief plain in his voice.

I head back into town, trying to avoid the streets I know have working CCTV cameras. (Not many.) I get back to the beachfront twenty minutes later and park about a couple of hundred yards from my flat. It's possible the SSA spooks still have it under observation. Don't reckon they will, though. They've probably just instructed Ranson to detain me if I turn up at Delphic Division. Still. Better safe than sorry.

The streets are empty this time of night. A calmness has stolen over the city. A lie. When the night crawlers have passed out and the early morning joggers haven't managed to drag themselves smugly out of bed yet. A stray cat crosses my path. Pauses once and glares at the dog before walking calmly on, unafraid. The waves are a soft susurration to my left, their presence calming.

The thought comes to my mind unbidden. *This would actually be a nice world if it wasn't for us.*

I walk up a side street that takes me off the esplanade and into a dirty alleyway running along the back of the beachfront buildings. Fast food wrappers and carrier bags pile up against the sidewalk kerb. I can smell urine, vomit. It's dark back here.

We pass the service entrance to one of the hotels, a pile of cigarette butts showing where the employees take their breaks. Past another hotel, then across a wider street and I'm behind my building. I use my keys to unlock the reinforced door at the rear. All residents have one so we can bring our garbage down to the metal dumpster outside. Although, judging by the mess on the road, it looks like some of my neighbours just drop their shit out their window and hope for the best.

Up the stairs and I pause before my door. It's been kicked in, the lock destroyed, then sealed shut with a hastily attached clasp and padlock.

I rip the clasp straight from the wood and push the door open. Light from the hall spills past me into the flat, revealing a scene of devastation. The SSA have been here all right.

I step inside, pushing the door shut behind me. I make sure the blinds are all down before turning on the light and looking around.

'Fuck me,' says the dog.

They've destroyed everything. Glasses and plates smashed, food and drink in the kitchen emptied and thrown across the floor. The sofa's been upended and ripped to shreds. Books torn to pieces. My comics in tattered ribbons. Even the DVDs. They've snapped every single one.

I head into my room, flick the light switch. Glass crunches underfoot. I look down. My photographs of Cally and Becca, from when we were a family. They've all been ripped from the wall and ground beneath heavy boots.

I carefully pick them up, shaking the glass fragments away. I right the bedside table and lay the photographs down, attempting to smooth out the creases. Cally smiles at me. Becca is winking, her hand behind Cally's head doing rabbit ears.

I stare at it for a while, then blink, look around. I pull the mattress back onto the bed. It's been shredded, foam and springs jutting through knife gashes.

I lie down and close my eyes. I feel numb. I want to get away. To hide away from life.

I don't get a chance. My phone rings half an hour later. I pick it up and check the number. I recognize it instantly.

Becca.

I swing my feet onto the floor and answer. 'Becca?'

Silence. Some heavy, laboured breathing. Something else— something brushing against the phone?

Then a man, shouting in pain, but in the distance. Far away. 'Becca?' I say.

The shouting is cut off. The breathing in the phone increases. I can hear the panic.

'Gideon.' A whisper. Filled with fear. Anger. 'Someone's—'

Sudden noises, like a tussle or a fight. Grunts of pain. Something heavy falling.

Then the phone goes dead.

I'm out the house and running towards the car before I realise I've left the dog behind. No time to go back. I pull out into the street, narrowly avoiding crashing into an early morning taxi, and speed off into town.

The number on my cell was Becca's landline. She was back at home. Back? Had she even left? I told her to get to safety, but did she listen to me? I punch the steering wheel over and over. I should have checked! I should have fucking checked on her!

The trip to her house passes at a frantic crawl. I'm hoping a cop car sees me, tries to pull me over for speeding. Just so I can lead them to the house. To stop . . . to help . . .

I slam on the brakes outside Becca's house, mount the kerb, slide across her front lawn.

Then I'm out, my sweaty fingers curled around the Glock. I stand at the bottom of the garden, breathing heavily, watching. The house is dark. No sounds except the sleepy chirping of birds starting to wake up. The sky is grey on the horizon.

I move forward. The automatic gates have been forced, lifted from their tracks and shoved aside. I hurry up the driveway, watching the house all the time.

The front door is standing open. I feel like I'm going to throw up. I push it slowly with my foot. It creaks slightly, the noise sounding like a scream to my frayed nerves.

I enter the house. It's silent. It feels . . . empty. That feeling when you know nobody's home. A glass door to my right opens into the lounge. There's been a fight. Pillows strewn everywhere. Glass coffee table smashed. LCD television lying on the floor. I move down the passage, heading towards the kitchen.

I flick the light switch. The fluorescent strip light glints and glares on teracotta tiles covered in blood, pooling from behind the kitchen table. I step inside, gripping the table. Peer over the edge and almost collapse with relief.

It's not Becca.

A man, slightly overweight, sightless eyes staring up at the ceiling. Her boyfriend? Bullet holes in his forehead and chest. Double-tap. To make sure.

No one else in here. I climb the stairs, check through the first door. A spare room. Next one a study. That only leaves one possibility. I approach slowly, push the door open.

She's lying on the floor next to the bed, her face turned away from me. I don't move. I shake my head in denial. No. No, please no.

I take a step. Then another. Skirting the body, moving around to the other side.

I fall to my knees when I see the bullet hole in her forehead. A sound of horror escapes me, a howling moan of rage and pain, of hatred and loneliness.

Her eyes stare at me accusingly. *Look what you brought to my door.*

I gather her up, grip her to me. I rock back and forth. My mind has switched off. All that exists is this moment of pain and agony. I've lost her. I've lost them both. I will her to be alive. I find myself stopping suddenly, holding my breath, staring hard at her chest, convinced I'd felt a movement. Even though I know it's impossible, my mind keeps saying she's just sleeping. Watch. She'll get up. She'll move. It'll be all right.

But she doesn't.

And it isn't.

It takes a while for the sirens to filter through my grief. I look to the bedroom window, see the blue lights flashing outside.

I blink. Look around. Down at Becca. She looks angry.

You're always told people look peaceful in death. That was one of the first illusions to shatter when I became a cop. They don't look peaceful. Most look terrified. Or furious. Or surprised.

Rarely peaceful.

I hear footsteps on the stairs. I don't look up. Because I know once I do, once I leave this house, I've lost her forever.

'You!' someone shouts. 'Hands in the air!'

I finally look up. See a cop standing in the doorway with his gun pointed at me.

I shake my head. Not to say no, just to say this isn't me. I'm not the killer.

But my mouth isn't working properly. More police enter the room. More guns trained on me. Lots of screaming.

Shouted commands. Then hands on my shoulders, my arms, pulling me away. Throwing me to the floor. Someone's knee digging into my spine. My arms are yanked behind my back, cuffed tightly.

Then I'm hauled to my feet and dragged down the stairs. Outside now, where the sun has risen, shining on Becca's flowers. Glinting on the police cars.

An hour later I'm sitting in a dim interview room at Durban Station. The table is wooden, pitted and scarred. Someone has inscribed the words 'I'm innocent,' into the surface.

I stare numbly at my hands, waiting while a detective makes himself comfortable in the chair opposite me. He puts a file down, then a polystyrene cup of coffee.

'How do you want to do this?' he asks.

I look up. I don't recognize him. Old. Grey hair and a goatee.

'Do what?' I say dully.

'Well . . . do you want to just give us your reasons?' He smiles grimly. 'It's not as if you can plead not guilty.'

I shake my head in confusion. 'What?'

'Why did you kill her?'

I stare at him. 'I didn't kill her. I loved her.'

'But your gun was at the scene.'

'Of course it was. She called me. She said there was someone in the house. I drove over there with my gun and found her like that.'

'Your Glock?'

I nod.

'Yeah. I'm not talking about that gun. I mean your *other* gun.'

He fishes out a crime scene photograph. A Beretta lying on the bedroom carpet.

'The serial number marks it as your secondary SAPS firearm.'

I drag my eyes away from the photo. 'That's not possible. My gun is in my work locker.'

'No, it's not.' He taps the photograph. 'Your gun is in evidence. Your prints are all over it. It's been fired recently. And let's not kid ourselves. The post-mortem will show the bullets are from the same gun.'

I blink. How? How could this be? I have a brief moment of panic where I wonder if I really *did* do it. Maybe everything just got to me. The scenes at the mansion last night. The pressure. It all just got too much and I went on a rampage.

I shake my head. No. I couldn't. Not Becca. Never her.

'I need to call my lawyer,' I say.

The detective frowns with disappointment. 'You sure you don't want to just confess?'

'I didn't do it.'

He purses his lips and stares at me.

I lean forward, stare at him. 'I didn't do it.'

They throw me in a cell identical to the one at Hillcrest Station. I slump on the bench, staring at the wall.

That's it. Everyone I ever loved is gone. My body is saturated with . . . emptiness. Despair. Numbness.

I'm beaten. There's nothing I can do anymore. Why even bother trying? The world is rotten. Filled with black pus and evil, and if I ever thought I could do anything to hold back the tide I was deluding myself. I'm nothing more than a kid with a plastic bucket, trying to throw the water back into the ocean. A waste of time. A waste of space.

Maybe God had it right with the flood. Just wipe everyone out and start again. We deserve it.

'May I extend my condolences?'

My head snaps up. Lilith is standing against the far wall of the cell.

I blink, shake my head, wondering if I'm suffering halluci-
nations now.

She doesn't go away. Just stands there watching me, her
eyes filled with pity.

When I realise it's really her, that she's really standing in the
cell with me, I lunge forward and try to wrap my hands around
her throat.

I don't make it. About two feet away I hit some kind of
barrier. There's a flash of pain and I'm suddenly lying against
the far wall, my head ringing from where it hit the concrete.

'I will allow you that one,' says Lilith, 'because you're not
thinking clearly. But only the one.'

A guard walks past the cell. He glances in, his eyes skipping
over Lilith, not even seeing her. He looks at me sitting on the
floor, frowns, then moves on.

'What do you want?'

'I came to offer you a deal,' says Lilith.

'A deal?' I laugh. 'You killed my wife. Why the fuck would I
make a deal with you?'

'I did not kill your wife.'

'Of course you did. You threatened—'

'Indeed, I threatened. But I decided my aims would be
better served by staying on your good side. What happened
tonight wasn't us.'

'Then who?'

'Who do you think? How many people did you cross last
night? And before then? You stirred up a hornet's nest by
looking into the sin-eaters. The powers that be don't like their
personal absolution service tampered with.'

I look away.

'How did your gun come to be at the scene?' asks Lilith.

'It . . . it was in my locker. At the Division.'

'Yes. The Division. Where my kind cannot enter unless
invited. So that alone should tell you it wasn't me.' Lilith walks

forward and squats down in front of me. She reaches out. I
flinch away but she just strokes my cheek. 'I want to talk to
you about something. About your world.'

'My . . . ?'

'Your world. Dayside. I want you to honestly tell me, right
here and now, that humanity is doing a good job looking after
it. Looking after the people. Governments, corporations. You
think these . . . things . . . have your best interests at heart?'

'I never said they did.'

'Look around you. Your whole world is corrupt. From the
ground up. The oil that makes the world turn is corruption.
Power. Nepotism. Bribery. Look at your people. They are
murdering, raping, doing . . . unspeakable things, things we
"monsters" find just as repellent as you do. And they get away
with it. Those things you saw last night . . .' She shakes her
head angrily. 'Those people are animals. No – less than
animals. Animals do not kill for sexual thrills. Animals kill to
eat. Some of us "monsters" kill to eat. Is that not more honest
than what you saw last night?'

I shake my head, not liking that fact that she's making sense.
After last night, after today . . .

I look away. I agree with everything she's saying.

'Humanity is out of control, Tau. There are three hundred
and forty births every minute and only one hundred and
ninety deaths. You do the math. How long before the world
becomes unsustainable? For *all* of us? In this country *alone*
the population is set to double by 2050. That's only thirty-five
years away. And it's not as if you treat those extra people well.
There are one hundred and forty-four reported rapes every
day. *Reported.* That's not counting those that are too scared to
go to the police.'

'I know all this!' I say. 'I'm a cop. I see it every day.'

'I'm just trying to explain why I want to do what I want to
do. A clean slate, London. It's not as if the whole world would

be wiped out. There will be no flood. This time, I will be by
God's side. I will wake him up to what is wrong, wake him up
to the world's sins, and I will guide him in his judgements.
This time the victims – the innocents – will be spared.'

'What are you asking me for?'

'I want Jengo's soul.'

I stare at her.

'I was there last night, you know. I saw you.'

'What were you doing there? Were you at the party?'

Her eyes turn cold. 'Do not insult me. I was there for Stefan.
But since you killed him, Jengo's soul is my last means of finding the Sinwalker. I can't find any of the others. They've gone
into hiding.'

'I wonder why.'

She says nothing. Just stares at me.

'What will you do? If you find the Sinwalker?'

'Kill it. Let God have his sins back, his memories. His wrath
will be great, but as I say, I will be there to guide him. And the
first to feel his anger will be the angels who created this
Sinwalker in the first place. The angels who let the world
become what it is. The angels who lied to him.'

'You want to destroy the world.'

'No. I want those who deserve punishment to *face* punishment. All the killers who walk free. All the corrupt
millionaires who profit from the pain of others. All the war
criminals, the generals who bomb hospitals and schools,
who murder innocent children. All the politicians who steal
while those they are supposed to serve do not even have
running water.'

She pauses to let her words sink in.

'Your world – Dayside – operates under one supposed
absolute truth. The word of law. But your law has proven to be
corrupt. It can be bought. Evaded. I want to bring something
else to Dayside. I want to bring justice.'

Her words ring in my ears. I stare at her, trying to deny the vague flutterings of excitement in my stomach. Her words . . . her words mirror my own thoughts. What she says is true. There *is* no justice.

'How would you rule? What kind of governments would be set up?'

'We would not rule. Once all the guilty are washed away, Night and Day can co-exist. Nothing will change. Elections. Democracy. All that will remain. The only difference being that my people, the Nightsiders, will not be forced to hide. Your kind has had their chance, Tau, and they broke the world. Let us fix it.'

My mind goes back to last night. To the depravity. To the innocents slaughtered. To the laughter I heard echoing around the mansion, the sense of . . . entitlement they all gave off. Like what they were doing was their right.

I see Becca's face. They killed her. They killed her to protect their sick way of life. I clench my fists. And what of Cally? The law didn't help her. Her killers got away with it. One doesn't even know he's done anything wrong. Where's the justice there?

But . . . no. This is insane. Who am I to decide this?

Anyway, it would just be more of the same. Nothing would change. Oh, maybe for a hundred years or so. But then entropy would set in. Those in power would want more power. Because that's the problem. It's never enough.

'Here's the thing, Gideon Tau. We will win one way or the other. You must have noticed the changes in orisha behaviour. We – they – have decided that enough is enough. The war is coming. Whether it happens this week, or next year, or five years from now. It's on its way. And unless you have an army of soldiers trained the way you and your squad are trained, you're going to lose. At least this way, you have a way to *control* the change. To be *part* of it.'

She gets to her feet, paces to the bars and looks outside. 'I'm going to find the Sinwalker, London. I'd like your help. It will make things simpler. But if not, I'll just have to search for more sin-eaters. They're around somewhere. Overseas, maybe. Might take a bit longer, but I'll find them in the end.'

I say nothing, thinking back to all those Monday morning items in the files. About the fae moving, about the creatures up north coming out of their hiding places. We'd all noticed the orisha were acting odd.

But a war?

'I can offer you an incentive,' says Lilith.

I focus on her.

'I can offer you the killer of your daughter.'

My breath catches in my throat. 'What?' I whisper.

'My sin-eater. He will know who the killer is.'

'What good does that do me? He won't even know what he did.'

'Once I locate the Sinwalker, I will kill my sin-eater. I'll have no need of him anymore. The sins he took will return to those who committed them. Your daughter's murderer will know what he has done. And you will know who he is. All I ask is for you to bring me the ramanga's soul.'

She waits. I stare at the floor, my thoughts racing furiously. A way to get justice. A way to put her to rest. Properly.

'You owe these people nothing, Tau. Look at you. They have framed you for the murder of your ex-wife. If you do not help me you will end up in prison for the next twenty years.'

I swallow against the bile in my throat. If I'm in prison, Cally's killer will remain free, not even knowing what he did. And all those bastards in power will carry on with their sick games.

Fuck it. The world deserves to burn.

'Fine,' I say, locking eyes with her. 'I'll do it.'

18

The thing about making difficult decisions is that once they're made, it becomes a matter of justification. And once you've got the justification down, it becomes a matter of acceptance. Convincing yourself there really is no other choice.

Lilith gets me out of prison. She simply pushes the cell door open and we stroll out into the late afternoon. No one even looks in our direction. We're invisible to them.

Which also means the fact that my car is impounded at the rear of the police station means nothing. Lilith leans past a cop watching repeats of *Isidingo* (one of the worst soaps on television and the dog's favourite), grabs the keys from the security booth, and we drive straight out the parking lot without a single challenge.

'Stop here,' she says after we've put a bit of distance between us and the station. I pull over. She watches me. I stare back.

'We still have a deal?' she says.

'The ramanga's soul for my daughter's killer.'

She nods. 'When will you get it?'

I check my watch. It's four in the afternoon. 'I'll go in after five. Won't be as many people then. Should take me an hour or so. Say . . . seven?'

She nods, hands me a piece of paper with a number on it. 'Call me when it's done.' She gets out the car. 'Try not to let your conscience gain a voice. I know your type.'

'Where has my conscience gotten me up till now?' I ask.

'You keep your end of the deal, I'll keep mine.'

She stares hard at me, trying to see inside my head. She's still not sure whether to trust me or not. If I could open up my soul to let her see I would. I'm tired. Let them bring the world down. What comes after the fall can't be any worse that what we already have.

I find a coffee shop close to the Division headquarters to kill some time. I nurse a cappuccino, watching the customers come and go. I should feel something for these people. I know I should. How many will survive the changeover? How many will have a life in the new world?

I *should* feel something, but I don't. I'm all out of emotion. I don't have anything left. Besides, if they're innocent, if they're good people, they'll be fine.

Let them be responsible for their own lives.

After five I head out, joining the rush hour traffic then turning onto the Division off-ramp. Down beneath the road and onto the dirt track on the other side, the gates approaching fast.

I steel myself, grip the wheel tight, ready for the pain, for the wards to push me out.

They don't.

I breathe a sigh of relief as they swing open and I drive through. I was worried Ranson would have taken my clearance away. Hell, maybe no one even knows what happened.

I knock out the coded greeting on Eshu's silo. The door appears in the concrete and I hurry down the steps.

'Weren't you arrested?' he asks, glancing over his shoulder at me.

'Misunderstanding. All cleared up.'

'Oh.' He turns back to his computers, utterly disinterested.

'Who's still around?'

'Armitage. She's in her office.'

Shit. I make my way along the corridor outside Eshu's prison, considering my next move. I could hide away, wait for

Armitage to leave. That would be easiest. But I owe her more than that. I want to see her. To say goodbye.

I take the elevator up and knock on her door.

'Go away!'

'It's me.'

The door is yanked open and a surprised Armitage stands on the other side.

'London?'

She grabs me into a tight hug. I stiffen, surprised. Her cheek presses against mine. Her skin is dry, cold.

She pushes me to arm's length. 'I'm so sorry. Are you OK? What are you doing here? I heard they arrested you.' She pulls me into the office and closes the door. ''Course, I knew it was all rubbish. You kill Becca? Do me a favour. No one here believes it. No one.'

'Thanks.'

She goes to her desk and pours me a drink. I take it gratefully, gulp down the whisky.

'So . . . what happened? I've been on the phone to the Divisional Commander since I found out. Which, I'll have you know, wasn't that long ago. The buggers were trying to keep it under wraps.'

I shrug. 'Not sure. Think they found another suspect. An eyewitness or something.'

All lies, but by the time Armitage finds out the truth, it won't matter.

'The Divisional Commander?' I ask. 'What about the arrest warrants?'

'Told him it had nothing to do with me. That if the SSA carried on trying to arrest me I'd go to the press.'

'That worked?'

'For the moment. Not sure if he's in on the conspiracy or not. If he is, I'll be arrested first thing tomorrow. If he's not, reckon the SSA will try something more sneaky.'

'And me?'

'You're still wanted.' She frowns. 'Which makes it odd that they let you go tonight.'

'You know how it is,' I say quickly. 'Police and government agencies never communicate. The locals won't know anything about the SSA situation yet.'

'I suppose.'

'Anything in the press?' I ask, hoping to distract her. 'About last night?'

She grabs a newspaper from her desk and tosses it to me. There's a picture of the manor house burning, flames reaching up against the night sky. The headline reads, 'Manor Inferno'.

I scan the article. Something about an electrical fault. A few fatalities, their bodies burned beyond recognition.

I toss the newspaper back onto her desk. I hadn't really been expecting anything else.

'I've been thinking,' says Armitage. 'This case . . . it's getting messy. These people – they'll do anything to protect their secrets. I wouldn't be surprised if this whole division gets closed down. Either that or we get taken out. No investigators, no investigation.'

'So – what? You saying we should give up?'

'Christ, no! I was murdered because of this case. You don't think they'll just find another house to throw their little parties?'

'So what are you suggesting?'

'We might need to take it off the books. We try and put some names to the faces we saw outside the house. When they took their masks off.' She sighs and rubs her face. 'We might have to target them one by one, see if we can pin specific crimes onto them. Maybe put them under surveillance. Catch them when they try to do it again.'

'You're talking serious operational manpower there.'

'I know.'

'And you think we can do that on the down-low?'

She shrugs. 'What other choice do we have? Slow and steady wins the race. As long as we catch them. As long as we stop them killing again, who cares how long it takes?'

'I suppose.'

She gets to her feet. 'I want a full report on my desk first thing in the morning. Let's get cracking on these names, eh? Let's focus on the SSA guy. What was his name? Dillon? If we can find something on him, we get them off our backs.'

I get to my feet, head to the door. I hesitate, turn back. 'Armitage?'

'What is it, pet?'

'Just ... see you round, OK?'

She waves me away. 'Aye. See you round. First thing tomorrow.'

I leave her office and close the door behind me. First thing tomorrow? I don't know what the world will look like first thing tomorrow.

It's for the best, says a voice in my head.

Here's the thing with the Delphic Division evidence room. It's filled with insanely dangerous occult artefacts: grimoires, hoodoo spells, desiccated Indian magi, Cthulhu demi-gods trapped within tetrahedron prisms, that kind of stuff.

Which means it's not really open to the likes of me. Only the higher ups have access. I'm not even talking about Armitage here. If she wants to get into the room she has to fill out Requisition Permission Forms, in triplicate, which then have to be approved by someone even higher up than her.

In our case, that means Ranson.

His office is on the top floor, in the biggest room of the building. His door is always locked, but right now I don't have time to worry about that.

I insert a screwdriver between the doorjamb and the lock,

putting all my weight behind it. The lock gives with a satisfying crack and the door flies open.

I glance around the corridor to make sure no one has seen me, then slip inside and push the door closed again. It won't stay shut so I grab his desk chair and push it up against the door to keep it in place.

I pause and look around. It's five times the size of Armitage's office, decked out with all the modern stylings. A glass-topped desk with chrome legs. A single painting on the wall covered with Impressionist swirlings, teal and blue, like the colours they use in movie posters. Metal book shelves with books arranged by size. An expensive looking filing cabinet made from brushed aluminum.

I head around his desk and open the top drawer. Locked. Nothing my trusty screwdriver can't deal with.

The drawer reveals lots of official forms. Nothing interesting. The next drawer is filled with the usual office detritus that collects over the years. Paperclips, rubber bands, pens and post-it notes. The third one down is filled with car magazines.

I check the other side of the desk. Nothing at all in the top two. And stationery supplies in the bottom one. I slam it shut in frustration and hear the sound of something metal sliding around inside. I frown, pull it open again and look beneath the envelopes.

There's a small key hidden there. I take it out and examine it. It looks like a safe key.

I look around. Only one place to hide a safe in here.

I lift the painting away from the wall.

Nothing.

I swear and let the painting drop back into place. A floor safe? Could be. I move slowly around the room, testing the carpet to see if it lifts up anywhere. No luck. It's stapled down all around the wall.

That only leaves the filing cabinet.

I pull the top two drawers open. Personnel reports. I resist the urge to look for mine. It won't be complimentary.

I try the bottom drawer and it slides slowly open to reveal that it's been modified to hold a small gun safe. I insert the key and open the door. A Glock firearm and suppressor sit next to a key ring filled with keys, some money, and Ranson's passport.

I take the gun and the keys, screwing the suppressor onto the front of the barrel. My guns are still with the police. Lilith hadn't bothered to get those back for me.

I'm closing the filing cabinet drawer when I hear a scraping sound from behind me. I turn around to find Ranson trying to get into the office, his head half-through the door, peering down in puzzlement at the chair stopping his door from opening.

He throws his weight behind the door, shoving it open, and enters the office.

That's when he spots me.

His eyes go wide. He tries to duck back into the corridor but I'm there in three strides. I hit him in the face with the butt of the gun and shove the door closed. He drops to his knees, blood dripping into his expensive carpet.

'Christ, but that felt good,' I say, ramming the chair back against the door. 'You have *no* idea how long I've wanted to do that.'

'Have you lost your mind?' he shouts, his hand pressed against the wound.

I grab him by the arm, try to pull him up. He jerks away, then falls back with a cry of pain. I frown, put my hand around the back of his neck and drag him to one of the two chairs in front of the desk. He cries out again as I do this. He's cradling his right arm, not even bothering with the cut over his eye.

I grab his jacket, pull it back over his shoulder. He tries to fight me but I push the gun against his head.

'Seriously, Ranson. You do not want to fuck with me today.'

He stops resisting. I pull the jacket off his arms, let it fall back over the chair.

'Unbutton your shirt.'

Ranson glares at me, but he does as he's told.

'Arms out.'

He pulls his arms out of his shirt sleeve. There's a transparent bandage over his upper arm. I can see a wound beneath it, a line of red that has been stitched together.

A bullet wound.

I take a step back, realization dawning. 'You were there,' I whisper. It was him. The one I shot in the arm. He was the one holding the girl down.

'Yes, I was there, you fucking imbecile. Do you have any idea how much damage you've done?'

The last pieces slot into place. It was Ranson who deleted the sin-eater references from GHOST. Ranson who turned the SSA onto us. Probably on the instructions of Stefan.

I can't believe it. How could I have worked under someone for so long and not know?

I look at the keys I took from his safe. 'One of these opens our gun lockers.'

He doesn't say anything, just stares at me defiantly.

'You killed Becca.'

I barely recognize my voice. It's a hoarse growl. I grab him by the neck, pushing the gun against his head. For the first time I see fear in his eyes.

'No! Not me. I just got the gun. Dillon killed her. The SSA guy. I swear it!'

I hit him in the head with the gun. He squeals and tries to shield himself but I keep hitting him. Blood flows over my hands, down his face. He moans, begs me to stop. It's only with a supreme force of will that I do.

He looks at me in a daze. His left eye is ruptured. A flap of skin hangs over his forehead like a fringe of hair.

'You . . . don't know what you're doing,' he mumbles. 'I . . . have friends. Powerful friends. They're going to catch you. They're going to hunt you down—'

I punch him in the mouth as hard as I can. His teeth tear into my knuckles. He falls to the floor, moaning, cradling his jaw.

I stare down at him, my breath coming in great heaving gasps. At the mess of his face.

I did that. I'm becoming just like them.

No. Not like them. I'm getting justice for all the people they've fucked over. That's what I'm doing.

A tiny voice in my head argues with me. That's not for you to decide, it whispers. But I shake it off. It is. It's for me to decide when this conspiracy spreads to judges and politicians, to those who are supposed to protect the innocent.

I hold out the keys to him. 'Which one opens the evidence room?' He doesn't answer. I slap him. 'Which one?'

He points weakly at an intricately cut key. 'Wuh . . . won't do any guh-good.'

'Why?'

'Eye scan. Bio . . . Biometrics.'

I stare at him.

There's a line here.

If I cross this point there's no going back. I mean, after last night, there's really no going back anyway, but this . . . it's a *personal* line in the sand. If I do this, then it's over for me. I have no moral high ground anymore.

I stare at Ranson, crying and threatening me with alternating breaths. This . . . parasite. This murderer. The things he's done. The things he's done and doesn't even remember!

This is where Lilith's justice comes in. No one else will do what has to be done. It's down to me.

I shoot him in the chest. He jerks, then lies still. I look around on his desk and find a letter opener, then I crouch down next to his body, push his head to the side so his good eye is staring at me.

Then I get to work.

The evidence room is down one of the corridors that branch off from the Hub. The Hub itself is covered by Eshu's cameras, so I know as soon as I make a move I've got to be quick. Eshu's sort of a friend, but even he'll be wondering why I'm making my way towards the Evidence Room when I'm not supposed to be able to gain access.

I consider writing a note and leaving it on my desk. Because, let's face it, this is the last time I'll be stepping foot inside Delphic Division. What with me murdering my boss and everything. But I decide against it. What's the point? Everyone will make up their own minds anyway.

I'm sad about Armitage, though. I want to explain everything to her, but I have no idea how to make her understand.

I don't think anyone will understand.

I'm stalling.

When I realise that I make a move, head out of the office and into the Hub. No hesitation. Straight into the corridor that leads to the evidence room. I use my body to block the door and hold Ranson's eyeball against the sensor. A panel opens up and I use the key to unlock the door.

I step inside and close the door behind me. A large room with floor-to-ceiling metal shelving recedes into the distance, all of them filled with neatly labelled plastic containers. I scan the ceiling. Cameras in each of the corners. Shit. Have to move fast. I check the closest boxes, moving by date until I find our case number. I cut the cable ties and unclip the lid.

The box is filled with transparent bags. The first hold Jengo and Caitlyn Long's clothing. Another bag holds her personal appointment diary. Another her handbag. But no soul.

I frown. Where else would Armitage put it? I check the box behind it. It's also labelled with our case number. I cut the ties and pull the lid off.

Miscellaneous effects. The ramanga's ID book. His wallet.

And, at the very bottom, a small plastic box.

I pick it up and shake it. What sounds like a marble rattles around inside. I check it just to make sure. A round ball, smaller than Armitage's soul had been. This one is a muddy brown colour.

I smile grimly, excitement and hope stirring to sluggish life.

I drop Jengo's soul into my hand and close up the boxes. I walk calmly to the door. Nearly there. Nearly clear.

I pull the door open.

Armitage is standing in the corridor, five paces away. Her hands sunk into the pockets of her old mac.

I freeze, my hand resting on the door. I search her face, trying to read her, see what she knows.

She looks . . . puzzled.

'Hello there, love,' she says.

'Armitage.'

A pause.

'Everything all right?'

I nod.

She smiles kindly. 'It's just . . . you're acting a bit weird, like.'

I straighten up. 'Weird? Armitage, I've just witnessed people getting murdered, violated – cut into pieces. Why the fuck *wouldn't* I be acting weird?'

She nods calmly. 'Right you are.' She glances at the ceiling. A slight frown appears, as if she's seen something up there she doesn't like.

'What are you doing down here?'

'Just . . . picking something up.'

'How are you doing that? We don't have access.'

'Ranson. He . . . gave me access.'

She nods again, then sighs and takes a step forward. I shift slightly, ready for an attack. Armitage stops and frowns.

'Is that blood?' Steel in her voice now.

I look down. My jacket has opened slightly. Ranson's blood is all over my shirt.

'Oh, London. What have you done?'

I sigh. 'Ranson was there.'

'Where?'

'At the manor. Last night. I saw him. He's the one who set the SSA after us. He deleted the sin-eater entries in GHOST. He . . . he set me up, Armitage. He . . .' I swallow past the huge lump or rage in my throat. 'He's the one who got Becca killed.'

Her face tightens with shock. 'You sure about that?'

I nod.

'Where's Ranson now?'

I shake my head slightly.

'London?'

'He's . . . he's dead. I killed him.'

Armitage's shoulders slump. She looks at me sadly. 'London. You stupid bloody bugger. That's murder.'

'It's not murder. It's justice.'

'That's not for you to decide!' she shouts, suddenly furious. 'We're the *police*, Tau. We don't hand out death sentences. We catch the bad guys and let the courts decide.'

I shout back. 'Are you insane! The *courts*? Most of the judiciary were at that manor last night! They don't prosecute the crooks. They *are* the fucking crooks. The inmates control the asylum, Armitage. There *is* no justice anymore. Not after what we saw last night.'

'So . . . what? You're going to decide, are you? Judge, jury, executioner?'

'Why not? I'm a good man. I know what's right and wrong.'

'No. You don't! You just murdered someone! You know what's right and wrong according to *you*. I might think differently. So might Parker. Or Russells. That's what the courts are there for.'

'The courts are compromised,' I say wearily.

'Fine. Whatever.'

She doesn't move.

'Can I go now?' I ask.

'That depends on what you're hiding behind your back.'

I sigh. There's still a chance. A possibility, however slim, that I can make her understand. 'Lilith got me out of prison.'

'Lilith?' She frowns sceptically, like she's trying to decide if I've gone mad.

'She's going to tell me who Cally's killer is. Get the information from her sin-eater.'

'What's the point? He still won't know what he did.'

'He will. She promised to . . .' I hesitate, realizing how terrible it all sounds. Then I straighten up. 'She promised to kill him. So all his sins return to the owners.'

'But . . . why would she do that? She needs him to find this first sin.'

'She doesn't. Not anymore.'

She sags slightly, compassion clear on her face. 'London,' she says softly. 'What have you done? Just tell me, lad.'

'Let me pass, Armitage. I don't want us to fight.'

'You know I can't.'

And then she comes for me. It's so unexpected I take a moment to react. This woman in her fifties sprinting towards me, her eyes dark with anger. I duck back into the evidence room, throw my weight behind the door.

She smashes into it before I can get it closed. There's a gap of about twenty centimetres between us. I grit my teeth and push. The gap starts to narrow.

There's a lurch and the door slams into my head. I cry out in pain, drop the box containing Jengo's soul. It clatters onto the tiles, clearly visible from the other side of the door. I swear, try to stretch out my foot to pull it back towards me. Armitage uses the distraction to push the door wider.

I take my weight off the door, yanking it open. Armitage stumbles inside, moving past me and righting herself against the metal shelves. I hook my foot around the little plastic box, kick it out into the passage, then lunge through the door and pull it shut, the automatic locks coming into play.

Armitage hits the other side.

'London, don't do this!'

I slide down the door onto my backside. She's banging on the door. Eshu will spot her soon. I need to move.

I push myself to my feet, pick up Jengo's soul, and make my way back along the corridor. I move through the hub straight into the entrance foyer. There's a security guard on duty. He nods at me. I nod back, holding the jacket closed across my blood-stained shirt.

Out into the warm evening air. As soon as I'm out of sight of the doors I sprint around the side of the building and head for the underground garage, leaping down the steps and into my Land Rover.

Up the ramp with a screech of tyres and heading towards the gates. They swing open and I release a breath I hadn't known I was holding. Out and down under the freeway, then loop up and around, feeding back into the traffic.

I take a shaky breath, pat my pocket where Jengo's soul rests.

The first part is done.

19

I meet Lilith outside a KFC on Victoria Street. She's sitting at an outside table that's been cemented into the sidewalk, watching the queue that snakes out the door and onto the sidewalk. There's an amused expression on her face.

I sit down opposite her. 'What's so funny?'

'That lot. All they're bothered about is filling their stomachs. I can look into each and every one of their minds and there's absolutely nothing there beyond attaining their next meal.' She shifts her dark gaze to me. 'I envy that.'

I frown. 'Why? That's not living. It's just . . . surviving. People with no goals. No ambition.'

She tuts at me. 'So judgemental, Gideon. Just because they are forced into survival mode does not mean they are not ambitious. It means they do not have the means to attain their ambition.'

'Blame the government, then.'

'There are any number of people to blame. Parents, teachers, themselves.' She shrugs. 'After tonight it will not matter.'

'What will happen to them?'

'It depends on whether they are good people or not. That's what everything will come down to. One simple question. Are you a good person, or are you not.'

I stare at her, then shift my gaze to the queue. Laughter. A couple arguing about something. A drunk staggering, leaning against the person in front of him. A little kid asking about the toy that comes with her kid's meal.

For the first time since Lilith's arrival in my jail cell I have second thoughts. What I'm doing ... there's nothing to compare it to, no way of knowing what comes after. With my actions I'm changing the entire world.

But the thing is, I'll take the blame. I'll stand up and say it was me, for better or worse. I'll own my actions. Which, admittedly, will be small comfort to those who don't come through it in one piece.

To be honest, I don't think *I'll* come through it in once piece. Not after I get my hands on Cally's killer.

Thinking of Cally makes me straighten up, my doubts forgotten. She's why I'm doing this. I reach into my pocket and take out the plastic box, lay it on the table between us.

Lilith stares at it hungrily. She reaches into her shirt pocket and takes out a folded piece of paper. She slides it over to me.

I can see her neat, cursive writing through the paper. I reach out. My hand is shaking. My fingers rest on it and I pull it towards me. Lilith does the same with Jengo's soul.

I open the paper and smooth it out. My heart is hammering in my chest. My mouth is dry.

My eyes skim over the words. I force myself to read them again and again.

Timothy Evans. 5 Hunter Crescent, Morningside.

My eyes burn as I stare at the name and address. For three years I've been after this guy. Morningside? That's only a few kays from where I'm sitting now. I've probably driven past the fucker on my way to work.

'Is it worth it?' Lilith asks.

'I don't know.' I drag my eyes away from the paper. 'How will I know? When he has his memories back?'

'I'll text you when I've found the Sinwalker. When I no longer need my sin-eater.'

I nod, get to my feet. I look down at her. 'You'll keep your word? Only people who ... deserve it?' I realise how stupid and naive this sounds as soon as I say it. I think back to that night in the car, when I tricked them into driving into the wards around Delphic Division. I'd been thinking that night about how naive I was for trusting Kincaid. Am I doing it again?

She laughs. 'Oh yes, Gideon. Only people on the naughty list will be judged.'

I shake my head. Hesitate. A feeling of unease building.

'On you go then,' she says. 'Go and get your revenge. It's what you've always wanted, isn't it?'

It is. Of course it is. I need to get this person. He has to be punished. Not just him, but all those people at the manor. All the people just like them.

I return to my car. By the time I climb inside Lilith has vanished.

Timothy Evans' place is utterly nondescript. A single-storey, three bedroom house that needs a coat of paint. Kids' toys litter a slightly overgrown lawn.

I stare at these toys from where I'm parked across the street. I'd never even entertained the thought that Cally's killer would have children of his own. How could anyone with his own kids do something like that? It doesn't make sense to me.

I open the glove compartment and take out a creased photograph of Cally. It was taken on the esplanade when she was trying to learn how to roller blade. She's soaring past the camera as I take the picture, her eyes wide with fear and exhilaration, screaming with delight.

She was dead five days after the photograph was taken.

I stare at her, study every plane of her face, stoking the fury, feeling the rage rising inside me like a tide of flame, burning through my veins.

A few minutes later a minivan pulls up outside the house. An Alsatian appears at the gate, barking and wagging its tail.

The electric gate slides open and the van drives in, stopping in front of the garage.

I lean forward, watching as two kids, a girl and a boy, hop out and run after the dog. A woman climbs out the passenger side, calling to the kids as she unlocks the front door and heads inside.

The kids and the dog follow her.

And then Timothy Evans climbs out from behind the wheel.

I stare at him, burning every detail of his face into my mind. He's about 5'8", balding, a pale blue golf shirt tucked into his jeans.

He looks utterly . . . normal.

I'd only ever seen the briefest glimpse of him, and he'd been wearing a cap at the time. But still. I didn't expect him to look like . . . like a school teacher.

I should know better by now, especially after the last few days. Evil can wear the blandest of faces.

He grabs some grocery bags from the back of the car and carries them into the house, closing the door behind him. I get quickly out of the car, wanting to make my move while the dog is inside the house. I climb over the gate, hurry to the front door. I listen, can't hear anything.

I carefully turn the handle and open the door a crack. I peer inside. A passage ends at the kitchen before turning to the left. The sounds of the Cartoon Network blast suddenly from the right. The kids are occupied. Mum and dad in the kitchen.

I enter the house, pause and peer into the lounge. The kids are seated directly below a massive LCD screen, utterly transfixed.

I move quietly past the door, heading towards the left turn in the passage. The kitchen door is wide open. I can hear plates clinking, the low murmur of conversation. The wife appears, her hand on the door, glancing over her shoulder as Evans says something to her.

I freeze, halfway between the kitchen and the front door.

'What?' the woman says. She waits. Then her hand leaves

the door and she turns back into the kitchen. 'Why did you promise them pizza? They had it yesterday.'

I dart past the door, left. Doors open to either side. Kids' rooms, bathroom, and . . . Ah. An office. Perfect. He'll either come here or the bathroom when the memories hit. I'm betting on it being here.

I sit in the darkness for the next four hours. I listen to the family sounds echoing through the house, kids squabbling, complaining about having to go to bed, being ordered to brush their teeth, that kind of thing. All the sounds a normal family makes.

That will all change. Because they aren't a normal family. Their father is a murderer and he's going to face his punishment before the night is out.

I try my hardest not to think about how it will affect the kids. They're not my problem. It's not my fault their dad is a psycho.

I won't be deflected. It's too late for second thoughts, anyway. Everything has been set in motion. When the sun rises tomorrow, the world it looks upon will be partially my creation.

How many will hate me? How many will curse my name? Will I be turned into some kind of demon? The Lucifer of humanity? The man who sold out the human race?

At some point while I'm waiting, my phone beeps with a Push news notification. I quickly mute the sound, but my eye is caught by the alert. It's a news headline about some street fights going on over at Albert Park. Nothing new there, it's a haven for users and pushers. But the reports say these fights are unusually violent. Over twenty people have died already.

During the next hour, more notifications come in. I keep my phone out, staring at the screen. Street riots, looting. Lovers' quarrels that turn violent. Family murders. The incidents cover the whole city, slowly getting worse and worse. Fires. Buildings being set alight. Flash mobs protesting God knows what. It's as if Durban has gone to war.

I feel a heavy knot in my stomach but I try to ignore it. This has nothing to do with me.

I switch my phone off and lean my head back against the wall. Nothing to do with me.

At about midnight, I hear a low moan. My heart quickens. I take the Glock out and lay it across my lap. I stretch my legs, twist my neck from side to side to loosen my muscles.

The office door swings open, the light from the hall spilling inside. Evans lurches in and shuts the door behind him. He staggers towards the desk, slumps into the chair. His face is hidden behind his hands. He's rocking back and forth, making a high-pitched keening sound.

I stare at him, enjoying his pain.

I get quietly to my feet. Pad across the carpet and flick the desk lamp on. White light floods the room. Evans jerks back, staring at me with wide, tear-filled eyes.

'W-who . . . who—'

I point the gun at him. 'How are the memories, Tim? Feeling good about what you did?'

'Wha— what? How . . . who told . . . ?'

I take the picture of Cally out of my pocket and lay it on the table. He looks at it and jerks away as if it's poisonous.

'Yes. You remember her, don't you?' My voice is shaking. 'She was my daughter, Evans. My *daughter.*'

'You . . . you don't understand. I didn't want to do it. I had no choice!'

'Funny how they all say that. The paedos. The murderers. The rapists.'

'No. You don't get it. I . . . I really had no choice. They said they'd kill my kids if I didn't . . . didn't do it.'

I frown. I hear the distant sound of a chopper outside.

Through the office window I catch a glimpse of a spotlight shining down from the sky, dancing across some distant hot spot.

The voice in my head is telling me to just kill him. To put a bullet through his brain. This is what you wanted! Three years you've been waiting for this. Three years. Just do it. End him!

But another voice, one I haven't heard since before the Manor house, is telling me to wait. This isn't making sense. It's not how I thought it would be.

'*Who* said they'd kill your kids?'

The tears stream down his face. 'I can't tell you. You wouldn't believe me.'

'Try me.'

'I *can't.*'

I push the suppressor into his temple, twisting it against his skin. 'Tell. Me.'

'The monsters! The . . . *things* . . . from my dreams! They're real, you see.' He giggles and cries at the same time, looking down at Cally in the photograph. He reaches out to touch it and I snatch it away. 'The monsters under the bed are real. *They* made me do it.'

I shake my head in confusion. 'What are you saying? That these . . . *creatures* made you murder those kids? My daughter?'

His head jerks up and he looks at me in shock. 'Murder? What are you talking about?'

'You know what I'm talking about. You killed the kids at the lodge.'

'We didn't kill them.' He sounds astonished. 'They're still alive. At least . . . I think they are.'

I stare at him. His words don't make any sense. My whole body reacts, starts shivering. My head pounds. I can hear a fierce wind whistling in my ears.

'What are you talking about? The blood . . .'

His face clouds. 'That was Simmons. The other guy. They made me work with him. He was sick. He thought we were doing that. Taking the kids there to . . . to murder them. It's what he wanted to do. I wasn't there. I'd left the room to let the sin-eater in. When I came back, he'd . . . already started.'

I shake my head. 'No. You killed them all. *That's* why the blood was there.'

'No! I *saved* them. Saved your daughter. When I got back Simmons was about to kill her. I pulled her away. He . . . came after her . . . after me.' He shakes his head in disbelief. 'Then a . . . a hole opened up. In the air. And these . . . *things* came through. They . . . said they were faeries. They had these . . . white faces. Long, like a fox. Black eyes.' He shivers as the memories come back to him. '*They* took your daughter. And the other kids. Stopped the bleeding. Healed them. Took them through the hole.' He reaches up, touches the side of his head. 'Then the sin-eater took my memory. That was the only way I'd do it, you see. They gave me a list of names. Threatened me. But I'd only do it if I didn't remember.'

My gun drops to my side. 'You're really saying they're still alive?' My voice is a whisper.

He nods. 'I asked those . . . things why they wanted them and they said something about needing their belief.'

I stagger backwards, bang up against the wall. The room is swimming, tilting crazily. The blood is pounding in my ears. Evans is talking, but I can't hear a word he's saying above the rushing sound.

Cally is alive?

Is that possible?

Can it be?

All this time she's been alive, somewhere in the Nightside? Kidnapped by . . . by the *fae*?

She's not *dead*?

I straighten up.

She's not dead.

My whole life suddenly shifts focus, coalesces into a bright, burning pinpoint. Everything changes. Three years of being driven by revenge, by grief, by loss. They all drop away, sloughing off me like a decaying snake skin. I find myself standing taller, my mind clearing.

Which is when I realise what I've done.

'What's happening outside?' I demand.

Evans glances out the window. 'It's crazy. Everything's gone to shit. Riots, fights, people killing each other.' He shakes his head. 'It's . . . it's like something out of a movie. When they get infected by a virus or something.'

Lilith.

Fuck. It has to be related to the first sin. She's found the Sinwalker. But . . . why are the sins leaking out? If she killed the Sinwalker like she said she would, all the sins would return to God. What's going on now . . . it's what would happen if the Sinwalker was woken up. Not killed. God's sins are leaking out into the world, infecting people. Just like Stefan said.

Which means . . . which means she lied to me about what would happen. There is no process here. No control. God's sins are infecting *everyone*, turning them crazy. Whether they're good or bad.

She betrayed me.

I point my gun at Evans. He flinches back, hands coming up to shield his face.

'Give me your passport and your ID book.'

He opens a drawer and fishes around, finally handing me his documents. I put them in my back pocket.

'What was the creature's name? The one that took my daughter.'

'I can't remember. But I don't think he was one of them. The fae. He looked . . . different.'

'I don't care! I just want his name!'

He closes his eyes, thinking.

'Come on, Evans. I'm not playing around.'

His eyes snap open. 'The Marquis! The others called him the Marquis.'

The Marquis? I've never heard of him. But still, someone will know who he is. Someone will know how to find him.

I take my phone out and dial Armitage's number.

She answers on the second ring.

'You are in so much trouble, lad.'

'Armitage. Listen to me. I think I've made a huge mistake.'

'You're bloody right you have!'

'Armitage, just shut up and listen. The riots? That's Lilith. She's waking up the Sinwalker. God's sins are leaking out, infecting everyone.'

'No shit, Sherlock. Because you gave her the ramanga's soul.'

'I know that! I want to fix this. Are you still in the evidence room?'

'No. Eshu let me out.'

'Meet me outside Durban Museum. Soon as you can. And Armitage – don't tell the others. I can fix this.'

I hang up. Evans is watching me. 'You're going to jail, Evans. You know that, right?'

He doesn't say anything.

'You can't go anywhere. And if you run, I'll hunt you down myself and I will slice your skin from your body. Understand?'

He swallows nervously. Nods.

'Open the window.'

He turns and unlocks the window, pushing it wide. I put my hand onto the frame, then pause. I turn and I hit Evans as hard as I can. Using every bit of the grief and horror and hatred that I've been carrying around with me for the past three years.

He hits the floor and doesn't move.

I hop out the window, run through the garden and climb over the high wall into the street beyond. I can smell smoke in the air. I turn towards the city and see an apocalyptic glow illuminating the undersides of the clouds from one side of the horizon to the other.

Durban is burning.

20

The apocalypse has come to Durban.

I want to say something cynical, like, I don't really notice the difference, but that would be a lie.

There's a roof of darkness smothering the city, thick columns of smoke that connect the sky with trouble spots on the ground. Hundreds of cars have been set on fire, the fierce heat shattering shop windows, setting off alarms. The stench of burning tyres is thick and cloying.

Shops have been utterly destroyed, looters grabbing what they can and making off with their spoils, ruining livelihoods without a second thought. As I drive along Church Street I have to brake to avoid ploughing into a mob of about thirty people running with flat screen televisions, Blu Ray and DVD players. They're met by another mob coming from the opposite direction, this one wielding knobkerries, knives, and guns. The two forces meet with screams and jeers. Gunfire rings out. The televisions become weapons, thrown at the enemy.

I turn down a side street to avoid the fight. The police radio is going crazy. Dispatch issuing increasingly panicked requests for backup along with updates on the worse-hit areas. Although, from the sounds of it, the whole city is under attack.

The mobs come after me a few times, forcing me to fire shots at their feet and drive through the gap this creates. I don't have time to stop and do anything more. I have to track Lilith down and stop her. I have to make amends.

My thoughts are going in crazy circles. From thinking about what I've done to thinking about Cally. She's still alive somewhere. There's still a chance to get her back. To save her.

The excitement and joy I feel at this is utterly at odds with what is happening, with Becca's death. My emotions are all over the place, a flurry of conflicting feelings.

I eventually make it to my destination. Aliwal Street. It's deserted, unlike the rest of the city. The power is out, the street shrouded in darkness. I slow down, my headlights picking out a stray cat as it runs across the road.

When I get to the museum I turn onto the kerb so the lights shine up towards the building. Armitage is sitting on the steps, a shotgun resting across her lap. The dog is sitting next to her. Armitage raises her hand to shade her eyes from the glare. I dim my lights and get out.

Armitage gets to her feet, the shotgun held in both hands. Is that for me?

'The fuck have you done, London?' calls the dog.

I ignore him, lock eyes with Armitage. I can see the betrayal there, the sense of hurt my actions have brought.

'Would it make a difference if I said I'm sorry?'

'Not really, no.'

'I am. Sorry, I mean. Lilith . . . she got me at a low point. I . . . She made *sense*, Armitage. A fresh start. Where the guilty are punished.'

She shakes her head sadly. 'That's a child's dream.'

'Is that what you think? Then why are we doing this? What's the point of . . . *us*?"

'You don't know?' She sounds surprised. 'We do this to protect the little people. To protect all those who can't protect themselves.'

'But that's impossible! We fail all the time.'

'But we have to keep *trying*. That's the whole point. If we don't, the bad guys win. That's what our job *is*. Trying to hold

back the tide. We'll never turn it completely. We can't. We just
have to hold it back enough so everyone doesn't drown.'

She's right. We can't cure the world's ills. But we protect
our people as best we can. From the corrupt officials, the dirty
cops, the crooks, the orisha who think we're their playthings,
the gods who think we're stupid meat puppets here for their
own amusement.

That's what we can do.

I forgot that. Forgot the one belief I told myself I still had
after Cally went missing. Belief in justice.

Not the law. The law fails. Every day of my life I see people
get away with crime. Killers walk free. Government ministers
ignore right and wrong, hand out tenders to friends so they
can get huge backhanders, and fuck the poor who are dying
of starvation. I see the rich cut corners whenever they feel like
it, using money to buy a life not earned. Those who, as soon
as their bank balances hit a certain number of zeroes, think
the law doesn't apply to them anymore.

And the shitty thing is, they're right. It doesn't. Money buys
you everything, the law included.

Money can't buy you love? Yeah it fuckin' can. And it can
buy you people to hide the body when it all goes to shit.

The law can be bribed. The law can be ignored. The law is
not equal.

But *justice* . . . justice is inside. Justice is what kept me going.
The idea that even if the world goes to shit, I can still do what
I believe is right.

I forgot that.

I can hear the sounds of distant gunfire. Voices raised in
anger. And, oddly, singing. It sounds like some group is
toy-toying. Probably facing off against a gang of looters. Or
facing off against the police. Who knows anymore.

'The thing is . . . I may have put an RFID chip on the box
before I gave it to Lilith.'

Armitage looks at me, eyes wide. 'What?' I can hear the sudden hope in her voice. 'You mean this was some kind of plan? You did this so she would lead us to the Sinwalker?'

I hesitate. How easy to say yes. That I planned everything all along. Problem is, she won't believe me. Sure, she might believe me *now*, but tomorrow morning? She'll wake up and realise the truth.

I planted the chip as an insurance policy. Plain and simple. Just in case anything went wrong. In case she double-crossed me.

Not because I didn't plan on going ahead with it.

Armitage sees the truth in my face. Her eyes go flat and she makes a move to my car. 'Let's go then,' she says brusquely.

The dog saunters past. 'You're an idiot, London. You know that?'

'Well, where were you? You're supposed to be my guide! You're supposed to help me. All you do is lick your balls and drink sherry.'

He squints at me before he jumps into the car. 'You say that like it's a bad thing.'

Armitage climbs into the passenger seat. 'He's right, you know. You are a bloody idiot.'

Yeah, that's becoming very clear.

I drive while Armitage uses my cell phone to track the signal. The location marker is taking us out of Durban, heading inland back towards Hillcrest.

But before we even hit Pinetown the marker switches direction, pointing towards the Pavillion shopping mall.

I take the Spine Road off-ramp and follow it around the perimeter of the huge structure. The road curves up, eventually bringing us up onto the rooftop parking. There are lights everywhere, pubs, sports shops, coffee houses, but all of them barricaded and closed off. Word of the Durban riots has spread.

The place is deserted, except for a group of about ten mini-bus taxis pulled into a circle at the far side of the parking lot. The drivers stare at us suspiciously. I look around. Not a bad place to ride out the storm.

'Over there,' says Armitage, pointing towards the entrance of the mall, a huge, glass tower covered with twinkling fairy lights. I drive slowly forward. I can see the distant fires of Durban beyond the tower, a fiery orange glow that lights up the horizon.

I remember bringing Cally here one Christmas for late night shopping. She wouldn't even let us go inside. She just wanted to watch the fairy lights. They don't look like they belong here now. Not tonight.

The warm wind gusts against my face as I get out the car. The breeze constantly changes directions, sneaking up on all sides like a mischievous sprite. Armitage holds the cell phone up as we approach the entrance. She stops and bends down, straightening up with something in her hand. I feel my stomach sink.

It's the box.

Armitage opens it and holds it in the air. Empty.

Nobody says a thing. We climb back into the car, drive out of the parking lot and head back towards Durban. How the hell are we going to find Lilith now?

The riots are getting worse. There are police on the streets in riot gear, trying to cordon off areas and kettle the rioters into cul-de-sacs and dead ends. But they're hopelessly outnumbered.

We're deep inside the city, but I still don't know where I'm going. We tried to listen to the police radio, to see if there was any kind of epicentre to what's going down, but there isn't. The whole city is in meltdown.

Armitage even called in to Dispatch to try and find out where the first incidents occurred. If we could track the first reports, perhaps that would lead us to Lilith.

Again, no luck. There were multiple incidents, all occurring at around half past ten, spread widely across the city.

I see blue lights coming up fast in the rear-view and quickly turn into a side street, braking hard and turning the engine off. A tactical police van screams past, chased seconds later by five civilian cars.

I watch the cars as they go past. On the bright side, at least these riots have embraced the concept of our 'rainbow nation'. In one car I catch a glimpse of three young blacks, two in suits, one in torn street clothes, an old white woman brandishing what looks like an AK-47, a young Indian kid who can't be older than twelve, and a skinny white dude wearing his cap sideways. The one thing they all have in common is the look of animalistic rage on their faces. They're screaming into the night, firing their guns at the retreating police van.

'Bloody hell,' says Armitage shakily. 'Feels like the end of the world.'

'So what's your plan, brainiac?' asks the dog. ''Cause, to be honest, I'm kinda getting the feeling you're winging it.'

I ignore him, turn to Armitage. 'Call up Eshu. See if he can access the CCTV feeds at Pavilion and find out what kind of car Lilith is driving. Maybe he can track it through the surveillance feeds.'

She takes out her phone and dials. While she's chatting I get out the car and approach the alley entrance. Smoke billows from a building at the far end of the street. A fire truck arrives, lights and siren blaring, and the first to jump off are private security guards. They form a ring around the truck while the fire fighters get to work. I'm impressed they're even trying. The whole city seems to be burning. How do they decide what buildings to save?

'No luck,' says Armitage behind me. 'All the systems are down.'

Typical. There *has* to be a way to track Lilith. Who would

know how to find her? With all the shinecraft and orisha contacts we have, there has to be something we can do.

A thought occurs to me, but I don't like it. I examine it from every angle, considering the implications. It could work. But the cost would be high.

We don't really have a choice, though.

'Phone Eshu again,' I say. 'Find out where Anansi is holing up these days.'

'Anansi?' says Armitage, her voice dripping with disgust.

I know the feeling. Nobody in the Division likes Anansi, but he's way too powerful for us to mess with. So we just watch him. Track his movements, and hope he doesn't do anything we can't put a stop to.

Armitage has her phone to her ear, but she's looking at me. 'Why him?'

'Because he's been courting the soul of Durban.'

And the soul of Durban – or Mother Durban as she likes to be called – knows everything about her city. Like, for instance, where specific people might be hiding out trying to wake up a Sinwalker.

The question is, will she tell us or not?

Armitage has turned away from me to talk to Eshu. I wait impatiently, listening to the sounds of the city. The gunfire, the shouting, the hooting of car horns. What will Mother Durban be feeling right now? Will she be enjoying all this? Will it be damaging her?

Armitage taps me on the shoulder. 'Eshu says Anansi runs a night club on West Street.'

'You got the address?'

'Yeah.'

She frowns.

'What?'

'Nothing. The address looks familiar, that's all.'

We get in the car and drive back towards the beachfront.

West Street straddles the line between the tourist side of Durban and the inhabitants' side, meaning most everything on this side of the line is pretty rundown. Boarded-up buildings, car body shops, liquor stores, pawn shops, loan sharks, and muti doctors who promise all kinds of things, from love spells, to a few extra inches you-know-where, to curses for love rivals.

We pull up outside one of many blank-faced buildings. There are no rioters here. There's nothing worth stealing. I can still hear the chaos around me. The rapid crack of AK-47 gunfire, the answering muted crack of small arms fire.

'I *knew* this address was familiar,' says Armitage.

I turn to her. She's staring up at the building.

'This used to be a night club. I came here a few times with a few younger members of the team. This was before your time, like.'

I frown up at the building, trying to imagine Armitage boogying down on the dance floor.

I can't.

'It was called The Rift,' says Armitage, heading towards the door. 'Quite a nice vibe. Alternate, like. Bloody nice people. Never any trouble.'

She pulls open the metal door. Loud music bursts out, a slow, heavy base. The song is familiar. I think it's from *Pulp Fiction*, one of the two good Tarantino movies.

The door opens onto an incredibly steep set of stairs. The walls are black, the paint peeling away with age. We climb up to the landing, then through a door into the club itself.

The music is deafening. We're in a huge dark room. A long bar to our right, the dance floor and stage to our left. The walls are covered with faded paintings of the X-men. Wolverine glowers down at me from above the toilets, his face mottled and peeling.

There are orisha dancing – vampires, werewolves, dark creatures with red eyes, misshapen dwarves covered in bristly hair. A strobe light flickers over them, monochrome shadows making everything look like a stop-motion horror movie.

I approach the bar and nod at the orisha handing out odd-looking drinks. Thick, viscous. No beers and whisky here.

'Anansi?' I say.

The bartender gives me a flat stare with bright purple eyes. I pull out my badge and show it to her. 'Delphic Division. I know you know who we are, so unless you want this place shut down, tell me where he is.'

She jerks her head towards a door to my right. It leads to a narrow corridor where all types of orisha are sitting on the floor, resting and chatting. The music isn't as loud here, but I can feel the bass thumping through the walls.

All eyes turn to the three of us as we navigate the maze of stretched-out legs.

The dog bares his teeth at them, nodding in greeting as we pass. 'Hi there. Good to see you. Looking good, girl.'

A second door to the left leads into the pool room. Eight tables, four to each side. Half of them are occupied.

I spot Anansi straight away. Tall, skin so dark it's the colour of night. He's clearing up the table against the far wall, effortlessly sinking ball after ball.

We wait, because it's well known you don't get between Anansi and his games, no matter what they might be.

He finally sinks the black and the guy he's playing against starts to cry. He looks like a human to me, no hint of magic about him.

'Please,' he says. 'Again. We can play again.'

'No,' says Anansi. 'You know the rules.'

'But my sister. I need her back.'

'Tough. You should have thought of that before you sold her.'

The man's face twists. He's tall, built like a gym bunny, beach bum hair pushed back behind his ears. He lunges towards Anansi, hands outstretched.

The walls burp out some kind of black oil. The oil forms into a huge creature about the size of the Hulk, and it grabs the man before he moves two steps. He struggles, but the more he moves, the more he sinks back into the creature, until only his face is showing, the black oil crawling across his skin.

Anansi puts his cue down on the table.

'You want to see your sister so much? Then you will join her, yes? A family reunion.'

He gestures and the creature steps back into the wall, pulling the struggling man with it. He's gone in an instant. A moment of silence, then the club-goers who stopped to watch carry on with their conversations.

Anansi glances at us without much interest.

'Who are you?'

I flash my ID. 'Delphic Division.'

'We'd like to know where Mother Durban is,' says Armitage.

He focuses on us with renewed interest. 'Why would you want to know where my fiancée is?'

'She's not your fiancée yet,' I say. 'Last we heard her people hadn't got back to you.'

'She's playing hard to get, that's all. She'll come around, yes?'

'Spoken like a true misogynist,' mutters Armitage.

Anansi grins at her. 'You are one of them, then?'

'One of them?' says Armitage, steel in her voice.

'A feminist.'

Armitage glowers and takes a step forward.

'Armitage,' I say.

She glances at me, purses her lips, and nods. She steps back again to stand next to me, but her glare doesn't go anywhere, and it's directed straight at Anansi.

'Do you know where she is?' I ask.

'I might.'

I sigh. 'Anansi, we have a whole filing cabinet devoted to you back at the Division. We know about your trafficking. We know about you using the taxi industry to funnel funds. We also know you use the taxis to transport stolen goods. If you don't want us to drop everything we're working on and focus all our attention on you, tell us where she is.'

He winks at me. 'If that is what you know about me, then you know nothing.'

'That's just the first file in the first drawer,' I say. 'Like I said, we've been watching you for a long time.'

His smile disappears. He stares at me, trying to see if I'm telling the truth. 'Why do you want her?'

'Have you seen what's going on outside?'

He shrugs. 'A few fires. A few riots. What is it to me?'

'It's not just a few fires. It's Lilith, starting a war between orisha and mankind. What do you think will happen to your precious little crime syndicate if that happens?'

'And think how grateful Mother Durban will be if she finds out you helped save her city,' says Armitage.

Nice one. Why hadn't I thought of that?

'Because as it stands,' continues Armitage, 'Durban is going to be doing a pretty good impression of Hell come morning.'

Armitage's phone rings. She answers, it, turns away to talk.

Anansi sighs, checks his watch. 'This time of night she'll be at the Playhouse.'

'The Playhouse? Doing what?'

He frowns. 'What do you normally do at the theatre? She'll be watching her play.'

Armitage leans close to me. 'We need to go,' she whispers. 'That was Eshu. He thinks someone's piggy-backed his comms.'

'SSA?'

Armitage nods. 'He reckons so. They know we came here.'

21

The sins of God leech into the collective psyche of the city. Forgotten dreams bubble to the surface. Old wounds open afresh, boiling with pus and resentment.

A man remembers when his brother stole his girlfriend, thirty-two years ago. He gets a kitchen knife, travels to the other side of the city, and drives it into his sibling's heart, screaming about lost love and what might have been.

A nun who teaches at the Our Lady of Fatima Dominican Convent School runs naked through the streets, screaming that she's in love with a woman who used to live next door to her.

An anorexic teen eats her family. She keeps going until her stomach lining ruptures and she dies from internal bleeding.

A television presenter who gained exactly 0.4 of a kilogram in the previous month goes on a rampage at the local television studio, locking his co-presenters in the editing suite and setting fire to the building. He then proceeds to cut the fat from his body with a blunt knife, weighing himself after every cut, muttering about it not being enough. It's never enough.

A failed businessman steals his neighbour's jeep and rams it into the closest ATM. When he still can't get the money out he shoots himself in the head.

The Playhouse, Durban's oldest theatre, is only about ten blocks over from the Rift.

It's an unassuming, old-fashioned building, fronted by a small portico supported by columns plastered with posters for upcoming plays and ballets.

The street is eerily quiet compared to the rest of Durban. No gangs here. No screeching cars. No fires. The street is deserted, quiet.

Calm.

Has to be Mother Durban's doing.

I try the front doors. Locked. I consider using my gun to shoot out the glass, but something makes me pause. There's an air of respect here. Doing something like shooting the doors to gain entrance seems . . . sacrilegious.

'There's another entrance round the side,' says Armitage.

We head down a dirty, cobbled alley. Apartment blocks tower up to either side. Washing lines straddle the air above the alley, strung up between cracked and broken windows.

The side entrance to the Playhouse is an ornate door at the top of five steps. Armitage is ahead of me. She pushes it open and we enter a narrow hall. The lights are on. The walls are lined with posters advertising *The Nutcracker*, *Aladdin*, *Swan Lake*.

The passage leads into a wide atrium, an area where people can wait for the plays to begin. Leather couches, cramped tables and chairs. A long bar to the left.

There are three different stages in the playhouse: the Loft, the Opera Theatre and the Drama Theatre. We climb the set of stairs that leads to the Opera Theatre, picking this one because it's the biggest stage and the most likely place we'd find Mother Durban.

We move along the rotunda that leads to the theatre itself. Concealed lights cast a warm glow across the red carpets. I can hear sounds as we approach a door. Loud voices, drums, heavy echoes.

I hesitate, wondering if we should be doing this. I feel like we're interrupting something private. Like we're stepping into a church during a stranger's funeral.

'Ah ... I'll wait here,' says the dog. 'Don't think I'd be welcome inside.'

I nod and gently push the door open. Armitage and I step inside.

The theatre is huge. We've entered right at the back, and a thousand seats spread out below us, a semicircle of high-backed chairs leading downwards. Painted Elizabethan buildings flank the brightly lit stage. A starry sky twinkles above actors performing to an entirely empty house.

'There,' whispers Armitage, pointing.

Ah. Not entirely empty. There's someone seated in the front row, a shadowy figure with head craned back, watching the play unfold with rapt attention.

We make our way down the sloped floor, heading towards the figure. My eyes are drawn to the play as we do so. The actors are running around, clashing in groups while red and orange ribbon, blown by wind machines, sway across the stage.

I suddenly realise I'm watching a play about what's happening in Durban right at this moment. The riots engulfing the city, the fires burning through the streets.

As we draw closer I see that the figure watching the play is an African woman. But then I blink and she's suddenly Indian. Then a white housewife. Then a small black kid. Another blink and she looks like a Dutch settler, sitting in old-fashioned clothes. And then she's an elderly Zulu tribeswoman, laughing with delight and clapping.

I suppose it makes sense. Mother Durban is made up of the entire history of the city. The souls and memories of all its inhabitants reside in her.

The face that finally turns to look at us is that of a smooth-skinned African woman. She looks like she's about twenty-five.

Her mouth is turned down, a crease in her brows showing her annoyance.

'You are interrupting my show,' she says.

I glance at the stage. In the time it's taken for her to acknowledge our presence, the sets and actors have changed. Now there are two people and a dog approaching a painted facade of the Playhouse itself.

I realise with a jolt that the actors are supposed to represent us. I watch as they enter the building. The lights fade to darkness. A moment later they come on again to reveal the actors and Mother Durban's double, standing against a painted backdrop of the stage itself.

The three actors turn to look at us.

'The story is waiting,' says Mother Durban, and the words come simultaneously from her and the woman on the stage. 'What will you write?'

'We . . . want to track someone,' I say. 'The person responsible for what's happening right now.'

'You mean Lilith?'

Armitage and I exchange looks.

'Yes. Can you tell us where she is?' I ask.

'I can.'

I wait. But Mother Durban says nothing. Instead she feels around in her seat and pulls out a box of Smarties. She pops the lid and tips the contents of the box into her mouth, staring at me expectantly.

'Well . . . *will* you?' I ask.

'Perhaps. What can you offer me in return?'

I stare at her in amazement. 'We're trying to save your city. We're trying to stop the Night from taking over.' A horrible thought occurs to me. 'Unless . . . unless you want the Night to win?'

'No. I do not want that. I'm quite happy with my city as it is.'

'Then tell us.'

'If you pay. Nothing is free, Mr London.'

'Jesus Christ. Fine. What's the price?'

'The price is always the same. That which is most valuable to you.'

She gestures at the stage. I glance across, only half-interested. But something in the layout of the set makes my head snap around.

It's an exact replica of Timothy Evan's house.

I look at Mother Durban uncertainly, but she smiles benignly and gestures back to the stage.

An actor enters the room from the wings and someone who had been sitting on the floor surges to his feet and grabs him.

There follows an exact re-enactment of what happened earlier that evening. I can feel Armitage's focus shifting between the play and myself. When Evans tells me my daughter is still alive, she reaches out and takes my hand, squeezing it tightly.

When the play reaches the point where Evans tells me the name of the fae who took Cally, Mother Durban raises her hand in the air.

The play stops abruptly, as if a pause button has been pushed on a DVD. Mother Durban turns to me.

'That is the price you must pay for the knowledge you seek.'

I blink, unsure what she's talking about. I look back to the frozen tableau, see the actor representing me staring at Evans with disbelief and hope clear on his features.

'I don't . . .'

'Oh, London,' whispers Armitage. 'I'm so sorry, pet.'

I turn to her. 'What?'

'Not too sharp, is he, honey?' Mother Durban gets up and comes to stand before me. Except now she's a little Indian girl, about ten years old. She gestures me closer.

I crouch down and she puts a hand to my ear, leaning in to whisper. 'The price is always the same, no matter who asks. I want that which is most valuable to you. In your case, the memory of who took your daughter.'

I lean back, stare at her in shock. 'No.' I shake my head, straighten up. 'No. You can't.'

She shrugs and goes back to her seat. 'Your choice.'

'You can't . . .' I turn to Armitage. 'She can't.' Back again to face Mother Durban. 'Three years!' I shout. 'Three years I've thought my daughter was dead! I've only just found out she's alive! Found out who did it! And you want me to just . . . forget that? Give it away?'

'Your choice,' repeats Mother Durban. She gestures at the stage.

I turn and see that the sets have been cleared, leaving behind empty boards. 'But you must decide soon. The play has not ended this night.'

I take a step forward, yank my gun out. Hold it in a trembling hand. 'Just tell me. Tell me where Lilith is!'

'London, don't,' warns Armitage. I feel her hand on my shoulder. I shrug it off. I'm trembling with fury. With fear.

'Tell. Me.'

Mother Durban looks at me calmly. She reaches up and curls her fingers around the barrel, moving it to her temple 'Best to make sure,' she says softly.

I put my finger on the trigger. Can feel it easing slowly inward.

'Gideon,' says Armitage quietly. 'Come on, love. Don't be a silly bugger.'

I grit my teeth. Mother Durban stares into my eyes.

I scream in anger and frustration, throw my gun aside. 'What is it with you people?' I shout. 'Why can't you just do something good? Why do you always need a piece of someone's soul?'

'It is not a price worth charging if it is not worth giving.'

I point a shaking finger at her. 'Fuck you and the bike you rode in on, you sanctimonious bitch.'

I turn to Armitage. 'I can't. I won't. The world can fucking burn. I won't give up the name.'

'I'm not asking you to,' she says softly.

'Why not?' I'm shouting again. Can't seem to make myself stop. I'm pleading with her. 'Ask me! Tell me I have to do it!'

'I can't.'

'No. It's all down to me, isn't it? Fucking marvellous.'

I stalk away from them, pacing in circles just below the stage. I can't do this. I can't lose hope again. I've just got it back. I can find her. I can get her back. We can be a family again. Me, Cally, Becca—

I freeze. No. Not Becca. I can't save her. She died thinking our daughter was dead, murdered by some sick fucking bastards who got their kicks out of torturing kids. She'll never know the truth.

But *I* do. I can get Cally back. I know I can. All I need to do is walk out that door.

I approach the door with the red EXIT sign above it. I pull it open, step out of the theatre, into the hallway. The door swings shut behind me.

Just keep walking. Find Cally. Leave the country. Go back to London. Start a new life. Leave everyone to sort out their own mess.

Except, this isn't their own mess, is it? *I* caused it.

I drop to my knees. After all this. After everything I've been through. Everything I've given away.

I sold my soul for this name. Fuck, I sold out *humanity* for the name. And oh, sweet irony, if I want *my* humanity back I have to give the name away again. I shake my head. Where's the justice there? Where's *my* justice? Can't I have something for myself, just this once?

I start to laugh. I can't help it. It's all a big fucking joke, isn't it?

I see Cally's face. What would she look like now? After three years. If I walk away now, what would she say when I told her how expensive her freedom was? Would she be grateful? Would she understand? When she's older and the world is gone to shit. When Night has taken over and humanity is ... what? Wiped out? Enslaved? What would she say to me? Because all that crap Lilith fed me about being fair, about letting the good survive, that was obviously all bullshit. She never intended to keep her word.

Unless everyone in Durban deserves punishment.

I run that thought back again. What was it she said? Lilith? The guilty will be punished. The innocent will be spared.

And there you have it. I straighten up. She's not breaking her word at all. She meant it. Because who, when you got right down to it, *wasn't* guilty of something, at least in their own minds? Whether it's cheating on a spouse, not paying their taxes, lying to their kids about being too busy to play.

Everyone's guilty of something. It's the human condition.

Lilith tricked me.

No, I'd *let* her trick me.

Ah, fuck. I slump back against the wall, rub my face wearily.

I can feel it inside. I'm going to give her the memory.

I have to. I can't sentence humanity to death in Cally's name. What kind of fucking justice is that?

I pull myself to my feet, push open the door. The stage has changed again. A painted backdrop of the hallway I'd just been in. As I walk into the theatre, my actor is moving towards me. His face is blurred, almost featureless. I don't stop as he leaves the stage, still walking. We move towards each other, neither of us slowing. I can see Armitage and Mother Durban watching behind him as we meet ...

... A sensation like pushing against the wind. I look behind me and see him glancing over his shoulder at me. I don't know what this means. It's symbolic of something, but I have no idea what. That the story is ongoing? We're all acting out parts?

I shake my head, turn back to Mother Durban. Now she's a tall Asian woman, watching me expressionlessly.

'Do it,' I say.

'London—'

'Armitage, it's fine. I have to.'

Mother Durban nods. 'You realise it is not just *your* memory? But that of the man who told you. Whoever knows. None will remember.'

I nod. 'Figured as much. Get it over with.'

Mother Durban puts her hands on my temples, closes her eyes.

I try to hold on to the memory. I repeat the name over and over in my head. But it's no good. I can feel it slipping away, like water through my fingers.

I don't forget that I once knew the name. I just forget what it is.

I'm not sure if that's a good or a bad thing. Good, I think. At least I still know she's alive. I just won't know who has her. Or where.

And then it's done. An empty space in my head that fills up with thoughts of regret and anger, with guilt and sadness. Mother Durban steps back and I scrabble through my memories, hoping she left something, anything.

She didn't. All I'm left with is the knowledge that I once knew how to save Cally and I gave it away.

'Lilith is beneath my streets,' says Mother Durban. 'There are storm drains that lead to the sea. In the place you call Whoonga Park. They will take you to her.'

I feel Armitage's hand on my arm, pulling me away. I pick my gun up from the floor and follow after her, out into the corridor, then back out onto the streets. Armitage says nothing. Hell, even the dog is quiet for once.

★   ★   ★

Whoonga Park is an inner city area off limits to the likes of
you and me, a dry, scruffy piece of land squashed between the
M4 and the train tracks.

The place is a nightmare. Even the police tend to stay
away. Every now and then you read news reports about
'clean-ups' and 'evictions', but it never lasts. The hundred or
so vagrants who live there – the homeless, immigrants, the
dying – all gravitate back to the spot like bacteria to an open
wound.

I've only ever seen Whoonga Park in passing. Every time I
look I see a huge group of people milling around like mindless
zombies, shuffling back and forth across the tracks, smoking
their drug of choice and looking like extras from *The Walking
Dead*. They always look like they're in some kind of trance.
Blank eyes, vacant expressions.

Until they rise to action. Until an intruder walks into their
midst. Then they go apeshit crazy, feral animals protecting
their territory.

Armitage, the Dog, and I stand on the bridge that crosses
the rail tracks. Over to our left I can see the addicts, shuffling
around, sitting around small fires. But the area to the right of
our location is clear, the train tracks pushing right up against
a steep bank.

'The storm drains are over there,' says Armitage, pointing
towards a freeway overpass beyond the vagrants. 'To the left
of that flyover.' She points to the right. 'Reckon we head along
the tracks by the bank and loop around behind them. No need
to intrude, eh?'

I nod. I'm surprised the vagrants are still here. I thought
they would have joined in the riots. They're getting even
worse. The cops have given up and word on the police radio
is the Defence Force is on its way.

Which means more guns and more deaths. Time is running
out.

There's a hole in the wall above the bank that borders the track. We duck through and slide down the grass into the gravel the rusted rail tracks are resting on.

A few of the whoonga addicts turn at the noise. We duck low. After a few seconds they turn away.

Armitage raises two fingers and points ahead. The dog doesn't even wait for us, probably thinking he's got more of a chance on his own. He moves into the darkness, vanishing from sight.

Armitage and I follow the railway lines for about two hundred metres, moving parallel to the vagrants. Once we get past them we cross over the tracks, moving towards the shadows of the concrete pillars supporting the overpass. They're covered in graffiti, pictures of an odd-looking rowing boat, signatures and tags one atop the other until all that's left is a confused mess.

The dog pads back to join us.

-*The opening into the storm drains is up ahead. Keep quiet, though. There's a few of them sleeping in the entrance.*-

We move beneath the flyover. There's no light here. Just shadows and darkness. We pass over broken rubble and old playing cards. Empty bottles and discarded syringes.

I hear a scuffing behind me. I freeze. Turn around. My eyes scan the darkness, but I can't see anything. The massive support pillars can obscure a multitude of sins, though.

Including the spot on the tracks where the addicts were milling around.

I wait a few seconds, peering into the night.

-*Come on, London.*-

I turn back. Armitage and the dog are waiting about ten paces ahead, backs up against another support. I join them, cast an uneasy look over my shoulder.

'You see something?' whispers Armitage in my ear.

I hesitate, then shake my head.

We move forward. Around the next pillar and I can see the entrance to the drains. A concrete culvert that delves below the ground. A dark opening, easily two metres by two metres.

A shift in the wind brings a vile stench our way. I jerk my head to the side, quickly clamp my hand over my mouth and nose.

-*Yeah. They use the entrance as a toilet. Tends to keep the cops away.*-

As we draw closer we emerge out from the shadows of the overpass. I can see the vagrants sleeping outside the drain entrance. About ten of them. No fires here, but then, none are really needed. It's a humid night. My own sweat is prickling on my skin, making my shirt stick to my back.

We move slowly, silently. Aiming our feet between the broken glass, the empty packets of Nik-Naks and Cheese Curls.

The opening is only about ten feet away when there's a sudden flare of white light behind us, etching our shadows into the ground.

We whirl around—

—To find a hundred or so vampires standing there, their eyes blazing with white light.

Fuck.

A noise behind us. I glance over my shoulder, see Armitage pulling out her wand. The 'sleeping' vagrants are rising to their feet, their eyes flaring to life like they've been plugged into electrical sockets.

Armitage and I close up, back to back. We turn in a circle, ready, waiting as the vampires start to close in.

Shit. These are numbers we can't win against. We need backup.

Real backup.

I lick my lips, nervous, wondering what to do. If I summon the dragons, I'm not sure I'll be able to put them away again. It's too soon after the last calling.

On the other hand, I don't really have much of a choice here.

I mutter the words of awakening and they stir to excited life on my skin. Green and red light bursts into the darkness as the dragons rise up and coil above my shoulders.

They spit and lunge, trying to pull me forward. Armitage grips my arm, holding me back. I dig my feet in, grit my teeth.

'Wait, you bastard things.'

I can feel the air shivering as Armitage draws in power to her wand. The dog is making some sort of unholy growling noise.

It's all a waste of time, though. How the hell are we supposed to fight off a hundred vampires? We're finished.

Maybe so. But we'll take a few of them with us.

'I want everyone to imagine I just said an incredibly witty comment about coming to your rescue, OK?' says a voice from behind us.

I glance over my shoulder and see Parker standing on top of the stone culvert of the storm drain, framed against the fire-tinged sky, holding some kind of old-fashioned shotgun.

Movement behind her, and another seven figures arrive to flank her, all from the DD. Allison, Lisa, Jasmine. Cole, Daltry. Cass. Even Russells, looking a bit nervous as he holds a flaming sword as far from his body as possible.

'And Armitage,' says Parker, 'I want this taken into account when you calculate my performance bonus this year. Shit! *That* should have been my opening comment.'

She jumps over our heads and lands directly in front of the surprised vampires. She fires the shotgun at the closest. Its head evaporates in a cloud of mist.

That's when all Hell breaks loose.

The vampires scream and surge forward. The other members of Delphic Division leap down from the culvert and start laying about them with whatever weapons they brought.

I run forward, releasing any control I have on the dragons. They snap forward, yanking heads and limbs from vampire bodies, pulling me around like I'm attached to a parachute in a gale. I have to just go with it. Orange flame and heat to my right as Russells waves the sword around, going for sheer determination and rage over skill.

I pull out my wand, draw in the aether presence and let loose with the anti-light I used against the Matchstick Man and his cronies. Speaking of which, I can actually see a few Smilers in the crowd, hissing and spitting as they come for us. I turn to them and release the black lightning. Purple after-images flash in my eyes as it vaults through the air and wraps around them. They drop, screaming, writhing on the ground. I pump more energy into the wand and the lighting branches out, hopping from Smiler to vampire, spreading through their ranks.

I whirl around, trying to find the others. Allison is fighting with a staff that turns everything it touches to dust. My tattoos are snapping and lunging in every direction. I think they're growing bigger. Armitage has stashed her wand and is now dual-firing her semi-automatics into the throats of any vampires that reach for her.

Russells goes down, the sheer number of attackers forcing him to his knees. I shove my way through the vampires, fighting the pull of the dragons. I yank back the head of a Smiler as it's about to rip out his throat. I jam my wand into its head and unleash the anti-light. The vampire basically explodes in my hands, coming apart in a mess of stringy meat and gristle.

I help Russells to his feet and he nods his thanks and scoops up his sword. It ignites as soon as he touches it and he swings it to the side, cutting a vamp's head off.

There's a new sound coming from behind us. Some of the vampires are turning around, trying to see what it is.

A row of powerful flashlights burst to life. Automatic gunfire rattles through the air.

And I see Dillon, the SSA guy that Ranson said killed Becca.

He's accompanied by about twenty-five SSA operatives. All of them wearing black tactical gear. They move into the fight calmly and cleanly, cleaving through the vampires.

I don't think. I run straight into the vampires. They reach out for me, trying to pull me down. I shrug them off, firing black lightning all around me. I force the dragons down to stomach height. They fight me all the way, but I don't give up. I pull them down low and use them like a long, double-bladed staff, letting them clear the way to either side, cutting a screaming swathe through the hordes of vampires.

All I'm focused on is Dillon. I catch glimpses of him through gaps in the fighting. He's shouting orders, pointing in our direction, trying to get his men to focus on us. He obviously has his final orders. Wipe out Delphic Division.

He sees me coming, turns, brings his weapon up. Fires. I yank a vampire in front of me. Use him as a shield as I push forward. Bullets thud into the creature. It screams and jerks. Cold blood spatters my face. I duck down, trying to make myself as small a target as possible. Then I throw the vampire forward. It stumbles into Dillon. He jerks aside, his gun shifting direction.

That's all I need.

I pull the knife out of my belt and ram it into his throat.

He stiffens, eyes widening in shock. He reaches out, fingers scrabbling for my face.

I yank the knife out. A fountain of blood gushes from the side of his neck.

He falls to his knees.

Then the vampires are on him, driving him to the dirt.

I watch him get torn apart, the vampires shredding his body, tearing limbs apart.

Someone grabs my shoulder. I whirl around, wand ready. Only to find Parker standing there reloading her shotgun.

'You know what's going on here, right?'

I nod.

'Can you stop it?'

'Maybe.'

'Maybe's not good enough!'

She pushes something against my chest. I look down and see she's holding a satchel of hand grenades.

'What about now?'

I grin. 'That might help.'

'You and Armitage go. Finish it. We'll hold them off.'

I hesitate, look back to the battle. Bright flares of light, high-pitched, animalistic screams of pain. Fire and blade. Magic burning the air. The sharp taste of ozone. The loud crack of gunfire as the SSA do their best to stay alive.

'Go!'

I slip the satchel over my shoulder and move off, grabbing Armitage as I go, backing up towards the storm drain. I try to find the dog, see him tearing through the vampires. Except, he doesn't look like a dog anymore. He's grown in size. Looks more like a demon on four legs.

-Dog. We're going in. Stay here and . . . do what you're doing.-

-Fine. But you owe me a shit-load of sherry after this.-

-Dog, if we get out of this in one piece I'll fill the house with sherry. You can bathe in it if you want.-

-The fuck would I want to do that for? Waste of good booze.-

I fire off more of the anti-light at a group of vampires lurking by the dark entrance to the drains. They hiss, drop to the ground, and the tattoos rip them apart.

Then we step beneath the culvert.

22

We sprint through the drains, but I haven't gone five steps before I'm yanked suddenly off my feet.

I land on my back in the water, twist around and look over my shoulder.

The dragons. They don't want to leave the battle.

They strain against me, hissing and spitting. They pull me back through the water, my fingers scrabbling against the concrete. Armitage sees what's happening and retraces her steps towards me.

'No! Stay back!'

The green dragon lunges at her. She jerks out of the way just in time.

I close my eyes, summon up all my strength, and shout out the words of rest.

The dragons screech in protest. They stop pulling, lunge at me instead. Neon green and blazing red mouths trying to tear off my head. But they can't do any damage that way.

I shout the words again. Pushing all my force, summoning up as much surrounding aether energy as I can and pumping it into the words.

The dragons screech and writhe around as if in pain.

But they're still not going anywhere.

I can't do it. They're too strong.

I slide back another few feet. Then I feel a sudden surge of power. My eyes snap open and see Armitage holding her hands out to me. It takes me a moment to realise she's pushing energy into me.

I pull the power into my being and scream the words again.

This time the dragons obey. They wind slowly back, still struggling, still screeching, and I finally force them back into place. They feel like sandpaper against my skin. I feel like they're trying to pull me with them, to draw me back into the Nightside where they'll tear me apart in revenge for trapping them.

The red and green light winks out. The screeching stops.

I throw up. My stomach heaves, emptying its contents into the storm water. I collapse, roll onto my back, taking in deep, shuddering breaths.

Armitage appears above me.

'You OK?'

'Not really.'

She holds a hand out and helps me up. I stagger, put a hand out to support myself against the curved wall.

'You up for this?'

I hesitate. No, I want to say. I'm not.

But I can't. We have to do this.

'Give me a minute.'

We wait while I take deep, steadying breaths. I shake my head, trying to banish the floating white spots.

'We need to go,' says Armitage impatiently.

I reluctantly nod and we head off, slowly at first, then picking up speed as the nausea recedes.

If I survive this I'm going to be out of action for a week.

Our footsteps echo as we sprint through the huge storm drains. We're using our cell phones as torches, the anaemic light picking out the graffiti on the rounded walls, the dirty, rancid water that comes up to our shins.

'Did you call in the reinforcements?' I ask as we pause at a junction.

'Of course I did. You think I want to get killed because of your stupidity?'

Fair enough. I look left, then right. Both directions look identical. But there's something to the left, a sense of . . . heaviness. I can feel something down there.

We both turn down the tunnel at the same time and keep running.

'How long are these tunnels?' I ask after a few minutes.

'At least six kays. Whoonga dealers use them to hide from the cops.'

We keep going. After another hundred metres or so I trip over something, almost fall flat on my face. I point my phone downwards. 'Think I might have found one of the dealers.'

Armitage pauses and retraces her steps. The light from her phone joins mine, picking out a young guy submerged in the murky water. His throat has been ripped out.

We pick up the pace, following the sense of . . . otherness that permeates the tunnels. The water gets deeper, coming up to our knees. The air is heavy, dank. We're both breathing through our mouths, trying to block out the stench of garbage and stagnant water.

-Dog? How's it going?-

Silence. Then: -Not too great, if I'm honest. Lisa's dead. So is Russells.-

Fuck.

'Armitage, we need to move. They're losing up there.'

We run faster, following our senses down side passages, up slime-covered ladders, along more of the wide drains. I begin to wonder if we're going round in circles, if we've been tricked into a wild goose chase.

Then Kincaid swings down from the shadows above us, grabs Armitage by the head, and flings her hard against the wall.

'No!'

I try to move towards Armitage but Kincaid drops, flips over in mid-air, and lands in the water with a heavy splash.

'My friend,' he says regretfully. 'I truly wish you had not come here.'

'Believe me, I'm feeling the same way.' I try to see past him, but he's massive. He completely blocks my view of Armitage.

'Let me past, Kincaid. We need to stop her.'

'I'm afraid not.'

'I'm not asking. I'm giving you the chance to step aside. For old time's sake.'

Kincaid smiles at me and his iron teeth glint in the light from my phone. '"For old time's sake" I will break your neck instead of gutting you. How does that sound?'

I bring my wand up but Kincaid's moving before I can raise it five inches. He hits me in the chest. My breath surges from my body and I fly backwards, landing in the water. My wand skids out of my hand. I'm wheezing, struggling to draw in air, wondering if he's broken all my ribs.

I hear splashing, force myself to my elbows to see him striding towards me. I get to my knees. He grabs me by my waistcoat, lifts me effortlessly in the air, and head-butts me.

My nose breaks. I scream in pain. Blood pours down my face. I scrabble around at the back of my belt, my fingers curling around my knife. Kincaid's lowering his head towards my neck. I can't see properly. My vision is blurred with tears.

I bring the knife up and plunge it into his chest.

He hisses in pain, drops me. Staggers back. He pulls the knife out. Blood bubbles from the wound. He looks at the blade with interest, noting the runes inscribed there.

'Holy weapon?' he says, his voice hoarse.

He staggers and I feel a surge of hope.

Hope that is quickly dashed. He straightens up and flings the dagger at me. I jerk aside and it flies past my face. It skitters against the curved wall, raising sparks as it vanishes down the tunnel.

I turn back and Kincaid is rushing me. His eyes have turned red. He's no longer smiling. Fuck. I fumble around for my Glock. Pull it out. Fire. One. Two. Three. The explosion of gunfire is deafening in the tunnels. Kincaid staggers, hesitates. The bullets should have dropped him. They're UV laced silver nitrate. But he just shrugs them off as if they were paintball rounds.

I fire again but by this time he's reached me. He grips my wrist, squeezing. Bones scrape together. I grit my teeth, try not to cry out. But he presses harder and a hoarse cry of pain tears from my throat.

I punch him with my free hand. He doesn't even blink. I go for his eyes and he grabs my other wrist, squeezing that one too. He stretches my arms out to either side, forces me to my knees.

Then he starts pulling.

My muscles scream in pain. My shoulders are on fire. The fucker is actually trying to tear me apart.

He snarls at me. I think I hear my joints pop. I grit my teeth against the horrific agony—

And then something bursts out of his chest, spraying me with his blood.

We both look down. It's Armitage's wooden wand. Right through his heart.

He growls, releases my arms. I fall back into the water, gasping in pain.

Kincaid drops to his knees. A black stain appears around the wand and spreads like veins across his entire body. He shudders once, the black veins reaching up his neck and across his face.

The red light in his eyes flickers and goes out. He slowly falls sideways to reveal Armitage standing there, still holding her wand.

'Good riddance. Never knew what you saw in him.' She wipes the wand on Kincaid's clothes and twists her neck from side to side, wincing as she does so.

I push myself to my feet, stagger towards her.

'You OK?' she asks.

I try to say, *I think he broke my nose,* but what I actually say is: 'I dink he boke by does.'

'Didnae catch that, pet. Hang on.' Before I can do anything she reaches up and gives my noise a sharp twist.

I scream again, even louder this time. I stagger back, cradling my face in my hands. 'Armitage! What the actual fuck?'

'That's better. Now. What were you saying?'

I hesitate. Straighten up. I wrinkle my nose a bit. 'I said I think he broke my nose.'

'Oh.' She shrugs. 'Least it's straight now. You think it's through here?'

She points to a massive hole in the tunnel wall.

We peer through and see a downward slope vanishing into the darkness.

I gather up all my fallen weapons. Even my knife, which is about twenty feet down the tunnel. Then we duck through the hole and make our way down the slope.

Every part of me is crying out in pain. My arms, my nose, my chest. I feel like I'm a single throbbing raw bruise. My muscles are seizing up and we haven't even found Lilith yet.

I look around as we descend. The tunnel is old. The walls worn smooth. We pick up our pace, so that by the time the tunnel levels out about half a kay down we're dripping with sweat. The heat has grown heavier, relentless. It sucks out every bit of moisture from our bodies.

I can hear sounds now. A low mumbling, as if a group of people are having a whispered conversation.

We keep moving, and eventually we see light coming from up ahead, a pulsing, lurid glow that leaks out into the tunnel from around a bend in the passage.

I pull out my wand and my Glock and we move slowly forward.

We follow the curve around and find ourselves a few feet from the end of the tunnel. A sickly, warm breeze touches my face, carrying with it the stench of gangrene and blood.

We edge forward, though every instinct is screaming at us to turn and flee. We pass through a rough arch at the end of the tunnel.

And stumble to a stop.

I look around in awestruck horror, feeling suddenly dwarfed, tiny.

We're standing at the top of a stone ramp, looking down into a massive cavern. Indistinct light comes from somewhere, purple and red. It glows strong then soft, strong then soft, like the beating of a heart.

The walls . . .

I look to my left, at the wall closest to me. I reach out and gently touch it, then snatch my hand back.

The walls are made of flesh. Not skin, but flesh, like someone has stripped away the top layer, leaving behind exposed nerves and glistening sinew. I lift my gaze, taking in the entire cavern. Every single surface is covered. Bloody, quivering meat.

'London . . .'

Armitage's voice drips with horror. I follow her gaze, see something else embedded in the walls.

Faces.

They're part of the flesh, growing from it. Insane eyes rolling, mouths opening and closing, moans of horror and terror issuing from them. My eyes scan the cavern. There are more. Hundreds of them – the source of the voices I heard.

'What the fuck is this?' whispers Armitage.

We edge forward, peering down the ramp. At the bottom is a mound of . . . *something*.

It looks like a heaving, cancerous mass of flesh, easily the size of a tank. And the mass is . . . connected to the walls. I look around. Everything is attached, part of a single organism that begins and ends with the mound below us.

Then I see Lilith. She's walking slowly around the mass, watching it intently.

She hasn't seen us. We move down the ramp, our weapons at the ready. She carries on walking around the mass, moving out of sight. We start to run when she vanishes, arriving at the foot of the slope just as she reappears into view.

She stops when she sees us. Frowns at me, but doesn't say anything.

'You told me there would be a selection,' I say. 'That only the guilty would be punished.'

'I spoke the truth. Your whole race is guilty.'

'Innocents are dying up there!'

'No one is innocent, Tau. You of all people should know that.'

I shake my head in despair. 'So, what happens? You wake this Sinwalker up? How does that help you? I thought you wanted the sins to return to God. That you would guide him in his anger.'

'Don't be ridiculous. How can I guide something as insane as God? You've seen what he's capable of. This way is better. The Sinwalker cannot hold onto the sins if he is awake. They will drive him mad. He will slowly push them out. They will seep into your minds. Your souls. They will spread across the world, infecting everyone.' She smiles. 'You will do our work for us. And we just . . . pick up the pieces.'

'But won't it affect your kind too?' asks Armitage. 'The orisha?'

'No. God is an orisha. Just like we are. His sins have no power over us. They only affect humanity.' She turns back to me. 'This was always the plan, Tau,' she says gently. 'You knew that.'

I shake my head. 'No.'

'Yes. You sat in that jail cell and you listened to me talk and I knew you wanted this. I could see it in your eyes. It will be tough. To begin with. But there will be survivors. A few at least. We will make sure they're taken in. Taken care of.'

I turn away from her, stare up at the heaving mass of the Sinwalker. She follows my gaze.

'Not pretty is it? He used to look just like any other angel. But God's sins have . . . changed him a bit.'

'Angel?' says Armitage sharply. 'You're saying this Sinwalker is an angel?'

'The first and foremost.' Lilith holds her arms wide, like she's opening a show for an audience. 'May I present to you the one, the only, Lucifer Morningstar.'

Lucifer?

I look at the Sinwalker in amazement. I take a step back, searching for anything recognizable in the pulsing tumour. A face. Arms. Legs. But there's nothing. Just black, cancerous growths leaking pus and blood.

'That's not Lucifer,' says Armitage. 'No way. Lucifer fell. He's ruling in Hell.'

'A cover-up. Or propaganda. Both are the same.'

'I don't believe you,' I say.

Lilith frowns. She cocks her head, thinks about it. 'I suppose it is a lot to take in. Hold on.'

She disappears back around the black mass, then reappears dragging something along behind her. It takes me a moment to realize it's a person who's had his legs cut off.

The figure trails dark blood behind it as Lilith props it up against the mass and pats it on the head.

My breath catches.

It's not a person.

It's the archangel Michael.

'Silly bastard was waiting here when I arrived,' says Lilith. 'Thought he could stop me. Always was a fault with that lot.

Arrogance, thy name is angel.' She leans down and slaps him till his eyes flutter open. He frowns and focuses on us.

'Tell them, Michael,' says Lilith. 'Tell them the truth about the Sinwalker.'

He closes his eyes, tries to turn away, but Lilith grabs his hair and jerks him back. 'I've already told them it's Lucifer.'

Michael still doesn't talk.

'No? I'll just tell them, shall I? Feel free to chime in if you need to.'

She turns back to us. 'I was there, remember? I was the first wife of Adam. Selfish bastard, he was. Misogynistic pig. He didn't even want me to speak, you know that? Wanted me to just sit there and be silent. To smile and nod and spread my legs when he wanted me to.' She shakes her head. 'I said no. So he went crying to God and I was disposed of. Kicked out of Eden as if I was nothing.'

'What's that got to do with Lucifer?' asks Armitage.

'Just that Lucifer was treated no better than I. He did everything God asked of him. He was the ultimate fall guy. You think it was he who slid into Eden to tempt Adam and Eve? Don't be stupid. It was God. Glorious God and all his wonderful insecurities. Always testing. Always trying to catch us out. He could never just leave it alone. He was convinced there was a conspiracy. That everyone was plotting against him.

'But the angels finally had enough. When God brought the flood they admitted he was being ruled by his sins. So they stepped in, came up with the idea of the Sinwalker. Only thing is, they needed a volunteer. Someone to spend the rest of eternity holding onto God's sins, letting them eat away at his being. No one would step up. Not a single one of them. Not Michael. Not Gabriel, Not Raphael.'

She shrugs.

'So Lucifer finally said he'd do it. Why not? He was already considered a pariah. The one who rebelled against God – which, by the way, was another test. God wanted to see who would stay loyal to him so he ordered Lucifer to rebel, to question his judgement in front of the others.' She shakes her head. 'There were other tests. The Watchers. The Grigori. All those angels, rotting away in prison just because God was paranoid.'

Michael finally speaks. 'We . . . we didn't force him to become the . . . Sinwalker.'

'No. You didn't complain, either.'

'It . . . made sense. He was already . . . tainted. His . . . loyalty will be rewarded.'

Lilith spreads her arms wide, taking in the entire chamber 'Rewarded? Look at him. Look at where his loyalty brought him.'

Michael turns at us. 'You . . . must stop her. He cannot wake up. If he does . . .' He coughs up some black blood and wearily shakes his head. 'Things are not as you think, Lilith.'

'No. They never are with you lot, are they?' She turns to me. 'Everything you hate about the world – the corruption, the evil, the lying – it all starts with them. The angels.'

'It . . . it is not like that. Please . . . listen to me.'

'Why?' She turns to Michael. 'I'll give you one chance. Convince me. Why shouldn't I wake him?'

Michael stares at her. 'You must . . . have . . . faith.'

'Faith?' Lilith bursts into laughter. 'Look at where faith has got us. Look at where faith has got *you.*'

I've heard enough. I point my gun at Lilith. 'Put him back to sleep.'

'How am I supposed to do that?' She gestures above the mass. I can see faint lines in the air, flicking around like headless snakes. 'The wards are broken.'

'So fix them.'

'I can't. I have no idea how they were built. I simply severed them.'

I turn to Michael. 'Can *you?*'

'Perhaps . . . Given time. And . . . the help of the other angels.'

'There *is* no time,' I say, frustrated.

'Quite the pickle,' says Lilith sympathetically.

I hear a moaning noise from the mass and turn my attention to a spot at about head height. There's something there. I
step closer. Is that . . . is that an eye? I lean in. It is. A single eye
that flicks between us all, then comes to focus on me.

Is that him? Lucifer? Hidden beneath the growths. I stare
into the eye, see the pain there. The pleading. I turn and look
at my surroundings.

The mass, this whole cavern, it's a . . . *tumour* on his body.
Sins given diseased form.

This must be what Stefan had been talking about. God's sins
are just too much for one person, even if he is an angel. The
sin-eaters needed to . . . draw them out, pull them into their
own being. Like a syringe drawing out pus from an infected
wound. To stop the sins from spilling out into the world.

But it looks like they weren't doing their job. All this disease,
it shouldn't be here. I bet it all started when the sin-eaters
themselves became corrupted. The cancers started to grow
when the sin-eaters shifted their focus to making themselves
rich.

I look up at the near-invisible wards. They're shrinking now,
disappearing into nothingness.

Which means there's really only one solution here.

I take out my gun and hold it against Lucifer's eye.

'*Don't!*' Michael falls over, tries to pull himself towards me.

'Why?' I shout. '*We* all have to live with our sins. Why
shouldn't God?'

'Please . . . I can't explain. Just do not pull that trigger.'

Lilith takes a step towards me. I lock eyes with her. 'Don't
you dare,' she says.

'London,' warns Armitage. 'Not sure that's the best idea.
Maybe we should think this through, eh?'

Michael points at me. 'Human!' he shouts. 'I *order* you to put that gun down. On the authority of God himself. The All-mighty. *Your master. Put. It. Down.*'

I tighten my lips. 'Mate, *nobody* is my master. Understand?' I pull the trigger.

The bullet bursts Lucifer's eyeball. Ichor and pus sprays across me, scalding hot. I snatch my hand away and lurch backwards, trying to wipe the mess off my skin.

The tumescent mass starts to shiver. Yellow powder forms in the air, drifting to the floor like fine snow. Armitage and I step back, covering our mouths and noses.

Michael is trying to drag himself away from the tumour. It's leaking yellow bile now, streams of it pouring onto the pulsating floor.

The faces in the walls start to shriek, like terrified inmates in an asylum.

There's movement in the rippling mass. Bulges pushing outwards like . . . massive blisters. The bulges grow larger, the skin growing thinner. Stretching . . . pushing. . . .

. . . Until they burst, blood and fluids falling in an unholy rain.

Seven translucent sacks slide out of the tumour, leaving behind gaping holes. They hit the ground and split open. Black, foul-smelling fluid spills across the floor, wisps of steam rising into the air.

I stare in horror. Lying in the fluids are seven figures, pale grey flesh covered with blood and mucous.

The figures rise slowly to their feet.

My heart skips a beat. The faces are empty, hungry, feral. Black eyes blink, survey the surroundings. The one closest to me opens its mouth and a bubble of black ichor bursts out and pours down its chin.

Michael is on his back, staring at the creatures in horror. 'I warned you!' he screams. 'I *warned* you!'

'What is it?' I shout. 'What's happening?'

Michael looks at me. He's in tears. 'It doesn't matter if you kill the Sinwalker! You *can't* send God's sins back to him.'

'Why?'

'Because God is dead!' Michael screams. 'We executed him.'

I blink in shock. I turn my attention to the figures as understanding crawls up my spine. The seven deadly sins. If God is dead they have nowhere to go, nowhere to return to.

And with the Sinwalker dead, they've taken on form.

Armitage grabs my arm and pulls me away. We back up slowly, watching as Lilith approaches the sins. She holds a hand out, almost as if she's giving a treat to a dog.

'Here now,' she croons. 'Aren't you all just perfect? A true gift from God. Would you like to help me? Would you like to help me destroy the world?'

In answer, the seven sins tilt their heads back and scream, an ear-splitting shriek that scars my soul. I clap my hands to my ears as Armitage and I move quickly back up the ramp.

The sins stop screaming. Lilith smiles, steps forward and reaches up to touch the face of the closest one.

Armitage and I are at the arch at the top of the ramp by now. I grab one of the grenades Parker gave me. I hold it up to Armitage. She nods. I pull the pin and throw it back towards Lilith and the seven sins.

The grenade hits the ground and rolls down the ramp. The sins turn to watch as it bumps up against Michael.

Lilith starts running. Armitage and I are already in the tunnel, sprinting as fast as we can. The grenade explodes, a terrific roar of sound. The concussion hits, throwing us both to the ground. A huge cloud of dust billows past us. We scramble to our feet and sprint up the slope, heading back towards the storm drains. The ceiling is coming down behind us. Rocks and stones sliding from the wall, hitting the ground, forcing us to leap and dodge to stay alive.

I can't see anything. My lungs are filling with choking powder. Can't breathe. I look around. See hazy darkness. I try to call out for Armitage, but I inhale another lungful of dust. My throat constricts. Flashes of white before my eyes.

A rock falls and hits me in the shoulder. I drop to my knees. Try to crawl on. But then I realize I don't know if I'm going up or down. I'm trying to breathe, but there's nothing left. No air.

I push myself to my feet, struggle on. Have to keep going.

And then we're through the hole in the wall, back into the man-made storm drains.

The choking dust isn't as bad here. We fall to our knees, coughing and spluttering, spitting up black phlegm.

We don't hang around. We struggle to our feet and get moving, retracing our steps towards the exit. After about a hundred metres there's a deep trembling beneath our feet, followed by a long, drawn out crash.

'That'll be the tunnel leading into that cavern collapsing,' says Armitage. She pauses, then smiles. 'It's over.'

I nod, then take a deep, shuddering breath. I'm finished. Exhausted. But we did it. We stopped Lilith. Stopped the seven sins. Dropped a cavern on their heads. Which hopefully means we stopped the battles raging through Poison City.

I allow myself a brief moment of self-congratulation.

Stupid.

It's only a few moments later when I hear the noise.

I pause, turn back. There it is again. A shuffling sound, then splashing water. Echoing back through the tunnels.

I pull in the last of my energy and send out my shinecraft, tendrils of awareness drifting back along the tunnels, trying to track the sound.

I eventually spot it. A figure making its way through the storm drains, limping, clearly hurt.

It's Lilith.

Fuck.

Should have known it wouldn't be this easy.

Armitage is pretty far ahead by now. She arrives at the next turning and realizes I'm not following.

'Come on then,' she calls. 'Haven't got all night.'

I hesitate. I could just keep going. Leave it. Think about tracking Lilith down another day.

Except . . . I can't, can I? I can't let her live. Not after what she did. It's up to me to finish it. I'm the one who brought her here. I'm the one who gave her the sin-eater's soul.

I look into the satchel. Two grenades.

I take one out.

'London? What are you doing?'

Armitage starts to walk toward me.

'Stop!' I shout.

She stumbles to a stop, checking her surroundings as if expecting an attack.

'What?' Her voice is urgent.

'It's not done.'

'What're you talking about?'

'I . . . have to finish this. It's my fault, Armitage. I have to end it.'

I pull the pin out of the grenade. The metallic sound echoes around the storm drain.

'What was that?' Panic in her voice. 'London? Don't be a silly bugger now.'

'Armitage.'

She hesitates, peers towards me. 'What?'

'You better run.'

I roll the grenade towards her. But not too hard. Armitage swears loudly and sprints into the adjoining tunnel.

I turn and run, water splashing up around me as I try to put as much distance as I can between myself and the grenade.

The explosion hits.

A tremendous roar, like a demon screaming fire and brimstone into the night.

I'm plucked off my feet. Sailing through the air as everything explodes with orange and red light. I smack into the ground, skidding through the water until I hit the wall.

I groan, roll onto my back. My ears are ringing but I can still hear a mighty rumbling and crashing. The light flickers and dies away, but not before I see more smoke and dust roiling through the air.

I push myself to my knees, my feet.

I try to peer back but the dust is too thick. I think the grenade has done its job, though. I've trapped Lilith this side of the drains.

We're trapped in here. Her and I.

23

I limp back along the tunnels and reach the spot where Armitage and I descended into the Sinwalker's cavern. The tunnel is gone, the opening blocked with huge chunks of rock. I try to pull one or two out, but they don't budge. The whole chamber is buried.

I carry on walking. I have my gun out. I've hooked the last grenade through the belt at the back of my pants. I don't think I have any energy left to use the wand. I'm not tracking her by shinecraft either. Only one direction Lilith could have gone.

Ten minutes pass. My nerves are on fire. Every part of me is straining to hear. Freezing at every sound. Spinning around at shadows. My cell phone light picks out a white powder on the walls. I touch it and it crumbles beneath my fingers.

Salt.

We're close to the end of the storm drains, where they empty out into the sea.

My left hand curls nervously around my gun. I turn the phone off. No point in making myself a target.

I wait for my eyes to adjust. There's light filtering into the tunnels from somewhere up ahead. Just enough to illuminate the curves in the walls.

What if I'm too late? Maybe she made it out the storm drains.

I start to run, follow the curve of the drain around . . .

. . . And there she is. Limping.

'Stop!'

Lilith freezes, then turns slowly around. She looks ... *furious*. There's blood on her face. A nasty gash in her cheek.

'You,' she growls.

'Yeah, me. Turn around. Keep walking.'

She doesn't move. I fire my Glock past her shoulder. The crack echoes around the drain.

'Turn around and keep walking. Don't make me say it again.'

She does as she's told.

'Hands in the air,' I say as I follow after her.

She raises her arms. 'You haven't saved them, you know.'

The tunnel is growing brighter, a grey-white light that picks out the bumps and crags in the concrete.

'The war is coming, Tau. The orisha are tired of being second-class citizens. We're taking back the occupied land.'

We reach a junction. Darkness to the right. The storm drain opening is to the left, the full moon visible in the sky beyond.

'Stop there.'

She stops. I gesture with the gun for her to move to the side. When she does as instructed I move to the opening. I keep her in sight as I peer briefly out the drain.

A thirty feet drop into the ocean. Fuck.

'Didn't think this one through, did you?'

'Shut up.'

We'll go back. I destroyed one way out with the grenade, but there have to be other entrances into the tunnels, from different parts of Durban.

'Turn around.'

Lilith doesn't move. She's smiling at me.

I hesitate. Why is she smiling?

Then a wave of emotion hits me. Hatred. Fury. It blanks my mind, turns me into an animal, filled with rage. I scream and shoot at Lilith. She ducks away, darts to the side. I empty my magazine as I try to kill her, try to end her, but my hand is shaking so much I don't get anywhere close.

When I've no more bullets I drop the gun and run at her, hands curled into claws.

Before I reach her I feel my insides twisting. I stagger, stop moving. Something is wrong. Something is very wrong.

I double over, crying out in pain. Hatred, lust, fear, they pummel through my body, shredding my nerves, leaving my curled up on the floor. I'm weeping, weeping for lost hope, weeping with desire, weeping with hatred and fury. The emptiness inside is like a devouring beast, sucking me dry. Like I'm being eaten from within.

The feelings surge through me, cut into my very soul, strip away everything that is me. Everything that makes me Gideon Tau, just . . . falls away, leaving behind an empty shell filling up with . . .

. . . With sins.

I force my eyes open and there they are. The seven sins. Standing in a semicircle around me, Lilith at the front.

The sins' faces are vibrating, moving so fast I can't see their actual features. Except for the black eyes. The eyes are filled with hunger.

'I just want you to know,' says Lilith. 'Before you die. You failed. We're still going ahead with our plan. We're still going to infect the world.'

I gasp for breath, attempt to pull the shattered remnants of my mind together. I push myself up. The sins aren't grey anymore. They look like they're made from oil. Their bodies slick with viscous fluid.

I can't let them get out of here.

I struggle painfully to my feet. I can feel their presence corrupting me, trying to wash away my humanity, wash away everything about me. I can't let them do it. Not yet.

I hold on to one thing. One thing I know will keep me human, will stop them pulling me down.

Cally.

Blood is pouring from my eyes, my nose. I can feel the sins hammering at me, trying to get past the wall, into my soul.

I don't let them. I keep my thoughts on Cally.

Her first birthday, when she pulled herself around the house in one of those kid chair things with wheels.

Her first day at school. Happy and smiling, ready to go. The tears were all mine. I didn't want her to go. Didn't want her to grow up.

Christmas, presents unwrapped by the tree, the smell of pine needles hanging in the air, then swimming in the afternoon heat of an African summer.

The sins are disturbed. They cock their heads to the side, looking at me curiously. Lilith frowns, glances uncertainly at the sins.

'What are you doing, Tau?'

The sins step closer, pushing Lilith with them.

Cally and Becca, playing at the Botanical Gardens. Cally on her bike and us getting told off by the security guard because bikes aren't allowed. We run away, laughing, Cally pedalling furiously because she's scared of going to jail.

Reading to Cally in bed. Every night since she was born. It didn't matter she couldn't understand. It was what we did. Either Becca or me, lying in bed, reading books with Cally until she falls asleep.

The sins move closer. Only a few steps away. I can feel their hatred battering against me, tidal waves of raw, primitive energy.

'Tau,' says Lilith. 'What are you—'

I grab the grenade from the back of my belt.

Goodbye, Cally.

I put my other hand behind my back and pull the pin.

I drop the grenade between us.

'No!' Lilith screams.

She rushes me, a blur of unnatural speed. Everything changes direction. I'm falling. I see the sins flashing around me, a tornado of black oil that soars up into the sky. Then light, and rushing air. The moon above me and I'm sailing backwards, falling, the storm drain receding above me.

The explosion roars out of the hole, bright orange flames soaring up into the night sky. Rocks and debris strike me, hit my shoulder, my face. My vision goes red: blood in my eyes.

We hit the water.

It's like hitting a slab of concrete. My head smacks hard against the surface, is shoved forward, hits my chest.

Lilith releases me, shoves away. I'm dazed, can't think straight. The vestiges of the sins are churning through my system, trying to overwhelm me. I try to hold onto Cally, but the pain drives her away. I reach out, but she recedes down a long tunnel, vanishing into a tiny pinprick of light.

Then I'm floating in nothingness. Sinking.

Allowing myself to just . . . drift away.

I'm done now. I'm too tired.

Time to sleep.

I close my eyes, but I can't let go. There's something nagging me. Something I haven't tried. One last desperate attempt.

I wonder vaguely what it is. I've used my ammo. No more grenades. My wand is gone.

I don't have anything left.

Oh, but I do.

The tattoos.

My eyes snap open. The darkness of the water surrounds me, weighs down on me. My lungs are straining, crying out for air.

The tattoos. I can use them against Lilith.

There'll be no surviving that, though. There's no way in hell I have the power to send them back. They'll pull me into Nightside and rip me to shreds.

But what have I got to lose? This is my mess. I have to fix it.

I start to sub-vocalise the words of awakening. I feel the tattoos writhing excitedly on my back, my arms.

Before I can finish there's a rush of coolness against my face. I blink, confused, and find I'm floating in the ancient, dark waters of the earth.

Yemanja floats before me, a curious look on her face.

-Why do you sacrifice yourself again? You are already mine.-

-I'm not sacrificing myself.-

-You are calling the ancient wyrms. I can sense your weakness.- She smiles. *-You are most definitely sacrificing yourself.-*

-I don't have any other choice. Unless . . .- I feel a surge of hope. *-Unless you want to take Lilith out for me?-*

-I think not.-

-But . . . you did it before. With the smilers. Back at the beach.-

Yemanja frowns. *-All I did was bless the water.-*

-But . . . the waves, they obeyed you. The water followed me. Came off the beach.-

Yemanja smiles. She drifts forward, her hair floating around her head. *-That was not me. You are mine, my servant. You are mine to command. But I am also yours. Yours to ask for help.-*

I'm about to say, 'that's exactly what I'm doing, asking for help', but she cuts me off with a kiss, driving all thoughts from my mind. It's a more passionate kiss than before. We lock into an embrace and I feel her tongue in my mouth, sliding over mine. Her lips are soft, forceful. I don't want it to end. I want to enfold myself in her presence and just never let go.

Our lips part and she drifts back into the dark waters.

-I hope to see you again, London Town.-

She laughs and fades from view.

Pain engulfs me. My lungs strain, clawing at my throat for air. I blink, come back to awareness, kicking my legs, trying to get to the surface before my lungs explode.

I explode from the water. Gasp in huge mouthfuls of air.

When I can breathe properly again, I look around. Lilith is about twenty feet away, clambering over the rocks, trying to get around the crags to the distant beach. I swim after her. She hears me coming and stops, turns to face me, her face a mask of rage.

'Why won't you just die?' she screams.

I reach the sandbank, wade towards the rocks. She's coming back towards me now, her eyes filled with murder. I look around, but the sins are gone, vanished into the night. Not good. Not good at all.

I can't think about that now. I reach the end of the sand-bank, climb out onto a flat shelf of rock. Lilith clambers over the crags. I notice that her hands have sprouted some seri-ous-looking claws.

I bend over, try to get my breath back. My body is finished. I can barely stand. My eye is caught by movement. A little fish caught in one of the rock pools formed by depressions in the crag. I stare at it for a while, contemplating Yemanja's words.

A thought occurs to me and I start laughing. I can't help it.

Lilith freezes a few feet away, looks around warily.

'What the hell are you laughing at?'

I don't answer. Just keep laughing.

'Tau! What are you laughing at?'

I force myself to stop. I wince and straighten up.

'What am I laughing at?' I raise my hands to either side, a conductor ready to guide the music. 'You really want to know?'

'Tell me!'

'Fine.' I grin at her. 'I'm a fucking waterbender, bitch.'

I fling my arms forward, summoning the water.

It rises up behind me in a huge wave, surges around my body. The water slams into Lilith, sends her stumbling back. But she's strong. She opens her mouth to scream at me—

—And I send the water down her throat, into her body.

She doubles over, coughing, spluttering. Choking.

I lower my hands. The water stops. Drops to the crags and rocks.

Lilith straightens up. Our eyes meet . . .

... I pull my hands apart.

Lilith disintegrates. Every molecule of salt water in her body surges apart, obeying my commands. She explodes into nothingness, a red mist that patters into the ocean, onto the rocks.

I drop my hands. Slump onto the rocks, sitting in the freezing ocean. My head droops. I see the little fish still swimming in its pool, and I carefully cup my hands around it, picking it up and releasing it into the ocean.

I lie back on the rough stone, staring up at the moon, the ocean lapping around me.

It's done.

For now.

24

The summer storm hit like a smash and grab at the traffic lights. A sudden burst of violence, then a silent, shell-shocked aftermath.

I, of course, got caught in the worst of it before managing to find shelter, which is pretty typical of my luck lately.

I nod amiably at the drunk sprawled against the recessed door of the pawnshop. He glowers at me and pulls his bottle closer to his chest.

There are tiny imps scampering across his shoulder, stealing his drink when he isn't looking. I lean down and flick one of them away, sending it cartwheeling through the air with a squeak of outrage. I give the middle finger to the others then step back out onto the beachfront esplanade.

I check the files in my leather satchel, making sure they didn't get wet in the storm. They're all fine.

The sun chooses that moment to burst out from behind the purple clouds. I lift my face, enjoying the heat on my skin.

It's been a week since I shot Lucifer. A week since I killed Lilith. Two days since I left the hospital. Cracked ribs, broken nose, dislocated vertebrae, massive bruising, infection in my lungs, sprained wrist, and a fractured scapula. Plus, a week of fever and delirium brought on by excessive use of the tattoos.

Still, reckon I got off lightly.

When Lilith died, her vampires did the clever thing and bailed. There weren't that many left by then. The SSA and their M5 assault rifles had already done a pretty good job at thinning the ranks. The spooks that were left did a runner as soon as they discovered Dillon's body. Reckon nobody was there on any official business. Hard to explain that to the cops.

It's going to be interesting to see what happens here now that Kincaid is dead. There's going to be trouble, power plays, turf wars, the usual shit as the vampires jockey for position, trying to become the King of the East Coast. Armitage put me in charge of it all. As punishment, she says. I also need to look into this war Lilith was talking about. Are the orisha about to try and change things? Is the Covenant no longer holding?

Ranson's body disappeared. No one knows who took it. Another mystery to look into. Who could get into the Division headquarters? Does it mean someone else was in on the sin-eater conspiracy?

The riots petered out over the following day. They were put down to the effects of an undiscovered gas pocket beneath Durban. A gas leak that culminated in a massive explosion somewhere beneath Whoonga Park.

Over five thousand dead.

That's not even the final count. They think there are more in the burned buildings they haven't managed to clear out yet.

Those deaths are on my head.

They're on Lilith's head too. But it was me that gave her the soul.

In a rare moment of kindness, in between her bouts of anger and recrimination, Armitage explained that this was actually the best possible way for it all to work out. Even without my help, Lilith would have found the Sinwalker eventually. And we wouldn't have been there to stop her. So if I hadn't handed over the ramanga's soul when I did, it could have been a lot worse. The war would have come and who knows if we'd have been able to stop it.

Still. Doesn't excuse it. Doesn't let me off.

Those deaths are on me.

Even more worrying is the fact that God's sins have vanished. None of our seers or oracles can track them.

I have no idea how, but we're going to have to find them. They can't be left to just . . . wander the earth infecting the planet with the sins of God. If everything Stefan told me is true, they have the ability to utterly destroy mankind. To infect us all with their poison until we give in and let the sins take over. How long will the world last then? How soon before someone launches the nukes in a fit of wrath?

No, they need to be caught. Destroyed or contained.

Something else that's down to me.

The dog looks up as I enter the flat. He sniffs the air. 'You forgot the sherry, dipshit.'

I drop the satchel on the kitchen counter. Shit. Forgot his booze.

'Ignore him,' says Armitage. She's sitting on my slashed couch, paging through files. 'I already bought him some.'

'Come on, Armitage,' complains the dog. 'You're cramping my style.'

My flat has been tidied up. As much as it *could* be tidied. I still need to restock with new furniture and . . . well, pretty much everything, really.

But that's for another day.

'So? Did you get them?' asks Armitage.

I grab the satchel, toss it through the air. She catches it, empties out the folders onto the couch where they join the rest. We must have a few hundred files by now. Any records, mentions, legends, or stories that have anything to do with orisha stealing children.

Because that's all I remember. Whoever took my daughter wasn't human.

I grab two beers from the fridge, crack them open. I pour one into the dog's bowl and sit down on the floor. (Armitage doesn't drink anymore. Doesn't eat either.)

I pull the closest file to me.

I can't remember who took Cally, but I'm going to find out.

Then whoever it is? We're going to have some serious fucking words.

ACKNOWLEDGEMENTS

Huge thanks to my agents Sandra Sawicka and Luke Speed, for going over the manuscript many times and offering suggestions that improved the book tenfold. And to my new editor Anne Perry. For getting exactly what I was trying to do with *Poison City* and for being so welcoming to me as I joined the Hodder family.

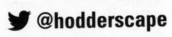